The Sword of Damascus

Also by Richard Blake

Conspiracies of Rome
The Terror of Constantinople
The Blood of Alexandria

RICHARD BLAKE

The Sword of Damascus

First published in Great Britain in 2011 by Hodder & Stoughton
An Hachette UK company

1

A CIP catalogue record for this title is available from the British Library

Hardback ISBN 978 1 444 70966 7
Trade Paperback ISBN 978 1 444 70967 4

Typeset in Plantin Light by Hewer Text UK Ltd, Edinburgh
Printed and bound in the UK by Clays Ltd, St Ives plc

Hodder & Stoughton policy is to use papers that are natural, renewable and recyclable products and made from wood grown in sustainable forests. The logging and manufacturing processes are expected to conform to the environmental regulations of the country of origin.

Hodder & Stoughton Ltd
338 Euston Road
London NW1 3BH

www.hodder.co.uk

To my wife, Andrea,
and to my daughter, Philippa,
with deepest love,
I dedicate this novel.

ACKNOWLEDGEMENTS

The verse in Chapter 3 is from *Ad Puerum Anglicum*, by Hilary the Englishman (twelfth century). Translation by the author:

O pretty boy – gorgeous as the flower,
Shining like a gem – I'd have you know
How the beauty of your face
Seems to me the very torch of love . . .

The words spoken at the crucifixion in Chapter 28 are from the Koran, 5:33, translated by George Sale (1697–1736).

The words ascribed to Euripides in Chapter 39 are actually from John Milton, *Paradise Lost*, I, 263.

The story recounted in Chapter 40 is the, 'Story of the Confectioner, his Wife, and the Parrot', from *The Book of The Thousand Nights And A Night*, translated by Richard Burton (1821–90).

The verse in Chapter 43 is from the *Diwan* of Ibn al-Farid (twelfth century), translated by R.A. Nicholson (d.1945), *Studies in Islamic Mysticism*, Cambridge University Press, Cambridge, 1921.

The verse in Chapter 53 is from Virgil, *Aeneid*, Book VI, 6–7.

Now, when the purple morn had chas'd away
The dewy shadows, and restor'd the day.

Translation by John Dryden (1631–1700).

The Latin quote in Chapter 62 is from M. Tullius Cicero (106–43 BC), First Speech against Catiline. Translation: 'How long, O Catiline, will you abuse our patience? How long is your madness still to mock us? When shall there be an end to your unbridled audacity?' Translation by the author.

The words ascribed to an ancient poet in Chapter 65 are actually from *Ozymandias* by Percy Bysshe Shelley (1792–1822).

1

Jarrow, Thursday, 27 December 686

'Is that wank on your sleeve?' I croaked accusingly. The boy opened his mouth and stepped backwards through the doorway. I gave him a bleary look and carried on with pulling myself together. If I'd supposed I could hide that I'd been dozing, this was – all else aside – the wrong boy. Out of habit, I'd spoken Greek. Edward was barely competent in Latin. I leaned forward in the chair. My neck was hurting where my head had fallen sideways. The beer jug I'd brought with me into my cell was empty, and I was feeling cold again.

'My Lord Abbot presents his compliments,' Edward opened in obviously rehearsed Latin, 'and begs your presence in the bell tower.' His face took on a faint look of relief before lapsing into its usual blankness.

'The bell tower, indeed!' I grunted. 'And Benedict imagines I can skip up and down his twelve-foot ladder as if I were one of Jacob's angels. One day, if he's lucky, he might have eight years of his own to every foot of that ladder.' But I stopped. It was plain I'd lost the boy. I groaned and reached for my stick. As I finally got to my feet, he tied the threadbare shawl about me. I ignored the offer of his arm for support, and made my own way into the corridor.

As I came back to what passes with me for life, I noticed that the banging had stopped yet again. I looked round. My cell was only a few yards along from the side gate of the monastery. It was still barred. However, the buckets of water I'd suggested were filled and ready for use.

'Do be a love, Edward,' I said, now in English, 'and have some more charcoal put in that brazier. It's perishing in here. If I'm to live long enough to have my throat cut, you'll need to keep me warmer than you do.' I looked again at him. Wanking would have been pardonable in the circumstances. But it was most likely snot.

I gripped at the rail and looked down at the rain-sodden waste that is Northumbria. On better days, you can see from here all the way down to the Tyne. This wasn't one of the better days. In the mist that had come up again, a few hundred yards was about the limit. There was a fire burning now close by the limit of visibility, and some of the northern beasts were dancing about it. I supposed they'd looted more beer from somewhere. Lucky beasts! I thought.

'So, what is it that's got all these old women in another panic?' I wheezed. I spoke once more in Greek. This time, I got an answer.

'It's over here,' said Brother Joseph in his flat Syrian accent. He guided me across the floor of the little tower and pointed down to a spot about fifty feet from the main gate. 'The Lord Alaric will see that we do indeed have a new development.'

'The Lord Alaric died when he left Constantinople,' I said, now softly. 'I must tell you again I'm plain Brother Aelric – born in Richborough, to die in Jarrow.'

'It is as Your Magnificence wishes,' he said, with one of his maddening bows.

No point arguing here and now, I thought. I looked out again into the mist. My heart skipped a beat and my hands tightened on the rail. Focusing isn't what it used to be. But I could see from his hair that they'd got hold of young Tatfrid. He was one of the boys who hadn't been able to make it through the gates before they'd swung shut. Now, he'd been dragged from whatever hiding place he'd found. They'd nailed him to a door and slit his belly open. His guts they'd arranged about him in the shape of an eagle's wings and nailed them in place. How they'd kept him alive was beyond me. But if he was no longer up to screaming, he was still twisting. The door was propped up at the angle of a pitched roof, and more of the beasts were dancing in front of it. One of them was pulling at the boy's trousers, and another was waving a knife up at us. It wasn't hard to see what they had in mind. It was all noiseless, and, with the progress of the afternoon, white mist swirled thicker on the ground like insubstantial snow, hiding the lower halves of the cavorting bodies.

I swallowed and looked steadily down. Oh, I've seen suffering and death enough to fill many more years than I've been in the world. One way or another, I've caused enough of it myself. But it isn't every day you see one of your best students butchered. Only five days before – no, it must have been just three – and he'd been construing Virgil downstairs. Now, the poor boy was – I forced myself to look away and turned back to Joseph.

'Can you get an arrow into the right spot?' I asked.

He looked and pursed his lips. He nodded and reached for his bow.

'In the name of God – no!' It was Benedict. He hadn't followed the words, but the meaning was plain enough. He snatched at the bow and threw it down. 'Has there not been enough killing?' he cried indignantly in Latin. 'If these benighted children have brought perdition on their heads, must we now do likewise?'

I bent slowly down and took up the bow. I gave it back to Joseph.

'Take careful aim,' I said. 'We can settle things with the Bishop as and when.' I stared at the Abbot until he looked away.

As Joseph fitted an arrow, there was a sudden commotion over on our right. It was the Chieftain and his retainers. They stood in a tight group, their cloaks pasted heavily about them by the fine rain. While I strained to see them properly, the herald stood forward and began another shouted message. The work of gelding laid aside for the moment, everyone nearby gathered round him to wave spears and shout fiercely at every pause.

'What's he saying now?' I asked. Benedict had assured me their language was close to English. I've known many Germanic tongues, and most of them have been pretty close to English if you can hear past the different inflections. This one was beyond me. It might have been a dog down there barking away.

'He says, Master,' someone whispered from behind, 'that they will all go away tomorrow morning if we but open the gate and let them take what they have come across the wide northern seas to obtain. They also ask for food.'

I looked round as far as my neck would turn. It was Edward. His words had come out in a strangled gasp, and I'd not recognised the voice. His face carried a look of alarm – which was natural enough, but also of confusion, and just a little of fascinated curiosity.

'They want food, eh?' I snarled. 'Well, they can go fuck themselves!' I looked back to Joseph. 'Any chance of getting an arrow in the big man?' I asked. He shook his head. I'd guessed already the wet leather was as good at this distance as plate armour. But it had been worth asking. 'Then see to poor Tatfrid,' I said. Before he could protest further, I took Benedict by the arm and moved with him until we were looking again at the distant fire.

'Where is King Aldfrith?' he wailed, pulling on the few strands of hair his tonsure had left. 'Why has he not sent men to protect us?'

It was a stupid question. Even if word had reached the royal court, they were all probably still too hung over from Christmas to set out to the rescue. And according to the villagers who'd made it through the gate, the attack party had come ashore at Yellow Tooth Creek. It was one of those darting attacks from across the northern sea that are over before anyone outside the immediate area even notices. We were on our own. If I'd believed a word of what I now daily recited, it was for us to huddle within the thick walls of the monastery and pray for a miracle.

'If we'd just done as they asked,' Benedict struck up again, 'if we'd but listened to their plea for food, they might even now be back on their ship.'

'Might?' I sneered. 'Might?' I paused at the twang of Joseph's bow and the soft thud a moment later. I listened to the low, terrified murmur of the other monks and boys behind us. I didn't bother turning. I'd already seen Joseph in action. He didn't miss. 'My dear Benedict,' I said with a change of tone, 'you *never* open a gate to these animals. You've seen what they did to the other villagers they caught. My age and your vows may have made them a superfluous treasure. But I rather fancy dying with my testicles still attached.'

I looked again at the fire. The mist was blotting out most of the sound. But if I listened hard, I could hear those dancers barking like a whole pack of rabid dogs.

2

Down in the great hall, Brother Cuthbert was making trouble again.

'O ye of little faith!' he bellowed, waving his arms in what he doubtless thought a dramatic gesture. 'Do you not see the sinful folly of sheltering within these walls? Are not these devils sent here to call us to our duty? Do they not hold out, though in reeking hands, the violet crown of martyrdom?' He wheeled round and, as if in supplication, held out both arms to the barred and bolted gate. 'Let us cast aside this pitiful shelter and receive the blessings that are without. Why fear ye death when it is but a second birth – a birth to a new and glorious life in the world that is to come? Every cutting and searing of the flesh, every snapping of bones, every dismemberment – what can it be to us but so many steps on the hard ladder that leads to Paradise?

'For all of us, our heavenly birthday is at hand. O Lord, Thy will be done! O Lord, Thy will be done!'

I got to him just as he was pretending to pluck out his eyes. With a hard prod of my walking stick to the back of one of his knees, I had him on the floor. As he rolled over, I jabbed hard into his belly and looked down at the face creased into a mask of unexpected agony.

'If you value your front teeth,' I said softly, 'you'll keep your cunty mouth shut.' I glanced briefly about the hall. The local villagers were huddled into a tight mass at the end furthest from the brazier. Cuthbert had been raving in Latin, and they hadn't followed a word. The other monks and boys, though, were looking decidedly scared. Worse, I could sense that many of them felt at least a vague duty to agree with him. I took in their pale, tense faces and looked back down to Cuthbert.

'Haven't you lived long enough already?' he jeered up at me, his breath recovered.

'No,' I said shortly. I could have quoted Lucretius on the unending sleep that is death. But it would only have confirmed his opinion about my own beliefs. 'Let me tell you,' I went on instead, 'that if I hear you so much as breathe another word of this nonsense, I'll set the boys on you with sticks. If you go anywhere near that gate, I'll have Brother Joseph strike you dead.'

'You wouldn't dare!' he cried, sitting up. 'You know that my person is sacrosanct. You know the damnation due to any who lay hands on a man of—'

I shut him up with the best knock I could deliver to his chest. He fell back again, his head smacking nicely on the flagstones. No point, for sure, in quoting Lucretius or any of the poets. Certainly none in pointing out the inconsistency of not wanting to be killed before he could commit suicide.

'Don't presume to tell me what I would and wouldn't dare,' I said, now louder. 'Joseph will have a knife in your back before you lay hands on that gate. And I'll see he gets the sort of penance for it that boys get for scrumping. If you don't believe that, you still don't know me.'

I left him nursing his head and made my way to the top of the table. It was evening, and we'd be safe enough now till morning. Benedict was up in the bell tower – as if the lookouts needed any encouragement to stay awake – and he'd not be down to claim his place. I carefully seated myself. Just behind me, the brazier was glowing bright. I looked round. Just three evenings before, Benedict had sat here. Then, he'd been all smiles and jollity as he dispensed the Christmas bounty of the Church to us and anyone else of quality who felt inclined to join us.

Now, the cups and platters were gone. The lamps were burning low. No one had thought to move the big table back into the refectory. But the few who were sitting round it picked nervously at the stale crusts that had been doled out. The other monks and boys stood about clutching at their rosaries or trying not to cry with terror.

Joseph poured me a cup of hot cider mixed with beer. I motioned him into a chair beside me and looked at the jug. He poured another cup for himself. We drank awhile, keeping to our own various thoughts.

'My Lord is still convinced,' Joseph asked eventually, his cup now empty, 'there will be no proper attack?' He spoke again in Greek – not that anyone was paying attention to us. I looked about the hall. It had been so very jolly on Christmas Eve. I'd been too pissy drunk at first to follow what the boy was saying when he'd burst in unannounced with the dreadful news. But I'd staggered out into the damp night air and had seen the flames of the village not a half-mile away. I'd seen the more fortunate villagers hurrying towards us with whatever they'd been able to pick up and carry. The arrival, come dawn, of the raiders outside the gate had finalised the gulf between the secure jollity of Christmas Eve and the impending horrors of the present.

'A regular storming of the walls?' I asked with a faintly satiric smile. 'By these wankers? Even with fewer men than the dozen of that rabble outside, you or I would have had the gate smashed open days ago.' As if on cue, the slow banging started again. The gate was at an angle to its porch that made a battering ram useless. Instead, it was a matter of trying to hack into three inches of seasoned oak. With the more vigorous blows, the bars on our side shifted slightly in their housing. We could hear the muffled shouting of the attackers as they went about their work.

'Oh, I'll not deny we're in a weak position,' I went on. 'We're in the middle of nowhere. There's only one of us who's up to fighting.' I nodded towards one of the monks. He'd covered his ears to blot out the sound of the horrors that just a few inches of wood held at bay, and was rocking backwards and forwards in his place. 'We can be sure these people won't fight. As for the villagers' – I wrinkled my nose – 'it's their people who got carved up out there. But they've no discipline or experience for fighting.' For just one moment, I let my defences slip, and thought again of that poor gutted boy. I squeezed my eyes shut and forced the bleakness and despair back out of mind. I looked Joseph in the eye.

'Against all this,' I said, 'the walls of the monastery are high and solid. We've no shortage of piss and shit to pour on the heads of anyone who tries climbing them. Gone at with hand weapons, the gates should hold till Easter.' I took a sip and burped. This was good stuff. Whatever it might later do to my head, it dulled my wits now. I giggled softly and took another sip. 'And do bear in mind that time is on our side. It's cold out there, and we know there's a growing shortage of food. Aldfrith will eventually get wind of the attack, and prestige requires him to do something about it. Given luck, he'll get here before these creatures can run back to their little boat. We can then look forward to a most edifying public spectacle. All we have to do is sit here and wait – and hope the gates remain shut on our own side.'

'My Lord thought more activity in order at his last siege,' Joseph responded, a strange tone to his voice. I raised my eyebrows and looked at him. The fire had now dried my clothing, and I could feel it was beginning to toast my shoulders. He looked back at me, then broke the silence. 'It was at the last moment in the crisis. The Great City, cut off from its remaining provinces, had the barbarians on the European shore and the Saracens everywhere else. They were outnumbered in men and ships. All food supplies within the City were exhausted. Just as the orders had been given for the final assault, I saw you appear at the highest point on the sea walls.' He shut his eyes and thought back. 'I saw you on a white horse, dressed in golden armour that caught the morning sun. I saw you raise your sword and how, in answer, the chain went up, unblocking the Golden Horn. Five ships came forth – five ships against ninety. Straight they raced at the Saracen flagship. The laughter of seventy thousand Saracens was like thunder that rolls across the water. Then I saw—'

'Fuck all good it did *me*!' I cut in with a bitter laugh. I scratched and looked at my fingernails. The light in here wasn't good, and I couldn't tell if there was blood on them or just dirt. 'And even if it were needed again, this isn't Constantinople. And that was an age ago and half the world away.'

'It was *eight* years ago, My Lord,' he prompted. 'Even then, the world believed you were half as old as time itself.'

I looked hard into the bearded face. Joseph had turned up in Jarrow six months before. I'd soon worked out he had military experience. But if it was nice to have someone around who knew Greek, I hadn't so far got this much out of him.

'Well, well, my dear Joseph,' I said. The heat was turning uncomfortable, and I got unsteadily to my feet. My stick was on the far side of the chair, and I couldn't be bothered to stretch over for it. I walked a few feet down the long table and paused beside one of the less unprepossessing novices. He stared up at me, seeming as scared of the syllables of an unknown language as of the horrors that lurked beyond the three-inch thickness of the gate. I laughed and turned back to Joseph, who remained sitting – still recalling, perhaps, how I'd made my dramatic gesture from the walls of Constantinople and saved an empire on which even the Church had given up.

'My dear friend,' I went on, now in Syriac, 'you've a talent for narrative. But to have seen what you describe, you'd need to have been up there on the sea walls beside me, or on the Asiatic shore in the main Saracen camp. I'd place your accent to Antioch – which, like all of Syria, has been in Saracen hands since before you were born. I'll agree that it's rude of one refugee to ask another too much about the past. But since you've raised the matter of my last public service to the Empire, I might wonder just how much of your fighting was done in the *Imperial* Service.' I sat down. I scratched again. This time, I tried not to look at my fingernails.

'Perhaps My Lord is right,' he said, still in Greek, with another of his bows. 'Perhaps the past is best not revisited.'

I nodded and pushed my empty cup towards him. He muttered something about my years, and I scowled at him. After a momentary hesitation, he poured out the second refill. He'd dropped the matter, and I'd not take it up again. I had little doubt, though, that Joseph had fought for the Saracens before taking holy orders. But where was the shame in that? Syria had been out of our hands so long, it could no longer be considered a shame for Christians to fight for its new rulers – even if it was to spread the Desert Faith. And I really was too old and out of things to care. It was all too far away – thousands of miles from Jarrow. Even with the Emperor's agents snapping at my heels, it had taken me months to get across the wild desolation that was the fate of what had been the Western Provinces. So what if Joseph had been on the other side in my last stroke of Imperial policy? I was glad to have him here and now. But for him, I'd be all alone with these wretched women – young and old – of the male sex.

'I'm going to my cell,' I said, heaving myself to my feet. I sat down again. 'No. Before I go, I want you to bear in mind the threat I made to Cuthbert. If he goes near that gate again, I look to you to see that he doesn't undo it. And' – I dropped my voice, although we were speaking in Greek – 'I want you to keep an eye on young Edward.' I noticed the slight questioning look. 'He's the pretty one with big hands.' I paused again. 'You kicked him out of mathematics for idleness.' Joseph nodded. I went on: 'Well, he may not be up to learning any of the languages I can teach. But he's good enough in whatever it is those savages speak. I'd like you to keep an eye on him as well.

'Now, it really is time for bed,' I ended, getting up once more. 'Do have a jug of that stuff sent in to me. I have work to do that always goes better with a slight lubrication.' I giggled tipsily again, wondering when I'd last held a pen without some mood-altering substance to ease its passing across whatever surface was available. I might have said something else. But as I went back to the chair to gather up my things, I heard Benedict behind me.

'Brother Aelric,' came the shaking voice in Latin, 'something more is happening out there, and none of us can imagine what it could be.'

3

With the fading of day, the rain had ceased, and the unbroken grey of the sky had somehow been replaced by a moon that shone from a sky of pure blackness. There was still a mist out there, but it had contracted itself to a dense whiteness that lingered, in the cold, breezeless night, perhaps nine feet above the ground. Here and there, it was broken by the tops of the rather scrubby trees that grew about the monastery. As far as my eyes could see, it was like looking over a field of ethereal snow. I listened again for the neighing that came from somewhere within that whiteness.

'If they did come ashore at Yellow Tooth Creek,' I said, cutting through the quiet babble of prayers, 'it must have been in one of those little boats they have with a shallow draught. Getting horses across the northern ocean in one of those things doesn't seem likely to me. Fitting in even the dozen men we've seen would be a tight squeeze. It's fair to say, then, that we have a fresh arrival.' I fell silent and looked down again over the smooth whiteness that concealed whatever might be happening outside the monastery.

'Could it be His Majesty?' one of the older monks quavered. 'Could it be that God in His infinite mercy has spared us for continued labours in the world?'

'Could be,' I said, without turning. 'You're all certain you heard a clash of weapons earlier, and then a scream?'

Someone beside me nodded eagerly in the gloom.

'Well, perhaps Aldfrith has sent over a warning for these people to leave now or face the consequences. Or it might be something else.' I fell silent and listened. Whatever had happened earlier, it now sounded less like a battle down there than a conference. That didn't rule out some intervention by the secular authority. Just as likely, though, the northerners had got lucky with their thieving, and there had been a falling-out over the horse.

'We wait until morning,' I said firmly to no one in particular. 'Until we can know what's happening down there, I don't see the point of further discussion.'

More to the point, I was in need of a piss. All that drink had gone in and done its job. Now, I could almost feel it trickling into my bladder like water through a rain pipe. I set trembling, frozen hands on the ladder and prepared to heave myself into another descent. After all this clambering up and down, I could feel a nosebleed coming on. As Joseph reached down to make sure my feet were properly on the rungs, I heard the faint braying of '*Deus uult! Deus uult*' – 'God wills it! God wills it!' Far below, Cuthbert was back in full cry.

'The moment of deliverance is at hand!' I could just make out. 'As the Lord smote the host of Sennacherib, so has He now smitten the northern devils who dared infest this house of peace. Let us give thanks to God for the preservation of our lives. Let us gather up the rich spoils that lie abandoned beyond these gates, and dedicate them to the Lord . . .'

'Brother Cuthbert seems to have much amended his tune,' Joseph observed drily.

'Not really,' I sighed, looking up at his moonlit face. 'It's all any excuse to open that fucking gate. Do see to him when you come down. I'd like *some* peace tonight.'

I nearly trod on Wilfred as I stumbled off the last rungs of the ladder. 'Why aren't you asleep?' I asked. 'It's been dark some while.'

The boy stood back from me and bowed. 'Is it true, Master, that the northerners are preparing to leave?'

I sniffed impatiently, then dabbed at my nose. I opened my mouth to speak, but caught another gust of '*Deus uult*!' from the great hall.

'What's that mark on your face?' I said eventually.

Wilfred stepped out of the pool of lamplight, and put up a hand to cover the bruise.

I heard a noise overhead, and looked up to see Joseph's little

Syrian feet on the upper rungs of the ladder. I thought of the increasingly imperious itching in my bladder. I set it aside. Given this opportunity, it could wait for the moment. I took the boy by his arm. I led him along the corridor to a point just outside my cell where there was a little recess in the wall with a wooden bench set into it. I sat down and carefully stretched my legs. Over on my left, I could hear people grunting and scraping away beyond the side gate. The table now jammed tight between it and the wall was as good as any bars. No one would get through that – not, at least, without a fire, and that wouldn't do much with all the rain that had been soaking into the wood. I pressed my hands into my armpits and waited for another of my shivering attacks to pass. Wilfred was wearing the new outer robe I'd demanded for him. Even so, his face looked pinched. If the light had been better, I might have seen the bluish tinge that had begun to frighten me. I wondered if the brazier in my cell had been refilled. I thought of going in to see. But the fit was passing, and moving was too much trouble.

'I did fall this time, Master,' Wilfred said defensively. 'It was the stairs into the pantry. I was fetching scraps to feed the people from the village, and . . .' He trailed off.

There was no point trying to corner him. It was obvious what had happened. But no one likes a grass, and Wilfred wouldn't turn grass on the other boys. Bede usually looked after him. But Bede was off with the King; we'd needed one of the boys to show off his Latin, and Bede was easily the best candidate. Not for the first time in these few days, I wished I'd also recommended Wilfred.

'How old are you?' I asked with a slight change of subject.

'I shall be fourteen in March,' he said.

I sniffed. Of course, he was telling the truth now. But no one could have guessed it. The boy's height didn't say more than ten, and he might have disappeared altogether by turning sideways.

'But, Master,' he said again, 'surely we shall not all soon be dead. Is it true the northerners will be gone by morning?'

'Could be,' I said, trying to sound non-committal. Then I leaned close to him and dropped my voice lower still. It came out somewhere between a whisper and a croak. 'Listen,' I said, now urgent, 'do you remember the gap behind the bread oven – the crack in the outer wall made by the heat? It can't be seen from the outside because of all the brambles. Well, I want you to gather yourself a bag of food and water from the kitchen and be prepared to get out through that gap.' I took hold of his arm and shook him as he began his protests. He trailed off into another of his coughing fits. A drop of opium in wine would fix that. Sadly, opium is just another of the civilised luxuries that can't be had in England. 'No,' I said, 'I know you can squeeze through. There's no point my even trying. All else aside, I still have the chest and shoulders of a big man. If anything happens, I want you straight out. Get out and run. Don't look back. Don't fall in with anyone else who may know about the gap. Get out, run, and don't stop running until you hear men talking English.'

'And you, Master?' he asked, trying not to cry.

I tried for a laugh, but felt it turning to a cough. 'At my advanced age, dear boy,' I said, 'I can't say death is such a loss as it might seem to you. I already stand far over its threshold. There isn't much the northerners can do that would make it more inconvenient than if I just stopped breathing one night in my sleep. Now, I want you to promise that you won't stick around if any of the gates are forced. And I want you to promise that you will help write the *Universal History* that I've been promising the world these past fifty years, and still haven't delivered.'

I sat back and gritted my teeth as the chill of the wall went straight through my bones. 'Listen,' I said, fighting for control, 'I don't know more than anyone else about what tomorrow will bring. But it never does any harm to prepare for the worst.' I got up. 'Now, you get yourself off to the kitchens. Get something proper to eat, and sit as long as you can in the warm. If anyone challenges you, just say that Brother Aelric sent you.' Wilfred stood before me in silence. I waved him about whatever duties had made him cross my path. I'd said what I'd wanted. There was no more to discuss. I listened as his racking cough vanished into the maze of corridors that spread out behind the great hall. Expecting him to run more than a hundred yards without falling down was optimistic. But I'd now done all that I could given the limits imposed.

I looked angrily at the fifteen feet between me and the closed door of my cell. Now I was up, my bladder was letting off trumpet blasts of urgency. I could already feel a warm dribble on my left shin.

It is much later. It may be around the midnight hour. It may be later still. With the disruption of regular observances, there are no bells or chanting to let me know the time of night. It may be a waste of my dwindling papyrus to sit here writing up new events. But I'm sure you will pardon me, dear Reader, if I dwell on the siege. So far, pestilence and the cold have been the main perceived dangers in Jarrow. Barbarian raids are not a common occurrence.

And there is yet more of the here and now to write up before I can settle back down to my narrative of the past. I got to my cell and had a piss. I sat awhile, warming myself and brooding over another cup of the beverage that inebriates and only sometimes cheers. I did then write the whole of the above. When I'd finished, I sat up and wiped the ink from the end of my nose. I looked at my pens. The steady scraping across cheap papyrus had blunted all the reeds. It was now I noticed that my knife was missing.

Fucking nuisance! I thought. For old times' sake, I had the usual suspicious attack, and began looking through my stuff. There are no locks on the cell doors. But since I'd been with Joseph – or been aware of his movements – all day, there was no cause for suspicion. He'd not been snooping through my cell. No one else can read the sort of Greek in which I normally write. No, someone had most likely been in to sharpen my pens and then simply gone off with the knife. Just to be sure, I had another look in all the likely places, then got up to see if anyone else might be awake and have a bladed instrument to hand.

I was about to lift the catch on the door to my cell when I heard voices in the corridor outside. It was Cuthbert, whose cell was next door but one to mine. For once, I was glad to hear his voice. He'd surely have a penknife. All I had to do was paint on a toothless grin and overlook our little differences of earlier in the day.

But he was in a hurry. By the time I'd got the door open, he was already disappearing round the corner towards the front of the monastery.

'I feel the hand of God on my shoulder,' he was saying to someone else – as if any Supreme Being might give a toss about the doings of some broken-down teacher of logic out here in the middle of nowhere. 'My work is plainly not yet done.'

Knowing Cuthbert, his work would be some while in the doing. I wasn't standing out here in the freezing cold on the chance he'd cut it short. There was a candle guttering away in his cell. So I shuffled down the corridor and pulled his door shut behind me.

Mine was hardly luxurious, but this place was bleak to the point of uninhabited. The cot was of bare boards. The one blanket was folded ostentatiously on the table, which was devoid of writing materials. There was a wooden cross hung on the wall. That was just beside the window – which was wide-sodding-open to the courtyard.

'God-bothering shitbag!' I snarled softly. Little wonder it was always so cold. 'No consideration for others,' I muttered again. 'Just self, self, self.' I thought of pulling the shutters to. Then again, Cuthbert would only reopen them, and wouldn't take kindly to the attack on his humility. I looked round the room. It really was bare. I couldn't see so much as a teaching note, let alone a penknife. I could feel the advance warnings of another shivering attack, and was about to go when I saw the box. The candle was at the far side of the room, and the box was the same colour as the bed boards under which it had been pushed. It's more of a surprise that I saw it at all than that I'd almost missed it. I stared at it a moment, wondering if it was worth the effort of bending down. But old habits die hard. If something was worth any degree of concealment, it was worth looking at. I opened the wind shield and pressed the candle into shape until its flame was clear. Setting it on the edge of the bed, I bent creakily forward and pulled the box into the open. About fifteen inches square, it had been adapted from some original use that I couldn't guess. There was no lid. Instead, a mass of stained rags covered whatever lay within. I sat carefully down on the floor. Taking care not to disturb any arrangement that might have been methodical, I lifted out the rags so far as possible in a single mass.

Oh, joy! I hadn't been so lucky with snooping since that time in Ctesiphon when, got up as a Nestorian bishop, I let myself into the diplomatic archive and found those letters that helped us win the Persian War. First thing I saw was a dildo. It was a big, alarming thing – twelve inches of finely stitched leather over a thick wooden dowel. I picked it up and sniffed. It had the smell of recent use. I sniggered and blotted the cold out of mind. I'd think about this thing stuffed up his arse as often as I saw Cuthbert in prayers. The way he walked about so stiffly, perhaps he had it with him in prayers. Remembering its position in the box, I put it on the floor. Ditto with the many-headed whip coiled up beside the dildo. That showed signs of less frequent use. Underneath was a little book of parchment sheets sewn together. There was no name or other details on the binding. I opened it at random and held it up to get what help there was from the guttering flame of the candle. It was the buggery small writing you get on parchment, and I thought at first it was beyond my old eyes. But I squinted hard and found a distance where the neat lines of blurriness resolved themselves into something legible:

Puer decens decor floris
gemma micans uelis noris
quia tui decus oris
fuit mihi fax amoris . . .

So it went on in a paean of love to some unnamed boy. As it didn't even try to keep to any of the quantitative rules, I'll not call it poetry. Still, it had a nice accentual rhythm, and the end-rhymes were interesting. Was this something Cuthbert had picked up on his travels before settling in Jarrow? Was it his own work? Hard to say. The script had a vaguely English look about it, and Cuthbert was a native. One thing, though, I could say, was that he'd have every word of this stuff whispered back to him the next time we sat together in prayers. That would wipe the pious look off his face.

I carried on looking into the box. The revelations were not exhausted. There was a bag of silver coins. They were the crude, heavily clipped money issued by the French kings. I counted thirty of them. I'd learned all I needed to know about Cuthbert's vow of celibacy. So much now, I'd found, for his vow of poverty.

Then, right at the bottom of the box, hidden under more of those disgusting rags, I found a canvas document pouch. Weighing about half a pound, it had once been sealed. It reminded me strongly of the pouches used in the Empire for sending out confidential instructions to provincial governors or generals in the field. The seals were now cut away. In their place, the pouch was closed with a set of tight knots. I pressed it all over, trying to guess the nature of the documents it contained. Of course, I didn't get much further than knowing they were written on parchment. Given time, I could get the knots undone. Getting them retied would be the problem. My hands might still be up to that sort of work – but not here, not now. I'd keep quiet for the moment, I decided, on the poetry. Instead, I'd come back with Wilfred. I knew he'd have scruples about snooping. I also knew I could get round those easily enough. I'd already lectured him half to death about a historian's need for an enquiring mind.

I was just about to put everything back as I'd found it when I heard voices in the corridor outside. Oh shit! I thought. It was Cuthbert, back already.

4

There was a time when I'd have heard the voices long before they were directly outside. But age is a terrible thing. There were perhaps four beats of my rather uncertain heart between hearing the voices and hearing the rattle of a hand on the latch. There wasn't time to squeeze myself under the bed. Even if I could get under there – some doubt to put it mildly – and then not wheeze away like a snuffling hog, getting out would surely be beyond me.

I thought of trying my confused act when the door opened. Looking blank and talking nonsense had got me out of trouble more than once during my escape from the Empire, and again on the roads through France. Or perhaps I should just heave myself up and confront them. More fun to do this later – but now might have its enjoyable side.

But the hand rattled the latch and then pulled back. Cuthbert was standing outside in deep conversation. I turned my good ear towards the door and strained to hear what was said. Gradually, the muffled whispering resolved itself into the jumbling of Latin with English that even the foreign monks have taken to using.

'You saw it? You saw it with your own eyes?' he was asking in a hushed but exalted tone. 'You saw the knife held aloft? You saw the spurting of blood and heard the long, terrified scream? You saw the bright, hopeful manhood severed from the body? You saw it held before terrified, barely comprehending eyes?'

'No, Master,' came the mournful reply. It was Edward. His own voice was coming on to break, and I'd have known it anywhere. 'The Old One got Brother Joseph to put an arrow in his heart before the knife could fall. I heard My Lord Abbot call that a sin,' he added.

'Sinful indeed!' said Cuthbert, now indignant. His hand brushed the latch again. I braced myself for the effort of getting up. But the door remained shut. 'To every one of us,' he said, in his lecturing voice, 'God has appointed a certain end. We must each of us face our end with cheerful faith in the love of Jesus Christ. For anyone to frustrate that end is a damnable sin – utterly damnable. I thank you, boy, for telling me about the sin and its attendant circumstances. The sin I will take up first thing in the morning with Benedict himself. His indulgence of Brother Aelric's ways grows increasingly scandalous. This must end in any event. But you have now given me a most opportune means of smoothing any scruples in My Lord Abbot's heart.

'But let us turn back to the attendant circumstances. You saw the slitting of the belly and the pulling out of intestines. Was there much blood? Did the boy scream? Was there a cloth soaked in vinegar held to his face?'

From the tone of Edward's answer, I now had no doubt it had been wank on his sleeve. Next time the lazy wretch misconstrued Cicero, I'd have the arse off him so viciously he wouldn't sit down for a month of Sundays. For the moment, though, he was getting me out of trouble with Cuthbert. That door hadn't yet opened, and probably wouldn't.

'Softly, softly, my son,' Cuthbert said. 'This is not the place for such conversations. You can see the light under the door of Brother Aelric's cell. We both know he never sleeps, but writes and writes in what is surely the catalogue of shame to serve as his last confession. I think again of the quiet place where the wood is kept. Let us continue there in our usual privacy. It will be – ah – spiritually uplifting for us both were you to remove your clothing and show me the spot where the knife was pressed into the unfortunate's body . . .'

I could hear the hushed voices grow quieter as they went back the way they had come. I heard much whispering and laughter. Before he turned the corner, I think I heard Edward talking about his need for a *whole* cup of honey.

I replaced everything as I'd found it and closed the door quietly behind me. I could have gone back to my own cell. But the thrill of that near discovery had perked me up again. On a whim, I turned away from my own cell and went towards the great hall. There was no chance of embarrassment. Cuthbert must already be hurrying the boy through the basements for their rutting session. It would be daylight before Edward was released to wash out his mouth with anything more substantial than water.

All was quiet in the great hall. The only light was from the now dying and quite smoky brazier. The villagers had bedded down in their own corner. The new baby had died the night before, and the mother just after breakfast. The rest of them were now snoring peacefully. The boys would be sleeping in one of the animal sheds. Everyone else was in his cell. Everything was as normal as, given the circumstances, it could possibly be. Above all, the gate was still securely barred and bolted.

'My Lord is unable to sleep.' Because he'd been sitting so still in Benedict's chair, I hadn't seen Joseph. Now, he stood and bowed to me across the hall. I could see he had his bow and arrows on the table before him. By the side of his chair came the dull gleam of one of the more ferocious knives from the kitchen.

'I need a penknife,' I said, as if I'd been looking for him all along. 'Mine has been taken.'

Joseph turned and rummaged through a small bag. He took out a wooden case and opened it. He handed me a small surgical knife. 'It is very sharp, My Lord,' he said. I looked at the black steel. I could see at once it had better uses than sharpening pens. 'Would you have me bring it back with you to your cell?'

I shook my head. I could still be trusted to carry knives with me, however sharp. Besides, Joseph was doing his best job here in the hall.

On my way back here, I went past my cell and stood by the side gate. I tried to ignore the white flashes my bladder was sending up once again to my eyes. I leaned hard on the table and fought to control the ragged gasps of my breathing. There was a half-inch gap at the bottom of the gate. Through this came the glare of what seemed to be many torches. I listened hard to the urgent and argumentative conversation beyond. I still couldn't follow a word. But there was a malevolent sound to those guttural exchanges that chilled me.

I'm now back in my cell and feeling better. I have Edward's charcoal and the remains of Joseph's drink to keep me warm. The papyrus sits, invitingly blank, before me. My pens are sharp. Time, then, to forget the horror that lurks and crawls outside the walls of the monastery – break in or go away, let me be clear, there's bugger all I can do about it. Time also to put aside those 'lovers' in the basement; though, if we're all still alive come dawn, I'll not overlook Cuthbert's plot against me: I'll have the whole truth out of him, and then him and his pretty catamite on to penances neither will forget. Yes, put it all out of mind. I have my papyrus. I have my memories. Let us see how many of these and how much of this I can join before death, in one form or another, stills my trembling hands.

Would you like to know about my first visit to Athens? It's tough titty if you don't, as that's what I now propose to write about. But, even after seventy-four years, it's a story worth telling.

5

It was Tuesday, 10 October 612. I was twenty-two and rejoicing in all the health and beauty of my early manhood. Well, perhaps rejoicing is too strong a word. My mission to Egypt hadn't gone as smoothly as I'd hoped, and I was beginning to worry about the supplementals Heraclius might have for me once he'd read the report I was carrying with me. Oh, I'd made sure to get Priscus to add his name to it, and we'd bullied Nicetas in Alexandria to attach his own seal as Viceroy of Egypt. Before taking ship, I'd thought that report a little masterpiece of evasion and tasteful self-glorification. I'd hugged myself at some of the wording. Martin had looked up several times from putting my final draft into his best clerical hand to compliment me. Now, a day or so off Cyprus, all I could think about was long faces in the Imperial Council, and that slow, moany voice at the head of the table, asking questions that didn't admit of easy answers.

But the sun shone from skies of cloudless blue, and the smooth waters of the Mediterranean sparkled as far around the ship as I cared to look. I was His Magnificence the Lord Alaric, Legate Extraordinary of the Emperor. And, for the moment at least, I was the youngest member of the Imperial Council in living history – 'not since Caligula made a consul of his horse' Priscus had sneered when the appointment was published. On and off, I'd been brooding on that ever since. Not bad, though, for someone who, just three years before, had been a native clerk helping his boss fake miracles in Canterbury. I was number four or five in the Imperial pecking order, and if I was currently stark naked from my swim, I had the robes to prove it.

'I fail to see why we couldn't have taken the land route,' Priscus groaned as he looked up from another of his vomits over the side. 'I did tell you more than once that I had work to do in Syria.'

I sat up in my chair and stretched my arms. I took another sip of wine and gave the cup back to the bearer. As another slave rearranged the cushions behind me, and yet another began fanning me a little harder, I smiled for the first time that day.

'I don't recall, Priscus dear, insisting that you should accompany us,' I said smoothly. My one joy of this voyage had been the discovery of his seasickness. In the two years or so I'd known him, this was the first human weakness I'd seen. At first, he'd tried concealing it. Then he'd worked heroically on mixing powders from his box of mood-altering substances. When those failed him, he'd tried praying before an icon of Saint Demetrius. I'd have been quite put out had that worked. Of course, it hadn't. I looked steadily into his withered face. With all the retching, patches of white lead had come off, revealing the true greenish tinge beneath. 'I told you I wanted the sea passage for speed and because of all the luggage. Besides, I don't trust the Persians not to be sniffing round Jerusalem. I've had enough of falling into enemy hands.'

'I can't recall how often I've told you, my lad,' Priscus said with another queasy look over the side, 'that hostilities ceased on the eastern front in June, and won't pick up until spring. I do know what I'm talking about.'

'All the more reason, My Lord Priscus,' I said straight back, 'for the Commander of the East to be inspecting the Syrian defences, and not taking his ease with a purely civilian minister of the Great Augustus.' As he turned to make yet more of those wonderfully disgusting noises over the side, I got up and walked down the length of the Imperial transport I'd commandeered. I'd made sure to arrange my quarters as far away from Priscus as was consistent with my own exalted status. I was still stuck with him as often as I ventured out and he wasn't groaning in his bunk. But this latter hadn't so far been a common occurrence.

'Something you *must* bear in mind, Alaric, is that we did save Egypt.' Priscus was hurrying beside me. There was an urgency in his voice that had nothing to do with the slight pitching of the ship. 'Even Heraclius accepts in his heart that there was nothing I could do to save Cappadocia. Oh, he's given me the blame because it's the only way he can get it off his own useless shoulders. But there's a limit to what he can say in the Council. There's no doubt, though, that we saved Egypt. Take that away – rob us of its corn – and the Empire disintegrates.

'Yes, whatever else can be said, we did save Egypt.'

I stopped and took a hard look at the ravaged face. So he'd also been reflecting on our less than glorious time in Egypt, and how to gloss over its details in Constantinople. He sat down on a handy coil of rope and groaned. But for that, I'd never have noticed the slight gust that was rippling the otherwise loose sails. He clutched at his stomach. I stood back in case there was anything left in there to bring up on deck. But the spasm passed.

'And don't forget, dear boy – I did save your life.'

I shifted position to steady myself as the ship moved slightly. Overhead, the sailors were now padding about on the masts. Far below, there was a tightening of the drum beat to keep the slaves rowing in time. I heard the lash used a few times and a muffled scream. I stared down at the shivering wreck that Priscus had become the moment Alexandria dropped below the horizon.

'My own recollection, dear friend, is that you got me out of one scrape that you wholly engineered, and chose not to murder me in Soteropolis when you'd decided I might be more useful alive than dead. Unless there are facts about our doings in the south that still haven't come to my attention, saving my life is the last description I could make of your behaviour.' I stared pitilessly down at Priscus.

Of course, none of this was relevant. We'd feed Heraclius a version of the truth so tarted up, it would amount in places to a pack of lies. But however incredible it might sound in places, none of it could be properly shaken so long as we both swore to its truth and didn't try bitching behind each other's back. Because he was the Emperor's cousin, there was a limit to what we could say openly about him. But we'd left Nicetas behind in Alexandria. It therefore stood to reason that everything was his fault. *He* was the one who'd let the mob get out of hand. *He* was the one who'd ensured there had to be twenty thousand bodies rotting in mass graves outside Alexandria, and a heap of burned-out ruins in much of the centre. *He* was the one who'd abandoned Upper Egypt to the Brotherhood, and who'd failed to stop the Persians from coming close to stealing the whole country from us. Certainly, he was the one who'd blocked the land reform law all the time I'd been there to get it implemented; and it was he who'd cancelled the implementation warrants Priscus had sealed in his own moment of power. We'd get the man recalled in well-merited disgrace – though not before we'd done a thorough job of shuffling our own failures on to his shoulders.

I was searching for something friendly to say when Martin came on deck. Like Priscus, he wasn't taking the voyage particularly well. He clutched at the doorway that led into the cavernous depths of the ship and, with a look up at what he plainly still thought the blistering sun, adjusted the two-foot brim of his hat.

'The cook is asking if you'd like boiled chicken for lunch,' he said. 'Since we'll be putting into Cyprus before long, he suggests we might as well finish the Alexandrian supplies.'

I nodded. Now the subject was mentioned, I was feeling rather peckish. Ducking and diving to avoid the motions of fifty heavy oars was all the exercise a man could need. And it had set me up nicely for lunch. Priscus forgotten, I looked round for the cup bearer. Priscus, though, wasn't to be forgotten. He dragged himself upright and took a tight grip on the rail.

'Ah, little Martin,' he cried with an attempt at jollity, 'I see the bandage is off.'

Martin put up a hand to where his left ear had been before it suited Priscus to have it sliced off. 'I thank My Lord for his concern,' he said stiffly. 'And I am most grateful for the recommendation of the man in Constantinople who can fit a leather prosthesis.'

'Think nothing of it,' Priscus said, now almost cheerful. 'Indeed, you could go for a ginger wig as well. That would hide the baldness as well as the retaining straps.' He took a step forward. But there was another slight pitch as the wind shifted direction, and he was back with both hands clamped on the rail. 'How did you manage the sea crossing from Ireland?' he asked.

I looked at the sorry couple and sniffed at the smell that was drifting up from the kitchens. It was a question I'd thought of asking – but, in deference to Martin's reluctance to talk about his past, hadn't. There was a feeble mutter about how he'd been too young to be troubled by the mountainous waves of the ocean that swelled and raged at the 'edges of the world'. But Priscus wasn't listening.

'Is it true,' he asked, with a change of tone, 'that the Irish are the Britons who could swim when young Alaric's ancestors turned up to steal their country? If so, could we describe the remaining Britons as the Irish who *couldn't* swim?'

Under the comical brim of his hat, I could see Martin's face flush so that the freckles all but disappeared. I had the first few words out of a sneer at the modern Greeks, when there was a shout from overhead.

'Ship on the starboard bow!'

By the time we'd worked out which way to look, it was above our own horizon.

'A trading ship,' I ventured.

'Too small,' said Priscus. 'Pirates more likely.' He took both hands off the rail for a moment and looked almost cheerful.

Martin sat heavily on the vacated coil of ropes and looked set to cry. But the Captain was now at hand.

'I think My Lords will find that it is an Imperial dispatch vessel,' he said.

I squinted and looked hard across the bright waters. How anyone could tell what it was at this distance defeated me. But I was willing to take the Captain's word.

'It's coming our way,' he added.

Priscus looked again at the seal on the letter – as if the thing weren't unquestionably genuine.

'What I'd like to know,' I said, replying to his own question, 'is how Heraclius could have known we were travelling together by sea. We must surely have outrun the fastest messenger from

Alexandria. And then there's the matter of getting an intercept from Constantinople to Cyprus.'

Priscus scowled. 'That's the fucking least of it,' he said bitterly. 'You really should know by now never to ask how an emperor gets his information.' He dropped his voice and led me away from the stiff Syrian who'd presented the document written all over in purple and gold. It may be one of those irrelevant details that stick in the memory, but I'd noticed how well it went with my official robes. 'What I can't handle is the substance of the orders. Where civilians like you get sent is of no importance. No – the further you are from Constantinople, the less alarming are the "reform" laws Heraclius publishes. But I do have a war to fight. I've business in Constantinople that can't wait. It may please you to be sent there – though I do assure you, it's a shitty little town far below its reputation. But I've better uses of my time than inspecting the defences of Ath . . .'

6

Jarrow, Friday, 10th January 688

Well, my dear Reader, where do I start again? It's over a year since I last handled the thin pile of manuscript on which I must now again set to work. My writing table has an unfamiliar feel about it. The chair seems to be at the wrong height. The candle smells fatty. Do I overlook all that has happened this year, and go back to the comfortable, if not always creditable, certainties of my youth? Or do I set out on what may be the still open issues of the present?

But come now – put in these terms, what choice is there? Interesting as it is, the story of heresy and perhaps ghostly blood-drinking in the Athens of my youth can wait. In its place, let us have the reasons why what, last year, were my most familiar things have become strangers to me. And so, let me close my eyes and wait for the quarter opium pill I've taken to have its effect. When I open them again, let me guide my pen over the wondrously smooth papyrus, boxes of which fill this room; and let me put aside the little matter of the oath of silence that all concerned have been required to swear on the Gospels.

I begin around noon on the day that follows my last entry. My first recollection is of lying slumped over my writing table. My pen, still clamped between chilled fingers, had poked a hole in the papyrus.

'Brother Aelric!' came the soft yet urgent voice in my bad ear. 'Brother Aelric, please wake up.'

It was Benedict. I tried to look up at him with bleary eyes, but I was too stiff with the cold to move. One of the novices with him gently pulled me into a seated position. Another set a cup of warmed barley wine to my lips. As I drank in its welcome goodness, I stared in Benedict's direction and waited for my eyes to focus.

'Have I missed prayers again?' I asked. I glanced at the chink of bright sunshine coming through the shutters.

'That doesn't matter,' he said flatly.

Now I could focus, I looked at the pale, sweaty face. I felt the faint stirrings of alarm.

'Are you able to stand up and come with me?' he asked.

Good question. I'd answer it when I felt ready. I took up the cup the novice had set down on the table and finished its contents. I kicked at the floor to push my chair back and was helped to my feet.

'What's happening?' I asked. Monasteries hardly ever bustle with activity. Everything but our own voices, though, was unnaturally silent. I looked again at the hard, cold sunlight that was making a pattern of colours on the contents of my inkpot and waited as my shawl was tied about me. Benedict's mouth twitched as if he were about to speak. But his jaw set again, and he said nothing.

Going into the great hall, I was at first blinded by the mass of sunlight that poured in through the now open gate. A couple of big men stood just outside. But all else about them other than their size was lost in the blaze. Looking back into the unwindowed dimness of the hall, I could see virtually nothing. One thing I did see, though, was the body. It lay face up, about six feet inside the gate. I let go of Benedict's arm and moved towards it.

'He had his reward for opening the gate,' Benedict said as he moved beside me.

I looked steadily down at the calmest expression I'd ever seen on Cuthbert's face. The absence of malevolence, or of any other passion, had made me wonder for a moment who it might be. But it was Cuthbert. For all death might have purged it of unpleasantness, that body had once, beyond any doubt, contained Cuthbert. He'd had his throat cut, and had landed on his back before dying. Blood had sprayed everywhere as if from a fountain. Those white flagstones Benedict always fussed over would need a day of scraping to get the stains out.

'You're telling me he opened the gate and was killed as the northerners rushed in?' I asked.

Benedict nodded, but looked inclined to move to other business. Plainly, the monastery had fallen. But since the northerners hadn't so far run wild, whatever business needed to be discussed could wait a while longer. Now my eyes had adjusted, I could see everything else in the hall. The villagers were nowhere to be seen. But the entire company of monks was sitting silent and terrified around the table. Sprawled on the ground or leaning against walls or on convenient furniture, the northerners had surely increased in number. There were more here than I'd ever counted from the tower. And there were still some outside. I looked at the weapons they had on show. As it had been outside, they mostly had small battle-axes. Otherwise, there were a few clubs and some largish knives. I saw nothing that might have been useful for cutting a throat as neatly and quickly as Cuthbert's had been.

I looked again at the flagstones. They were blotched or spotted with blood right up to the stone threshold. Though light and shining in the sun, this was unstained. It was the same with the darker stones of the porch. The gate wasn't pushed entirely back against the wall, but had a clearance of about three feet. I walked over and looked at the inner side of the gate. It was bad light again, but I could feel the congealed mess on one of the drawn crossbars.

'Since poor dear Cuthbert didn't open the gate,' I said, turning back to face the monks, 'is anyone able to tell me who did?' I turned again to Benedict, who was looking confused now as well as worried. 'But do pardon me – old habits of enquiry die hard.' And I had to admit that I'd not been dragged out of my slumber to explain the death of the worst logic teacher England might ever have produced or might ever produce. I nodded at one of the northerners who'd come over to get a closer look at the body. He stood beside me, his face like leather where the beard didn't cover, his hair rancid with butter.

‘A more relevant question might be why everyone else is still alive?’ I looked round yet again. This time, I noticed Joseph. As before in Benedict’s chair, he was now bound and gagged. His kitchen knife lay perhaps a yard from his feet. I could see where blood had dripped from it on to the floor. Rather big for cutting a throat, I imagined it was bloody from some attempted resistance. He looked back at me, rage and bafflement streaming from his face. Yet, if his clothes were torn, and if a bruise seemed to cover his entire forehead, even he was still alive. ‘What is going on?’ I asked Benedict.

I felt someone tugging at my sleeve, and I was helped on to a little stool that had been brought forward. I carefully stretched my legs and waited for the blood to rearrange itself. I twisted round and saw a jug of something on the table. I pointed at it and waited for the cup to be brought over. Bad luck – it was only water. I rubbed my head and tried to think. But Benedict was now staring down at me.

‘Brother Aelric,’ he said, then looked suddenly away. ‘Brother Aelric, how the gate was opened is a matter I am not able to explain. But these men tell me that their natural inclination is to strip the monastery of anything valuable and then to burn it with all of us still inside it. However, they have said that they will leave us in peace if we give up what they have come to take.’ He paused and swallowed. He began and his voice failed him. He began again: ‘Brother Aelric, I am told that they want you to go with them.’

I heard one of the monks burst into a stream of incoherent prayer. Someone else let up a wail of terror. From somewhere in the gloom over on my left, there was quiet sobbing. I closed my eyes and tried once more to think. With the evidence available, I’d not have got very far at my best. Now, it was just a matter of suspicions I could barely articulate even to myself. I grabbed at the monk who stood beside me and got to my feet. I looked round at the gathered company.

‘Are there any of you savages,’ I asked as loudly as I could manage, ‘who know Latin?’ I stopped and then laughed. ‘Anyone who knows Greek?’

'They speak through me,' Edward replied slowly in Latin. He came from where he'd been leaning against a chair and stood before me. The ragged shirt and trousers that had been growing increasingly too small for him had been put aside. In their place, he wore a suit of travelling clothes that were just a little too big. 'I understand their language, and they have made me their interpreter.'

I gave him my best look of disgust and pointed at the corpse. 'And I suppose,' I said with heavy irony, 'that you can rejoice in having been Cuthbert's "appointed end". I only hope the poor bugger died with his balls well-drained.'

The boy's smooth, unblemished face tightened for a moment. Then he shrugged and barked a few words at one of the northerners. The man laughed and said something to the others that set them all off. He got up and left the hall. Benedict pressed shaking hands to his chest and prayed softly.

'Brother Aelric,' he said at length, 'I cannot force you to anything. You are a free agent. But I ask you to consider that there are forty-three other people in my present care. There is no reason why these men should not have killed us all at once and then taken you by force. If they are asking you to leave of your own free will, there is reason to suppose that they will keep to their word. As an individual man of God, I hardly need assure you that I would suffer any martyrdom before doing or counselling evil. But I am responsible for the safety of everyone here – and for all the work we have done and may yet do . . .' He trailed off and looked towards the chapel.

He didn't need to go on. Even with cold water in my cup, I'd got there first. Silly of me, really, ever to have thought that Jarrow was far enough to run. If I'd managed to get here at my age, it was plainly not far enough to deter others. Certainly, Bishop Alexius and the three senators had managed the journey. They'd turned up one Easter in clothes that I could see were spoiled by travelling, but that everyone else had thought ravishingly magnificent. And they'd stayed the better part of a month, variously whining and nagging. If I'd sent them back with a flea in their collective ear, I should have realised that wouldn't be the end of the matter. You don't say no to an emperor. You certainly don't to an emperor like Constantine.

I looked once more about the hall. This time, I saw the leader of the northerners. Not the big Chieftain from outside – I'd not seen him yet – he hadn't been one of the low creatures who'd made a spectacle of themselves during the siege. Most likely, he'd been the one who arrived the night before. Smaller than the others, and dressed with more concern for the niceties, he sat quietly a few yards along from Joseph and was looking at me with close attention.

'Do you speak Latin?' I asked.

He shook his head. I tried him in English. He nodded towards Edward. I pulled myself straight and looked down at Edward. He wasn't yet fully grown, and I was still a tall man when I took the trouble not to stoop.

'Do these savages not realise,' I asked, 'that even ten miles in this weather would kill me? If they expect to get me on to their open rowing ship, they must be either mad or desperate.'

'That has been considered,' he said, now giving up on Latin for English, 'considered and answered. We have decided that Wilfred should accompany us.' The man he'd spoken to now reappeared. He was holding a pale, silent Wilfred by the scruff of his neck. 'Wilfred will come with us. We will do all we can to make your journey safe and easy. If you manage to die, however, he will be killed as Tatfrid was. This time, there will be no Brother Joseph to speed his death.'

You little shit! I wanted to snarl. *If you expect either of us to last long outside this monastery, you haven't thought very hard.* But I could see there was no point in arguing. With Bede away, there was no one else here who meant enough to bend me to another's will. So instead: 'I suppose you think pretty well of yourself,' I sneered. And, to be fair, it seemed Edward had every reason so to think. He'd got himself admitted here. He'd put up with months of my snarly abuse at his lack of progress in Latin and God knows what from Cuthbert. All this time, he'd bitten his tongue and waited for a prearranged time – or perhaps for an opportunity that might never come. I'd run networks of professionals in my time – against the Persians, and then against the Saracens. I can tell you the hardest thing with tradecraft is keeping your embedded agents from going native. If Edward was now mightily pleased with himself, he had every reason. I'd underestimated the boy. Such a pity. At the very least, if he was up to this, I could surely have found a better way than I had to get Cicero into his head.

And he had got rid of Cuthbert! Of course, where he and his thirty pieces of silver came in was beyond me. Plainly, he hadn't known of Edward's involvement. Perhaps he'd been some kind of dupe. But why kill him? Questions, questions, so many questions – and not much chance here and now of an answer. But Edward had been a very clever lad. That much was clear. I smiled and sat down again.

'When are we supposed to leave?' I asked.

Edward looked out into the sunlight. 'The King and his men are already on their way over,' he said. 'We must leave at once.' He pointed at a couple of bags that had appeared. 'This will be enough for your journey.' The leader got up and gave a short command. I heard the crack of a whip outside and the neighing of a horse. 'The carriage is heated,' Edward told me. 'I will sit with you on the journey to the coast. Wilfred travels with the others.'

The horses made hard work of pulling the carriage through the mud of the track that led from the monastery. I had plenty of time for looking back through the open flap. It was one of those chill, cloudless days you sometimes get in a Northumbrian winter. Everything was lit with a bright intensity that allowed even my eyes to take it in. I pretended to ignore the body of the Chieftain and the two other bodies that lay a few yards from his. As before, since I'd get no answers, there was no point letting on that I had any questions. I chose likewise to overlook Edward's mention of 'the coast'. Once over the hundred yards of the track, we'd set out to the south-east on the old military road – in the opposite direction to Yellow Tooth Creek.

I looked steadily back in silence. Benedict and the other monks stood outside for a long time, crossing themselves and praying as they watched our departure. At last, they went slowly back inside. Once I'd seen the heavy gate swing shut behind them, I slumped back on to the rough, charcoal-warmed cushions and breathed more easily. Whatever was to happen with me – whatever was to become of my little Wilfred – the monastery stood, and its precious work of civilisation could continue. It wasn't work as I'd have arranged it. But it was the best that England was likely to get, and it hadn't yet gone up in smoke.

I tried to ignore the smell of wet embers as we passed by what had been the village. I listened instead to the thin calls of the winter birds. Northumbria isn't blessed with the kind of scenery that anyone would wish to look on before leaving for ever, so I turned my attention to the contents of the larger bag that had been dumped beside me.

'Should I compliment you,' I asked Edward, 'on the appositeness of your packing the Acts of the Apostles in Greek? It does contain the best account I've ever seen of a shipwreck. Or was this a random selection?'

He gave me a thin smile. 'You poked me hard with your stick when I suggested in class I might wish to learn Greek,' he said. 'You told me a scarecrow would sooner pass into your world of light than I could. Taking me there can now be the project that keeps you from more desperate thoughts.'

'So you have a very long journey in mind?' I asked with mock earnestness. Except for the hands, he was a pretty boy. One unbiased look at those regular features and the very blond hair, and it wasn't hard to see why Cuthbert had fancied the arse off him. Twenty years – no, ten years – earlier, and I'd have been up to making a pass of my own.

'How old were you when you got out of England?' he asked.

'I was eighteen,' I answered, thinking back an age to King Ethelbert and his gelding knife, and good, kind Maximin who'd held him at bay by pure force of personality. 'I was five years older than you are now.' I smiled. He was no longer just pretty. The slow boy we'd all mocked and flogged through our various classes might have been stretched out as dead as worthless Cuthbert had been in the monastery. I was sitting now beside an entirely different young man. So far as I had any say in the matter, not dying on him might be interesting.

'Did you ever intend coming back?' he asked again.

'No,' I said. 'As you will read of Saint Paul in Corinth, I shook the dust of England from my clothes and got on with the rest of my life. It has been a longer one than I think yours will be.' I smiled. 'But I suppose now is as good a time as any to begin your education.'

7

'You really must both get it out of your minds,' I said, still in lecturing mode, 'that the Empire "fell" in any meaningful sense. There is no doubt that, several hundred years ago, our own people and their cousins invaded the Western Provinces, and that these places – partly as a result – ceased to be administered from either of the Imperial capitals. The Eastern Provinces, however, passed unscathed through that long crisis; and the remaining Emperor in Constantinople continued as head of the richest and most powerful state in the world.'

'But, surely, Master,' Edward broke in, 'the Saracens are completing the work of destruction. For the East, the fall has merely been delayed?'

I thought of correcting a misused deponent, but thought better of it. If the boy's progress in Greek had been encouraging, his Latin had really blossomed. Even before we'd put in at our first Spanish port, he'd caught up with Wilfred. Now, none of us had used English in over a month. No loss there, to be sure – who'd speak a language like that from choice?

I shifted slightly in my daybed. The sun had moved, and the canopy above me no longer kept it from shining on me. Wilfred leaned over to rearrange the blanket that covered my legs. Another few inches, and it would be in the bowl of water where I was soaking my feet. I closed my eyes for a moment, and then tried to see across the two hundred yards that separated our ship at anchor from Cartenna. It was a useless effort. I looked back at the two boys who, waxed tablets in hand, stood before me. I noticed black stains on the thumb and two main fingers of Edward's right hand. Practising his penmanship again, I thought approvingly.

'I wouldn't dismiss the Empire so casually,' I replied, coming out of my little reverie. 'We lost Egypt and Syria, and no one nowadays expects we shall get them back. We're losing Africa a bite at a time. When that's been all swallowed up, I expect the Saracens will cross into Spain. But Spain isn't our problem, and Africa has for a long time been more trouble than it's worth. If Egypt and Syria are to be regretted, we did stop the desert whirlwind from overblowing the Asiatic Provinces. Within those, plus European Greece and its islands, we now nurse our shattered strength and await the recovery of health. I do assure you that Constantinople will not fall to the Saracens. If you think it will, you haven't comprehended the passive strength or the long ambitions of an impersonal and regular government. You also haven't understood how, reduced to territories almost wholly Greek in language and Orthodox in religion, the Empire has found an internal unity it had not possessed in centuries – if ever. No, young Edward, don't suppose the Empire will go away any time soon. It certainly won't go before you've had your reward out of it.'

I looked at the boy's face. It remained impassive. Not even the repeated 'we' had ruffled him. Before we could continue the lesson, one of the northerners came over. Edward was wanted by the 'Lord' Hrothgar, he barked in his own language. That, I saw, broke through the icy calm. If only briefly, the boy's face took on a troubled look. Well it might. Some of the beatings he'd had in private from Hrothgar had kept me up at night.

Regarding language, by the way, Benedict had been right. What these people spoke was pretty close to English. It was a matter of paying attention and listening past those horrible consonant sounds. You can be sure I hadn't let on I could understand them. Some knowledge is not to be advertised.

'Can you forgive me, Master,' Edward asked with ceremonious courtesy, 'if I take further instructions?'

I made my best effort at a gracious bow and leaned back on to the cushions. If Edward was to have the stuffing knocked out of him again just because no one on the ship seemed to have the faintest clue about navigation in these waters, that was his problem. I at least could try to make the best of things.

'May I begin now, Master?' Wilfred asked.

I opened my eyes again and nodded. My feet had been soaking long enough. Wilfred got down on his hands and knees and set about me with his block of pumice stone.

'You're a good boy,' I said with a contented yawn. 'Don't spare your efforts on the left big toe. The hard skin there is beginning to hurt again.'

'It will be as you wish, Master,' came the obedient reply.

I looked down at the boy as he huddled over my feet. The gentler sea and the growing warmth of the February sun were doing me no end of good. If I say that twelve days in the Mediterranean had restored me to vigour, I'd be exaggerating. But there was no doubt I was feeling better than I had in several years. I wished I could say the same for Wilfred. Below that head of matted, greasy hair, he was still little more than a bag of bones.

'Have you been here before, Master?' he asked.

'No,' I said. I paused and allowed myself another sip of bad Spanish wine. 'In all my years of service to the Empire, I made only one trip to Africa. That was about twenty years ago, when I came west with Constans. He was father of the present Emperor.' I thought fondly of my last Lord and Master who'd really appreciated my services. Yes, he'd raped a nun in front of the Patriarch, and generally hadn't gone out of his way to win friends and influence people. But he'd slowed the Saracens and left internal affairs to me. I hadn't been making it up when I spoke about the Empire's recovery of health. You can enable wonderful things with lower taxes and less control. If only his wretched successor hadn't . . .

But I brought myself back to the present. 'While he was on his looting pilgrimage in Rome,' I said of Constans, 'I spent a few months in Carthage trying to sort out the finances. I was so busy there, I never actually went beyond the walls. But I know Cartenna from the description of its double church. The place is a few hundred miles west of Carthage.

'If we aren't making direct for the capital, it may be the place has been lost to the Saracens – though, with Carthage gone, I'm not sure how anywhere else in Africa can be held. Mind you, I am assuming what is by no means beyond doubt – that these people know where they are going.' I stopped again and thought of the rising tension aboard this big, heavy ship. In the open seas beyond the Mediterranean, I'd been impressed by how well Hrothgar and his crew of hired trash had worked the ship. Despite the endless and insane pitching, there had never seemed any chance that we'd go down. Ever since we'd entered the great, enclosed sea around which all civilisation had arranged itself, however, it had grown increasingly plain that we were lost. What could have been in Hrothgar's mind when he'd come through the Narrow Straits without a pilot? It was almost funny that I'd been the only man aboard able to give our whereabouts as Cartenna.

As I opened my mouth to try for a bitter laugh, Wilfred dropped his pumice stone and gripped hard for a moment on my left foot. I took hold of the daybed and pulled myself forward to see him. He'd let go of my foot and was now huddled into a tight ball on the deck. His body shook with suppressed coughing. Then, with a soft groan, he opened his mouth for another long vomit. There was no retching this time. It was just a mass of clotted blackness that stank of blood. I pushed him with the head of my stick so he wouldn't collapse into it, and got myself upright.

'Drink this,' I said with soft yet urgent authority. I'd got myself down on to my knees and was trying to straighten the boy. Even I was able to hold his head and shoulders up in one arm as, with the other, I held my cup to his lips. 'Drink and look hard up at the sky,' I commanded. I dipped the sleeve of my outer robe in the wine and dabbed at the bloody froth on the grey, bloodless lips. He clutched at his stomach with shaking hands and squeezed his eyes shut.

'Open your eyes, Wilfred,' I commanded in my firmest voice. 'Open your eyes and look at that rope swinging from the front mast. Have you never noticed how often I've sat here looking at it? Have you never noticed how, whatever the distance it covers, each motion back and forth takes the same time? There is an inverse relationship between speed and distance. Think how there is an order in the world about us, and how this can be explained in mathematical terms.' I'd got the boy's attention. While he looked at the rope held taut along its length by the block of wood at its bottom, I repeated myself and elaborated on a set of ratios you'll not find anywhere in the writings of that fool Aristotle.

'It is proof of God's providence,' he gasped at length. That wasn't quite how I saw it. But this was more a distraction than a lesson, and I nodded eagerly. 'It is a sign of God's boundless love for the world,' he added. I painted on a smile of agreement, and cast round for some appropriate text from Scripture. 'But, Master, surely God has abandoned me,' he wailed, going straight off the path I'd appointed for him.

I sighed. Unless I could think of something fast, we'd be back to the confused ramblings of our journey through the grey, mountainous waters that lay beyond the Narrow Straits. Then, barely noticing myself, I'd forced him into my own heated cot, and plied him with soup and encouraging words, as he'd snivelled on about the torments that surely waited for him beyond the grave. Edward hadn't been at all pleased: I, after all, was the one who *had* to be kept alive. In truth, I'd been pretty pissed off at times. I didn't fancy any return to that.

8

I was saved from having to deliver another lecture on theodicy and teleology by a loud crash over on the right. Someone had cut another of the dangling ropes, and the block it was supporting now fell heavily on to the deck. His spasm over, his reflections on the coming fires of Hell forgotten for the moment, Wilfred sat up and looked round. That was my chance. I got my arms about his chest and dragged him to his feet. I guided him over to the side of the ship and got him to breathe in and out. In and out, in and out, he breathed. I could feel the return of his limited strength. Relieved, I looked over at the shore.

And this was Cartenna. I could have no doubts of that. I shaded my eyes and again tried to look through the glare of the morning sun to see the details of the place. There were a few trading ships in the harbour, and I could see the two churches. I could say nothing beyond that. The city might still be a busy port. Just as easily, it might be as derelict and as empty of people as everywhere else we'd touched on this voyage.

'Look, Master!' Wilfred cried weakly.

I followed his shaking finger. Fifty yards over on the right from the direction I'd been looking, there was the rowing boat the northerners had seized during one of their supply raids on the French coast. With a couple of the biggest northerners to pull on the oars, Edward and Hrothgar had set out for the shore. Edward sat very still, his body radiating sullen hostility. Hrothgar's voice had its slurred, nagging tone about it. I couldn't hear what he was saying. But I had no doubt there'd be another beating tonight. Bad luck, Edward, I thought complacently. Still, until he faded to a blur, Edward looked most fetching in his white tunic. It wasn't just his Latin that had blossomed since leaving Jarrow. In that fairly short time, he'd grown from pretty boy into a rather scary beauty.

And I wasn't the only one who'd noticed. It didn't take perfect vision to see how the northerners currently on deck had left off their work and were leaning over the side, the lust plain on their horrid faces. Forget the lack of any pilot, I told myself: this alone would be trouble for Hrothgar. None of it, sadly, would be of my making. When I was younger, I believed the conventional wisdom that lust is abolished by age. I then found that, if lust may be dulled, all that really goes is the ready means of satisfying it.

'I suppose we need more supplies,' I said, trying not to sound as morose as I suddenly felt. 'Since it's just the two of them, we can assume some intention to pay. I wonder why we've anchored so far out, rather than gone in to dock?' I looked again into the harbour. If the exchange was to be made here, I was surely worth a convoy for taking back to Constantinople. There wasn't so much as a single Imperial galley moored against the docks. It probably was just a matter of supplies.

But I pulled myself together. I plucked at Wilfred's sleeve. I tried to ignore how loose it hung on his arm. If possible, he might have been still smaller now than he'd been three years before, when he'd been sent to me with Bede to improve his Latin. I pointed at my slippers that I'd left beside the bowl, and waited for him to struggle back to his knees and get them on to my feet. We were going on another of the slow circuits of this ship that served for my daily exercise. Since the boards were new and not properly planed, I had no wish to pick up any more splinters.

'Listen,' I said, 'this is our first proper time alone in over a month. It may well be our last. There are things we need to discuss. It's pretty obvious I've been lifted by the Emperor, and we're on our way to Constantinople. What will happen there with me is impossible to say. But the moment we dock and the palace officials take charge of me, your own value as a hostage will be at least diminished. When that happens, I want you to grab the first excuse for a getaway. This time, I rather hope you'll be a little faster than you were in Jarrow. I want you to get yourself to the Nunnery of the Blessed Theodora. It's where the main wall joins the Golden Horn. The Abbess there is the great-niece of someone I knew well in the old days. Tell her I sent you. She'll see you come to no harm. Whether you see Jarrow again, or even Rome, is another matter. But that much I can do for you.'

'Surely, Master,' came the predictable reply, 'surely, I shall never see Constantinople or anywhere else. Long before then, I shall be paying for my sins.'

I thought of bringing him to his senses with a hard poke in the chest. But that might easily have knocked him to the deck. Besides, his face was taking on a more cheerful look.

'And,' he began again, 'I remember how, the Easter before last, we were visited in the monastery by the Emperor's representatives. You told me then that they had made fair promises. Whatever refusal you made at the time, I cannot see how the objective circumstances will have changed. Your state of health could not be known in Constantinople. If you are wanted for punishment, it would make better sense to have killed you in Jarrow. If you are now going back, therefore, it is unlikely to be for punishment.'

It was a fair point. I thought again of that clerical shitbag Alexius. Silly of me to have supposed he was the last I'd hear from the Empire. Certainly, if I'd paid attention to him then, we'd not be here now. I stopped and took hold of the ship's rail. We hadn't gone far from my daybed. Now, guessing my wishes, Wilfred went back for my cup. He brought it back invitingly full. Sadly, it carried more promise of cheer than performance – one part wine, three of water. I pulled a face. Edward was far more generous about refills. But I smiled and looked into the bright if sunken eyes.

'You could be right,' I said. 'I haven't discounted that possibility. At the same time, we do need to prepare for the worst.' I looked hard at the boy. What was the worst? I wondered. I changed the subject. 'Is there anything you can tell me about Edward I don't already know?' I asked. Wilfred looked steadily back at me. He waited for me to continue. 'I know,' I said, 'he really is English. But can you tell me anything about how he fell in with these northerners? Has he said anything to you that we can spin into actual knowledge?'

'I have heard him speaking English with Hrothgar,' came the reply.

That was interesting. I hadn't been able to catch anything of their conversations beyond the shrill cries for mercy. Was there a blood relationship? They didn't look very alike, though that was no bar to the hypothesis. I pressed Wilfred on the nature of their conversations. But they'd mostly been connected with the day-to-day running of the ship and keeping four dozen dangerous wild beasts from tearing us all limb from limb.

Otherwise, there wasn't much Wilfred could give me from Jarrow that I didn't know for myself. Edward had turned up at the monastery after the last harvest, and been taken in by Benedict without questions. He'd maintained an appearance of plodding idleness that had raised no suspicions with anyone. Since then, his manner had changed markedly. Whatever conversations he and Wilfred had managed out of my hearing, though, were entirely about grammar and history and all else he'd evaded in class. He hadn't boasted about the brilliance needed to keep up his pose. He hadn't even gloried in the horrid end that might await the pair of us. This wasn't the place for dispassionate judgements. But I had to admire the boy. *If only!* I thought again. *If only!*

'But, Master,' Wilfred asked with a gentle smile, 'are these enquiries leading anywhere? Is there any plan of escape from this ship?'

I laughed carefully, waiting for my chest to explode. No – the Mediterranean was working more of its magic. The cough I'd thought many times during the early days of the voyage would finish me off was gone. I laughed again and looked at the boy.

'I might once have conceived a daring plan,' I said with an attempt at brightness. 'See those two savages over there by the mast? The others are below, taking advantage of Hrothgar's absence to break out the beer. I could take up that lump of wood that has fallen so conveniently on to the deck and brain one of them, and grab his axe to finish off the other. Meanwhile, you could jam the hatch shut on everyone else. You and I could then rearrange the sails and take the ship off to some place of safety.

'Leave aside, however, that I might have trouble lifting anything as heavy as that piece of wood, let alone being up to a desperate but brief struggle with a man who can probably lift me with one hand while wanking with the other.' I smiled at the dark look that passed over Wilfred's face. 'Leave all that aside. Do you know anything about the management of any ship, let alone one this big and heavy? For myself, the only attention I've ever paid to ships is a purely abstract interest in the balance of forces. And this one really is bigger and heavier than anything I've ever seen below supply carriers. I never thought barbarians might be up to building anything so large. As for a place of safety . . .' I trailed off and allowed myself another laugh.

'Oh, my dear boy, I'm not saying we should entirely think ourselves into the heads of beasts prodded along to the slaughter. I've been alive a long time, and one reason for that is that something always turns up – if only you know how to recognise it. For the moment, though, with or without its two head gaolers, this ship is a floating prison, and we might as well put aside all thought of escaping. We wait here for Edward and Hrothgar to come back. I'm beginning to hope they'll bring some decent wine to have with dinner. In the meantime, I'm off to my cot for another nap. Get me up when the sun casts a four-foot shadow of yourself, and we'll have a Greek lesson. I think you will now understand why I've been putting so much emphasis on the spoken language.

'So, help me to my cot if you can,' I said curtly. 'I feel a good dinner coming on for tonight, and I'd like to be up to its full enjoyment. One of us needs to stay in reasonable health.'

9

But there was no good dinner. The crew waited until the stars looked down from a moonless sky. When Edward and Hrothgar didn't return, they served up something disgusting and went back to their beer. I was kept up half the night by their bawled singing and by their yapping, increasingly ill-natured arguments. When I eventually woke the following morning, the sea was calmer still and the sun hotter. I sat on the deck under my awning, looking over to the land. I still couldn't see much of Cartenna. And I could see no suggestion of a returning boat. It would soon be a day since it had set out.

'I think we should pray, Master,' Wilfred said, coming over to stand beside me.

I gave what I hoped was a casual sniff, and looked harder at Cartenna. I couldn't tell for sure, but there seemed to be movement of some kind on shore. I leaned forward and held up a hand to shade my eyes. It might have been a boat. Or it might have been something else. I looked back down at the deck. Without Hrothgar to nag, of course, nobody had seen fit to clean up Wilfred's vomit from the day before. Though dry, it was beginning to attract flies from the shore.

'We must pray for Edward, and I suppose for Hrothgar,' Wilfred elaborated. 'But I fear the time has come to pray for ourselves. I have sins that I wish I had been able to confess.'

I ignored him, hoping he wouldn't get back on to *that* worthless subject. I turned my head slightly, wondering if a new angle of vision might bring some improvement. It didn't. I tried to think of something witty. I did better with keeping the wine cup from spilling its redness all down my chest. At least no one would think I was either palsied or cold inside from the fear. If I couldn't be bothered with twisting round to look, I could plainly hear the muttering on the deck behind me.

'Do tell me,' I asked calmly, 'if we are just to be thrown overboard, or if the crew proposes to carve us up first.'

'I think it will be the latter,' came the infinitely sad reply. 'The weapons they carry would be superfluous for the former.'

I tried not to laugh. This was, after all, a crisis. 'Oh dear,' I said. I took another sip and put my wine down very carefully. 'Have the kindness, dear boy, to help me round so that I can face these people.'

It may be that familiarity had blunted the horror of their appearance. Or it may be that Hrothgar had done outstandingly well in transforming them from a pack of beer-demented barbarians to a crew of cut-throat pirates. Whatever had been the case, though, they weren't now an encouraging sight. They looked pretty much as they had on their first appearance in Jarrow – only there was no monastery wall this time to keep us apart. They stood in a closely packed rabble a couple of yards from my daybed. One of them leaned forward and jabbered something I couldn't catch. Someone at the back began making weird animal noises. How Hrothgar had kept them in any line at all said much for his skills as a leader. How he'd dared trust them unsupervised on board was a mystery. Now he was gone, and might not be back, they were all reverting by the moment. I clutched for my stick and got unsteadily to my feet.

'Gentlemen,' I said in my best approximation to their own language. No one seemed surprised I could speak it. 'Dear friends.' I smiled and held out my free arm in a gesture of regard and affection. 'I appreciate your concerns for what may have happened ashore. But I do suggest that a day is not long enough for drawing untoward conclusions. Let us wait until evening. If nothing has happened by then, let us consider returning to England – where I can promise a generous reward from the Lord Bishop of Canterbury for my safe return.'

'We want our men back,' someone shouted.

'You've fucking stitched them up with the Greeks,' someone

else added with a certain want of reasonableness. There was a general humming of assent.

I didn't bother with probing. It was plain that 'our men' covered the two oarsmen alone. Edward and Hrothgar could be written off as lost. My stick wobbled with a slight motion of the ship, and I had to grab hold of Wilfred to stay on my feet. Since he was clutching at me for the same reason, it was almost a wonder we didn't hit the deck together. As it was, I was able to carry on with my probably useless oration.

'You must consider,' I said, 'that I have no knowledge of conditions on shore. You surely know that I am a prisoner on this ship, and have no contact with anyone. If your friends are in trouble there, I cannot help them. All I can do is repeat my promise of reward for my safe return to England.'

'You'll get them back,' the man at the front shouted again. 'You'll get them back – or the boy dies!'

Against my better judgement, I laughed. I thought raiding undefended towns was their job, not mine. What did these creatures now expect of me – that I'd swim ashore in the absence of another boat, and then back with an oarsman under each arm? They might as well butcher us on the spot. I sat quickly down and fussed with my blanket.

'Master,' Wilfred whispered in my ear, 'I've often heard them talking about you. They are all convinced you are a wizard of great power. They really believe you can help them. And I also want you to go ashore. If we must die together now, I am prepared to watch your own ascent to Heaven. But you might be able to save us both. All else aside, why should both of us die when one of us has the chance of escape?'

'Don't be stupid, boy!' I snapped. Evidently, he'd been too impressed by stories of my past life to realise how long ago all that had been. 'Give me another moment, and I'm sure I can think of something else to offer these animals. Perhaps they could deliver us to one of the bishops in France before negotiating our ransom with Theodore . . .'

But if they were still sufficiently collected not to commit any actual violence, nothing I offered was enough to stand them down. I did think of putting the eminently reasonable argument that if I had magical powers sufficient to get their men back, I'd hardly have been their helpless prisoner since Christmas. But there's no reasoning with the barbarian mind. You'll get more sense out of women or idiot children. One way or another, at least one of us was going over that side. I took off my hat and scratched my scalp. My thoughts raced as, like a failing litigant in court, I tried to think of some other argument that would turn things in my favour. But nothing came.

'Wilfred,' I asked, 'can you tell me what is going on ashore?'

'There is a boatload of armed men setting out,' he said.

Interesting, I thought, and potentially useful. I'd said that something always turned up. Perhaps it just had. Without being able to see more than a blur at this distance, I couldn't tell how many armed men there were. From the manner of the crew, however, I could guess they weren't enough to raise any alarm here. I thought hard again. I shrugged. I turned and pointed at the more presently alarming crew members.

'I want you all below,' I said firmly. 'I want just three of you on deck when that thing comes in hailing distance. You will treat me with exaggerated respect.'

'The boy stays with us,' the man at the front said. 'We give you until dusk.'

'You are under arrest,' the senior official rasped at me in Latin as the little boat docked. 'You will order your crew to surrender.'

'On the contrary,' I replied in Greek, as smoothly as my remaining teeth would allow, 'you will send news to His Excellency the Prefect that I should be received with all respect due to the Emperor's servant.'

He looked down at the shrivelled creature swathed in dirty rags who'd addressed him from the boat. His mouth fell open.

'You will also provide me with a covered carrying chair. I don't at all fancy those stairs up to the main square.'

As I'd half expected, Cartenna was largely derelict. With the decline of population, it's much the same everywhere in Africa. All the buildings on the west side of the main square were already in ruins. On the other three sides, they were, so far as I could tell, mostly empty. There were a few stalls set out to sell food, and there was a weak apology for a slave market in progress. I could see a couple of naked, half-dead blacks prodded into dancing by the Berbers who'd brought them in for sale. No one was bidding for them. No one seemed to notice they were for sale. About a dozen children played in the dust. There were a few looks in my direction as I was carried past. No doubt, the big and decidedly odd ship moored outside the harbour had been the main talking point in town. There didn't seem to be enough people for a mob of the curious to gather round me. But there were curious looks. I sat in my chair, trying to pretend I looked other than an old beggar. The smells were comforting, though – the familiar mix of early flowering shrubs and of broken sewers.

'Who are you, that you presume to dirty our waters with your presence?' the Prefect asked in laboured Greek. 'This is a peaceful place. We'll have no trouble here.'

From his accent and his faintly Germanic appearance, I guessed he was a local man. He was also very young. If he was twenty, I'd have been surprised. This had its advantages. A sharp little Greek seconded from somewhere that mattered might have been more sceptical. The hall of audience had been piled high with smashed furniture, so I was being received in the man's office. I pointed at the water jug and sat myself unbidden on the other side of his desk. A dark slave looked at the Prefect. There was a moment of uncertainty. Then he nodded. I drained the cup and put my hands together on the stained wood.

'I am on a mission from the Emperor himself,' I opened. 'It brooks no delay.' I stared into the man's confused face. Keeping a strongly Greek accent, I switched into Latin and repeated myself. 'I think you have the Captain of my ship. If so, I need him back at once.' While the Prefect took this in, I glanced about the room. Plaster had come off the upper reaches of the wall behind him, showing the remains of a mosaic. Over on my left was a filing rack that contained perhaps a dozen dust-covered circular letters. With a little shock, I found myself looking at the icon of the Emperor. This wasn't in its proper place on an easel beside him. It was instead propped against the far wall.

So, Constantine is out! I thought. Imperial images are never true to life, and the face that looked stiffly back at me might have been of almost anyone. But it wasn't of Constantine: I'd commissioned that portrait myself. Most likely, this one was of his boy, Justinian. He must now be only seventeen, I calculated. Still, he was no fool. More to the point, unless all his tutors had been changed after my fall, he'd not be so hostile as his father had been to finishing off the old nobility and handing out their land to the people who actually defended the Empire.

'The Augustus Justinian is not a man who tolerates interference in his business,' I said with more confidence. 'You have held me up outside your harbour for an entire day. Do therefore release my men and ensure that we have the supplies needed for an immediate departure.'

The Prefect glanced uncertainly at his secretary, who pulled a face and shrugged. I didn't like the look of him. He was probably a Greek. Though not bloated, he might have been a eunuch. His face streamed suspicion. There was a long silence as they looked at each other. While I drank again, the secretary scribbled a note and brushed it in front of the Prefect. He read it and sat in silence a while longer.

'Your orders,' he said eventually. 'I shall need to see your orders.' I could feel the tremor going out of my hands. Whatever else he'd been made to say, at least Edward hadn't shared anything material in Cartenna.

'My orders are here,' I said haughtily, tapping my head. 'Your orders are to follow my instructions without further question.'

There was another long silence. I sat placidly while the Prefect stared at nothing in particular and his secretary scratched away at another note.

'Your name at any rate,' he stammered.

'There is no need for you to know that,' I said. I had turned over various possibilities. Leontius of Smyrna had seemed a good idea before I'd seen the Imperial icon. But when a new emperor comes in, you never know what names might have found their way on to the list of the purged. I'd been out of things too long. Who could tell if some Leontius wasn't on the list that would have been transmitted to every provincial authority? I glanced again at the filing rack. If any of those circular letters had been consulted in a year, I'd have been surprised. I looked up at the tatty, smoke-darkened ceiling. I gave a bored yawn and looked at my fingernails. I'd forgotten how shameful they were and put my hands hurriedly down.

'Look, my dear young fellow,' I drawled, 'there really are just two possibilities. One is that I'm a pirate chief masquerading as a rather aged Greek of the higher classes. The other is that I'm telling the truth. I'll leave it to you to decide which is the case. But please don't spend too long about it. The Saracens are planning a raid on your city. Only I can stop this.'

Anyone with an ounce of imagination could have raised several other possibilities. But this was a prefect with no imagination at all.

'You will excuse me a moment, My Lord,' he said. He got up and bowed and led his secretary over beside the icon. I couldn't hear any of their whispered conversation. But it was easy to guess its frantic course. Every so often, they'd turn and give me a suspicious or merely frightened look. The wine I'd finished on board to steady my nerves now decided to announce its presence in my bladder. I left the remains of my water cup untouched. I wiggled my toes and wondered how long all this would take.

It wasn't that much longer. I could see the secretary was still for demanding further and better particulars. The Prefect, though, had decided his best course of action was to get rid of me at the earliest moment. He sat down opposite me again and smiled nervously.

'You must appreciate that I don't have responsibility for every detail of the administration,' he said, speaking fast. 'I will, of course, order a full enquiry. Even if it will report after your departure, I promise it will spare no one if guilt is to be laid on any individual. If there are lessons to be learned . . .' He spluttered on more about the *independent* enquiry he'd order and how no one would be spared.

What was the wanker about to tell me? I went cold all over. I set my face into a mask of bureaucratic immobility and stared straight at him.

'You see,' he continued, 'your men came ashore yesterday morning. They didn't come here to give their purpose, but went straight to the market. There was some – there was some altercation. The reports didn't tell me exactly what happened. But it seems that one of your men was hanged yesterday afternoon. The others are in prison awaiting my justice.'

'You hanged one of my crew?' I asked once I was able to trust my voice. Never mind the piss I was increasingly desperate to have – I nearly shat myself. 'This may be a serious matter. Are you able to tell me which of the four you hanged?'

'You will appreciate, My Lord,' he said, now blustering again, 'that one shouting barbarian is very like another. It required five men to get his neck into the rope. As it was, he nearly tore down the gallows.

'Would you like to see the body?' he asked suddenly. 'It's still hanging. I think the birds . . .' He trailed off.

Sixty-odd years of dealing with higher level administrative trash than this had left me in no doubt of how to put the frighteners on. I kept up the look of chilly distaste and thought frantically. If they hadn't hanged Edward – and, even if he were the most expendable of the four, I was relieved about that – there was a two in three chance that Wilfred would be in the clear back on board the ship. If it were Hrothgar, though . . . I trailed off myself. Wilfred would assure me it was all in the hands of God. As for me, I'd find out soon enough.

'I will sign an immediate order for your men to be released,' the Prefect said after another whispered row that I hadn't been able to follow. 'Sadly, it may not be until mid-afternoon that they are released. You see, the gaoler is a most devout man. Every morning, he goes off to pray before the shrine of the Blessed Rugosius, and takes the keys with him. Until he returns, you must regard yourself as our guest.'

'Very well,' I said briskly. 'I want them out of prison at the earliest.' I looked closely at the secretary. There was something unpleasantly thoughtful about his face. 'In the meantime, I shall be grateful for a bath and a change of clothes. Get me something plain but respectable. Your secretary can take down a list of other items that I want and you may have available here. Oh, and for the avoidance of any doubt, I will be staying for dinner.'

10

Even in early February, the sun hadn't been kind to Hrothgar. His gibbet swung gently in the breeze, flies crawling in and out of the open mouth. I shrugged and looked down again at Edward, who'd taken the hint and was now kissing my slippered feet. There were some nasty bruises on his arms. His tunic was ripped, showing on his back the cuts and bruises that come from being dragged across a rough surface. What wasn't ripped was still soaked in the foul-smelling mud that I've only ever come across in prisons. What I'd caught of his face as he emerged from the gloom was puffy with repeated crying. If you can imagine anything beyond their normal appearance, the two oarsmen looked probably worse. Covered in bruises where they'd been clubbed into submission, wrists chafed from endless struggle with the manacles that had kept them in submission, they'd emerged blinking into the bright sunshine. Credit where due, though, they'd taken the hint even sooner than Edward. Cowed and respectful, they knelt in silence beside him.

'Their weapons will be returned on your departure,' the secretary explained in answer to my unvoiced question. 'As His Excellency said, this is a peaceful place.' He gave me an openly hostile look, and then bowed ironically. Plainly, he thought the prison traffic he'd been ordered to oversee should have been in the other direction.

I smiled at him and raised my arms. The slaves stood obediently forward and lifted me back into the carrying chair.

'The Lord Perfect will surely not object if I continue the boy's education with a tour of your beautiful city,' I announced. 'I, for one, shall be grateful of the exercise before dinner.'

The secretary pulled a face that might have curdled milk and muttered something about supervising the gathering of stores. I watched as he went back over to the gaoler and rapped a few quiet instructions. Holding himself steady against the gatepost, eyes bleary from his 'devotions', the gaoler bowed at every pause. As the slaves got my chair aloft, and I leaned forward to poke my cane into the back of their leader, I saw the gaoler produce a sheet of what may have been folded parchment – hard to say with my wretched eyes. Without looking at it, the secretary stuffed it into a satchel before disappearing back in the direction of the Prefecture Building.

'Come, Edward,' I announced grandly – and sounding grand in any language with most of your teeth missing is quite an achievement. 'We must inspect the Church of Saint Varicella.' I leaned forward again and, this time, tapped all the carrying slaves with my cane. The boy and the oarsmen keeping up beside me, we began our slow progress towards the larger of the two semi-ruinous churches.

'Behold,' I said after about fifty yards. 'You see here the most ancient of the monuments of the city.' We stopped beside a battered arch. 'Cartenna is a place of measureless antiquity. Its name is derived from the Carthaginian words for "City on the River Tennus". It is said to have been the birthplace of the mother of the Hannibal who so beset Rome in ancient times. In its present form, however, it is a foundation of the First Augustus, who, after the close of the civil wars, designated it as a colony for soldiers of the Second Legion.' I pointed up at the pompous inscription. Over time, many of the bronze letters had come away from the stone. But it was still possible to read the words from their context and from the pattern left by the holes.

Edward played along with a question about the roofless temple beside the triumphal arch. While I went into much elaboration about the deification and worship of emperors before the establishment of the Faith, I pushed the blond wig back and mopped at my freshly shaven scalp. Cosmetic paint was beginning to run down my cheeks, but was best left untouched. I looked back at one of the oarsmen, who was picking his nose, and checked to see if we were being followed. Sure enough, there was that bloody secretary. He was lurking behind the pediment of what had been a statue of Septimius Severus. He was stooping forward to get as much as he could of the cover. But if he lacked the colossal obesity of the third sex, it would have taken a larger pediment than this entirely to conceal him.

We continued our slow progress through the silent, abandoned streets of what had once been a substantial grain port. Here had been the public library. Here had been the baths, a gift of the Great Constantine, that could accommodate five thousand. Here was the shrine where Saint Augustine had witnessed the miracle of the stroke suffered by an heretical preacher. My throat was feeling raw from the continual raising of my voice. While Edward passed me up a cup of water drawn from a fountain, I lapsed into quiet English.

'We're approaching the harbour from the western side,' I said. I'd noticed the stepped incline on my way up to the Prefecture. 'The moment I take off this ridiculous wig and put it back on the wrong way, I want the oarsman with the broken nose to lift me out of this chair and run with me straight to the docks. It will mean jumping down half a dozen steps each with a four- or five-foot drop. The ship's boat is still moored where you left it, and may still be unguarded. I must rely on the three of you to use your own initiative as required. But the idea is to get us back to the ship before anyone thinks to ignore the Prefect's orders and tries to arrest us.

'Do you understand?' Edward's mouth had fallen open. 'Oh, Jesus!' I whispered with another look round. 'Stop looking so gormless. If you don't want to end up like Hrothgar, you'll do exactly as you're told. Do you understand?'

His face took on his impassive look while he thought. Whatever he was thinking, it took longer than I fancied. Then he nodded. He took the cup from my hands. I heard him muttering to the oarsmen as he replaced it above the bowl of the fountain. I brushed a speck of dust from my tunic and wondered how well I could trust these people. If they decided to run off and leave me in the chair, it would be sod-all punishment for any of them. On the other hand, if gratitude is rather much to expect of barbarians, they were all three of them in considerable awe of the Old One. Even if not a wizard, I was the one who'd had the Greeks anoint him and clothe him in raiments of shining white, and who'd also sprung them from a prison from where they must have thought they'd only be taken out to be hung. I reached up and patted my wig back into place. I'd find out soon enough how I stood with these people. In the meantime, there was a charade that still had to be played. I peered at an inscription above a bricked-up doorway that we were gradually approaching, and cleared my throat.

'Here is the place where Saint Flatularis suffered the first part of his martyrdom.' I turned and made a loudish aside to Edward: 'He was a youth of exquisite beauty, yet was also solid in the Faith. When the tyrant Diocletian ordered all to sacrifice to the demons of the Old Faith, Flatularis refused. In order to break his will, he was chained naked in this house on a bed of roses while three beautiful courtesans assaulted him with their sinful lips and fingers. What did our Most Holy Saint do? Why, he quelled the rising temptation by biting off his tongue!'

I wanted to follow this with an account of how the young man was then rolled – still naked – in live coals mixed with broken potsherds, and end with a homily on what an example this should be for the youth of today. Sadly, the look on Edward's face was too much, and I found myself having to cover my laughing fit with coughs. By the time I was able to breathe again, we were halfway along the terrace I'd seen from the harbour. Before us, I could see a handful of armed men. It wasn't worth looking to see behind. On our left was the blue of the sky and the deeper blue of the sea, and, against both, the dark blur of our ship where it rode at anchor. It was now or never. I pulled myself back into order. I took a deep breath and lifted my hands up to the wig.

Before I could even turn the thing round, the oarsman had lifted me clean out of the chair. The next few moments are beyond any ordered description. There was a bone-shuddering crunch as the man landed on the first step of the terrace. It was enough to knock all the air out of my lungs, and I fought again for breath. There was another, and then another. I could hear wild shouting above us, but couldn't even think of trying to look back. Like a frightened child, I clamped my arms tighter about the oarsman's neck and pressed my face into rancid, prison-soaked clothing.

Our fast, jerking motion came to a sudden end about ten yards from the jetty. With a scream that reminded me of a pig when the knife goes into its belly, the oarsman went down. We hit the granite slabs together with me on top of him. I rolled off and only just saved my face from striking on the stone. I heard the man, still screaming, as he dragged himself to his feet and staggered the remaining distance to the boat. I struggled up and looked back at the crowd that was racing towards me. Suddenly very calm, I relaxed and looked up at the sky. Going like this hadn't been the end I'd imagined for myself. Then again, it was a sight better than snuffing it in bed, back in the freezing cold of Jarrow.

'Give me your arms, Master.' It was Edward! I'd seen him run ahead of us across the docks. Now he'd come back. He took hold of me and heaved me on to his back. He wasn't yet fully grown, and I was – as I like to keep saying – still a big man, even if decrepit. But, swaying about like a slave under a grain sack, he ran with me across what now seemed the impossibly long distance to the boat. But we got there, and fell together into its deep centre.

'Stop that boat!' I heard someone shout. As I gripped the side of the boat and tried to haul myself up, I heard, just overhead, the whizz of an arrow. Another thudded into the planking not six inches from my right leg. I looked up at the blubbering oarsman who'd dropped me. He was nursing a deep gash an earlier arrow had made in his arm. But, as I looked back to the jetty, I could see the Prefect's secretary frantically pushing the bows down, and shouting madly as he waved everyone towards the boat that had brought me ashore. It was nice to know, I told myself, that, even now, the price on my head was higher alive than dead. I pulled myself up into a sitting position and patted my wig into place. I smiled and blew a kiss at the secretary, who now stood on the extreme edge of the jetty. I couldn't make out his face. But it wasn't hard to guess the mixture of disappointment and boiling anger.

'Put your backs into it!' I croaked at Edward and the able-bodied oarsman. 'If we don't get a move on, they'll try to cut us off.' But the chaos of shouting and running back on the docks hadn't yet resolved itself into effective action. By the time their boat was setting out, we were already three-quarters back to the ship. I could see the anchor as it was pulled up and hear the beat of the drum as every man raced to take his place at the oars. Four arms of differing strength lifted me up and pushed me against the side of the ship. Two hands from above took hold of my wrists, As I was jerked into the air, someone else grabbed the waistband of my tunic. In an instant, I was back on deck and pushed into the arms of Wilfred, whose only response was to try carrying me back to the daybed from which I'd been plucked so very long ago – or so it now seemed. Needless to say he failed, and it was Edward who finally disentangled the pair of us and placed me with some show of reverence on the stained cushions.

An atrociously ugly but admiring face snarled down at me as I lay, exhausted, back on to the cushions.

'Have you managed to drink all the wine yet?' I asked weakly.

The face looked at me a moment longer, then vanished.

11

'So, apart from this exchange off Kasos,' I asked again, 'you have no idea what Hrothgar was about?'

Edward looked across the table with tear-swollen, still terrified eyes. He shook his head.

'Well,' I said with a hard smile, 'you can take that as a lesson to have something in writing.' There had been nothing. There should and could have been nothing. Most likely, Hrothgar had been illiterate even in the runes our people used before the light of Rome broke in to shine so benevolently upon us all. But I'd watched as Wilfred and Edward went through the man's cabin. Not a scrap of writing. And I believed Edward when he insisted that he'd been kept throughout on a need-to-know basis.

I pulled my wig off and dumped it on the table. Wilfred's first act once we were away from Cartenna and he'd recovered from his fainting spell had been to wash the paint off my face and pull my new clothes back into shape. I was vastly tired. I was beginning to hurt all over from the strain and the bruises. But I was enjoying myself far too much to give in to that. Yesterday, I'd been poor old Brother Aelric, schoolmaster and close prisoner. This morning, I'd nearly been food for the larger fish. Tonight, I was again – or as near enough as mattered – His Magnificence the Lord Senator Alaric. Now, the three of us sat in what had been Hrothgar's cabin, deciding what to do next. Correction – *I* was deciding.

There was a polite knock at the door. One of the less ferocious northerners sidled in. Had I any orders for dinner?

'I'll have some of the pickled lamb,' I said with a lordly wave. 'Do make sure to cut it up small and cook it tender. With it, I'll have bread soaked in whatever milk you have.' There had been no supplies from Cartenna, and I didn't feel that hungry. But prestige called for a dinner of sorts. And I could do with some more of that Spanish apology for wine.

'Oh,' I added, 'and do please send in your friend with the green eyes. For want of anyone else, I've decided to appoint him pilot of this ship. We need to discuss a change of course for tomorrow.' I waited for the door to close, then turned back to the boys.

'I'm not going back,' Edward said yet again. He squeezed his fists tight. 'I'm not going back. Any orders you give I'll countermand. You forget that I'm now in charge of this ship.'

'I beg to differ, young man,' I said grimly. 'The moment Hrothgar choked out his last breath ashore, you lost whatever position you had on board this ship. *I am the master now.*' There was a slight exaggeration here. If its crew was treating me with scared reverence, it was plain I was barely more in charge of the ship than a rider was of a bolting horse. Yes, everyone had been awed by my achievements ashore. They appreciated that I actually knew where we were. And they hadn't refused my offer of twice whatever Hrothgar had been paying them – twice that, and payable in gold the moment we made contact with Theodore in Canterbury. But calling myself their 'master' was putting things rather strong. Still, I was as near as mattered in charge. Certainly, Edward would have to adjust to his altered position on board. And I had no intention of making it other than a bitter demotion.

'Richborough strikes me as by far the most suitable destination,' I went on, 'by far the best for all of us.' Edward opened his mouth to argue again. I glowered at him until he shut it. I thought he'd burst into more tears. But, though his shoulders shook, he fought off the attack. 'So Richborough it will be,' I said with a nasty smile. 'For Wilfred and me, it will be special prayers of thanks for our safe return. For you, it won't be quite that. But I'll get you a very gentle penance. I'll even have you back in my class – this time under your own name, assuming it's other than Edward. Before then, however, there will have to be some kind of penance. I am mindful of your services earlier today. But it doesn't make up for your part in getting Wilfred and me on to this lunatic voyage. And killing a monk isn't something the Church can wholly overlook.'

The boy looked up. 'I don't know what you're talking about,' he cried.

'Come now, boy,' I snarled. He shrank back before a glare that had terrified emperors. 'Don't try denying something when the facts speak for themselves. You sucked Cuthbert off till you puked. Then you cut his throat so you'd be the one who opened the gate. I don't think anyone is missing a man like that. No doubt Benedict has already found a better teacher of logic among the surviving villagers. But since no one probably gives a shit about poor young Tatfrid, you can take the blame for Cuthbert. I'll ask you some other time about the two groups who turned up outside the monastery. For the moment, you're an accomplice to what I consider bloody murder, and penance you'll do for it.'

'There will be no trip to Constantinople?' Wilfred broke in. The shock of my coup on board had forced all thought of dying from his mind, and there now seemed a hint of disappointment in his voice.

I shook my head. Being ambushed in Cartenna was neither here nor there. I could put that down to local causes. The real problem was the change of emperor. Justinian might be friendly for old times' sake, and I could be sure that any Circus execution was right off the agenda. But I didn't suppose there would be any plans to kill the fatted calf in the event of my return. The new ministers could be trusted to see to that.

'Your place is in England,' I said reassuringly.

Wilfred nodded, now obedient.

'Besides, we don't really know what was agreed with Hrothgar. Edward is sure there was talk back in Jarrow of an exchange in Kasos, but has no idea where Kasos is, or when the exchange might be. Is that so, Edward?'

He nodded.

'Well, Kasos is a little speck that lies between Crete and Karpathos. It has a nice harbour, but is also rather close to the seas where the Saracens may again dominate. We aren't going there.

'No,' I said firmly with a little gloat at Edward, 'we're going home. For all the wind may be blowing from the west, it's back west we're headed.'

The gloat was too much for Edward. He reared up and shouted, 'I'm not going back to England! I'm never going back. I've got this far into the world. I'd rather die than go back to England.'

'Be that as it may,' I sneered, 'you're going back. You're going back to do whatever penance I get you. After that, you can study for the Church, or go off and fight for someone, or, failing that, dig in the fields. And if you try anything naughty between here and Richborough, I'll have you flogged and then clapped in irons.'

I overate at dinner. Or perhaps I drank too much. Whatever the case, I had what I suppose I should think the most awful dream. I was back on my diverted ship to Athens. The sun shone bright overhead. The waters sparkled all about. I was naked again. I held my arms up and bathed in the glorious warmth. I thought of my own appearance and felt the usual stiffy coming on. It swelled and swelled into a mighty erection. I looked about me. The sailors were all hard at work with their ropes. No one was looking. I thought of my cabin below. But this was an urgency that wouldn't wait even the brief drop down the ladder into the cool darkness. Again, I looked about. Even if every eye had been turned in my direction, I was too far gone to care. I flopped down against the mast and gently stroked myself. I almost went off at once, but squeezed my eyes shut and concentrated on delay. When I was ready, I began again with the lightest strokes. My nipples were stiff with excitement. I could feel the sweat running down my back. I groaned and paused again.

'Let me help you, Master,' I heard Edward say in English.

I opened my eyes and looked at him, trying to work out who he was, and then how he could be here with me.

'You haven't been born yet,' I said through dry, trembling lips. As he smiled silently back at me, the clothes melted from his body, and he knelt naked beside me. I put a damp hand on his back and pulled him towards me. I kissed him and breathed in the smell of his body. He took hold of me and pressed very hard. I put my hands on to his shoulders and looked into his eyes. He smiled steadily back. I looked at him until a great ball of white fire went off behind my eyes and bleached out all other visual sensations. All sense of time, of space – even of personal identity – followed, as I passed deep into the blaze of annihilation the more insane mystics try and fail to describe.

At last, it was over, and I lay trembling on the deck. Still looking at me, Edward smiled with a calm tenderness. And rested a hand lightly on my chest.

As I finally relaxed and let my eyelids droop, he said, '*Ya a'khy, anta ygeb a'n takon alkhalifa.*' I opened my eyes and looked at him. With a strange smile, he repeated himself. He was speaking, I realised, in Saracen. 'O, my brother, you shall be Caliph,' he was saying. How could I understand what he was saying? I asked myself. What did it mean? But he smiled again and pointed down at my crotch. I followed his pointed finger. With a cry of terror, I was on my feet and brushing at myself. Writhing in the sticky mess that covered my belly and thighs were thousands and thousands of black maggots. I brushed at them, and they fell on to the deck. I looked at my right hand. They squirmed and wriggled between my fingers. Already, some were crawling on my wrist and forearm.

'Welcome to Hell!' I heard Priscus call from behind me. 'Isn't this what you've always deserved, you corrupt bastard? Yes, welcome to Hell, my shitty young Alaric! This is the beginning of the punishment you've long deserved.'

His grating laughter still sounding, I woke with a start and lay sweating in my cot. I tried to sit up, but found I couldn't move. Gradually, I came back to my waking senses, remembered who and where and when I was. Except for the steady grinding together of new timbers, all was now silent about me. Instinctively, I reached down to my crotch. Certainly, I'd had an orgasm. Still cold with horror, I rubbed the watery-thin liquid between forefinger and thumb. For all the seed I'd cast off, I might have pissed myself. But I was alive and here and very, very old.

I laughed. Was that any improvement on the dream? I laughed

again, and now felt the griping in my belly. It was the disgusting food, I told myself – that, or the still more disgusting drink. I lay in the cot, farting softly. That gave some relief, but wasn't enough to settle me. I carefully relaxed my sphincter muscle and waited. I was right. That sour milk had gone straight through me, and was now sloshing insistently against its final exit. Unlike the dark, semi-cupboard below in which I'd previously been shut at night, Hrothgar's cabin up here on the deck had no night bucket. I could choose between shitting the bed and going in search of the common bucket on deck.

I pushed back the blanket and sat up. Since old Aelric had never yet fallen into geriatric incontinence, His Magnificence the Senator Alaric would definitely have to go for a walk. I reached out in the darkness for my walking stick and got unsteadily to my feet. The weather had cooled astonishingly since Wilfred and Edward had carried me to bed. I felt about for an old under-tunic that had belonged to Hrothgar, and stepped out on to the deck. I didn't suppose I'd be all alone out there. As usual with this rather strange ship, we hadn't put into shore for the night, or even dropped anchor, but were drifting in open waters. That meant there would be someone up on the mast to keep watch. But even if I were to be seen, my helpless doddering old fool act was now superfluous. There was a gentle but increasing motion of the ship, and I'd need to keep hold as I felt my way down to the stern, where the night bucket was placed. But I could and would easily manage that for myself.

12

Most of the pleasures that men discuss, and write books to praise or analyse, are best enjoyed when young. Just as satisfying in your nineties, though, as in your twenties, is a good shit. Indeed, my dinner was nicer to evacuate than it had been to swallow. I relaxed and savoured the relieved emptiness in my guts, and, seated on the bucket, looked up at the splashes of light that I saw in place of stars. All things considered, I had no reason to complain. Forget my bizarre dream – I'd just had a wonderful shit. And, if I was hurting all over, I hadn't broken anything in the escape from Cartenna. I was reasonably clean. If there had been no supplies in the end, I was now master of a crew that had, only that morning, been prepared to butcher me. Above all, I was still alive!

Yes, still alive. None of this abolished the fact that I was so bloody old. And being old, I can tell you, is rather like being ill – except there's no hope of getting better. Again, though, I had no valid reason to complain. Age had crept slowly up behind me. It was a matter of a white eyebrow here and there, a growing bald patch, a bit of a belly for a while, the gradual wearing out of teeth. Other men around me had sickened and died in various and usually horrid ways, and I'd drifted serenely through middle age with barely diminished vigour. Even when I did finally reach the age that men called 'half as old as time itself', I remained too busy to notice the falling off of bodily power.

But age had finally crept up. I leaned back against the mast and thought of my aborted narrative of the Athens trip. I'd been so young and strong, so healthy and so confident about facing the world. In the space of time separating then from now, men had been born and had grown old and died; so, in many cases, had their sons. But it didn't strike me as such a very long time since I'd stood on the deck of that other ship. Now, I was unambiguously decrepit. I'd seen as much back in Cartenna, when, for the first time in years, I looked into a proper mirror. Apart from the eyes, which were much as they always had been, the face looking back at me had reminded me of nothing so much as the unwrapped mummy I'd seen a few times of the Great Alexander. Little wonder everyone thought me a creature of magical powers. I hadn't called for the wig and the paint to cover up the truth. Neither, though, had I waved them away. The racing chariot of my life was reaching the end of its final lap.

Even so, the final lap wasn't ended yet. I'd survived the journey from the Tyne to the Narrow Straits. If only poor Wilfred hadn't nearly died, I'd have found the journey preferable to another winter in Jarrow, and I'd conceived a grudging respect for whatever race of barbarians had been able to design and build so large and capable a ship, and even for the barbarians who, if beastly in all else, had been so capable in handling it. We'd now be retracing the voyage out in much improved weather and with me in charge. It was worth looking forward to my reception in Canterbury and then in Jarrow. I thought again of the day just past. I thought of that ridiculous Prefect, and then of his secretary's despair on the jetty. I'd have to ensure that something unpleasant came of the useless lump of meat who'd tried to leave me behind. But the whole thing had been as neat an operation as anyone could have wished. I thought again of that absurd story about the martyrdom of Saint Flatularis. And I thought of the look on Edward's face. Yes, I was alive, and life still wasn't so bad that I wanted it over.

I thought again. Yes, I was alive. But let it be assumed that there was a Hell, and that I'd just had some vision of my place there – even that might have its moments. I put my head back and laughed. And I let out a long, gratified fart.

'You are unable to sleep, Master?' It was Wilfred behind me on the deck. I finished my laugh and hoped the fart hadn't been too embarrassingly loud. But he'd announced himself with a coughing fit, and probably hadn't heard anything.

'But what keeps you awake so late – or so early?' I asked. 'I did tell you to drink all your wine and get a proper night's sleep.' From habit I raised my arms each side of me in the gloom. He reached weakly forward and helped me to my feet. He cleaned me with the sponge and pulled my clothes back into order.

'I was looking at the lights over in the west,' he said. I followed his pointed finger, but saw nothing. 'I think there is more than one.'

I sniffed and suggested it might be a fishing boat, or some merchant ship that wasn't hugging the shore. Even in the Mediterranean, most seaborne trade doesn't start again until the late spring. But that doesn't mean the seas are empty. I wondered – now that Hrothgar wasn't around to keep the ship moving in its vaguely eastward course – if the crew would go back to full-time piracy. Once I'd taken charge of things, I'd spent some time with Wilfred on an inventory. We were running short of everything, including money. If we were to get back all the way to Richborough, we'd need a top-up from somewhere.

'Something you may not have appreciated, Master,' Wilfred added, 'is the danger that Edward took on himself when he went back for you.'

I said nothing, but let him help me over to the side of the ship – rather, we helped each other. Then I kept an arm round him while he finished coughing.

'Until the man in the green robe stopped them,' he continued once he was able to speak again, 'the archers were raining arrows on to the docks. Edward was already in the boat – already holding an oar – when the big northerner dropped you. When he reached you, there was an armed man only six feet away.'

I nodded. I hadn't been able to take in the whole picture at the time. But it was easy to see it all now. I'd led the main body of guards far into the upper part of the city, then had taken everyone by surprise with the speed of our getaway. Even so, the docks were an easy killing ground. It needed a very cool nerve to go deliberately back there.

'You were looking forward to Constantinople, weren't you?' I asked.

Wilfred shrugged. 'To pray in the Great Church there, to consult libraries so vast that the catalogues alone fill more books than we have in Jarrow, to walk through the endless streets and squares that you have described so well – who would not wish to see the New Rome built by Constantine as capital for his Christian Empire?' He paused and looked again into the west. 'But you are right that there is work to be done in England. It is sinful to wish for a place in the world other than the one appointed by God.'

It wasn't the answer I'd have given at his age. But it was useful to have only one resentful boy to keep in line. And I did want him in a place of safety as soon as we could get to one. If we could safely put in to Africa, I'd have considered even that for him instead of this ship, where he was slowly dying.

'And what place,' I asked with a smile, 'do you suppose has been appointed for Edward?'

'He may not be quite so great a sinner as you believe,' came the reply.

I thought of jumping in here with some questions, but didn't want to break the flow.

'Perhaps I should have told you at the time, but Edward did ask many questions back in the monastery about your earlier life. I broke no confidences, but now realise he was gathering background information for his mission. I think, though, he was inspired by the stories told by the other monks of your progress from Kent to Rome and then to Constantinople, and of how you rose from dispossessed orphan to greatest commoner in the Empire.

'You once told me, Master, of how you were expelled from Rome after your first few days there. You managed to have the decree cancelled, but you surely remember how it felt.'

I sighed and thought back to that meeting in Rome all those years ago, when the Dispensator told me he was throwing me out of Rome. As with all the man's dealings with me, it was a ruse to get me to do his dirty work. But I'd cried like a child when I thought I was to be pushed out of the glorious new world I'd found on leaving England. However, Wilfred hadn't finished.

'We prayed together after you fell asleep over dinner,' he said.

'There are things I am not able to repeat. But the plan was for Hrothgar to be present when the northerners first arrived at the monastery. If there had not been some confusion that Edward cannot explain, the capture would have gone as smoothly as it eventually did. There would surely have been no killing outside the monastery.'

'Very well,' I said. I'd already worked this out for myself. Whatever the case, Tatfrid was dead, and there was no bringing him back. Edward hadn't been any kind of principal in the capture. And he had saved my life. 'Let Edward know that I will send him ashore at our first Spanish port for supplies,' I continued firmly. 'If he chooses to make off with the money I give him, I shan't think any the worse of him.' There was a wind picking up, and the ship swayed just enough to make me clutch harder at Wilfred, and then to steady him. Was the sky clouding over? Hard to say. 'The Saracens will break into Spain sooner or later. When that happens, there will be opportunities for the man he will surely become.

'Now, do help me back to my cot. If I sleep late, I don't suppose my presence will be actively missed.'

13

I stood between two of the northerners. A third stood behind, holding up a wooden shield to keep the fine drizzle from soaking me.

'It's an Imperial battle fleet,' I said, looking west across the mile or so of choppy sea that divided us. 'I can't say what it's doing in these waters. And it's pretty unusual for it to be out of harbour at all this time of year, and on a day like this.'

'Could it have followed us from Cartenna?' Edward asked. He was the one who'd got me out of bed at dawn, and had then been darting up and down the mast so he could relay the details of the fleet's elaborate gyrations. I could see these now for myself as it struggled ever closer while keeping in attack formation.

'Might have,' I conceded. But that wasn't very likely. There had been no warships in Cartenna the day before. I knew of no naval base within easy communicating distance. And if this was what Wilfred had seen in the night, it would have been coming from the west – perhaps the north-west. The fleet might possibly have touched in on Cartenna after we'd left and then set straight out again in pursuit. But it struck me as a very faint possibility.

'These waters are full of Saracen pirates and other raiders,' I said, after another long inspection of those small, dark shapes. I couldn't see the rise and fall of the oars, but the wind was now bringing the faint and ominously rapid beating of drums. Unlike our ship, these were propelled by well-trained – or well-whipped – slaves. 'But do search your memory, Edward,' I asked with a change of tone. 'Did Hrothgar say anything about possible alternative meetings before Kasos?'

The boy shook his head. He repeated that the plan had been to use the design advantages of this ship so far as possible and keep away from the shore. There was no reason why Hrothgar should have shared any more with him than I'd already been told. But I did know that, ever since we'd had to put in to gather wood for a broken mast, we'd never managed to recover the course Hrothgar had had in mind.

'Do you suppose, Master, we are to be attacked?' Wilfred asked from deep within the folds of his hood. He might have been asking if the wind was about to change.

'No reasonable doubt of it,' I said. I glanced at Edward. He at least was looking scared. 'Do you see how the fleet is bearing down on us in that crescent formation?' I tapped the deck with my stick to show our own position, and then traced an invisible crescent a few inches beyond to show the formation of the fifteen battle ships. 'The idea is for the outer ships to overtake us. You see how small and light they are relative to their sails and the number of their oars? On a smoother sea than this, they can move with astonishing speed. The bigger ships in the centre don't move so fast. But you really don't want to come within a few hundred yards of them. The biggest ship of all will be controlling all the others – coordinating their moves into a single and quite deadly weapon. The cusps of the crescent will overtake us. The whole thing will then close in on us like some giant pincer. If we don't surrender at once, there will be grappling hooks fired at us from the larger ships. After that, it's boarding.'

Wilfred calmly folded his arms and fought to suppress the renewed coughing fit. I looked round at a noise behind me. It was Edward, now carrying a spiked mace so heavy, it bumped on the deck beside him.

'Will there be fighting?' he asked, trying to look fierce.

Where his rain-soaked clothes clung to him, he looked absolutely lush. A shame he'd not be going back to Jarrow, I thought again. I smiled.

'I'm sure the crew is up to a fight,' I said. 'But once those grappling hooks slam into the side of this ship, it's numbers that will count.' Edward's face fell again. Before I could really enjoy the sight, I sniffed at the rising wind that had brought the sound of the drums. 'Can you smell burning?' I asked.

'There are things on the larger ships that look like big spoons,' Edward replied. 'Do you think they might be catapults? They've been loaded with what look like bundles of burning cloth.'

I gripped the side of the ship and tried harder to see across the water. 'Tell me,' I asked, a cold feeling rising out of my stomach, 'can you see bronze tubes projecting from any of those ships?'

Edward shook his head and gave a better description of the charged catapults.

I was only slightly relieved. Even I could see the speed at which the fleet was approaching. I'd never have thought it possible for the formation to be kept up in weather like this. No one but a fool could think this was to be a prearranged or even peaceful meeting. If orders had been given for a capture, this was an odd way to go about obeying them. This was an attack. Bearing in mind the price of those pitch bags, the catapults hadn't been charged to scare us into surrender. It was an attack preparatory to sinking. I turned to the pilot, who was standing a few yards to my left.

'Cancel the order to try going round those ships,' I said. 'Can we outrun them?' I thought again of the hundred or so oarsmen aboard each of the attacking ships. I thought of them against fifty strong but semi-drunken northerners – fewer if we were to keep any fighting ability on deck.

'Piece of piss!' The man laughed. 'But why not just ram through them?' He cleared his throat and spat appreciatively.

I thought about his suggestion. He knew more about his ship's capabilities than I did. It was a heavy ship, and I had no doubt it could smash up even a big battle ship. But we'd be rowing into the wind. We were too heavy and hadn't the oarsmen to keep up the required speed once we'd broken through the crescent. But we did have that big sail, and the wind was picking up by the moment. The battle ships, I knew, were good for sprinting and darting about. If we could get away, they didn't have the means for extended chase. And in this sea, they'd take in a lot of water if they tried for speed over any distance.

But the wind was blowing from the west. If we raised the sail, we'd be hurrying further into a sea that I badly wanted to leave. If we did outrun it, that fleet would still be about, potentially blocking any further attempted dart to the west. If we did manage to get past it, we might still find ourselves chased from the east by another fleet. Then we'd be fucked for sure.

I strained to look into the dark skies to our west. That way was Richborough. All my plans had been based on a slow rowing into the wind. Once through the Narrow Straits, the northerners would be back in waters they knew and could manage with the sail. I'd been almost counting the days off to the moment when we could touch shore at Richborough and send word for Theodore to come down from Canterbury with his money bags. Now, that bastard fleet blocked the way. I sighed and nodded to the pilot. While I was helped back to my sodden daybed, the ship pitched and rolled horribly as the sail came flapping down and took the full power of the wind.

It wasn't before time. Even as I looked up again, I could see the bright streak of flame against the grey of the sky. As the burning pitch bag came closer, I could hear its fluttering buzz through the air. It fell short – though only by a few dozen yards. But then I felt the shudder as one of the six-foot iron-tipped arrows crashed into our side. Had I left it too late with my dithering? If we didn't pick up speed soon enough, or if the wind dropped down, there was every chance of a lucky hit. One hole in that bulging sailcloth, and the whole would split from top to bottom. With everything wagered on the sail and its already damaged mast, we couldn't afford a lucky hit.

But if the ships on the arms of that pincer came closer and closer, the distance did eventually widen. Other huge arrows flew overhead or smashed into the side. More of those fiery bundles landed behind us – and I could hear the hiss as they struck the grey water. But now the great sail was filled with air as if it were an inflated bladder, and the mast held. It held for all the dubious upward looks, and for all the continued distribution of arms about the deck. One moment, the battle ships were so close that even I could see the little figures darting about on the upper decks, and the archers watching us from the rigging. Another moment, and the whole battle fleet was a receding blur.

The crew let up a ferocious cheer. Perhaps the largest man on board sucked his moustaches in as he took a great lungful of air for shouting something long and obscene back towards the failing pursuit. Someone sat me roughly forward and patted my back until I coughed. Someone else pressed a wine cup into my hands. Whatever might be said against the notion, I was their wizard. For the second time in two days, they somehow believed I'd got them out of trouble. Whatever lay in wait at the end of this dash to the east would need more than the magic I'd shown them so far. I'd have to think of something. But that huge, articulated pincer was half a mile behind us. It could open and shut as it pleased. We were beyond its reach.

'Take me to my cabin,' I called weakly in Latin. No one came to help me to my feet. I looked over to the stern of the ship. Just beside the tiller, Edward and Wilfred were locked in what looked like a tremendous row. I strained to hear them, but the flapping of the sail overhead drowned out the snatches of shouted argument that blew towards me. I waved at them, but neither paid any attention. Wilfred suddenly gripped his chest, and I saw his body shake with coughs. But he never let up his own side of the shouted argument. I turned to the man who'd given me the wine. 'Take me inside,' I ordered. 'Also, do have the pilot attend on me before the celebratory beer is handed round.'

14

'What the fuck do you suppose you were doing?' I snarled at the two boys. Holding on to each other against the continuous pitching of the ship, they stood before me in my cabin. Outside, the wind was raging, and great belts of spray crashed against the walls. 'What little control I have over these animals depends on my pretence of calm assurance. Can you imagine the effect on this pretence when the two of you start a public shouting match and nearly come to blows?' More for warmth than any hope of a youthful appearance, I clapped the wig on my head and glared at the boys.

A defiant look on his face, Edward stared back at me. Legs shaking from the effort of holding his place, Wilfred looked intently at a spot on the floor.

'I tell you, it *was* him,' Edward repeated.

I raised a hand to silence him. 'Very well,' I said. 'I discount that you're lying to put me off any return to England. If you think you saw him, that's good reason in itself. I won't question the sharpness of your eyes, or your ability to recognise faces when they aren't where they ought to be.' And I didn't think it worth questioning either in Edward. I looked at Wilfred. He was pale and still trembling after his attack, but otherwise holding steady. 'You tell me, boy, why you don't believe it was Brother Joseph.'

His answer, if reasonable, was wholly unsatisfactory. He couldn't deny that the man who'd stood on the prow of the battle ship, at one point not fifty yards from us, had looked like Brother Joseph. All he could say against Edward was that it couldn't have been Brother Joseph. If we'd been discussing alleged miracles, the argument from common sense would have been decisive. But there was no need of any miracle for Joseph to have been looking at us from across the water and urging on a battle fleet that had been ordered to sink us. If we'd got this far from Jarrow, why not he also?

Of course, I was at one with Wilfred in hoping it hadn't been him. It wasn't that I shared any of his sense of scandal that a man of the Church could be urging on our destruction. Rather, it was the endless range of possibilities – all equally disturbing – that would be raised from admitting that Edward might not have been mistaken.

'Very well,' I said, trying to look unrattled, 'let us allow that it might have been Brother Joseph. I know more of his background than you do, and he would not have been out of place where Edward believes he saw him.' I was now thinking aloud. An audience even of boys made for more connected thought than if I'd withdrawn to my cot with a flask of heated wine. I motioned them into their now usual places at the table, and closed my eyes to fight off the returning tiredness.

'Edward,' I asked, trying to sound in control of things, 'I will ask you again if your kinsman Hrothgar told you anything about the details of my abduction. I want you to think hard and tell me anything you know. Anything – no matter how trivial you may think it – may be of use in our present circumstances.'

'He wasn't really my kinsman,' Edward replied slowly. 'He took me on after my parents died of the sweating pestilence.'

I thought back. England is a wretchedly unhealthy place, and there isn't a year without something nasty to thin the population. But the epidemic he mentioned had touched Jarrow two years earlier. That might in itself have been interesting. I sat forward. 'Did you know him before he took over your care?' I asked.

The boy shook his head. Hrothgar had arrived in the village a few days after most of the people there had died. He'd carefully inspected all the surviving boys before giving food and drink to Edward alone. He'd then paid for some kind of education from a drunken hermit before pushing him in the direction of our monastery.

'Would it shock you,' I asked again, 'if I supposed Hrothgar had chosen you for a scheme he already had in mind?'

Again, he shook his head. Between beatings, there had been some regard between them, but no real affection. He accepted that his childhood had ended with that visit of the pestilence. From that moment, he'd been simply the instrument of a stranger's will.

'He promised me that I'd see the world,' Edward told me. I let my face soften for a moment before pulling it back into my pitiless stare. 'He said I'd see cities paved with gold and silver, where no rain ever fell, and where food was given to all who were hungry.'

With the partial exception of this last, that didn't sound like the Empire I knew. But I continued probing. Had he ever collaborated with Brother Joseph? Had he been given any indication that Joseph might be part of Hrothgar's plan?

'He beat me when I didn't understand his triangles,' came the reply. 'He called me a moron, and said he'd get me thrown out of the monastery.'

Wilfred nodded in support. Brother Joseph, he added, had believed that Euclidian geometry was not only self-evidently true, but also intuitively known – with a little beating – to anyone but the mentally deficient.

I'd get round to asking more about Joseph. I'd often been puzzled how the most reasonable of men could turn, in front of a few dozen schoolboys, into a gloating tyrant. For the moment, it was enough to know that, if there had been more than one conspiracy afoot in Jarrow, they had been entirely separate. I'd already extracted from Edward confirmation of what I'd already guessed – that there had been two separate attacks on the monastery. Hrothgar had turned up with his own men to find others already in place. There had been an argument and then a fight in which the Chieftain had been killed. None of the survivors of the Chieftain's band had been in the know about what was going on, and those who didn't go back across the sea in their own boat had joined willingly enough in Hrothgar's mission. Edward had been told nothing of any timings. His instructions were simply to wait on events. It would never do to call in the crew for questioning. In any event, they too were on a need-to-know basis. If Hrothgar had not set out with any pilot, was that because the other attack had forced him to bring everything forward? If only Edward had been able to answer my questions . . .

That's one of the problems of need-to-know conspiracies. The advantage is that they're much harder to discover. You can catch the agents. Even under torture, they can generally say nothing of the principals. On the other hand, given any space of time or distance such conspiracies can turn very brittle. Here, there had been immense spaces of both, and just about everything had gone wrong.

When the two boys were alone with each other, they might recall or infer something else. For the moment, I'd got out of them all they had to give. There was a burst of wild shouting on the deck outside, and the ship gave a sudden shudder as if it had hit something. But if the shouting continued, the ship resumed its headlong race before the still rising winds. Whatever else was happening outside, we didn't seem likely to sink. Without thinking to point at it and look helpless, I bent creakily down and took my wine cup from where it had been rolling on the floor. I looked round for something to put in it. No luck there. I sighed, and fought to summarise our present state of knowledge.

'It seems reasonable to believe,' I opened, 'that Hrothgar was engaged at least two years ago to supervise my abduction from the monastery. It is possible that the Master of the Offices in Constantinople was behind this. It's the sort of coup that got him preferment in the first place. This could have run parallel with a later change of heart by Constantine himself – he did send that delegation the Easter before last with promises of full rehabilitation that I'm not inclined to disbelieve. Now that Constantine is dead – or just out of power – his heir Justinian may have decided against having me back and sent orders to have me killed. That would explain the earlier attack on the monastery that Hrothgar foiled.'

'So Brother Joseph was working with the first group to have you killed?' Wilfred asked. He ran trembling fingers through his hair and looked for a moment as if he might start vomiting blood again.

I supposed he was still coming to terms with such enormity from a man of God. I shrugged. In truth, though, I'd had Cuthbert in mind for this. I thought again of that sealed packet of documents he'd had hidden away. I wished I'd opened it when I had the chance.

Would they have explained his eagerness to get the gate open? Was he the insider for that failed attack? If so, I didn't see any evidence for contact with Edward beyond the carnal. Nor could I think of any evidence that suggested cooperation with Joseph.

And Joseph was the hard one to explain. Hrothgar and Cuthbert made sense within the hypothesis. Each was certainly or probably attached to one of the two bands of raiders. I knew one was there to capture me. I guessed the other was there to help get me killed. But what had Joseph been up to? If Edward was right, he'd just now been trying to kill me. Yet if he'd wanted me dead in Jarrow he had only to put something in my drink, or press a folded cloth into my face as I slept.

Of course, if there had been two conspiracies, each with different principals, there might easily have been three. And once these things came in contact, there was no predicting or even explaining their course. But this was the sort of tangled web that I'd seen long before, when Phocas was Emperor, or in the early days of Heraclius. If this was how the Imperial Secret Service worked now, it was evident that my own reforms had gone backwards since my departure.

I took my wig off again and scratched. I noticed both boys still looking expectantly at me – as if they believed I could explain everything to them as neatly and authoritatively as I might in class with some difficulty of word order in Horace. I smiled and dabbed at my nose – thin snot, I was glad to say, not blood.

'The problem with most hypotheses,' I wearily said, 'is the presence of facts that don't fit within them but can't be ignored. We could agree that Edward was deceived earlier today. And it was a time when the eye can see much that isn't there.' I raised a hand to silence Edward's objection. 'But I do think it was Brother Joseph on the deck of that Imperial battle ship. This raises difficulties that I will neither outline nor attempt to resolve. But they indicate that we must either reject our present hypothesis outright, or elaborate it to the point where it breaks down for want of further supporting evidence.' I stopped and thought. 'There is another possibility that I do not yet think worth exploring – though it does begin to trouble me.' I stopped again. Yes, it was troubling. But I would have to think more about that one.

'One thing is for certain, however,' I concluded. 'It's unwise to continue on our present course. There is nowhere safe for us in these waters. We must find some way of getting back to the west. England remains our most likely place of safety. If, as I suspect, the Narrow Straits are closed to us, we shall need to choose between hoping for a change of wind so we can break through, and travelling overland across France. If this latter, we need to consider how well the crew will take to being abandoned.'

I put my hand on a plate of hardened bread that had risen several inches in the air with another roll of the ship. I was now uncontrollably tired. In a while, I had a meeting here with the man who served as pilot. The only map he had was in his head and didn't correspond with any recollections I had of the maps I'd seen in Constantinople. And, regardless of how we'd get back to England, there was the increasingly pressing matter of supplies. If there was a renewed price on my head, it might make no difference if I turned pirate. But that might bring difficulties of its own . . .

'Go,' I said, waving the boys out of the cabin. 'I must rest a while.'

15

It was two days later. A mixed blessing, the wind still blew strongly from the west, though the sun now also shone from skies of unbroken blue. I stood unaided, my hands resting on the stern. I looked westward at the setting sun.

'So they are still back there?' I asked.

Edward nodded. He'd spent much of the day aloft and kept me informed of the ships that, unable to catch up, had remained on our tail.

'Well, I'm still servant enough of the Empire to rejoice that the navy is being kept at full efficiency,' I muttered in Greek. 'So long as we control the seas, the Saracen fleets must stay in their Syrian and Egyptian ports, and can't assist the land-based invasion of Africa.

'But I do assure you, they can't keep this up much longer,' I said, louder now and back in Latin. 'Those ships aren't built for this sort of pursuit. Their water must be running out even faster than ours. With short rations, and the removal of all unnecessary hands, they might be able to keep going another day – perhaps two . . .' I trailed off and thought of our own situation. There was still food of a sort. But much of the water was spoiled. Somewhere, and soon, we'd need to put in for supplies.

I turned and looked at the rowing boat. The moment it was plain we were being followed, I'd had it pulled out of the water. That had given us a slight improvement in speed. Now, it was being used as the container for a mass of inflated water skins. I'd had these tied together and topped with a little mast and sail. I thought again of the angle the sail needed to be to the line of the bladders. Would the tiller I'd designed be enough to keep the line straight? Hard to say. None of the crew, I was annoyed to learn, had been of the slightest use. The pilot plucked anxiously at my sleeve. According to his calculations, he whispered, we'd be approaching Carthage in the next day. I smiled encouragingly at the man. It was plain that, whatever his abilities in the northern seas, he was now out of area. Even I could tell that, on our present course, the most likely land we'd see was Italy – and that would be days of fast sailing yet to go. I thanked him for the news and looked back at the setting sun.

'We'll do it once the light is about to go completely,' I said loudly. 'Until then, I will lie on my daybed.' Without looking round, I lifted my arms and held them out. Unknown hands lifted me from behind and laid me down with reasonable gentleness. Wilfred stood forward from nowhere and pulled my blanket into place.

'What is that noise?' I asked Edward. The chanting had started down in the hold shortly after lunch. I'd so far decided to ignore it. However, it had now been going on and on, and the volume of sound might, if prolonged, get in the way of my cunning plan.

'It's something to do with their religion,' came the pretty near worthless answer.

I'd hardly supposed they were rehearsing an entertainment for the Exarch of Carthage. I scowled at the boy and pointed to the patch of deck just before my daybed.

A troubled look on his face, he gave up on his latest trip aloft and stood where directed. 'I spent a summer in their land with Hrothgar,' he said after a little prompting. So that was where he'd picked up their language. 'I don't understand the words of what they're singing – I think it's very old. But they did this for days at a time when they thought a sorcerer had spoiled their crops. Eventually, I saw them grab the eldest son of a chieftain and burn him in a wicker cage.' He brightened at this recollection. 'It was a slow fire, and he screamed until his lungs melted.'

'Interesting,' I said drily. 'Which one of us do you think they'll burn first?' That wiped the smug look from his face.

He opened and shut his mouth, and looked nervously round at the few grunting creatures who hadn't joined the prayer meeting below.

'Do you believe in sorcery?' I asked. Even in Jarrow, he'd never shown much enthusiasm for Christian prayer. That didn't make him a philosopher, of course. But I thought the question worth asking.

He stared at me for a moment, then nodded.

'Then you're as big a fool as everyone else!' I snapped. It may have been silly to expect more, but I was disappointed. I closed my eyes for a nap. But I could feel the boy's continued presence.

'Very well,' I said, reopening my eyes. 'If you assume that we are surrounded by invisible beings of immense power, some of them good, some of them evil, it makes sense to believe that we can, by using the right words, or making the right offer, acquire some of that power for ourselves. That was the view of Plato and his followers. With the added claim that all these beings are evil, such is the view of the Church. I have never come across a barbarian race that didn't generally agree. However, the basic assumption of a spirit world is unsupported by credible direct evidence. It is only made to explain events that would otherwise be inexplicable. If, on the other hand, you take the view of Epicurus, that everything that happens is a product of natural laws that can be investigated and understood through the use of our reason, the assumption may not be disproved – it is, nevertheless, made superfluous.'

I hadn't lost Edward. I simply hadn't convinced him. 'Take it from me,' I said again, 'that words and fanciful actions cannot change the natural order of things. There is no sorcery. Now, boy, go about your business.'

I no sooner waved him away than he was back up that mast. This time, he went right up to the top and clung there. I'd not have seen much from this distance at any time. In the fading light, it was harder still to see anything. I had the impression, though, that he might have been crying. Of course, my lecture had been beside the point. Just because there is no sorcery doesn't abolish the fact that everyone believes in it, and acts on the belief. And most of their acts are demented. I smiled grimly and glanced at the evil faces turned in my direction.

I pointed at the closest of the northerners. 'Take me back to the stern,' I ordered.

With a reverential bow, he stood forward. He swept me effortlessly into his arms and carried me the twenty yards to where Wilfred had continued his steady watch.

'I can see three sails, Master,' Wilfred whispered as I was propped beside him.

I nodded. Was it worth observing that, since our conversation was in Latin, and was about nothing confidential, we had no need of whispering? Probably not. His cough had let up for the moment, and he seemed to be enjoying himself. If Edward had been his usual self, he'd have been calling down how many more he could see. I found it hard to believe the entire battle fleet was still in pursuit. But if it was even half a dozen ships, the slightest diminution of the wind might be disastrous. I looked up at the sky. It had already turned a light purple, and was darkening rapidly from the east.

'Have you considered the possibility,' Wilfred asked, 'of evangelising these men?'

I gave him a funny look.

He stared calmly back at me. 'When they have completed their training, all the monks in Jarrow will be sent across the northern ocean to rescue those who live there from satanic darkness. This aside, do you not think converting the crew might bring tangible advantages to ourselves?'

Was he supposing that the faint chance of their conversion would make them less dangerous? Or was he looking about for some set-off for his doubtless imaginary 'sins'? It wasn't a question I felt up to asking.

'Let us consider the matter again once we have taken on supplies,' I said with what I hoped was a reassuring smile. 'For the moment, since they all seem pleased enough with their Great and Omnipotent Yadina, I suggest it might be expedient to leave them a while longer in the darkness.'

Wilfred nodded inscrutably.

Not for the first time, I felt a slight but growing disapproval in his manner. Well, that would have to be. Like Edward, he was still a child. As with Edward, I had a tendency to forget this. Their only difference lay in the nature of their childish suppositions. I lifted my wig and scratched at the patches of stubble that had grown back since Cartenna. The light was going fast. I looked west and strained until my eyes began to water. There was a faint light back there. I didn't want to show weakness to anyone by asking for confirmation. Instead, I accepted there was a glow of lights.

'Get that thing over the side,' I said to the two northerners closest to where I stood. 'Get the others up on deck. They can help.' Ignoring the sudden burst of activity, I switched back into Latin. 'Do go and call Edward down.'

Wilfred pursed his lips and looked thoughtfully at the towering height of the mast.

I smiled. 'No, boy, I'm not asking you to go up there. Just call up to him. Tell him the appointed time is upon us.'

There was a general shuffling and grunting as the whole crew came up on deck and stood before me. I waved them towards my contraption. I looked at it again, wondering if it would drift apart in the sea. Too late, however, to direct more ropes. It would have to do. I repeated the order and pointed over the side. It fell the ten-foot height of the deck and made a loud splash in the sea. I pressed my hands into my thighs to cover their shaking. No – it held together. I breathed out and smiled weakly. I looked about for Edward. He was leaning over the side, trying to take hold of the tip of the makeshift mast.

'Oh, come on, boy,' I shouted, beginning to feel as pleased with myself as I was trying to look. 'Just jump down there and do the business. The sea is hardly freezing – as you'd have found to your profit had you taken your clothes off.'

With a hurt look, Edward jumped lightly down on to the larger of the inflated water skins. He slipped on the wet leather, and seemed about to fall into the sea. But he steadied himself on the mast. I glanced round. From the looks on the faces of his audience, I realised it was probably for the best he hadn't stripped off. Rider of a bolting horse might be too sober an image to describe our situation. If we ever did get back to England, would these creatures be after a reward or a ransom? Could I hold things together even as far as the Narrow Straits?

I forced myself back to the matter in hand. I looked far into the west. As the last beams of the setting sun sank below the horizon, I clapped my hands together. Edward pulled the cover off the lantern that hung halfway up the mast. As he jumped back aboard, someone gave the bundle of skins a smart push with a piece of the broken mast, and it was soon moving steadily off on a divergent course from our own.

'We have until late tomorrow morning,' I said to the pilot. 'We may have less time than that before the trick is discovered. I know it's night, and we have no lamp of our own. But I want you to set us on a course due south. How fast can this ship go with the wind on our right?'

The details of his answer made bugger-all sense in terms of dynamic analysis. But he had no doubt we could crack on at a good speed even without manning the oars.

'Then let's have the tiller pulled round,' I said. 'And can you get everyone else to moderate the chanting? You may have noticed how surprisingly well sound can travel at night over the sea.'

16

'It might be Tipasa,' I said in Latin with another strained look at the shore. 'From your description, it's too small to be Caesarea. Anyone who says it's Carthage is ignorant of geography, and probably has shit in his eyes.' I made myself not look at the pilot. He'd been increasingly out of sorts with me ever since the African shore had come back in sight. If he couldn't follow my words, he could certainly get their broad meaning.

'Edward tells me the place looks deserted,' Wilfred replied.

Possibly it was. He had sharp eyes and a better view from aloft than any of us. Tipasa had been on the road to extinction when I went through its tax rolls. Twenty years later, it might well be dead. That might have its advantages.

'Will you be coming with me to get supplies?' Edward asked as he came up beside me.

I frowned at the boy and pointed back to the top of the mast. He was better employed in looking out for more of those occasional but still distant sails than in assuming any part in the running of the ship. One of the northerners laughed unpleasantly at him as he walked with head bowed over to the mast. Another made a strange cooing sound. I pretended not to notice and sat back on to my daybed. The northerner who'd laughed leaned forward to arrange the cushions and then handed me a cup of what might once have been fairly decent beer. I looked at the brown scum on the browner liquid and put the cup down on the table beside me.

'I do urge you to see the reason behind my plan,' I said, now back in the language of the northerners. 'As in Cartenna, it would not be wise to put into the dock – not until we know the place is safe. This being so, four of you should go with Edward. He can interpret. You can see that he comes to no harm and help with loading whatever he buys into the boat.'

It was a reasonable plan. But I'd already guessed they would have none of it. The two biggest and nastiest of the northerners stood before me on the deck. It was only because we were now down to barely another day of water that they'd consented to putting in at a city, rather than row along the African shore in search of an unguarded river mouth. For all we were growing desperate, though, they were now scared stiff of the cities. And I hadn't disabused them of the notion that Tipasa was a fully occupied city. I made another effort, this time suggesting that Wilfred and Edward should go with them. Still no success. A small crowd had now gathered on the deck, and there was a low muttering that I couldn't catch. I sighed and held up my arms. Two pairs of hands helped me gently back to my feet.

'Very well, gentlemen,' I said with a look of slight annoyance. 'We can't afford to wait around arguing. At the same time, we must at least have water. As I've said, we will anchor a few hundred yards from the shore. I will then go ashore myself. I shall need two rowers for the boat. I shall also need both boys with me if I'm to cut any decent figure on land. Everyone else will remain on board and out of sight, but fully armed and in full readiness to row back out into the wind if required. If five of us wave from the docks, the ship will put in. If we don't all appear on the dock within a reasonable time, I leave further action to the discretion of those still on board. Do I make myself clear?' I asked firmly.

There was a renewed buzz of low and now sinister muttering as my words were discussed. But there was no active disagreement. Then someone laughed and said it was all as the gods desired. There was an outbreak of vigorous nodding. A voice at the back of the crowd burst into the refrain of a song, telling how a wizard on dry land was twelve times more powerful again.

Once more, I pretended not to notice. I held up a hand for silence. 'Excellent,' I said with my best effort at briskness. 'I will gather my pitiful strength while the boat is being prepared. This time, I must insist on no weapons for the rowers.'

I went back alone into the cabin. I sat down and poured out the remains of the wine. It was vile stuff, but I drained the cup in a single motion. If there had been more, I'd have had that too. I took off my wig and patted the hairs back into shape. As I was finishing, there was a gentle knock at the door.

'Come!' I cried. I'd expected the pilot, sidling back for another argument about our position. But no, it was Wilfred. 'We are indeed going ashore,' I said with a smile when he'd finished his question. 'I think this will be your first touching on foreign soil.' I cut off his reply. 'Do run along and find Edward,' I said, clutching the table as I got up. 'Tell him what's been decided, and see if he still has that tunic he outgrew.'

Wilfred sat down and coughed. He coughed again. As he wiped his mouth, I saw specks of blood on the cloth. At least he wasn't vomiting. If he'd sunk still further since his last attack, there hadn't yet been another. He ignored the blood and looked at me.

'I've just come from Edward,' he said, dropping his voice so I had to turn my good ear in his direction. 'He was talking with some of the northerners. They all shut up when I approached. He told me that you and I should go alone in the boat. He will stay and manage things in your absence.'

I sat down again and fussed a little more with the wig. I might look better if I wore it backwards. A shame we had no mirror.

'Go and tell the little fool,' I said eventually – I'd surely lay hands on a mirror somewhere in Tipasa – 'that I expect to find him waiting in the boat when I eventually step out on deck. Remind him that I'm not a man who welcomes contradiction. And I'm not talking about my classroom in Jarrow. Tell him all that in clear English. There is a chance the northerners will understand. I don't think they will countenance disobedience to the Old Wizard.

'Now, whatever the case with how he chooses, do go and see about that spare tunic of Edward's. You really would stick to the wall in what you're wearing. Keep your outer robe with you in case we need to stay ashore into the evening. You may need it against the chill. Otherwise, I want you in something light that will let you have what goodness you can get of the sun.'

Once the door was closed, I settled down to some hard racking of my memory for that letter I'd been given so many years before in Carthage by the citizens of Tipasa. I'd been in no position then to reduce their tax assessment in light of its contents. If I could recall its precise details now, it might help me.

Down below, the chanting had started up again.

Back on deck, I smiled benignly at the assembled company. Most of the northerners bowed. A few sank to their knees. I waited for someone to take my arm and hobbled slowly over to the side. Wearing a grubby tunic that showed flesh the colour of aged parchment everywhere it didn't cover, Wilfred sat calmly at the stern of the rowing boat. A look of sulky ill-humour spread over his face, Edward sat beside him. He'd combed his hair very nicely, and the sparkling reflection from the sea sent little flashes of silver across his face. If he hadn't looked so dejected – and so nervous too – he'd have been almost as beautiful as I was at his age.

'I still have a bruise from my last entry into that boat,' I quavered at the northerner who'd taken my arm. 'I trust you will show more care on this transfer.'

He bowed and pointed to an elaborate harness of ropes that had been put together for that purpose. I smiled again and stepped back into the outstretched arms that were already waiting to put me into the thing.

'So we have the same oarsmen as in Cartenna,' I said as I was placed with great gentleness on to the arrangement of rather damp cushions at the prow. The men grinned back at me and took up the oars. 'I will think more of our escape than of your problems there,' I continued happily, 'and regard this as a good omen. Edward, have you brought all the money with you?'

He looked up and nodded blankly, then went back to a close inspection of the dirty planks at his feet. How they were already wet was an oddity. Perhaps the boat's long spell out of the water had caused some of the planks to shrivel. Well, they'd surely soon expand again. Edward misunderstood my stare and nodded again.

'Then let us be away,' I said. I looked up at the ship's deck. Two dozen nasty faces grinned down at me. 'Do please remember my instructions,' I called up at them. 'Stay out of sight, and don't think of approaching the docks until we've all assured you that it's safe to do so.' I might have spoken Latin for all the effect my words had. But I smiled again and waved at the oarsmen. With a few heavy grunts and a splash of oars, we were under way.

'You know, my dear boys,' I said, speaking past the silent oarsmen to the boys huddled at the far end of the boat, 'that the African sea is always a delight.' I stretched down with my right hand and patted the broken smoothness of the water. It was as warm as any noon-day bath. Of shimmering green, the sea bottom was refracted to look no deeper than six feet – though it must have been thirty. 'I won't remind you of how Jarrow must be at the moment. But can you believe that Rome is probably now so cold that people have to smash through the ice to get water from the Tiber? In Constantinople, I have no doubt there is a foot of snow in all the side streets. Indeed, it was at this time of year once that we had to put up wooden partitions along the Colonnade of Maurice so the beggars could huddle there and not freeze to death in the February cold.' That was true enough, though the 'we' was more collective than personal. It was that worthless toad Croesus who'd bent the ear of the Imperial Council for that waste of timber – less, I might add, out of charity than to curry favour with the mob. My own view had been that, with the Saracens at the gate, the fewer idle mouths we had to stuff with bread, the better it would be for the rest of us. But no matter that. It was a lovely day. The ship lay perhaps fifty yards behind us. In a moment, I'd twist round for a look at the silent, ruined docks of Tipasa.

'Mind you,' I went on, 'the sun can be a terrible trial come July. It's then that, in the old days, persons of quality would pack up and move for a few months to the more temperate climate of Sicily.' The boys seemed as if they were shrivelling into themselves. Edward's mood had communicated itself to Wilfred, who looked ready to start coughing again. I glanced back at the ship. The chanting had resumed almost the moment we were off. Now, I could hear a regular beating of cooking pots. If I strained, I could make out the blurred figures on deck as they danced about to the rhythm. I smiled again and patted my wig. 'I was in Sicily for about a month, when Constans had his court there,' I said, pointedly ignoring the breach of my orders. 'I'll grant that Syracuse can be as hot as Carthage on a bad day. But if you go up into the mountains, you can easily imagine yourself much further north. In a single day, given the proper relays of carrying slaves, you can pass from the palm trees of Syracuse and Catania to the chilly cover of the pine forests that fringe the craters of Mount Etna.'

As I spoke, all noise and movement back on the ship ceased. One moment, I was raising my voice to compete with the din that drifted across the widening distance from the ship. Another, and we were alone but for the regular splashing of oars on the warm African sea.

And then the oarsmen stopped rowing. One of them slithered round in his seat to face me.

17

'Is it to be thus?' I asked of the oarsman who'd dropped me in Cartenna. Already, Wilfred had started another of his calm prayers. Edward was clutching himself and beginning to rock backward and forward. I paid them no attention. 'You're scared of my ghost if you do the work on board the ship. Isn't that it? And you don't believe that I can be killed at all on land.'

No reply from that sweating, yellow-bearded face. His colleague sat still, his back to me. Of course, I didn't need any answer. When you've spent as much of your life as I have dissecting the various modes of superstition that complicate the politics of mankind, nothing is a mystery, nothing a surprise.

'So how is it to be done?' I asked again. 'Will it be the cutting off of my head? Is that to be thrown into the sea, and my body left on land for the wild animals to devour? Or is it to be drowning?

'Oh – and which one of you gets first crack at Edward's arse?' The boy looked up at that. His face was pleasingly scared and miserable. I grinned and went on. 'I don't know about you, but a pretty face doesn't mean much when you're at the back of the queue for a gang rape. You get more friction if you cut a hole in a dead pig and try fucking that.'

The oarsman who'd dropped me in Cartenna got unsteadily to his feet. Then he braced himself against the rocking of the boat and reached down for me. He carefully avoided looking into my eyes. The knife he held at the end of his outstretched arm was as much an iron charm to protect against anything I might do to him as the weapon with which he was to dispatch me. I uncrossed my legs and looked up at him.

'You do realise,' I said, with an easy wave over the sea, 'that, without me as your leader, you'll be stuck in this sea. You'll move about at random until the Imperial battle fleet catches up with you. I imagine you've seen men flayed alive. But I'll bet you haven't seen the finesse that the Imperial Government can bring to the operation. Heavens, my dear fellow, I've seen a man kept alive for days, quite screaming mad from the pain as blood oozed slowly from every inch of his peeled body. Lay hands on me, and that's what you'll get – though only if you're lucky. You won't believe what torments have been perfected over the centuries for those who try crossing the Empire, or its servants.

'But enough of unpleasantness. Come, come, my fine young fellow – if you'll only proceed on our supply gathering mission and return me safe to the ship, I can promise you gold as big as your fist once we're back in England. It really is an offer you'd be silly to refuse.'

Of course, it wasn't an offer he or any of the other dear fellows would dream of accepting. Their god Yadina wanted my blood. Nothing I could offer in its place would do for getting them back home. But I thought it worth going through the motions. The man reached down and took hold of me by the stiff brocade of my Cartenna robe. With a single hand, he pulled me to my feet and kept hold as, with an expectant look back at the ship, he held his knife about a foot in front of me. All at once, the pots began their clatter again, and – now as triumphant as the psalm at a victory celebration in church – the chanting rolled at us in swelling waves of sound across the water.

The man opened his mouth for some gibberish of his own, and held up the knife for what I guessed would be a downward stroke between my collar bones.

Now, my dear Reader, do you recall that vicious little knife that Joseph had given me far back in Jarrow to sharpen my pens? When Benedict had finally got me to my feet the next day to go and face whatever grim fact awaited me in the hall, I'd stuffed the thing out of habit into a fold of my clothing. No one had thought it worth bothering to search a poor old creature like me, and I'd ever since then been carrying the knife in its leather sheath next to my skin.

To be sure, I hadn't known how or when it might come in handy. But no one with any pretensions to calling himself a free man should go out – not even in the most civilised place – without some means of defending his life, liberty and property.

There was a time when, no matter how small the blade, I'd have carved the fucker's head off. But ninety-six is ninety-six. Even so, if age had withered my muscles, it hadn't dulled my wits. That two-inch gash, in just the right place on his neck, and he was down like something slaughtered in a butcher's market. I fell on top of him and gasped in the joy of looking close into those horrified, fast-dulling eyes. I felt the warm blood splashing in diminishing bursts on to my chest and face.

It was all very quick, and I was back on my cushions before the other oarsman had so much as turned to see what could have gone wrong. I held up the dripping blade and smiled at him. Over on the ship, the clattering and chanting had given way to a wail of most gratifying terror. If there hadn't been the other oarsman to deal with, I'd have staggered up and blown them a kiss. But there was outstanding business on the boat that was unlikely to wait.

'You want some of this?' I snarled, holding up the little blade. 'Just you come and get it, you piece of barbarian trash! Come on, then, shit for brains – don't just sit there with your mouth open.' With the first oarsman, I'd had the advantage of complete surprise. It really had been as if a sheep had turned and savaged the wolf that was about to eat it. This one couldn't so easily be tricked. That didn't mean I proposed to sit there, waiting for the beast to fall on me and complete the work of freeing his band from the evil fortune or whatever that had brought them all into the enclosed sea. Shouting with rage and fear, he was on his feet and screaming at me. He pulled out his own knife, and stepping carefully to avoid the still twitching corpse that lay between us, took a step forward.

You can be sure it was his last step. I'd been sitting with my back against the prow of the boat. I now reached both arms behind me and clamped myself as best I could to the one place where even I could make a difference. I threw my weight to the left. As the boat returned to balance, I threw myself to the right. It was a feeble rocking. The difference between my own effort and its results might have been comical had it not been so depressing a reminder of the obvious. But it was enough. The oarsman tried to drop to his hands and knees. He tried too late. With a heavy splash, he was straight over the side. He surfaced about six feet from us. Like every other seaman I've encountered, he'd never bothered with swimming lessons. For all it could help him, six feet out might as well have been sixty yards out. And the smooth African sea might as well have been the northern sea in a storm. He surfaced with a frightened gasp. He splashed ineffectually about. He sank again. He came up a few more times before he finally disappeared. But I'd already seen enough. Without bothering to wait for his end, I leaned forward and picked up my fallen wig.

'Don't just sit there,' I said to the confused, silent boys. 'This boat won't row itself ashore.' I looked over at the ship. Though not yet to much purpose, figures were already running about on deck and shouting. We needed to get inside the safety of the little harbour. If, by the time of Constans, gradual silting really had reduced the draught to about a yard, the ship could never follow us in. With no boat for a pursuit, I doubted anyone would want the risk of wading ashore. Until we were within the harbour, though, it was just a matter of turning the ship about and getting the oars in time with each other. Even scared barbarians were good for that. 'Come forward, turn about and take an oar each,' I urged the boys. To emphasise my words, I shook my wig at them.

An idiot expression on his face, Edward looked away from the dying but still occasionally surfacing oarsman, and stared down at the bloody streaks I'd splashed all over his tunic.

It was now that I actively noticed the inch or so of bloody sea water that was sloshing round my feet. All boats let in water. Perhaps the timbers of this one really had shrunk. But even without the pint after pint of lifeblood that had dyed it bright red, this wasn't the sort of leakage you'd expect in a boat so small – nor after so short a journey in calm water.

18

I dumped the wig with a dull splash into the filthy waters and leaned back. I could now see that I was myself covered in blood. It was all over my hands, and soaked into my robe. It must have covered my face. I could feel it dribbling down the back of my neck. So much for wanting to look my best for whoever still scratched a living in Tipasa! I laughed weakly and pointed again at the ship. It was all panic on deck now. Men were pulling frantically on ropes and tripping over each other. I could see the uncoordinated swirl of oars. The sound of almost insane shouting drifted across the several hundred yards of water that separated us.

'Look, my dear boys,' I said, now very feeble after the excitement of the kill, 'I really can't row this thing by myself. I've done what I can for our common salvation. I really do urge you to consider taking up these oars and putting your scared little backs into getting us inside the harbour.' I was looking for words to describe what would happen to us if we were overtaken by the ship that would provoke a response other than scared paralysis. But Wilfred had twisted round to his left and was silently pointing.

I peered dubiously into the horizon. No point asking if that was a sail perhaps five miles off. Now I look the trouble to look at the ship without the obvious preconception, it was clear that we weren't the object of the panic. If the northerners were getting ready for a pursuit, it was with them as the pursued.

'What is the ratio of the sail height to the perceived length of the ship?' I asked in my best classroom voice. That brought Wilfred at least to order. From his answer, I could guess that we had a scout ship in sight. It was just the one ship, so far as he could see. This would never be up to taking on something as large and well-manned as our ship. Its function was to dart quickly back and forth across the seas, to pick up and to relay information to a main fleet that might be half a day or even more over the horizon. Ignorant of Imperial battle tactics, the northerners were behaving as if already under attack. We were forgotten in the panic to get out of the calm. Our own oars trailing loose in the water, held only by their leather retaining straps, we drifted in the calm waters and watched the chaotic movement of the ship outwards to where the breeze blew strongly from the west.

'Can you please take up those fucking oars?' I tried again with the boys. There was no danger now of being overtaken and recaptured. If we ever saw that departing ship again, it would be a matter of bad luck. All we needed now was to be out of sight. Anyone looking in our direction from the scout ship would have the sun almost directly in his face. It would be unusual if we'd been spotted from that far off. And that was how it had to be left. *We had to get out of all possible sight.* So long as they kept up some basic standard of seamanship, and so long as the wind held, those northerners could outrun almost anything sent against them. If the Imperial authorities could keep believing I was in it, and so long as there was water taken on from somewhere, the ship could disappear right off to the coast of Egypt or even of Syria. That would give me time to consider what to do next. And I'd need plenty of time to think my way out of this one.

I looked down at my feet. They, plus ankles – plus calves halfway to my knees – were now hidden by the warmth of the bloodied sea water. There was no doubt we were sinking. I could see one of the arms of the dead oarsman moving slightly as each heavy motion of the boat lifted it in the water.

But Edward was now stretching into the water on his side of the boat to try to pull the oar into his hands. After some pained looking about, Wilfred was making less determined efforts of his own. Setting two jittery boys of uneven weakness to a job that really needed two big men didn't make for a fast or even a direct journey to the shore. But foot by foot, and with much drift towards the more ruined end, we did at last make our way into the harbour. My last view of the open sea, as we disappeared behind a rock, showed our ship, now quickly disappearing into the east, and the scout ship in cautious pursuit.

'Anyone waiting for us on the docks?' I asked, feeling the need with ever greater urgency for a long doze. I believed Edward's impression, and my own memory of its circumstances, that Tipasa was pretty well abandoned. Still, it would never have done to put in with a fresh corpse at our feet, and me looking like something from one of the flagellation ceremonies we used to put on when another province fell to the Saracens, and no reasonably convincing excuse for these facts.

No answer. Edward's face was straining like some overburdened athlete as he tried to pull effectively on his oar. Wilfred was far advanced into a dry coughing attack. The boys weren't ignoring me. They just hadn't heard me. I might have been sad Tithonus, whose lover, the Dawn, asked Zeus for him to be immortal without asking also for him to keep young and beautiful. At last, when loathsome age had leaned full upon him, the goddess locked him away in a cupboard. There, the ancient poets sang, he was left for ever, sounding like a cicada, to babble his senile nonsense. So I might have been as I leaned back against the prow and looked up into the bright sky. The sun was beating down on me with full strength. Tired out by the excitement of the kill, I closed my eyes. The muttering away in English of two incompetent, frightened boys, and the gentle lapping of the sea against the sides of the boat blended together and became more and more distant.

In my dream, I was back in Constantinople. It must have been just after our triumphant return from the Persian War. I was looking down over the Circus from my seat in the Imperial Box. We were in one of the intervals between races. Certainly, the racetrack was deserted. Behind me, the Great and Ever-Incompetent Heraclius was seated on his throne. If I glanced left, I could see one of his jewelled slippers where he sprawled, characteristically bored by anything that wasn't a church service. Far below, on the great oval that surrounded the racetrack, an impossibly large number of human faces looked expectantly up at us. Nothing unusual in that, I suppose. In a moment, the chanted request would start – for a free bread distribution, perhaps, or for one of the finance ministers to be put to death. If I had any say in the matter, the answer would be a firm *no* to either. But my gaze was drawn to the Senatorial Balcony, about twenty feet below my own level. I could see the bare heads of the hundred and fifty leading men of the city. I could see the backs of their gorgeously embroidered white and purple robes. All would have been as it should have been – only there was an empty place. It was about the middle of the front row. I tried to remember who was missing and why. And I struggled to tell myself why it was so desperately important to me that the ivory stool was vacant.

As I began to dift back into the present. I suddenly realised it wasn't Heraclius behind me, but his grandson, Constantine. And it wasn't after the Persian war, but some other more recent conflict. Yet, if times and persons were altered, that ivory stool remained solidly vacant . . .

'We thought you had died, Master,' Wilfred said, his head just blocking the sun.

Edward had put his arms behind me and was trying to raise me. There was a smell of heat and dust and of all the other things you never miss until you've been long at sea. Wilfred bent down closer and set a cup of dark, brackish water to my lips.

'Die, my dear young boys?' I said at last in a surprisingly firm voice. 'Dying is not something for those who still have work to do.' Clutching at Edward's shoulder, I pulled myself to my feet. We'd by now shipped so much water that the boat hardly trembled under the shifting of weight. Working together, the two boys lifted me over the side of the boat so that I could stand on the white beach where we'd finally come in to shore. I looked down at the dull eyes of the big man I'd killed. The Imperial scout ship nowhere to be seen, I looked at the vanishing bulk of the ship that had, since England, been both home and prison. I turned and took a confident and unaided step on the beach towards the remains of the Tipasa docks.

'Well, come along, my pretties,' I said without looking back. 'I really could do with something to eat.'

Dear me! Dear me! Keep a cool head on your shoulders, and something always *does* turn up. What to do with it was something I'd consider as and when.

19

I sat in the smooth, natural bowl the brook had, in its ages of spring flooding, carved out of the rock, and splashed happily in the water. If it had seemed a little chilly at first, I'd soon grown used to that. The afternoon sun was at its welcome best. I glanced at my moderately clean robe where Wilfred had hung it up to dry. I was hungry. As I'd expected, Tipasa was completely abandoned – not so much as one God-bothering hermit living in the ruined houses of what had, just a hundred years before, been a flourishing centre of the trade in fish sauce. Darting here, darting there – almost glowing with admiration of my double kill – Edward had gone all over the city while I rested with Wilfred in the shade. All the public buildings remained in good repair, he'd reported back, but the private houses had no roofs, and there was grass growing undisturbed in all the main streets.

Now, we were back where we'd first come ashore. We'd found a rocky inlet two hundred yards or so across the dazzling sands from where our boat seemed immovably stuck. Some fifty yards further on to the land, an ancient monument had sunk deep into its foundations. The rigid, almost incompetent statue still looked down from an odd angle. The inscription on its base was almost effaced by time. In any event, being in Punic, I couldn't read a word. It had once been the centre of an older city. The one built as part of our own civilisation had been centred further along the shore – I supposed, on weak evidence, because of the sands that had shifted within the harbour all through history. We were alone, but for the birds and various small animals that scurried unseen in the undergrowth where the shoreline ended. I was about to mention what would soon become the pressing matter of food. But Edward was peering into the water.

'What is wrong with your – your' . . . He struggled to find the Latin word before lapsing into the English 'cock'.

I took a deep breath and dipped my head under the water again. It was making my bad ear hurt, but the delicious cool of the water was too much to resist. I came up and rubbed my eyes. I looked blearily down at the sad remnant of an organ that had, for so many years, served me so well. I smiled and looked into Edward's eyes.

'The word you seek,' I said gravely, 'is *mentula*. Mine is disfigured by an operation anciently required of the Jews and Egyptians, and now of those who convert to the faith of the Saracens.'

Edward nodded. I'd answered his question. Wilfred's face, though, took on its sour expression. He still hadn't been parted from his own robe. It was as much as he could do to look with half-closed eyes at my own naked body. At Edward's he hadn't once dared to look. I put my head back and stretched lazily in the water. If, even now, Wilfred couldn't overcome his horror of nudity, that would have to be his problem. Where Edward's nudity was concerned, it was also his sorry loss.

'Oh, don't suppose I believe in the claims made by their false prophet,' I said with an easy laugh. 'But an apparent conversion was politically useful once for the Empire. It also helped me recover monies that would otherwise have been lost when the Antioch banks all failed at the same time.

'But do observe,' I continued, 'the two white scars at the base of the glans. You may not be able to see them through the water. They are there, even so. I will warn you now, should you ever feel inclined to turn to the satanic Faith of the Desert, that circumcision can radically diminish feeling in the organ of increase. This may have advantages for some purposes – and there are those who swear that it prolongs and enhances the act of love – but it was never wholly to my taste. However, the circumcised races go far to compensating for the diminished sensation by piercing the organ and fitting a curved golden rod with little balls at each end. I wore this with much pleasure until, together with my gold and ivory teeth, I had to trade it for what I thought would be my final passage across the sea to Richborough.'

I ignored Wilfred's passable imitation of a death rattle. I took another deep breath and went under again. I came up with a mouthful of water. I made a little fountain with it, and splashed hard on the surface. I looked down happily as the reflection of the overhead sun broke up into sparkling fragments and then reformed. Though tired, I was feeling justifiably pleased with myself. Most people who reach my age don't do much at all. I'd just killed two men in short order. I hadn't acknowledged Edward's breathless praise. But I certainly deserved it.

'Why is the city deserted?' Wilfred asked.

I looked at his face and noticed how the sun had turned it the colour of an Egyptian mud brick. That's what happens if you must dress up all year in heavy black. Except where he'd kept some clothes on aboard the ship, and where he was still getting over his stay in Cartenna, Edward had the nice golden tone that the sun can give to young northern skin. But this was no time for feasting my vicious old eyes. Wilfred had asked a rational question – even if it was to take me off a matter that he plainly found unwelcome – and he deserved a rational answer.

'After Scipio had taken and destroyed it in ancient days,' I began, once more in lecturing mode, 'the city of Carthage was refounded by Julius Caesar. From a heap of uninhabited ruins, it grew within a hundred years into a city of half a million. It was the biggest city in the West after Rome itself. The whole Province of Africa, of which it was capital, became the richest province in the West. After the Empire was divided, it was Africa that supplied Rome with seven million bushels of corn every year, Egypt being now reserved for the feeding of Constantinople. This whole shore was crowded with cities, great and small. The Punic heritage was eventually swept far out of sight. In its place arose a school of Latin and specifically Christian literature. You will recall that both Tertullian and Augustine were Africans. Cyprian, the first bishop to be martyred, was also an African.

'The bad times began just under three hundred years ago. The province was conquered by a race of Germanic barbarians called the Vandals who had swept through Spain. They were unsystematic in their oppression. But what they did coincided with an advance of the desert and of the desert races that swallowed up formerly wealthy regions. If you go fifty miles south of here – perhaps less now – you'll find great cities abandoned in the desert. When built, they were surrounded by the richest farming land in the West.'

'But, Master, these cities on the coast,' Wilfred broke in, 'surely they should still be rich?'

I ignored him. I was thinking of the long memorandum I'd written for Constans when he demanded more taxes out of Africa. Was it misrule that had destroyed the interior? Or was it some autonomous change in the climate? It did seem part of the world had grown colder since ancient times. Certainly, grapes grew no more in Jarrow. Was it the colder weather – and not Imperial decadence – that had brought our ancestors out of their northern forests? Assuming, as Eratosthenes had, that the sun was an inconceivably large ball of fire millions of miles away, could there be some periodic change in the heat that it issued? If so, how could a cooling in the north be accompanied by a heating in the south to turn black land into dust? But I pulled myself back to the present.

'The plague depopulated Africa worse than any other region,' I said. 'Our tax demands didn't help. Until I abolished them as useless, there were emigration controls to keep people from escaping to Spain and France and other regions beyond the reach of the tax gatherers. Tipasa was just a little too small to survive the depopulation. The silting up of the harbour didn't help. I imagine the population shrank and shrank over about two hundred years. You've seen how some of the old fortifications were taken down to build another wall around the centre. As time went by, the population must have fallen below the point where city life is viable. At that point, the survivors would have moved twenty miles along the shore to Caesarea.

'What you see all round you is a great void. The multitudes who once swarmed along these shores are long since passed away. In Constantinople, we still translate the laws for our last substantial province where Latin is spoken. But there is hardly anyone left to read or obey them. Africa pays no net taxes. If we do a little here and there to slow the Saracen advance west from Egypt, it is for the sake of prestige. Quietly, we are glad of the diversion of their strength from the Imperial heartland.'

I made an effort to stand, but the bottom of the pool was slippery. 'Come,' I said with a change of tone, 'help me out of here.' Once I was standing on the hot, smooth sand, I pointed for my stick. As Edward handed it to me, I looked again at his perfect young body. When I'd finished giving my undeniably wicked eyes their most gorgeous feast since the last one, I rammed the stick hard into his stomach. As he went down spluttering, I kicked him hard in the balls, and gave him a few hard blows to his shoulders. Knees drawn up to his chest, hands covering his face, he cowered whimpering at my feet.

'Master, Master!' Wilfred cried behind me. 'Have you lost your senses? Master, I beg you—'

I wheeled round and cut off the complaint with a poke into his own chest. That had him straight down on the ground, gasping for breath.

'Don't you ever presume to question what I do,' I blazed at the boy. He tried to get up, but fell down again and crawled before me on all fours. I breathed in and then out and counted the beats of my heart. 'Go back over there,' I said heavily, 'and get my clothes ready for when I want them.'

With a frightened wail, Wilfred crawled off to where he'd hung up our clothes to catch the sun. I turned back to Edward, who hadn't moved.

'You little snake!' I snarled softly. I looked down for some conveniently unprotected soft area I could go at again with my stick. He squealed something I didn't catch and began to cry. 'You treacherous bag of shit!' I added, with a hard whack to his buttocks. He screamed with the sudden pain and curled harder into a ball. There were some vicious little stones on this part of the beach, and they were doing to his underside what I was to the exposed areas. With every jerk of his body, he screamed at the double pain. 'If that soft bugger Hrothgar had known half as much about you as I do, he'd have left you alone in your village to starve – or to drag yourself up into the churl that nature surely intended you to become.'

'Master, I must insist.' It was Wilfred again. He'd recovered his nerve and was now pushing himself between me and the terrified Edward. I struck at his face with my free hand. He winced at the pain, but now took hold of both my hands. 'Put that stick down, Master,' he insisted with quiet force. 'You'll give yourself a seizure.' He pushed me gently but firmly down on to a convenient boulder and took the stick from my hands.

I did think to knock him aside and set about Edward again. But there was no resisting that unexpected strength, and I could see I'd already produced the effect I wanted. Letting the rage continue would be a waste of effort – and Wilfred might be correct about my own state of health. Already, I had a nosebleed starting. I wiped the blood with a piece of cloth he handed me. I took the cup he'd carried from the boat and drank down the fresh water. I looked again at Edward. He was staring up at me from between spread fingers. I took deep breaths and waited for my heart to stop banging like a smith's hammer.

20

'Behold our Judas and our double Judas!' I said ironically to Wilfred. I stared down at Edward, who'd uncoiled and, whimpering, now looked up at me like a beaten dog. 'Hrothgar saved him. Hrothgar gave him bread. Hrothgar bought him an education. Hrothgar took him away from a land that offered him nothing. At his first opportunity, he got Hrothgar hanged.'

Edward uncoiled slightly and began some attempt at objection.

I silenced him with a cold look and continued. 'Oh, I'll grant I have no evidence that he's the one who got Hrothgar into that gibbet. But I do know that he took a written statement ashore at Cartenna, informing the authorities that His Magnificence Alaric of Britain was on board the ship.

'Isn't that so, Edward?' I asked, with a brief lurch into the direct mode of address. 'You weren't happy with promises of your share of the reward when Hrothgar eventually and somehow got the ship to Kasos. You wanted it all for yourself. And you wanted it at the first port of call within the Empire. Isn't that so?' I stretched out a foot and kicked him lightly in an exposed part of his belly. He said something muffled that sounded less like a denial than a plea for mercy. But I found that I was overbalancing, and being caught and set right again by Wilfred took away both opportunity and inclination to go beyond my own guesses.

'The problem with this act of treachery,' I continued, 'was that his note wasn't passed to the right authority until it was too late to do the little rat any good. When I gave him the choice between joining our escape and staying behind to explain what he might have been able to deliver, he chose to stick with us.

'Even so, he didn't like that he hadn't stepped into Hrothgar's shoes. He hadn't realised that I'd be the one who took over, and that I'd insist on a fast return home. So, as they worked themselves up into whatever frenzy we've just escaped, he made a deal with the northerners. I don't know what its nature was – brokering my head to the Imperial Government? Promising his arse to whoever might be big enough to save him from the others? I don't know and don't care. But we can both be sure he knew what was coming on that boat journey, and it wasn't his wish to be there with us.

'Double Judas! And let's not overlook his treason against Benedict, who took him in, no questions asked, to study in the world's finest school west of Ravenna. Treble Judas! And, if we include the little matter of Cuthbert, quadruple Judas! And how many others has the boy fucked over in his short life?'

I leaned back into Wilfred's arms. My nose was bleeding more, and I felt ready to drop. In one day, I'd gone far beyond the limits anyone might have thought my age allowed. Now, it was time to pay the debt incurred and all the heavy interest.

'Set me on the ground over there,' I said, pointing to where some rocks made a shadow on the sand. 'Put me there and get my clothes ready for when I can stand again.'

'I'd already guessed the same, Master,' Wilfred said quietly as he tucked my now dry robe about my legs. 'Edward has grievously sinned. But all we can do now is ask him to repent. I might also suggest' – he paused and looked for his words – 'that the text "Let he who is without sin, cast the first stone" might have some value here.'

Though half comatose, I sat up here and looked hard at the boy. He took one proper look at my face and went into another of his coughing fits. He sat down heavily in the sand and clutched miserably at his knees.

'Wilfred,' I said sternly once the boy was back in some kind of order, 'I am aware that what little you know of my life fills you with horror. There are things you don't know that would make you sit up and stare. But never – never in all my time, not even for reasons of state – have I shat on those who helped me. If I don't force myself back up to flog that boy to death, it's only because he saved me in Cartenna. I could argue that he was only rescuing valuable property that he could try selling again later. But I won't. At the same time, if I've had to put up with worse from others in the snake pit of Greek politics, I'll not put up with behaviour like that from those under my control.' I let Wilfred help me to my feet and walk me over to where Edward was stretched out and weeping uncontrollably. Forcing myself not to shake with exhaustion, I stared down at him.

'Get up,' I commanded him. 'Go and wash yourself in the sea. It'll hurt but do you good. Then get dressed. Now that we are free – now that we hold together solely by free choice – I propose to write off all that has happened to date. It cannot be undone or excused. But it can be put out of mind. If my respect means anything at all, you can start earning it from this moment on.' I went by myself and sat again in the shadow of the rocks. 'Now go and clean yourself up,' I said. 'You might also look how much water that boat has shipped. We may still have need of it.'

'Do you think, Master, *anything* he told us was the truth?' Wilfred asked once we were alone.

I took another sip of water – oh, for a jug of wine! – and wiggled my toes in the sand. I passed him the cup and watched him drink. His own clothes had long since dried off from his cautious dip in the sea. Now, I was looking to see any sign of a sweat. Except when forcing himself to life to attend to my own needs, he was increasingly listless. If I was hoping he'd improve once off the ship, I hadn't yet seen any evidence.

'Yes,' I answered, turning to his question. 'I do think he's mostly been telling the truth. I have a good nose for insincerity. He really does know as little about things as he's said. It's at least because of ignorance – fear of those drunken beatings may come into it – that he stitched up Hrothgar. Don't suppose I really hold that betrayal against him. The man had it coming.'

'But, Master, do you think he was telling the truth about Brother Joseph?'

I smiled at that one. For myself, I hadn't the slightest doubt Joseph had been on that warship. I could close my eyes and see him standing there, looking across the narrow space of water that separated him from a man who shouldn't have survived the dark, towering waves of the open sea, let alone have made it so far into Imperial waters.

'You saw what Edward saw,' I answered. 'Put aside your own wishes and preconceptions. Do you think it was Brother Joseph?' I didn't need his answer.

Troubled, he looked away. 'If it *was* Brother Joseph,' he said, 'what does that mean for our return to England?'

Good question. Ever since I'd taken charge of the ship, I'd been wondering that myself. I shrugged. 'You are assuming, my dear boy, that we shall return to England,' I said. 'We have no ship. If we do put to sea, we have the Imperial Navy combing every mile of water to find us. If we take the road west, we'll be going through various deserts and dead zones. We'll end at the Narrow Straits, which are still controlled by the Empire. If we do get across those, we have Spain and France to get through, and then a sea trip to Richborough. If we'd had enough water aboard the ship to get us to Italy, it might have been different—'

'But you have a plan, Master,' he interrupted. 'You always have a plan, even if you don't at first know it.'

I smiled at the boy's fierce conviction. It had even brought some life into his cheeks. Here we were, on the beach by a deserted city. There was the ludicrously aged remnant of the Magnificent Alaric. There was a sick child – how sick I'd been trying to avoid having to realise. The only one of us in good health was silly, treacherous Edward. We were hunted by an Empire desperate to lay violent hands on me. If somewhat past its best, that Empire surrounded us in every direction, and had full control of the sea. We had barely enough cash to buy food for twenty days. And I was now trusted to get all of us out of the Empire, across two seas, and through any number of lawless territories to face who could say what on our eventual return to England. If I didn't give way to laughter, I'd burst into tears.

But Wilfred was right. I did have a plan. It had come to me in little flashes of enlightenment as I set about Edward. That vicious beating which had started in anger had ended as an act of policy. I might be ludicrously old, but I was still the Magnificent Alaric – Hammer of the Persians and barbarians, unyielding anvil of the Saracens, support and survivor of four legitimate and variously useless emperors. As for being old, I had just killed two men, each one of them a third my age and three times my weight. I'd killed them without so much as raising a sweat. So long as I didn't fall down dead somewhere along the next fifteen hundred miles, I had a plan that might just work.

I got up and allowed Wilfred to dress me. The brown stain that covered the whole front of my robe would never fade. Though washed and washed again, the blond wig was also brown. Since I had no hat, I'd have to make do with it against the sun. At the most charitable, I looked somewhat reduced in circumstances. I leaned against the rock and watched as Edward jumped up and down in the sea, washing the blood and grime from his body.

'Did you need to do all that, Master?' Wilfred asked. He looked across at Edward.

I sniffed, and then poked a finger into my nose to remove the clotted blood. I was feeling better by the moment. I wished I could say the same of Wilfred. Much more of that coughing, and it would be a question of who was helping whom along this shore.

'That boy isn't fourteen,' I answered. 'Already, he has a trail of corpses behind him. I don't intend either of us to join them. I do nothing without a purpose – something you would do well to remember.'

We watched in silence as Edward finished in the sea. Afterwards, he went and looked a long time into the boat. Then he fished around inside. After more washing in the sea, he walked back holding what I could see from the blurred glitter was the knife that had been meant for my dispatch. In his hands, it seemed more like a short sword than a knife. By the time he'd crossed the expanse of sand that separated us from the sea, he was already dry. I looked at him. Another day, and he'd be covered in bruises. If I hadn't broken any bones, he'd ache for days after that.

As the boy came within a yard of where I stood, he went down on his knees and, silent and with downcast head, placed the knife at my feet. Still looking down, he reached clasped hands up towards me. I stood a moment in silence, looking down at the small, naked figure. He was rather young for this sort of thing – and I rather old. But, regardless of that or the lack of any relics or anything else holy, there could be no doubt of its meaning. I considered for a moment, then leaned forward and took his hands between my own.

'I promise on my soul that I will in the future be faithful to My Lord the Senator Alaric,' he said quietly, 'and never cause him harm, and will observe my homage to him completely against all persons in good faith and without deceit.' He stopped and looked up at me.

I stared silently back and kept my own hands about his. So the magical essence – the *Hail* or *Heil*, they call it in the Germanic languages – that he'd never less than passionately adored, but never yet felt clean enough to acknowledge, in the Old One, passed from outer to inner hands. I smiled and tightened my hold on his hands. All round us the desolation of the beach and the unkempt land, and the broken, deserted city and the sunken forgotten statue, we stayed silently frozen in the highest – though long since Christianised – ritual of our ancestral, northern forest.

At last, I let go of the boy's hands and reached creakily down for the knife. Wiping off the sand, I held it aloft towards the sun, then presented it hilt first. Though I took care with the blade, the thing was more deadly for the chopping force of its weight than by its sharpness. Edward took it, still on his knees. I helped him to his feet.

'Take this, and use it well,' I commanded.

He took the knife and went back on his knees. I stood silent again, accepting his long, no longer abject obeisance. The ritual was complete. The boy was a man, and – by the power that was mine by descent from the tribal gods of Kent, and by positions in the Empire that no Emperor could abolish – was a man of some quality. His past was blotted out. If in different ways, he was now the equal in my eyes of Wilfred. Perhaps he was more.

'The boat is full of water,' he said once dressed. 'Also, the man you killed has swollen up in his stomach, and the water around him is turning dark. Should we not bury him?'

I shook my head. 'Leave the body for the animals – there are always plenty of those,' I said, looking up at the birds beginning to circle in the clear sky. They'd have the choice bits even if nothing on four legs would go down to the water. 'He deserves no better resting place than the other one who must float for ever beneath the seas that swallowed him,' I added. You can be sure I believed no such nonsense: dead is dead. However, though I'd have liked to remove all trace of our arrival, the body was too big for one boy and two invalids to move. And even if we could have emptied it and plugged its leak, the boat was useless for what I now had in mind. I could see that Wilfred was aghast at the idea of just leaving the body to float, face upward, in the juice of its own corruption. But he probably hadn't liked anything that had happened since Edward's return. Still, I was in charge, and that was my decision.

'I think we'll have a proper look round Tipasa,' I said, now brisk. 'If there is indeed no one living here, we can dine from whatever wild fruit trees may be in season. Otherwise, I'm sure something small will present itself for killing. As for shelter, we'll make a fire in one of the smaller churches.' I scowled Wilfred into silence. Taking up my stick, I tottered slightly as I set out along the beach towards the broken docks.

21

Taking into account the twisting of the road as it hugs the shore, Tipasa is about twenty miles from Caesarea. A man of reasonable vigour can cover that in a day. With me bumping along in the wheelbarrow Edward had rescued from a church, it should have taken two days. Halfway through the first day, however, Wilfred had his worst attack yet. I'd already decided he wasn't up to helping Edward with pushing me. But, though I'd insisted on a slow progress along the road, even that, in the unaccustomed heat of Africa, was too much for him. After our first long noonday stop, he couldn't get up again. This time, what began as coughing turned to a long choking. As I wiped the foul-smelling froth from his lips, I decided it was time for the Magnificent Alaric to show the world he was still up to taking a walk.

So, for three days, and not two, we journeyed along that baking road, the blue sea sparkling always on our right, drinking much, eating little, with barely another human being to pass or overtake us. Though our most understandable concern was the sea, and what ships there might be upon it, my own private concern was bandits. The days when a citizen might walk the roads of the Empire in reasonable safety – Saint Paul, for example, in Asia – were so long since passed away that it was hardly worth enquiring when. But I knew the African roads were especially dangerous. Professional thieves, escaped slaves, raiders from the south, the occasional band of Saracens – those were the real danger. We had no credible means of defence. We had no chance of running away. As for money to appease anyone who might accost us, those clipped coins would have sent any thief into a frenzy of disappointment.

But, unaccosted, we came at last within sight of the walls of

Caesarea. Unlike Tipasa – unlike even Cartenna – this hadn't shared in the general emptying out of Africa. Instead, by taking in the remnants of other communities, it had maintained the ancient circuit of its walls. Bearing in mind its evident lack of commerce with the hinterland, it was hardly flourishing. It had, nevertheless, survived.

'State your business, Citizen,' a guard called out from just inside the gateway.

I'd seen the wooden bar come down on our approach, and had my story already made up and rehearsed. I shuffled forward and peered into the dark gateway.

'It is surely the mercy of God,' I opened in an elderly whine, 'that I should ever again hear the voice of authority.'

Deep within the gateway, there was a sound of leather scraping on wood. Then the guard emerged. Fifty, fat, shifty, he blinked in the sunlight. The metal strips had come off his breastplate. His sword was broken away near the point. But he was taking no chances. He gave me and the boys a hard, suspicious look, then turned his attention to the road behind us.

'I am Seraphinus,' I said proudly, 'a man of some repute in Carthage. I am travelling to Cartenna with my grandsons. Since the last visitation of plague, I am all they have left in this world. You will see that the younger boy is sick. We are advised that his only hope is to roll in the holy dust before the tomb of Saint Flatularis.' I did a fair job of laying the mannerisms of the higher classes over an African accent. As I was hoping, it placed me nicely as what I was pretending to be.

The guard came over to us and leaned hard on the wooden bar. It groaned beneath the weight, and the folds of his belly not contained within the breastplate wobbled with every breath.

'That's a sick lad you have there,' he agreed with a look at Wilfred, who, covered with his faded robe against the sun, slept fitfully in the wheelbarrow. Sleep had suppressed the coughing attacks. Now, it was a matter of how long he could keep up the shallow gasps of his breathing. 'I suppose it was the doctors got him this way. They always do in my experience. You'd better get him to the saint before it's too late. Hard journey along the road?' he added with a nod at my clothing.

I thought of the brown stain and smiled. 'We fell among thieves,' I said. 'They stripped us of our possessions. But my healthy grandson fought like a desert lion, and put the thieves to flight.' Edward nodded vigorously in agreement and held up the knife. 'I now beg at the gates of this most opulent and well-protected of cities for entry. We cannot face another night on the road. All else aside, I must have a bed for the sick child.' The guard continued looking for a while at nothing in particular. I raised my arms in supplication. I began to wonder if it was worth the risk of falling to my knees. Perhaps I could spare a few coins. But the guard eventually heaved himself upright and fiddled with the bronze hoop securing the bar.

'Mind you,' he said as the bar went up, 'you'll get nothing within unless you've managed to keep a little money in your own hands. More important, that knife stays with me. City ordinances don't allow no weapons. This is a peaceful place. No weapons for nobody – just the authorities.' It took a surreptitious but hard jab with my stick before Edward handed the knife over.

There was a time – perhaps not that long before – when Caesarea had been one of the most elegant cities on the African shore. Coming through that heavy gateway, you'd have found yourself in a long, wide street that passed right along to the central square, around which the churches and the main public buildings were arranged to avoid the full power of the sun. Each side of the street would have been lined with a colonnade. Behind this, about four feet above street level, the pavements would have allowed pedestrians to move back and forth, safe from the dust or any filth cast up by the wheeled traffic. Running parallel with each colonnade, long granite basins would have splashed and sparkled from a dozen fountains that cooled the hottest day.

That was before the long tide of African prosperity had finally withdrawn, and Caesarea became the last refuge of a dozen other cities. Now, the colonnades had been closed up with crude brickwork, the pavements behind made into habitations for the poor. The fountains were dry and the basins choked with rubbish. Every ten yards or so, the ancient statues – some dressed in all the opulence of merchants made good, some nude – still held their plinths. Whatever paint and gold leaf had been applied to heighten their semblance to the living was gone. It was replaced by the grime of many open fires and by white streams of shit from the birds. The nudes had been disfigured to accord with modern ideas of propriety. But they all still looked from their sightless eyes on the broken-down jumble their city had become.

I picked my way carefully across the uneven and impacted dust that now coated the paving stones of the long street. Its smooth line had been broken by a row of makeshift houses that wandered down the centre and forced all traffic into six-foot passageways on either side. By much shoving and bumping, Edward was able to force the wheelbarrow through the crowded ways.

The central square was an improvement on Cartenna. At least all the buildings were still standing, and there were a few signs of a more organised civic life. Looking at the shabby crowds, though, it was plain that the public baths hadn't been open for some while past. I rather think that, of all the hundreds there who pushed and shouted as they went about their business, we were the cleanest.

'Don't look at those young men with your mouth open,' I whispered at Edward. 'You're supposed to be from Carthage. It doesn't do to behave like some barbarian in a border fort.' But, since Cartenna didn't really count, this was the first city he'd ever seen. To me, it was just another disappointing slum, interesting only for a spot of highly selective viewing of ancient sights. There was, for example – or once had been – a column put up by Hadrian with a trilingual inscription that might say something about Punic. If, however, I thought myself behind his eyes, I could see how it appeared to Edward. The largest human settlement he'd probably seen didn't contain more than a few hundred people or above one brick building, if that. For him, this place was everything Hrothgar had promised him when he'd been forced to hand over all direction of his life for purposes he wasn't given to understand. He stared round and round at the people in their mean finery, and looked at the huge, solid buildings that had come down to us from better days. And – fair's fair – clean up both people and buildings, forget the surrounding streets, and the place wouldn't have looked half bad.

'I think we should try again to force some water into poor Wilfred,' I suggested.

Edward nodded and reached for the water skin. He was paying rather less attention to us, though, than to a couple of the local whores who'd drifted over for a look at the newcomers. To me, every bloated wrinkle screamed contagion. But, again, I was a jaded old me. They doubtless appeared otherwise to a boy who hadn't managed sex with anyone but himself in over two months. I thought of the money hanging from his belt and decided to take charge.

'Come, Edward,' I said firmly. 'There's no good served in dawdling here. If we don't get him under cover soon, poor Wilfred will dry up in this sun.' I turned to someone close by who was trying to sell dried fruit from a bag.

'I shall be grateful,' I said in my assumed accent, 'to know the whereabouts of the Jewish district.'

The man scowled and spat. Then he pointed at the largest church in the square.

Silly me! I thought. Of course, the Jews would be clustered behind the main church. It was the best place for bribing the priests when the mob turned ugly. I peered in the dazzling sun for evidence of an alley or some other exit from the square.

22

When I began frequenting them as a very young man, I always used to find Jewish districts alien. I suppose that sounds rich coming from someone who was a barbarian until he was nearly twenty, and who never quite fitted into the ways of the Empire. But if I didn't believe in either, I'd come to regard the Christian Faith and the Old Faith that preceded it as inseparable from civilisation. The churches, the crosses, the statues, the converted temples – they were all part of the furniture of everyday life. It was a shock to find that the Jews had none of these things. More than this, though, it was the dark eyes and the darker beards, the words and gestures that might have one meaning for outsiders and another between the Jews themselves. And even when long familiarity and the joint acquisition of wealth had made them almost normal, I could never forget, as a servant of the Empire, that I was dealing with a people who were in the Empire, but who could never regard themselves entirely – not, at least, since Christianity was established – as of the Empire.

Stepping into the Jewish district of Caesarea was in one sense a homecoming. In another, the long absence from any Jewish place of residence brought back that early feeling of its being a world parallel to but separate from the one that had been mine.

If hardly spotless, though, this place was a sight better than the streets we'd now left. There was no longer need to look out for pyramids of dog shit or puddles of congealed saliva, or for the omnipresent cutpurses. The streets here were decidedly quieter. But what had brought me here? I told myself for the dozenth time that I was mad. I hobbled forward, Edward pushing the wheelbarrow and himself behind me. He was a strong boy – no doubt of that. However, even he was now wilting in the powerful noonday sun.

Then, as we turned a corner, I came upon an old man. He couldn't have been my age, or anything approaching that. But he was old and shrivelled. Sitting in the middle of the street, surrounded by boys of about Edward's age, he was scowling into a linen roll he'd arranged on his lap, and droning away at them in one of the Eastern languages. I stopped and leaned against one of the high, blank walls of the houses. I listened hard. I'd thought at first it was Hebrew. But this old Jew wasn't so learned in his people's ancient language. It was Aramaic, and he was reading out something nonsensical from one of the more recent prophets. It was no worse than anything you hear in church every Sunday. But even if you aren't a believer, foreign religions always sound more stupid than your own.

No one noticed me, and I stood there quite a while, trying to keep a smile off my face as the boys repeated the bottom-wiping instructions one phrase at a time, and copied the gestures that accompanied them. Then, without waking, Wilfred moved slightly in the wheelbarrow and groaned. The old man looked up and glared at us.

'Your sort isn't allowed in here!' he cried indignantly in Latin. He stood up and clutched the roll to his chest. 'Get out now, or we'll have the magistrates on you.' He bent slowly down, his hand reaching for a stone.

'I'll go where I fucking please, you bag of *apikoros* dirt!' I replied in Aramaic.

He shrank back as if I'd thrown lime in his face. I don't know if it was because I'd spoken in his own language, or because I'd used the worst insult one Jew can give another – as if, mind you, calling someone a follower of the Great and Wondrous Epicurus, Master of All Wisdom, can be other than a compliment. But I'd shut the old man up. He glanced nervously down at his linen roll, and crushed it harder against his chest.

I stepped forward and beat the ground with my stick. 'I need help,' I said. I was glad Wilfred wasn't awake to see this. It wouldn't do much for his faith in my ability to come up with plans if they involved begging off old Jews chosen at random in the street. But, if there are times when you're given one, there are times when you have to take a chance.

'Help you?' the old man gasped. 'Some piece of pork-chewing Nazarene shit?'

'Better that than a baldy-cock Christ killer,' I answered without a pause.

'Jesus sodding Christ?' came the inevitable reply. 'Jesus sodding Christ? Some "Son of God" he was, I can tell you! Mary was a whore. Joseph was a fool for believing her.' He waved the linen roll at me, the beginnings of a smile on his face.

I heard a gentle scrape as Edward moved the wheelbarrow out of the sun. What he thought of two old men obviously swapping insults in an unknown language I didn't bother wondering. He wasn't Wilfred.

'So, will you help me?' I asked again.

The old man came closer and looked carefully into my face. 'I guessed it was you when you first came in sight,' he said. 'I saw you once when you were ruling in Carthage. You do know this entire coast is buzzing with rumours of your return? Do you know what is being offered, no questions asked, for your head?'

'Less than it's worth, I'll be bound,' I said. We looked at each other. I smiled and leaned back against the wall. 'I can see you're a man who doesn't forget injuries to your people. Are you as keen to remember favours? Will it count for nothing now that I spent sixty years not enforcing the penal laws against your faith?'

There was a long silence. Then: 'What's wrong with the boy?' the old man asked.

I looked down at the sleeping face and the pale, cracked lips. 'It's a consumption of the lungs,' I said, trying to keep my voice from shaking. 'I did hope he'd pull through this attack. That doesn't seem likely at the moment.'

The old man looked up and down the street. Except for us, it was empty. He pulled at his untidy beard and rolled his eyes. He bent down and gathered the coins they'd earlier left at his feet, and waved the boys about their business.

'You'd better come quickly,' he said with a resigned shrug.

I stared at the house of old Ezra. Nowhere that Jews live is ever made to appear prosperous from the outside. My friend Simon of Magnesia was an exception. But he, of course, had lent money to emperors. And he'd made his youngest son convert so he could become Bishop of Nicosia. By and large, though, Jews don't live in palaces and flaunt their gains. But if those outer walls could have done with a lick of whitewash, it was plain that selling old clothes to finance his work as a rabbi had been a thoroughly profitable line for Ezra, son of David.

After a few hard taps with his stick, the door opened and, with a last look round the empty street, he ushered us in. I found myself in semi-darkness, under an arch that led from the gate right under the upper floors of the house to a central garden. I looked along the ten yards of brick archway to the greens and yellows of the garden. I thought I could hear the splashing of a fountain.

'Welcome to the impoverished hovel that I must call home,' he whispered in a weak attempt at irony. 'Normally, I'd have my lazy bitches of granddaughters come down and wash your feet. Then we'd have all the ritual bits of hospitality to keep us going till dinner. In view of the circumstances, you will forgive me for hurrying you all into my counting house. No one dares disturb me there.' From inside one of the doors that led on each side of the arch into the house came a sound of sandals flopping on stone. Ezra pulled me into the opposite door, and ordered his doorman to lift Wilfred out of the wheelbarrow and then carry him.

'We'd better hurry,' he said. 'All my children live here with their families. My wife's father has rooms straight across the courtyard. Until he gets really drunk, as opposed to just pissed, he can be a right nosy sod. We can save introductions till later. For the moment, let's keep things private.'

We passed through a succession of corridors and various storerooms. There was a continuous smell of fresh bread and spices.

The rhythmical thumping of feet on board above our heads told of children at play. At last, we were in a tidy little office. There was a roll of Jewish scriptures half open on the desk, and, beside this, an open parchment ledger marked with entries, I think, in Greek. Opposite the window that looked out to the garden was a bright mural – an apparently formless jumble of birds and flowers, with a large building on one side and a lion on the other. Ezra ordered Wilfred to be laid out on a couch and sat me in a soft chair that he pulled out from behind the desk. He perched himself on the desk and looked across at me.

'You know,' he said in a Greek that sounded more natural than his Aramaic, 'I did idly wonder, when I first heard you might be in Africa, if you'd come to us. It would make sense, I told myself. After all, the Christians won't help you. And it doesn't look like you've two coppers to rub together when it comes to buying help from them. But you're right that we owe you. We owe you big – and you're right that we don't forget these things.' For the first time, he smiled properly. 'I thought you might come to us. I never thought for a moment you'd come to *me*!

'Now, let's drop all this talk of owing and favours. When I welcome guests into my house, they want for nothing. Nor do I ask questions of them. Welcome, then, Lord Alaric, to my house. Welcome to all I can give you, for as long as you want it.'

He clapped his hands at the doorman. 'Go to the kitchen,' he said. 'Go and arrange food and drink for our guests. Tell Miriam the Master would have her keep her mouth shut.'

I sat back in the chair. It was the most comfortable resting place I'd known since leaving the ship. No, it was better than the ship. Here, no one was plotting to kill me – or to poison me by accident with slops and stagnant beer. I was hungry, and I wanted to give proper thanks for a stranger's kindness. But the strain of those days on the road, and that long walk through Caesarea suddenly caught up with me. One moment, I sat there watching a shaft of sunlight creeping towards my feet. Another, and the office was in gloom. I could sense Edward asleep at my feet. I wanted to stretch and pull myself upright in the chair.

But Ezra was behind me in a whispered conversation with someone.

'For what little it may count with you, my dear and honoured father,' a man said in Greek, 'I think you've gone round the twist. A ship put in yesterday afternoon with a good description of him and the two boys. The price on his head's been doubled, and may go up again. So you've brought him into the house and are proposing to give him sanctuary. Have you forgotten you have a family?'

'And have you forgotten that we have duties?' I heard Ezra reply. 'We'll tell the family at dinner. Rather, we'll tell *something* to some of them. All else aside, can you imagine what our people would think of the family that turned in Alaric the Just? How long do you suppose the Empire will keep this town? One year? Two? Sooner or later, the Saracens will turn up, and then we'll be free of the Greeks forever. In the meantime, I know my duty – and I suggest you remember yours.'

I now decided to go through the motions of a slow waking up. The conversation behind me ceased, and Ezra was standing before me.

'You slept a long time, My Lord,' he said with an attempt at sounding natural that didn't quite come off. 'You missed lunch. But I'm sure you will be glad of a little wine.'

I took the cup. Its contents were somewhat sweeter than I'd have enjoyed in Constantinople. But it was the best I'd had in years. I savoured its heady strength and waited for life to flow back into my limbs.

'I heard you talking,' I said. I decided not to say how much I'd heard.

Ezra pulled a face and nodded. His son came and stood before me. He was one of those short, very sleek Jews you see supervising rent collections. His oiled and plaited beard reached down almost to his immense belly. I'd never have guessed he was a son of Ezra. But he bowed and touched his forehead in the Eastern manner. Obviously, he'd have been pleased to see me and mine booted back out into the street. Since that wouldn't happen, he'd put up with me. To be sure, he'd not be turning me in to the authorities.

'My Lord will be pleased to know that he has not been forgotten by the Emperor,' he said. I waved my cup at him and waited for a refill. He took it back to the top and helped it to my lips.

'I didn't expect any less on my return,' I said with a laugh. 'Can you tell me what might be the current price on my head?'

'A lot,' he said shortly. 'Why a man of your years should have brought half the Imperial Navy to the West isn't a question you will be inclined to answer. But we must get you out of here within days at the most. We have family in Cartagena. Even if you are recognised there, Spain is beyond the current grasp of the Empire. You'll not object, I think, if I endorse my father's treason – that I wish Africa were in the same happy position. Even the Christians are getting fed up with this.'

I shrugged and tried to get up. But I still hadn't woken properly from the long nap, and I had to be helped up.

'You'll not take it as a slight on your hospitality,' I said, 'if I tell you that Spain sounds delightful. That assumes you can get us there. I might also mention . . .' I looked round for Wilfred. For the first time in that increasing gloom, I noticed that he was gone. Ignoring all the stiffness and aches, I stepped forward, a terrified question on my lips.

'My son Jacob is a physician,' Ezra said with an effort at the reassuring. He put a hand on my shoulder.

His son took up the explanation. It was no more than I'd already guessed. But it was a shock to hear it set out in those flat, professional tones.

'How long?' I asked after another full cup. 'How long has the boy got?'

Jacob put on a vacant, professional face. 'That I can't say,' came the answer. 'The right lung is already gone. The left could go tomorrow. How he lasted the journey from Tipasa is a wonder. The young can be resilient, I'll grant, and there may still be a partial and temporary recovery; we're talking months, by the way, nothing more. It's a question of nursing and of the right diet to rebalance the humours. But I do assure you he wouldn't last a day of any crossing to Spain.'

He'd been woken while I slept, so watery broth could be poured into him. He'd then been dosed with opium and put to bed. I was told I could see him in the morning. It was then that we'd discuss what was to be done with him.

As I fought to control myself, Edward came back to life. He got stiffly up and looked at the long, quiet faces round him. I pointed at the clothes set out for us on the couch where Wilfred had been lying.

'If you would have the kindness to direct us to our room,' I said to Ezra, 'and have water sent in, we'll get ourselves ready for dinner.'

An old man's tears are pathetic things to behold. I'd let Edward see them, but no one else. For the moment, I fought hard to compose myself.

23

The Imperial court still keeps up the old ways. So do some of the grander nobles in Constantinople. Ezra, fortunately, either didn't know about the old ways, or chose to follow the modern pattern of dinner seating – so much easier on the body, I can say. Of course, I was at the top table. I sat on Ezra's right, between him and his wife. Neither seemed unhappy with the arrangement. At right angles from us, two much longer tables filled the rest of the dining room. I didn't ask what had been said to explain my presence, but nearly the whole family must have been there. Including the women, I counted fifty people. They varied in age from a girl of about sixteen to a man even older than Ezra – the wife's father, I presumed. Naturally, the children I'd heard earlier weren't present. They, plus the slaves, would have taken the population of the house to something like that of the monastery at Jarrow.

Edward sat a long way down the left table, though not quite at the end. He'd been put between two of the plainer girls. Opposite him was a cluster of the older women. I looked several times in his direction. But he didn't disgrace me. He didn't tear at the meat. He didn't touch the bread platter on which he piled the cut slices of meat and vegetables from the steaming pot. He sipped politely at the watered wine, and took the more than polite attention of all the women with proper modesty.

No one thought it odd that I joined in the Hebrew prayers. When it became plain that I was the only one there able to understand their exact meaning, I found myself in a long conversation with two intense young men seated a few places down the right-hand table. Without meaning to, I slipped into my lecturing style, though had trouble keeping my voice heard above the surrounding babble of happy talk.

There was no point trying with Ezra for any conversation beyond the formulaic. As the great man of the household, he had no end of duties throughout the dinner. There were serving and other instructions to be given. Then there was the matter of sending little tasters of the food served at our table to a favoured few among the other diners. Fairly early into the proceedings, Ezra's medical son, Jacob, had been called away by one of the slaves. He'd thrown down his napkin, and, with a look at me that I couldn't interpret, was off. To take my thoughts off his look, I turned to the right and opened a conversation with Ezra's wife.

Fat, like most Jewish women, she spoke loudly and at terrible length about the achievements of her sons – of whom I learned there were seven. Jacob was her favourite, and if just some of her cure stories were true, he should have been fished straight off to Carthage, or even Constantinople. Otherwise, there was the youngest, whose musical talents I'd surely be able to judge later in the evening. Once or twice – though it never stopped her from gushing away like a broken water pipe – she fixed a thoughtful eye on Edward. He was still keeping up the diplomatic charm. But I could see those girls were having trouble keeping their hands off him. Oh, I've had my own day, I thought. Let him have his. It passes before you know it. But Ezra's wife was still loudly chattering. She had some faint notion of who I had been, and none whatever that I wasn't that any more. She thought it only natural that, on visiting Caesarea, the greatest subject in the Empire should also drop in on her husband.

So the dinner rolled on, through more courses than I could even think of eating. Edward steadily munched everything offered, including the honeyed cabbage in hot sauce that Ezra took care to send him. After the first meat course, I kept myself to bread soaked in wine, with occasional dipping into a large dish of barley pottage. The spices would repeat on me later, I knew, but the olive oil in which the pottage swam was beyond resisting for anyone who'd just spent more years than he should have making do on mutton fat.

'My Lord.' It was the voice, behind me, of Jacob. 'My Lord.' I twisted round. His voice had been enough. But there was one of those coldly professional looks on his face that ripped away all the cheer I'd absorbed from that brightly lit gathering. 'I must ask you to come with me at once. I think you can manage them, but I will help you with the stairs.'

My hands shook as I wiped them on the napkin. I made my excuses to Ezra and nodded to Edward to stay in his place.

'I agree that the symptoms listed by Aretaeus shouldn't be taken as a fixed definition of the illness,' Jacob replied. I didn't break in this time. Whatever I might have read on his subject, he was the expert. 'But, while every patient is different, and while this boy is wholly different from my usual patients, I don't think this is an ordinary case of consumption.' He lifted the blanket and, in the barely adequate light of the three lamps beside us, we stared down at the sleeping boy. I hadn't before seen Wilfred without clothes, and hadn't paid nearly so much attention to his clothed appearance as I had to Edward's. Still, the boy looked barely half the size he'd been aboard the ship. It was as if something had been hollowing him out, and what remained had collapsed into the resulting void. Except for the rapid rise and fall of his chest and the subdued gasps from his throat, he might have been dead already. Even I must have looked healthier. I swallowed, but Jacob hadn't finished.

'I won't ask you to probe for yourself, but you will see the contours here on his stomach of a tumour that goes right through him. If I were to turn him over, you'd see a blue mottling on his back where the tumour has distended the skin. There are also these lumps on his thighs. This one on the right is the size of a duck's egg. The others are substantial. These symptoms, with others, and the absence of the delirium that is almost invariable in advanced consumptions, lead me to believe the boy's to be a different and more rapidly fatal condition.'

'Two months ago, in the northern part of Britain,' I said, 'he'd been coughing on and off for about a year. But few of the inhabitants there can be called really healthy. The climate is cold half the year, and damp throughout. Except for the growing discomfort and frequency of his coughing attacks, I'd not have said he was other than a weakling.'

'With respect, My Lord,' Jacob replied to my unasked question, 'the size of these growths within his body indicates a terminal decline that began long before the journey you describe from his country. On the one hand, the strain of travel may have accelerated the decline. On the other, the more favourable climate of these regions may have compensated for the earlier hardships.

'Whatever the case, I do assure you that the boy wouldn't have lived another year – whatever his movements, wherever his location. If I knew the reason, I'd give it. All I can say is that, as others are born to live longer, some are born to live shorter than the three score and ten promised in our common scriptures.' He fell silent as, carrying a bowl and sponge, an old woman came back into the room. He moved closer to the lamps and fussed with a mixture of opium and mandragora.

There was no point in asking now anything other than the obvious. I'd seen enough. Groaning from the bodily aches of the past few days, I sat carefully in a chair.

'How long do you think?' I asked.

Jacob put down his measuring glass and shrugged. 'You should forget what I told you earlier. That was before I'd made a full examination. It's a wonder the boy is still alive. If he makes it through the next couple of days, I shall be surprised.'

There was a muffled burst of laughter and applause from the dining room. I'd not heard him, but perhaps the youngest son had now begun his performance. It was all ghastly – a boy with so much promise and, until recently, so much quiet joy from his life, so soon to die. And what made it worse was that his death would make things easier for those who survived him. We couldn't travel with Wilfred. We couldn't leave him behind. We couldn't stay too long in Caesarea to wait for him to die or recover. If he died soon, those choices could be forgotten. Edward and I would be free to make our own selfish choices. There's no point feeling guilty over matters outside your control. Nevertheless, I did feel guilty. I felt guilty that this problem was to be solved. I felt guilty also that I might soon have my answer to the question Wilfred had asked on the beach at Tipasa. If there was no telling what reception we'd have in England, why go back there at all? The longer I'd been back in my old world, the less enthusiastic I'd felt about a return to horrid, cold Jarrow. I'd been so fixed on returning purely because it was Wilfred's home. Edward had no wish to go back. I had little. Did we need to make our way back west? Did we even need to stay together? I'd be dead soon enough – even another few years was too much reasonably to expect. I could hide myself in some desert monastery that took in the aged. I could do any number of things. So too Edward. I looked at Wilfred. The drugs had suppressed his cough. He slept easily. Since it couldn't now be avoided, his death might as well be peaceful. That much I could arrange for the boy.

'Jacob, you seem convinced the Saracens will soon be here?' I asked to change the subject.

He sat heavily down just opposite me. He opened his mouth to speak, but then got up and went over to a table, where a jug and a couple of cups promised refreshment. He poured out the wine. Into his own, he carefully added twenty drops from his glass measure. He looked at me and held out the measure for me to sniff. I held up three fingers. I'd been so long without the joys of opium, it would be best to go easy on the reunion. He shrugged and added the drops. Turning back to his own cup, he gave up on counting, and just topped it to the brim.

I sipped at my own cup. Unlike downstairs in the dining hall, this was a poor vintage. Then again, we were drinking it less for its own substance than for the dull under-taste of what had been added to it. Jacob drank about half his cup in one gulp, and settled into his chair.

'You had no news while away of developments in the war?' he asked.

I shook my head.

'Well, the Saracens had another go at Carthage last year. They had to break it off for lack of naval support – the Empire had another big victory off Cyprus, and the Saracens haven't the ghost of a fleet. But the land forces are building in strength. Being Saracens, they can run supplies from Egypt straight through the desert. No one believes Carthage can hold. Once that goes, this whole shore goes with it. Without you to hunt, the naval base at Syracuse is barely enough to keep down piracy – let alone protect us from siege.'

'And you look forward to this?' I asked again.

He laughed bitterly. 'Why not?' he said. 'The moment you weren't there to keep things in order, the Greek Church went mad. The African Church is now run by Greeks. They're discouraging the use of Latin. They've made up some new heresy to seek out among the Latins.'

'*Another* heresy?' I interrupted. 'We sorted out the dispute over the Double Will of Christ six years ago. Surely not something else?'

'There's always another heresy,' Jacob sneered. 'These priests could find heresy in a bread queue. But don't ask a Jew about its details. I only know that the Greeks have started making a fuss about the use of pictures. The Latins want their pictures. The Pope in Rome is screaming blue murder. But no one in Constantinople listens to him nowadays.

'More important for us, the Greeks are talking of another forced conversion law. Remember the one you "forgot" to publish in Carthage all those years back? Well, they've blown the dust off it, and are talking of setting up brass copies in every African city.

'You ask if we want the Saracens? Of course we do! They lower all the taxes, and they leave us alone.'

'And a thousand years of shared history,' I asked again, 'that means nothing?'

No answer.

The drug had hit us both at the same time. I leaned back and closed my eyes as, like a tide sweeping over a rocky beach, the velvet of the opium blacked out the physical pains of age and over-exertion and the moral pain that flowed from a belief that everything Wilfred had been suffering was somehow my own fault. For the first time since we'd met, Jacob put on something like a happy smile. He took a little sip extra from his cup and leaned slowly forward.

'A thousand years of history!' he said with a laugh. 'Let's have a think about that, My Lord. The old Greeks would only put up with us if we stuck on artificial foreskins and cavorted nude like them in public. One of the madder Roman emperors nearly made us worship his own statue in the Temple. That only got called off when he was murdered by his guards. Another Emperor burned Jerusalem and destroyed the Temple. When it turned Christian, the Empire began telling us how to edit our own scriptures and treating us like lepers. It's a thousand years of history some of us would like to forget.'

I sat, looking at Jacob, and wondered at how good a few drops of dried plant sap could make me feel.

'But My Lord knows all this,' he sighed after a long and appreciative pause. 'Let's stop arguing about the Empire. We both know it's the best common home for the peoples of the civilised world. If only you'd been Emperor these past sixty years – why, we'd have gladly helped kick that upstart rabble back into the desert. The Saracens tolerate us. But they don't mean us any good. They're coming here, and we'll turn out and welcome them. But, if only – if only . . .' He drifted off into the sort of waking dream only enough opium to kill a dozen of the uninitiated can produce.

We both sat awhile in silence. For myself, I was reflecting on the many advantages of not being in Jarrow: no cold, no prayers, plenty of water for bathing, all the amenities of the civilised pharmacopoeia. Really, why had I gone there?

'But you will forgive me!' Jacob cried softly. The great poppy inspired orgasm was passing out of its intense phase, and would soon enter its much longer afterglow of delicious and untroubled comfort. He opened his eyes and sat forward. 'The reason I asked you to come here was that the boy was asking for you before his sedatives took hold. He was insistent that he had things to say that only you could hear.'

'I imagine the poor boy knows he is dying,' I said with a serene look at Wilfred. 'Among my many qualifications is the authority to hear confessions and absolve the dying from their sins. I can't think what sins Wilfred could have that press on him so. But those who believe very strongly do worry about matters the rest of us might barely notice.'

As I spoke, Wilfred threw back his covering blanket and sat up. I saw the lamp flames reflected by the sweat on his body as he jumped onto the ceiling. Except it was in the wrong direction, it was like watching a cat jump down from a wall. He paused there on all fours and looked down at me, his eyes glowing an internal red. He grinned triumphantly and showed canines that glittered white far beyond his lower lip. He opened his mouth as if to speak, but only smiled again. He got up and, without bothering to look at me, walked rapidly over to the closed door. There, he stopped and stretched vainly down to get at the handle. It was too low for him to reach. He stood back one pace, and then forward again. He slapped one hand hard against the wall, and then the other. Like some lizard on a rock face, he began crawling down to reach the handle.

I squeezed my eyes shut and concentrated. When I opened them again, Wilfred was back under his blanket, still but for the continued rise and fall of his chest. I rubbed my eyes and looked again. Yes – the boy hadn't moved an inch. I made a note to ask Jacob, when we were both more with it, how he prepared his opium.

There was another faint commotion downstairs, then a louder thudding of feet on the stairs. It might have been close within the house. It might, on the other hand, have been back in Tipasa. Had I just heard it? Might I be about to hear it? Interesting questions, these. Give me a day or two to think them over, and I might have some kind of an answer. I was wondering if the upside-down reflection of my own face in one of the lamp flames was somehow connected with the noise, when the door burst open. It was one of the young men who'd been so interested in the difference between the jussive mood in Hebrew and the imperative.

'My Lord,' he gasped, 'you must hide at once. There are men in the house. They have orders to take and kill you.'

24

You may assume, dear Reader, that opium, like wine, tends to incapacitate those who use it to the full. If so, you are wrong. It does stupefy – but only when stupefaction is desired. One sound of that heavy, collective tramping on the stairs, and Jacob was straight out of his chair and running about. I was, you can be sure, a little slower. But, once I'd realised the young man was no part of my hallucination, the blotting out of all the aches and strains of the past few days allowed me to get with surprising speed and resolution into the medical contagion robe and then on to my knees before the sleeping body of Wilfred.

'This is a room for the dying,' Jacob snarled as the door flew open again. 'I will not have my patient disturbed.' He fell silent while perhaps a half dozen pairs of feet tramped in and came to a disciplined halt a couple of yards behind me. Hoping I'd pulled my hood on properly, I kept my hands, palms upward, in the praying position. In a low mutter, I intoned as much as I could recall of the fifty-third chapter of Isaiah. The silence, and now the stillness, behind me seemed to last an infinity. Then I heard a faint sound of leather soles on the wooden boards. There was another loud scraping as the men already there pulled themselves up to attention.

'What is your patient's condition?' a voice asked in Latin.

I froze. It was all the effort I could manage to keep my upstretched arms from shaking. I'd have needed as much opium as Jacob had downed to keep calm. Even with the few drops I'd taken, I found myself wondering if this was another delusion. But I was fully with it, and that voice – in Latin or Greek or Syriac, or in English – I'd have recognised anywhere. I felt rather than heard Joseph come and stand behind me. He peered over at the shrivelled, sleeping boy. To be sure, Wilfred had changed radically since Jarrow. But the wispy blond hair said anything but Jewish. Even in the gloom of the dying lamps, it would take a miracle for him not to be recognised. But Jacob was now beside him.

'It's a new contagion that killed both his parents the day before yesterday,' he said with professional firmness of tone. 'I doubt he will last beyond tomorrow morning. The medical arts are exhausted on him. Prayer is all that remains.'

There was another long silence. I heard only the gentle scraping of military boots as the other men in the room removed themselves as far as possible from the vicinity of a sickness that might somehow communicate itself across the few yards that separated them from the dying boy. Joseph stayed put. I felt his long stare into the uncovered face.

'He was oppressed, and he was afflicted,' I droned on in Hebrew, trying not to shake; 'yet he opened not his mouth: he is brought as a lamb to the slaughter, and as a sheep before her shearers is dumb, so he openeth not his mouth.' If Joseph was Syrian – correction, since Joseph knew enough Syriac to pass for Syrian, he might understand enough Hebrew to know this wasn't a valid prayer of the Jews. I dropped my voice lower still.

'You will be aware,' Joseph said, speaking soft and to no one in particular, 'of the reason for our visit. The traitor whose name I hardly need mention is said to have landed on the African shore – here to raise disaffection against the God-anointed Augustus. The orders are that he is to be killed on sight. He is to be killed on sight – he or anyone who resembles him. For his head, the reward is its weight in gold. For any mistaken identity, the promise is full civil and criminal impunity. Against those who harbour the traitor the full penalties of treason are threatened.

'There is a report that a man matching the traitor's description was seen to enter the Jewish district. Have you anything to add in light of this information?'

It was no longer the relaxed, frequently bored, voice I'd known every day for months and months in Jarrow. The fellow spirit – the refuge from the chattering fools – I'd so often sought out in the monastery was no longer the Joseph who stood behind me, looking down at Wilfred with an incomprehensible lack of recognition. This was a man of obvious power within the Imperial Secret Service. Though terrified by what Jacob had told them, his military support didn't dare do as nature prompted and flee that room of possible contagion.

'I assure you that no traitor is harboured within this house,' Jacob said quietly. He leaned over me to adjust the blanket. Not realising that the boy had sat every day at the front of Joseph's class – and in every lesson had earned his grudging praise – Jacob pulled the blanket down, exposing more of the ravaged body to view.

'Dead?' Joseph asked. 'He'll soon be dead?'

Jacob pointed at the mottling that had now come out all over the boy's chest like barbarian tattoos.

'Well, death in one so young is always to be regretted. The Empire makes no war on children.' It was hard to judge the tone of his voice. But he took a step backwards.

'Your father tells me that he has an immunity from the Prefect against entry and search,' he said in a less ambiguous tone. 'As you know, this means nothing where reason of state is concerned. However, I am satisfied that there is nothing in this house to take up more of my attention. I will only repeat that there is no safety within the Empire for the traitor we seek. Wherever he may fly, we will follow. Wherever he may hide, we will find him. For him, there will be no second trial – no appeal to the uncertain mercy of Caesar. His friends in the Capital are dead or scattered. His technical skills are no longer required. His sentence was pronounced on the first discovery of his treason. All that remains is for sentence to be executed.' He turned and walked from the room. With a renewed clatter of boots on wood, the soldiers followed.

I continued in my place, hands upstretched to Heaven, listening to the increasingly faint tramp of boots and the shouting of orders. Only when the outer gate slammed shut, and the house fell into a deep silence, did I let myself drop forward to rest on the little cot. I felt Jacob's hands close around my chest. He pulled me to my feet and guided me back to the chair. He refilled the cup and held it to my lips. Nothing in it now but wine, I drained the contents with a single, chattering gulp.

'That was a close one,' Jacob said with a ghastly smile. 'Still, I think we managed to deceive a pretty senior Greek.' He relaxed and sat heavily in his own chair.

I didn't feel up to explaining what had happened. I didn't *know* what had happened. My hands and wrists on full view – Wilfred stretched out before him – and Joseph had contented himself with an oddly helpful warning before going off again into the night. I'd need to think a good deal harder than I'd yet managed before I could tell even myself what was happening. If only I'd been able to tell myself this was another product of the opium. But it wasn't. Joseph really had stood behind me.

'Tell me, Jacob,' I asked once my voice was reliably in order. 'Tell me what was that Greek official wearing?'

Black with a hat that may have had a purple trimming, came the answer – the light made colours hard to tell. I nodded. I knew it was purple. I'd helped choose the design when, after the death of the tyrant Phocas, Heraclius had put me in charge of reordering the Intelligence Bureau. Over the three generations that followed, abuses had crept into my original scheme. One of the most annoying of these had been the custom for everyone to put on the uniform of the grade immediately above. But, even assuming he'd been dressed two or three grades above his own position, there was no doubting that Joseph was at least – to use the Latin title – a *Magister Scholarum.* He was, that is, one of the departmental heads of the External Ministry. No wonder he'd been close enough to see my every move on the walls of Constantinople as I'd unleashed that irresistible tide of destruction on the Saracen fleets. Not for him to risk it in the killing zones I'd created.

And he'd been sent all the way to Jarrow to watch me. Every day for months, he'd been my chosen companion. And I'd never once suspected he could be other than just another refugee from the world of civilisation. Perhaps age had caught up with me. Alaric in his prime would never have been taken in as old Brother Aelric had been.

'Moses and all the prophets!' Ezra cried as he bustled into the room. He looked at Wilfred and dropped his voice. 'We certainly deceived the Empire then. The tax collectors were nothing compared with this!' Beneath his tone of relieved cheerfulness, there was something more complex. I looked closely at him. He turned away.

'Where is Edward?' I asked to change the subject. If Joseph had, for his own reasons, overlooked me and Wilfred, his men would have spotted those northern looks in less than a single heartbeat. Even if, after a few centuries, the remaining Vandal blood in Africa hadn't been darkened by local mixture, there would still have been the obvious question of what he was doing in a company of Jews. But he'd been spirited straight off, Ezra assured me, into the women's quarters. He'd be safe enough there. I nodded, trying to ignore the obvious further question about his safety there. It was enough for the moment that the Empire, in a majesty that no one else had been able to notice, had come into the house, and had gone out again.

'It would be for the best if we left this house as soon as possible,' I said. As one, all three of us turned and looked at Wilfred. His lips had now drawn back in a snarl that it required no doctor to interpret. Sooner than I'd expected, the shock of the search was wearing away the delicious yet conscious oblivion of the opium, and I could feel the return of guilt. The more I speculated on the meaning of this approaching death, the more crushing the burden of guilt became.

'We're safe enough for the moment,' Jacob assured me.

And, if what judgement I'd so far been able to make was correct, he was right to a degree he'd never understand. Yes, we were safe for the moment.

Jacob took up his half-empty measure. 'No one will disturb us more this evening. And I do assure you, the boy will continue at least till morning. If there is any change, I will wake you. For now, I will, as your physician for the day, prescribe for a peaceful night.'

25

Waking was like the beginning of consciousness in the very young. It was gradual, and was unmarked by any sense of its own arrival. Tucked in bed, I lay for an indefinite time without moving or opening my eyes. Two men beside me had been talking forever in Aramaic. I knew, in some instinctive way, that they were servants. I knew they were there to watch over me. What they were saying had, until just moments before, been unintelligible and without importance. Those five additional drops from Jacob into my wine cup had struck me like the blow to a slaughtered animal. Almost before I'd noticed how soft the pillows were, I was swallowed into a serene and infinite blackness. There had been no visits that night from the many dead I'd known, nor from the yet unborn; no visions of my own grave; no severed hands feeling their way over my face – the opium had brought me sleep and nothing more.

But now I was awake. And, if not willing to show that I was awake, I was fully aware of my surroundings.

'I told you, Reuben – I told you many times – the Master's going soft in the head,' one of the servants was saying. The words aside, I had the impression this was more than his first repetition. 'He turns up yesterday with three goys, all of them wanted by the Empire. He's now got another one hidden away in his counting house, and we're under orders to say bugger all about them. This here old bag of bones is the guest of honour. One of the boys is dying. The other one – well, you've heard it for yourself from Miriam. We're two inches from all being dragged off to Carthage and pulled apart with hot pincers. If you ask me, the Master's gone fucking mad.'

'He was up till dawn with Doctor Jacob,' I heard Reuben say

defensively. 'They was talking and talking. I didn't hear much of what was said. But trust me – the Master ain't no fool. He's done right by the whole house. Just you keep your mouth shut and do as you're told. You'll see a Passover yet without no bastard Greeks to tell us our ways.'

'*Another one hidden away in his counting house,*' I'd heard. It would have been worth hearing more on that. To hear more, I'd gladly have lain there, my face conveniently half buried under the coverings, till evening. But I heard the door open and a heavy tread on the boards. Both servants were on their feet.

'Isn't he awake yet?' Jacob asked. There was a silence that I guessed was a reply of shaking heads. He clicked his tongue impatiently, then went into Greek. 'Not another overdose!' he said in the quiet tone of a man who knows he is speaking only to himself. 'I really must cut down on things.' I heard him approach the bed. I felt his hand brush lightly on the unshaven stubble above my ears. In a moment, he'd probably have one of my wrists out to see how close to death he'd really dosed me. Nothing else for it. I groaned and moved slightly. I felt him draw back and I went through the motions of opening my eyes and looking confused.

'You're among friends,' Jacob said.

A priest – no, make that a toadying courtier, or, better still, some diplomat sent out to make trouble among the barbarians – would have had trouble matching the absolute conviction in his voice. Then again, he was a doctor and a Jew. One of the servants helped me as I struggled to sit up. I looked about the room. The bed set up for Edward was as neatly made as it had been the night before. I could tell nothing from that, mind you. Everyone else had been up and about for ages. There was no direct sunlight in this room. But the light that came in from the garden had an afternoon quality. I drank from a cup of honeyed wine diluted with fruit juice and asked about Wilfred. Jacob pulled a long face and took on a more openly professional appearance. He didn't need to say much. It hadn't been to get my lunch orders that he'd come to see if I was awake. On a chair by the window, there was a newish robe set out for me. Unlike the one I'd been given in Cartenna, it was neither faded tat nor too big. The colour was too light for what I had in mind. But it would do.

'I think we'll have to skip the confession,' I said in Aramaic. Jacob nodded. I wondered if he hadn't been a little enthusiastic with the belladonna. But Wilfred, I'd been told, had woken in considerable pain while I slept, and a doctor's recognised duty is to his patient's body. Now, he lay before me, semi-conscious but rigid from the administration of this and the other drugs.

'Confirm to me, if you can,' I said loudly, now in Latin, 'that you have received all other rites of the Faith. These include baptism and communion.' Just in case, I repeated myself in English. It was a redundant question, but had to be asked if the last rite was to be correctly administered. The pale eyes blinked slightly. 'You know, then,' I continued, 'that I am qualified by virtue of my priestly office to administer these rites.' No doubt, my qualifications were decidedly iffy. But, since no one in England had seen fit to question them on my arrival there, now wasn't the time to disabuse poor Wilfred of their validity. All told, I'd sooner have had a real priest brought in. I hadn't bothered raising this with Jacob. He could certainly have got me one – just as he'd managed to gather the necessary props. But now wasn't the time for introducing more Christians into the house. And all that really mattered was that Wilfred believed me. If death really was other than an infinite sleep still deeper than the one from which I was lately recovered, it would be a most perverse God who took against him on my account.

With dramatic emphases and pauses that any real priest would have envied rotten, I went through the prayers as I'd heard them said by others any number of times. The gaunt fingers fluttered ever so little on the wooden crucifix, and a thin trickle of the olive oil I'd just blessed ran down from his forehead on to the bed clothes. At last, I produced a fragment of the Host. I broke it in two and placed the smaller part between the dry lips. As I did so, they trembled and a faint effort was made to move them.

And it was now done. All that remained was the final prayer. I opened my mouth again and, Edward joining in, launched into the ancient words:

'O Almighty God, with whom do live the spirits of just men made perfect, after they are delivered from their earthly prisons: We humbly commend the soul of this thy servant, our dear brother, into thy hands, as into the hands of a faithful Creator, and most merciful Saviour; most humbly beseeching thee, that it may be precious in thy sight. Wash it, we pray thee, in the blood of that immaculate Lamb, that was slain to take away the sins of the world . . .'

The lips moved again. This time, Wilfred was able to speak.

'Brother Aelric,' he whispered. 'Brother Aelric.'

I moved closer to the dying boy's mouth. 'Be at peace, my child,' I said in my reassuring voice. 'There is nothing now to fear, in this world or the next. Of all you might have confessed I have now absolved you.' That should have sorted things. But, no – the lips moved again.

'I have sinned, Brother Aelric,' he gasped with urgent though failing energy. 'Such sins have I committed and never confessed to you. It was my plan – but God has called me so soon . . .'

He trailed off, and I thought this would be it. Jacob moved forward with a beaker of something aromatic to put under his nose. But the boy struggled with the feeble ghost of one of his coughing fits. I waved Jacob back.

Then, with an immense effort, Wilfred continued in a desperate croak: 'You must know that Brother Cuthbert – yes, Brother Cuthbert . . . He commanded, and I obeyed. He told me – he said . . . I discovered . . .'

He trailed off once more, and now closed his eyes. Jacob moved forward again, beaker still in hand. There was no point letting him try anything more. I've seen the shadow of death pass over any number of faces. It's not so much a darkening of colour as a loss of something. I've also held the hands of the dying so often. With its usual rapidity, I could now feel the mysterious transformation of living flesh and bone into the sort of meat you buy in a butcher's market. I didn't need to see the eyes turn up, or the mouth open wide for that last, rattling sigh, to know it was all up with the boy. He was as near gone as mattered. Even if some spark of life continued deep within, there was no point in supposing he was aware of anything outside himself. Still, I continued with the prayer to the end. Deathbeds are as much for the living as the dead. Besides, if what Edward believed was his own affair, there was a Jew present, and a certain appearance had to be kept up. I finished the prayer, then waited. As the lips sagged fully, and all tension went out of the body, I stood back and allowed Jacob to press his mirror to the boy's face. He drew it back and held it up for me, still unmisted. It really was over.

I sat down and took the full cup in both hands. I looked at Edward, who was still staring, still impassive – except, I was pleased to notice, for the single tear he'd managed to squeeze out – at the lifeless, shrivelled body. If you hadn't known that his fourteenth birthday would have been a full month later, you'd have thought this the body of an old man, broken down by years of sickness. On his arrival in the monastery, Wilfred had told me of his ambition to train for the priesthood, and join the mission the English Church was fitting out for the conversion of the Germans. Except for the collapse of his health – only slightly arrested by our passage through the Narrow Straits – I rather thought he'd enjoyed the adventure forced on him by Edward. In place of all his hopes, though, here he lay dead. And I, more than seven times his age, had prayed him over the threshold of death. How many more of those round me would I outlive before I finally turned to rancid butcher's meat?

But it was a pointless question. I drained the cup and held it out for a refill. Jacob pulled the sheet up over the face and muttered something about arranging a funeral. For a Jew, he had surprising contacts in the Church. Then again, he was a doctor, and few who need the healing art bother with which God – if any – its practitioners may care to worship.

'This has been a sad event,' I said lamely – and what point was there in making a fuss? What point in saying what might be really in my heart? 'But let us be inspired as Christians by the calm resolution with which Wilfred was taken unto God.'

No – that wouldn't do! It was a worthless pretence. Including the two old women who'd step forward in a moment to lay out the body, there were five of us in the room. Three of us weren't even supposed to be Christians. The other two believed bugger all. My words didn't touch one of us. When something as empty of meaning as death happens, silence may be the best response. I wanted to get out into the garden, and walk round and round in the sun, looking at the flowers and the fountain, and thinking about what to do next.

'Edward, I will speak with you later this afternoon,' I said. 'What has just happened – together with other matters – alters all our plans. I need to discuss these with you. There are some decisions that only you can make. Until then, I suggest you go to our room and lie down.' He had the dark circles under his eyes of one who hasn't slept. If I cared to notice this at all, I might prefer to think that grief had kept him awake.

26

'His illness was, I am assured, one of excessive internal heat,' Jacob said firmly. 'It was brought on by a reaction to the excessive cold and wetness of his native land. That would explain why its like has never been known here in Africa. It also confirms that the illness had its roots in his native land.'

I nodded and gave a non-committal grunt. Jacob sighed and continued walking beside me in silence. I had completed five circuits of the garden, and, now rested from a long pause beside the fountain, had begun a sixth. The sun and the return of every-day normality had failed to lift my spirits. I might as well still have been sitting beside the deathbed.

'It was the opinion of Aristotle himself, that dry heat—' Jacob tried again.

I stopped at the mention of the hated name and scowled at him. 'If he'd confined himself to literary criticism and pure logic chopping,' I said coldly, 'Aristotle might be more deserving of our respect. As it is, the man corrupted every natural science he touched. All knowledge of things, as opposed to the manipulation of ideas, begins with a rejection of Aristotle. I don't believe that story about how the Saracens burned the library in Alexandria. But if they really did heat their baths with the collected works of that man, they surely made the world a more enlightened place.' I looked at Jacob's shocked face. For the first time that afternoon, I smiled. I untensed my shoulders and put a hand on his arm. He was trying to help. He was the son of a host who'd saved my life. I stepped forward again on our sixth circuit.

'But, surely, My Lord Alaric,' he said, keeping pace, 'the Philosopher is the common heritage of all civilised men, regard-less of origin or faith?'

'Common curse, more like,' I replied. Now less wintry, I smiled again. I meant what I'd said about the man's writings. This being said, the story about Omar and the Alexandrian Library was quite untrue – I knew that much, as I'd been its first author. I smiled once more. Jacob had done his best by the boy. If that hadn't been enough, it was no fault of Aristotle or of anyone else in particular. It was certainly no fault of Jacob's. I looked up and breathed in the warm, scented air of an African spring. Since we'd hit on a subject that didn't lead back to the deathbed, or some other matter we'd tacitly agreed not to discuss, I might as well carry on with the lecture.

'Both our faiths,' I said, 'have incorporated the more acceptable teachings of Plato and Aristotle regarding the natural world. They have both decisively rejected the teachings of Epicurus. Since these teachings tend very strongly to atheism, it is a rejection that I can well understand. The teachings are, however, interesting in themselves.' I stopped before the fountain again and looked at the splashing waters. Jacob said nothing. So far as I could, and without giving any impression of rudeness, I'd lead him away from the self-recriminations he was plainly seeking to escape.

'It was a thousand years ago that he taught his doctrines in Athens,' I went on. 'He taught that the universe consists entirely of matter and void, and all matter is composed of atoms. These atoms are too small to be seen – they are all nearly infinitely small. Even so, they can be classed according to their differing sizes and shapes. They are all rushing infinitely fast through an infinite void. Because their motions are not uniform – indeed, their motions are in some degree indeterminate – they tend to collide. Because they are all hooked, their collision is able to produce the larger structures of the visible world.

'Now, while nearly infinitely small, these atoms can be classed according to their different sizes and shapes. These may correspond to the fundamental materials of the visible world. All other materials are compounds of these atoms in differing variations.'

'And the soul?' Jacob asked.

I'd got him! Like one of those atomic swerves, I'd knocked him off course. And I'd keep him there.

'What of God?'

'The soul is composed of very small and highly indeterminate atoms,' I explained. 'Organised in the right structure, they are capable of conscious thought and the exercise of free choice. But, as with all other atomic structures, they eventually break down, and the individual atoms begin their rush over again through the void, until such time as they recombine into some entirely different soul.

'There is no room in this scheme for any God. The atoms have always existed, and always will exist. No truly legitimate social order requires a divine sanction, but will emerge and be sustained through the enlightened self-interest of individuals. The only legitimate social order is one in which the lives and property of individuals are protected so they can pursue the happiness that is not merely the highest, but also the sole, purpose of life. Any law that constrains the actions of individuals is legitimate so far as it protects the equal rights of other individuals. No other laws are binding on the conscience, and may be disobeyed as individuals think appropriate.'

'No God? No immortal souls? No Judgement? No obligation to obey beyond personal convenience?' Jacob wondered. And wonder is all he did. He didn't look even moderately angry – no denunciations of the satanic *Apikorus*, no defence of his own faith. It was as I'd expected. For the moment at least, I'd left Wilfred and the guilt we variously felt at his death upstairs with the corpse. I sat wearily on a bench placed before the fountain. Jacob snapped his fingers at a slave who'd put his head out into the garden, and called for wine and cakes.

'None of those things,' I answered. 'Because death is the end of all things for us, we have no need to worry about what follows from it. Because there is no supernatural judgement, our only reasons for respecting the rights of others can be the sanction of our own consciences and fear of the law.'

'And supposing I have no conscience?' Jacob broke in, finally argumentative. 'What is there then to stop me from murdering my elderly patients so I can inherit from them? What if the law is too defective to be feared?'

'Nothing at all,' I said with a smile. 'Can you tell me that all the talk of divine punishment has rid the world of crime? And have there been no crimes prompted by religion itself?

'But let us come back to how all this differs in its view of the material world from the mainstream opinion. Both our faiths – plus the new Desert Faith of the Saracens – place God at the centre of things. He creates our souls, and endows us with a physical world within which we can seek salvation. This being so, the purpose of knowledge is to understand the mind of God and the nature of the divine substance that underlies the accidental manifestations of the world about us. Therefore, all that happens can be explained in terms of specific acts of the Deity – or, at best, as a working out of secondary causes. Therefore, we populate the world with invisible spirits, sent here to do good or ill. Therefore, we command attention to the good spirits, and make laws against communion with the bad spirits who bring evil promptings and evil events.

'However, does any of this correspond to the reality that we perceive with our natural senses?' I continued with illustrations that might appeal to a Jew – of coins worn away by much handling, of bodily increases brought on by overeating, and the like. I ended with an explanation of how happiness can be enlarged by a study of the atoms and their combinations, and the turning of this study to our own advantage.

There – I'd come full circle. Now using his drugs as my example, I was discussing how the right combination of atoms could produce known and desired effects on the human body. And there would be no more of Aristotle of Stagira and his ludicrous talk of heat and cold and wet and dry as the fundamentals of existence. Sickness was a disordering of the bodily atoms. The purpose of drugs was to bring about a collision and mingling of atoms to reorder the body.

Jacob drank heavily of the very heavy wine. I took mine watered, and passed up the offer of more drops from the bottle he carried about with him. He looked steadily forward at the streams of water that shot into the air and cascaded back into the stone basin, each one now an individual, shining drop.

'I regret that you must soon leave us,' he said, speaking as if in a dream. 'If I but close my eyes, I can see your atoms, rushing forward like grains of sand blown up by the desert wind. I really would hear you speak more of them. And I'd hear you speak also of your world without empires to tax and oppress, and without religions to divide us. Are there still writings on all this?'

I shrugged ruefully. In a lifetime of collecting, I'd managed to gather up just over half of the three hundred books the Master had produced. They'd been carefully repaired and arranged in my library in Constantinople. But all my property had been confiscated. Had the books found their way into some other library? Or had the ancient rolls been cut up so accounts could be kept on the blank side of the papyrus? Constantine surely wouldn't have had them cast into the fire. The only thing he'd ever shown much interest in burning was people.

'Has my father said that you have two places booked on the first spring sailing?' Jacob asked. 'It leaves the day after tomorrow.'

I hadn't seen old Ezra since the previous evening. Whatever arrangements he'd made were of the present day. But Jacob was drifting into the sort of state where details of time were decreasingly important. I thought again of the boy laid out in the shuttered room upstairs just behind where we sat. I didn't suppose Ezra had even gone through the motions of reserving a third place.

'My father negotiated hard,' he said. 'You know he got you the best deal.'

I nodded. That was an unstudied ambiguity best not resolved. I should have thought here of the mysterious figure shut away in Ezra's counting house. I found my thoughts pulled back to Wilfred. Jacob would get him buried in hallowed ground. In this heat, we'd surely have the funeral before the next dawn.

'The world can be a shitty place,' I said. I thought of many things, though chiefly my own guilt. Why had I never once in my life grieved for someone I loved without also feeling that I was in some way to blame? If there was an answer to that one, I made sure to drown it with a double mouthful of wine. 'The world can be a right shitty place,' I said again.

'Never a truer word,' Jacob sighed. He put aside any pretence of wine, and let a few drops from his bottle fall directly on to his tongue.

We might have sat there in the appearance of silent communion until the lengthening shadows had taken all colour from the flowers. But I could now see Edward. Visibly limp with exhaustion, he was creeping through a doorway that didn't lead to our rooms. Exhausted or not, he could come and help me back inside. It was time for our discussion. I wouldn't tell him everything I'd now pieced together. But there were still those decisions I'd mentioned. He'd have to make those.

27

'Says here you're a Jew – right?' The Captain stabbed a dirty finger on to my passport and looked up at me.

I nodded. I could have tried the exaggerated Jewish whine I'd been practising all the previous day. But, if Ezra had assured me I'd convince everyone but another Jew, I thought it best for the time being to grovel in silence before this bloated, insolent pig of a man.

'Well, we ain't taking no chances,' he added with a laugh. He tipped his head back and hawked. The flob landed about an inch from my left sandal. I resisted the urge to look down, and focused on the passport Ezra had bribed out of the Prefecture. 'If you are what you say you are, you won't mind hitching up that fancy robe for me.'

Bastard shitbag! I thought. If ever I were in a position to do him ill, I'd have him chained to one of the slave oars of this ship. And I'd not have him moved to the other side every month. He could grow as lop-sided from continuous exercise as he'd let the other slaves I'd seen as I came on board. Then, the free oarsmen could come up and piss all over him. But I smiled greasily and did as I was told. I steeled myself not to set about him with my stick as he barked out another laugh and invited the other passengers to get a look at my circumcision. It was enough that the grim, unsmiling guard beside him bent down for a long inspection, then went back to his continuous scanning of everyone else boarding the ship.

'The boy's not a Jew, though,' the Captain added with a statement of the bleeding obvious.

Still not speaking, I pointed shakily at one of the lower sections of the passport. It confirmed my permission to own a Christian slave.

'And I suppose you'll be trading him with the enemy, won't you?' came the reply. He took up the sheet of papyrus and waved it around. 'Boys like him fetch their weight in silver among the debauched Saracens.' He raised his voice and repeated the witticism. Someone behind me laughed. Well he might laugh. If we hadn't all been granted permits to trade with the enemy, why else was the ship filling up with merchants in the first place? Just because there's a war on doesn't mean trade has to stop.

'Oh, fuck off, then,' he snarled, waving me on board. 'But I don't want none of your Jewboy caterwauling on deck. I run a Christian ship, and I'm proud of it.' He waited until Edward had gathered all our documents back into his satchel and we were moving off in search of our cabin. 'It's salt pork for dinner,' he bawled after us. 'It'll be served just after prayers.'

After what seemed an endless wait, the ship pitched horribly to one side, and we were moving slowly away from the docks. Still gripping hard on the side, I stood beside Edward and looked back at Caesarea. The whole family had turned out to wave goodbye. There was old Ezra, capering about like a schoolboy as he waved his stick at me. There was Jacob, sitting dazed on an abandoned crate and looking intently at something in his hand that I couldn't see, but could easily imagine. And there was a whole tribe of sobbing women. I strained to see more clearly. Was that Ezra's wife blowing kisses at us? I looked at Edward. His face was as impassive as it had been on that day, so long before, in Jarrow. Not bad for only thirteen, I'm sure you'll agree.

'How long to Beirut, My Lord?' he asked.

I looked up at the clear, blue sky, and at the large birds that screeched and careered against the backdrop of the sky. Storms and pirates allowing, I told him, we'd be there in fourteen days – sooner if the wind held up.

'And it is ruled by the Saracens?' he asked, in English. He went back to his inspection of the receding docks.

'Yes,' I said. 'It's been in their hands over fifty years now. When I was your age, it was a thoroughly Greek city. Any Syrian with ambitions who settled there had no choice but to learn Greek and fit in. Why, it once even had the third largest law school in the Empire. It's still the main port for that part of Syria. But it's well outside the Empire nowadays. And that, my dear, is why it's to be Beirut for us. It has all the civilised amenities – without any Brother Joseph to cut short my decline.' I tried to scan the docks. They'd receded too far now to be other than a blur. 'Anyone else back there you might recognise?' I asked, switching too into English.

Edward gave the docks another long and general inspection. He shook his head. 'Whom else were you expecting me to see?' he asked.

Since he knew perfectly well whom I had in mind, I ignored the question. I looked closely at the boy – and, seen in profile, he still was rather boyish. I looked over the side. We were now perhaps a mile out from Caesarea. Unless he'd secreted himself on board – not impossible, bearing in mind how big this ship was – Joseph was far behind us. It was just the passengers on this ship, plus the attendant slaves. I changed the subject.

'Tell me, Edward,' I asked, 'have you any idea what poor Wilfred was trying to confess before he died? He mentioned Cuthbert several times. Is there any light you can shed on his final words?' Though just a little, the face tightened. I could see him thinking and then choose his words.

'Though I don't believe he understood the full meaning of what was put to him,' came the measured reply, 'he was promised safety by Cuthbert from the first group of raiders.' He paused. 'You do know that Cuthbert was involved with them?'

I nodded. 'Do you know who was employing him?' I asked. I mentioned the cash under his bed. The other objects Edward might already have seen.

He shook his head. 'I didn't guess he was involved until the night before Hrothgar walked into the monastery,' he said. He paused and chose his words again. 'Wilfred came to me that night. I'd been – I'd been kind to him ever since I realised he was your second favourite after Bede. I knew we'd need a hostage, and I wanted to make sure that Wilfred would be close by me when the gate opened.' He stopped and gave me a defiant look.

What was I supposed to do? Set about him again with my stick? I raised my eyebrows and shrugged. Wouldn't I have done the same in his position?

'Wilfred came to me that night,' he repeated. 'He told me that Cuthbert had propositioned him, offering safety as the reward. It was then that I guessed the first group was sent just to kill you – you and everyone else in the monastery. Cuthbert would let them in when he was able, and would himself be spared.'

I smiled and leaned harder on the rail. Hrothgar had been hard enough put to keep order among his own men of that breed. Any deal Cuthbert might have had with the Big Man would have come unstuck the moment he'd got the gate open. Everything he'd gloatingly predicted for the others would then have been his too. Almost a shame Hrothgar had turned up in time.

What I was now learning was interesting. But, since Edward couldn't give me the answer I needed, it wasn't that important.

'It was Cuthbert who knocked Wilfred about?' I asked. Edward nodded. 'He told you about the rejected proposition and the beating?' Another nod. 'You guessed what was happening, and attached yourself to Cuthbert to see what you could learn.'

'I got nothing,' the boy said stiffly.

Did he know I'd overheard their 'courtship'? Best not to go on.

'Is that all Wilfred told you of his dealings with Cuthbert?' I asked. 'Since the proposal was almost certainly not accepted, Wilfred doesn't sound much of a sinner.' I looked closely at the boy's face. Once more, he was thinking what to say.

'He told me nothing more,' came the final answer. We looked awhile in silence at the birds, which were now swooping out of the sky to pick among the refuse thrown behind us. 'What will we do in Beirut?' he suddenly asked. 'I know Ezra has given you some money – his wife told me that much. But what shall we do once that has run out?' For the first time in days, the look on his face was genuine. My slippery young Edward was on his way back to frightened boy.

'Oh, think nothing of that,' I said, taking my turn at the enigmatic. 'If you manage to live as long as I have, you too will realise that something always turns up. It's just a matter of recognising it.'

I turned and looked up again at the sky. Even wearing a hat with a wide brim, I found the sun rather much. We'd go and see what foul-smelling cupboard we'd been assigned for our quarters. I had thought it was time to fill Edward in on a few of the details that made Beirut so attractive, now Spain was off the menu. But that, I now decided, could wait until we were there. For the moment, it would be best to keep him busy with his Greek. Yes, I'd work him on that till he wished he could take one of the oars on this ship. Just because Beirut was no longer an Imperial city, didn't make the Empire's language any less important – not, at any rate, so long as it remained the official language of Syria. For now, though, I let him stand, looking silently back at the vanishing docks of Caesarea and all the happy memories that would keep him warm at night until such time as he might renew them in Beirut.

The main part of the voyage was without any incident worth recording. The wind still blew briskly from the west, and, while that was behind us, we hardly needed the oars. By day, we made excellent time. At night, we put into shore for safety. This wasn't a northern ship, after all, that was built for crossing the open sea. It was an elegant little galley. More important, it was filled with persons of reasonable quality who'd not have taken kindly to more risk than was unavoidable. We stopped at Cyrene for supplies, and then for a couple of days in Alexandria, to offload some of the black slaves who'd been moaning away in the hold, and to take on additional passengers. I did think to get off and walk about the city I'd helped, so long ago, to rule. But it would only have upset me. I might have felt some obligation – if only to Omar's memory – to see what really had become of the library. Further thought told me to stay on board. It was enough to squint at the sights as we sailed into one of the harbours. They all seemed in order – the Lighthouse, of course, the gigantic Palace from which representatives of the Caliph, and not of Caesar, now collected the grain tribute, the high pillar erected by Diocletian: these were all still in place, whatever changes might be seen around them. About me in the harbour, there was the same jumbled shouting as seventy years before of

Greek and Egyptian. But after that one inspection, I went back to my cabin, where Edward read haltingly from the collection of Plutarch biographies that Jacob had given me as a parting gift.

Our only excitement came on the second day of our long, direct jump from Alexandria to the Syrian shore.

'Oh, Master!' Edward cried as he rushed into the cabin. He tripped over a chair and landed with a heavy bump about a foot from my little cot. I opened my eyes and looked blearily at him. I'd put half a drop of Jacob's amazing opium juice under my tongue for breakfast, and had ever since been enjoying myself in a sequence of dreams that seemed never to end. I saw that it was Edward and focused on the dreams, trying to keep them from vanishing like a morning frost. But all I managed to snatch before it was too late was something erotic that involved a crocodile.

'Master, there's a ship coming alongside,' he said, stretching out his arms to help me from the cot. 'I heard someone say it was an Imperial battle cruiser.'

'Edward, you forget yourself,' I said automatically. 'I am to be addressed now as "My Lord", not as "Master". You last saw Brother Aelric on the Tipasa beach.' He ignored the correction and went into an agitated dance. I groaned, and, since he'd now withdrawn his arms, heaved myself up and made for the open door.

Imperial battle cruiser indeed! You didn't need perfect vision to see that it was hardly bigger than a scouting ship. Our own deck was a good six feet higher, and the Captain had passed down a ladder for the Greek official who was already on board.

'You'll see that our permit is sealed by His Highness the Exarch of Africa,' the Captain said in the most reasonable tone I'd yet heard from him.

The official glanced at the document and nodded. There was no point questioning its terms. It carried the seal of an exarch. That meant the ship was virtually under orders from the Emperor. The official turned instead to a set of standard questions about contraband. Were we carrying silk thread? Had we taken on spices in Alexandria for Beirut? If yes, had they been listed in the appropriate ledger for payment of the external carriage tax?

So the litany went on. I'd caught some of Edward's alarm and had come on deck quietly going over my cover story. But I could see there would be no inspection of passports. A thousand miles to the west, half the Imperial Navy might be combing the seas for the returned Alaric. Here, it was simply a matter of advertising which of the two warring powers controlled the seas. It seemed we had outrun the Empire.

'Now you've got me awake,' I snapped, 'we can go back to your favourite game. This time, though, I'll not bother with Plutarch or any of the Gospels. We'll take one whole sentence at a time from Virgil, and you can put that into Greek.' Edward's mouth turned down. I looked at him. The tan he'd got from two voyages in a strengthening sun suited him no end. All very well. But a pretty face without education can be picked up on any slave block. I'd have that boy fluent in Greek if it killed me.

28

We put into Beirut on the sixteenth day after leaving Caesarea. I ignored the last and now almost demented burst of abuse from the Captain and allowed Edward to help me from the plank that connected our ship to the pleasingly solid docks.

'I did tell you to put more clothes on,' I said. Though the rain had finished, the sky was still overcast, and there was a chilly wind coming down from the mountains. 'It will be hot enough soon. But this isn't Africa.' I let go of the shivering boy, and, leaning on my walking staff, took a few paces forward. I took a deep breath, savouring the smell of grilled meat and of freshly brewed kava berries, and looked around. A jolly little port with no pretensions nowadays to a wider importance, Beirut lies at the point of a triangular projection from the Syrian coast. I'd been here first in my thirties to take the unconditional surrender of all the Persian invasion forces. I'd been here again several years later, once the Saracens had snatched Syria, to settle the lines of truce. I'd been back on any number of occasions since. You see, the place is easily reached by sea from Constantinople, and has a good road connecting it with Damascus. It's the ideal place for informal discussions between the two great and usually warring powers of the modern world.

And now I was back. I felt good, not least because of the kava smell. What memories that brought back! I raised my walking stick and knocked it twice very hard on the granite slabs of the dock. Time was when half a dozen porters would have come running. Time was, though, when I didn't turn up on the docks dressed as some closed-purse Jew. The one porter who did eventually slope over gave me a nasty grin and pointed over at the main gate leading from the docks. Keeping what dignity I could,

I frowned back at him and turned to where Edward sat on the dockside with our things.

'I'll be just a moment,' I said. From what little I could see of him, he seemed too cowed by the full bustle of civilisation to have noticed my own embarrassment.

Over by the gate, there was an execution in progress. This had attracted a moderate crowd, including, for some reason, just about all the dock porters. I glanced at the young man who'd been nailed to the cross. Since he looked as if he'd been racked and scourged first, it was hard to say how long he'd been up there. From the voiceless movement of his lips, though, and from the impression I'd been able to form of the weather, he might have been there a day. Despite the colour his skin was turned, it was unlikely he'd been up there much longer – he still had enough strength in his arms to keep himself from hanging forward off the cross. I looked harder and pursed my lips. The bastard executioners had put a platform just under his feet.

I don't imagine you've ever seen a crucifixion, my dear Reader – they were abolished wherever the Christian Faith was established by the Great Constantine. They have been brought back, though, wherever the Saracens have conquered. Since its first use by the Carthaginians, the punishment has been much the same. You fix two lengths of wood in the shape of a T – the cross shape is a refinement made by the artists of the early Church. You nail the victim's wrists to each end of the top length, and his ankles to the down length. If it's done fairly, he shouldn't last much beyond evening, though cool weather can stretch out the agony. And the agony is extreme. You see, if he wants to breathe properly, the victim has to pull himself upright. With nails through his ankles, he can't do that for long. So he sags forward. That makes breathing hard, and he must try again to get upright. The continual movement on the cross, and the sun, soon wears the victim out. Look at Jesus Christ. He lasted barely any time at all; this being said, his legs had been broken to hurry things along. But this poor bugger had been given a support for his feet. That and the weather might keep him going for days. Everyone in the crowd knew that.

So did he. If he was no longer screaming, or twisting about, he was still conscious, his lips moving in some voiceless prayer. Even without Joseph's arrow, poor Tatfrid had been luckier than this. Nothing barbarians can do will match the refinements of a civilised punishment.

There was a steady muttering in Syriac from the crowd about the unfairness of the execution. Several men comforted a sobbing woman. The Saracen guards stood about the cross, edgily fingering their swords. Just before them, some scrubby brown creature stood looking over at the public sundial. As I was about to ask again for a porter, he cleared his throat with ceremonial relish and struck a pose.

'By orders of His Highness Meekal, Governor of Syria,' he cried in Syriac, 'you behold one who has dared wage war on God.' He repeated himself in Saracen and then in a kind of Greek. As he finished, someone with an even browner face, though a clean turban, stood forward with a sheet of papyrus.

'But the recompense of those who fight against God and His apostles,' he read in the strained squawk the Saracens use for recitals of what their Prophet is claimed to have said, 'and study to act corruptly in the earth, shall be that they shall be slain, or crucified, or have their hands and their feet cut off on the opposite sides, or be banished the land. This shall be their disgrace in this world, and in the next world they shall suffer a grievous punishment.' He didn't bother with the Syriac translation – the two languages are pretty close anyway – but went straight into an astonishingly corrupt Greek.

'It is the will of God!' someone breathed into my bad ear. Someone behind me whispered that it was murder, and that Meekal the Damned would be repaid seven times seven in the world to come.

I resisted the urge to ask what crime had been committed. This was none of my business. Instead, I knocked my stick again on the paving stones. Everyone, including the unfortunate on the cross, looked in my direction. One of the foreman-porters came forward. He looked at my robe and gave a half bow.

'Those three moderately large boxes over there are mine,' I said in Syriac. I pointed back to where Edward was still keeping a nervous watch over our things. 'Do you know the Golden Spear Inn?' The man nodded. 'That's where I want everything carried. You can also arrange a carrying chair for me.' I thought, then added, 'No – make that two chairs.' I tossed him a silver coin and waited for his much lower and more respectful bow. I turned and went back over to Edward. He was staring at the execution. I ignored him and had a final look at the ship that had brought us here. The customs officials had now finished their searches, and were pointing out faults in the documentation of the few idiots who hadn't known the appropriate tariff of bribes. It would have been nice to see the whole ship impounded. But the Captain was no fool. The Exarch of Africa had sealed his documents. That was as good for these officials as it had been for the Imperial blockade.

Our chairs carried at shoulder height, we moved slowly into the crowded, wealthy streets of Beirut. As in Caesarea, I'd warned Edward not to look about with his mouth open. But it was difficult not to be overwhelmed by the place. After so many years in the West, even I had forgotten how glorious a city still in full order could be. Of course, there had been changes. The long row of emperors had been taken down from their plinths that lined the main street. The bronze letters had been carefully prised from all the past victory and commemoration monuments. In place of all this, huge green banners fluttered from almost every public building. Every one of these carried pompous inscriptions in Saracen about the present and the coming Triumph of the Faith.

We stopped awhile by what had been the Church of Christ the Redeemer. The swarms of other chairs and of wheeled traffic had stopped easy access through the central square. I squinted in the powerful light and looked at what had been built as a smaller version of the Great Church in Constantinople. The golden cross had been taken down, and the mosaics above the entrance were painted over. No one would be allowed to know in future that it had been the gift of the Great Justinian after an earthquake had levelled the much older church there. Men with huge, dark beards stood outside, washing their hands and feet before going in. One of them looked up at me with grim hostility. Except his face was much darker, he might have been a big, ferocious Jew. I looked away and, fanning myself, peered instead at what had once been the main library. It was a couple of hundred yards across the square, and was largely a blur. I wondered if there were any books still in there worth reading.

But what of it if there weren't? The cloud cover had now broken up into great puffs of whiteness, and the sun shone down on us. I was back in the civilised world. Once more, I sniffed in the welcome smells of Beirut.

'My Lord,' Edward cried softly in English. I waited until the carriers had brought our chairs closer together. 'Why are all those men wearing blue crosses?' He nodded over towards one of the smaller churches.

This hadn't had its use converted, and I could see the black robe and beard of the priest, who was glowering across at the mosque. I looked hard at the crowd of men, all dressed in white, who were talking and waving on the steps of the church.

'Those are Greeks,' I said. 'No – it's better to call them the Orthodox. The locals call them Greek, but most actually speak Syriac.' That wasn't much of an answer, and the boy was looking at me to continue. 'Virtually all the Syrians are Christian,' I added, 'but most are heretics of one kind or another. Like the Jews, they all have to pay tribute to the Saracens as members of a tolerated but despised faith. However, only the Orthodox minority are required to distinguish themselves in the streets by wearing a special badge.' I was now making an effort to see about me. I pointed over to my left. 'Look at that one over there,' I said. 'See how he's got out of his chair to bow to the Saracen riding past on the black horse? That sort of thing pisses the Orthodox off no end. Then again, they do get full toleration – which is more than they ever granted to anyone in their own day.'

I heard the spattering of stones against masonry. I wasn't up to seeing where this was or who had thrown them. But I recognised well enough the sudden and intent stillness of the "Greeks" and Saracens as they looked across the square at each other, and the quickening of the chairs and other traffic as the crowds of pedestrians began to thin out. We were almost out of the main square when an armed Saracen on horseback got in our way and stopped there. The head carrier looked nervously back at me. I ignored him, and gave the Saracen a long, haughty stare. I thought for a moment I'd have to lose face in front of Edward. But I had no badge of disgrace on my clothing. There was no telling who I might be. After a short look at me, the man scowled and got out of our way.

'My Lord! My Lord!' the innkeeper cried in Greek as our chairs came to a stop beside the entrance to the Golden Spear. So our stuff and my scribbled note had got there in good time. 'But we had no letter,' he cried. 'After so many years, we assumed that you—' He broke off diplomatically and creased his face into a smile. Unless he was being very diplomatic indeed, there was a chance he'd not heard the news of my fall. 'We had no letter, and your normal rooms are occupied by another. But' – he smiled again and bowed – 'but for you, My Lord, all things can be arranged.' He turned to one of his people and rapped out a stream of rapid Syriac. I acknowledged their renewed bowing with a lordly wave.

Edward now walking behind me, I was carried through the gate into the entrance hall. As I was helped down into a padded chair, someone presented me with a cup. I sniffed at the heated contents and sipped. It was an infusion of ginger and garlic with honey sweetening. It tasted reasonable. But I gave a puzzled look at the innkeeper. My eyes had now grown used to the gloom, though, and I could see round the little hall. Where was the icon of the Virgin? Where the silver cross in the place where, centuries before, the household gods would have sat?

'Zacharias?' I began.

He cut in. 'I am known now, My Lord, as Zakariya,' the innkeeper said with a pious leer. 'I rejoice in my conversion to the True Faith of God.' He looked heavenward, and haltingly uttered the Saracen words: 'There is no God but Allah, and Mohammed is His Prophet.'

Oh dear, I thought, there'll be no wine in this house! But I smiled and nodded. Why not convert? It saved him from the Infidel Tax. And it would surely mean no more of the enthusiastic if ill-informed sermons he'd used to preach to all his guests against the Acts of the Council of Chalcedon. I was less happy about the delicate enquiry regarding my own 'conversion' at the hands of the Caliph Omar himself. I stood up swiftly and gripped at Edward to avoid falling over.

'That was half a century ago,' I said hurriedly. 'And it wasn't so much a conversion as a diplomatic understanding.' I turned the conversation to family matters. It seemed that Zakariya's old wife had walked out on him when he converted. He'd replaced her with four others, each a quarter his own age, and these had now given him a whole litter of sons. I cut short his opening remarks on the unity of God with a toothless smile and congratulations on his good fortune.

But whoever had been occupying my rooms was now kicked out. It was simply a matter of making them ready for me with all proper haste. While this was done, two black slaves took hold of my chair and carried me towards a door at the back of the hall for a tour of the enclosed garden.

'But where is the fire, My Lord?'

I laughed as Edward looked round, confusion on his face. 'My dear boy,' I said, pulling him back out of English into Latin, 'we are now deep within the civilised world. You'll find nothing so vulgar in houses of quality as a hearth or a brazier. Observe.' I kicked off one of my slippers and stepped forward on to the tiled floor. I pointed at Edward to do the same. 'You see, there is a single fire outside the main building. From this, heated air is sent through ducts underneath the floor and inside the walls. There's never a wisp of smoke to spoil your clothes or get in your eyes; no chance of suffocation while you sleep; none of fire. Why, ten years ago, when I was here, there was a snowstorm that took everyone by surprise. Out in the streets, the poor were losing their toes to frostbite. In here, I even had one of the windows open. But this is nothing. Let me show you the bathing rooms and latrine attached to this most luxurious suite. You'll find both hot and cold running water.'

I would have taken him over to the window that looked out to the garden. Not even in Ezra's house had he seen how pieces of glass could be set into a lead framework that allowed light in while blocking both noise and draughts. But it was now that I saw the jug and cups placed discreetly on a table before one of the smaller sofas. Zakariya might have got himself a new religion: he'd not forgotten how to make his guests feel at home. I turned to the slave who'd come in with us.

'My compliments to your master,' I said in Syriac. 'I will sleep until evening, when I'll have a light dinner in here. Before I nod off, however, do have a clerk sent in. I have some letters to dictate.' I looked at Edward. He was staring up at the high ceiling with its painted view of clouds and a rainbow. Once we were alone, I could feel, he'd start asking how much this place would cost. 'Get someone who knows Latin to take the boy on a tour of the city,' I said. 'If the museum is still there, I want him to see the paintings of the Great Alexander. After that, I want him taken to the brothel beside the Church of Saint Eustachia – or whatever the place may now be called. Limit his drink there, and don't let him gamble.' I sat down and reached for the jug.

'Oh,' I added. 'Do also arrange for a tailor to attend on us tomorrow afternoon.' I took a sip of pale wine and closed my eyes. If I chose not to open them again, someone would be bound to come in and put me to bed.

29

The banker and two of his clerks stood respectfully before me. After half a morning of massage, I stretched out a foot with reasonable firmness and planted it on the stool.

'We were made aware, of course, of the confiscation decree,' he said in coldly formal Greek. 'However, while this applied to all monies on deposit within the Empire, it had no force within the Caliph's dominions.'

I sniffed nonchalantly. If I hadn't known that, I'd hardly have sent for the man. But I left him to do the talking. In particular, I wanted to know how much I was still worth. I thought of reaching for my refilled cup, but didn't want to show that my hands were beginning to shake.

'Matters were complicated by the restitution of your goods that followed your temporary pardon by His Late Imperial Majesty Constantine,' the man went on. 'Your representatives in Constantinople took advantage of this to remit several large sums to your main account in Antioch.' He now settled into a regular drone of explanation of how this had been done. I might be aged, but I wasn't yet senile. Yes, there was the annual tribute paid by Caliph to Emperor while the two empires were at peace – it was the price the Saracens paid for Egypt and Syria not to be raided everywhere we could float a ship. Yes, some of my money had been paid over to the Imperial Government in place of a physical shipment of gold from Damascus. In return, the Caliph had paid an equal sum to my Antioch account. Yes, I knew all this. I didn't need any lectures on finance from someone whose grandfather had been shitting his nappies when I was already rich beyond counting. But I kept quiet.

At last, the man got to the important point. I had to pretend a coughing fit to hide the astonishment. I thought he'd slipped up on his Greek numeral adjectives. But I looked at the parchment account he'd finally handed over. Added all together, the Empire could have fought a war on two fronts with that lot. The conversation had been at a level that his own Greek didn't reach, and Edward gave me an anxious look. He took up the cup and held it to my lips.

'It would normally be a matter,' the banker continued, 'of sending to Antioch for sealed confirmation of funds. However, since the transfers were made through Beirut, and since I am personally assured that all is in order, I have decided to act in advance of formal confirmation. I have taken the liberty, therefore, of bringing over a sum that may be of use to My Lord for his daily expenses.'

One of his clerks reached forward and dumped two leather bags on the table set before my chair. There must have been four pounds of metal in each of them. I nodded to Edward, who looked about for a knife with which to cut the seals. At last, he got one of them open. He nearly fainted at the sight of the golden stream that poured through his fingers. Ignoring the main pile before me, I took up one of the new-minted coins and looked at the portrait.

'A poor likeness of Justinian,' I said. The banker gave me an indifferent look. If I'd mentioned the smell of the oiled leather, he'd not have been less interested. Let me see, I thought. Seventy-two solidi to the pound. Eight times that makes five hundred and seventy-six. I smiled. There'd be new silk for both of us when the tailors came round – Chinese, not Imperial – and plenty of change left over.

'Any chance the Caliph will start minting his own coins?' I asked, while I kept myself from jumping up for a creaky dance about the room.

'Not so far as I have been informed,' came the chilly answer. 'His Late Majestic Holiness Muawiya was concerned to avoid any act that might suggest a loss of interest in the eventual movement of his capital to Constantinople. His Present Majestic Holiness Abd al-Malik has announced no change in that policy.'

No change of policy – that was interesting, assuming the banker had his finger on the right pulse. Would these people never give up? They'd lost control of the seas, possibly for ever. And if Africa was theirs for the taking, they'd have a bloody fight if they wanted another go at Asia Minor. As for Constantinople, that was surely off the agenda.

But that was other business. The business in hand was complete, and Zakariya could be glad of my custom until I decided otherwise. I motioned the banker and his clerks out of the room and snuggled back into the sofa.

'Master,' Edward asked when we were alone. I ignored him. 'My Lord,' he asked again. I smiled and opened my eyes. 'My Lord, is all this money really yours?' As if not daring to touch it again, he waved a hand over the shining pile that covered the table.

'All that, and very much more,' I said with a wave of my own. 'I did tell you not to worry about finances.' I reached into the pile and took a handful of coins. 'Here, take this and hold it,' I said. 'Let the coins run through your fingers. This is what sets the world in motion. It's for this that men kill and cheat and lie and steal – and sometimes do good and necessary works. It was for the promise of less than this that Hrothgar set to work. Compared with this little hill of gold, Cuthbert worked for nothing at all. Go on – take it. Hold it. Have it for yourself.'

But Edward continued standing before me, looking down at the coins. 'If all this money really is yours,' he said eventually, 'why did you flee to England rather than here?'

'That is a most interesting question,' I said. I sat up and stretched, and reached for a date that had been preserved in honey. I popped it into my mouth and rolled it about with my tongue until it broke apart. 'It may be that I was mistaken,' I added indistinctly. I swallowed the sweet mass and took another sip of wine. 'Perhaps, on reflection, Jarrow was not the best place of refuge for me. Perhaps – if unwittingly – you and your dear friend Hrothgar did me a considerable service in giving me a second chance. I doubt, all things considered, I shall have the choice. But I have no intention of seeing that dreadful monastery ever again. How about you?'

He shook his head.

'You are a most sensible young man,' I said with another smile. 'It may be no bad thing that I failed to see this during the first months of our acquaintance. You are also, I might add, a young man with great expectations.' He gave me one of his blank looks. 'Oh, there is no exact parallel in the civilised world for our concept of fealty. But I do plan in the next few days to adopt you as my son, and to make an appropriate will.' If I'd said there would be olive paste on bread for dinner, I might have seen more of a reaction on the boy's face. I smiled. There was no point telling him that this wasn't an idle whim, and that I'd made my decision on our second day out of Caesarea. No point also warning him that the terms of my will were not always couched in terms of endearing love. I changed the subject.

'Now, dear boy,' I said, 'I do urge you to make yourself familiar as quickly as you can with this new and glorious world. That does mean learning proper Greek. I suppose it will also mean learning Saracen. I am already looking for instructors.' His face clouded over at the thought of yet another new language. 'But did you enjoy yourself in the brothel last night?'

I'd got him there; his face went a bright pink, and he stammered as he tried to come out with a polite answer.

'Excellent,' I said, not waiting for him to say anything. 'You will pardon me, then, if I trouble you with some immediate advice. You can fuck any slave that takes your fancy – girls, boys, women, even full-grown men, just as the inclination takes you. The Saracens are pleasingly untouched by our modern ideas of continence. But I must warn you to keep your hands off the free women. The Saracens – and the Syrians, come to think of it – dress their women in ways that would make the fine ladies of Constantinople look indecent. They can be madly possessive, and don't you ever forget that. Whatever may have happened back in Caesarea was an exception that I may one day explain to you. It will not be repeated here.

'Another piece of valuable advice is to keep away from gambling. Though their faith forbids it, I've never yet seen a Saracen who wasn't mad about dice. But just tell them you're a Christian, and they'll leave you alone. The best way, I assure you, for the inexperienced to make a small fortune from dice is to start with a big one.

'Now, go and pull that cord over there. I saw you splashing water on yourself this morning, and that just won't do. You can get yourself taken down to the main baths in this house – go there for a spell in the hot room and all that follows this. I, on the other hand, must content myself with a lukewarm bath in our own facilities, and then a siesta until such time as the tailors come round with their samples.'

And that should have been it. As he fiddled with the door handle and the elaborate closing mechanism behind it, Edward turned round.

'Why do they call the Saracen King "Your Holiness?"' he asked. 'I thought only the Pope was called that.'

I smiled and got up. 'The Caliph,' I answered, 'is not a merely temporal ruler. He is also Commander of the Faithful. He is the direct successor – though not in blood – of the Saracen Prophet. As such, he claims a status superior even to that of a Roman emperor. An emperor is to be addressed as "Your Imperial Majesty", a caliph as "Your Majestic Holiness". You may meet neither, but these things are worth bearing in mind.'

I sat down again. I had thought to cross the floor to help Edward with the workings of the door handle. But he'd now managed to work this out for himself. I waited for the door to close. Once I was alone, I reached forward and grasped handfuls of the coins. I let them run in golden streams through my shaking fingers. At some point on their journey from the Imperial Mint, the bags had been shaken. I held my hands up in a shaft of sunlight and looked at the specks of gold dust that now adhered to them. I rubbed them into my face. I licked my fingers. I could even feel the ghost of a stiffy coming on.

But I sat back and rested my head on the cushions of the sofa. I looked at the ceiling and laughed softly. I'd had what I thought at the time very good reasons. But it really was worth repeating Edward's question: what had possessed me to stagger halfway across the known world to shiver in Jarrow when all this was waiting for me here?

30

I dreamed that I was back in Jarrow on the day the northerners got into the monastery. This time, instead of lifting me, they'd killed all the monks and set fire to the place. I didn't see the killing. I only knew that it had already happened. I stood about a hundred yards outside the main gate, and was watching as the flames licked and flickered about every upper opening. Still wearing the clothes in which he'd died, Wilfred floated just before me, about three yards above the ground. Though his lips moved frantically, I couldn't hear a word he was trying to say. At last, he gave up on words and was reduced to pointing – now at the burning monastery, now towards the sun that was still low in the south-eastern sky. There was no solidity about his body. It was more like a mass of shaped and coloured smoke. In places, I could see straight through him to where smoke from the monastery was rising into the blue sky.

'Go away,' I cried at him. 'You're dead.' I waved my stick at him, and, without feeling it strike on anything solid, saw it vanish into his chest before re-emerging. The boy twisted about in the air so he could look fully at me. There was the hurt look on his face that I recalled so well from whenever he thought me less enthusiastic than himself about the lunatic doctrines it had been my duty to expound to him.

As I drifted back into wakefulness, the smell of burning travelled back with me. I knew at once I was far from Jarrow. There was the soft kiss of the silk on my body where slaves had put me into my bed, and the still, warm air of a Syrian afternoon in spring. I was plainly Alaric, rich-as-Croesus, resting in the house of Zakariya. Jarrow was far off, and the monastery there could take a running jump. But there was still an omnipresent though faint smell of burning. Was the house on fire? I opened my eyes. The slave who'd sat beside me while I nodded off was gone. I sat up and cleared my throat loudly. I was alone. No point shouting for assistance. No point struggling out of bed just to pull the bell cord. I waited while my legs came back to life, and I drained the cup of fruit squash that had been placed on the table beside my bed.

My rooms were all on the first floor, and my bedroom window looked directly down into the central garden. As I got it open and looked out, I breathed in a stray gust of smoke that had drifted up from the garden. I fought to control the coughing fit and squeezed my eyes shut. I was about to push the window closed again, when I heard the voice of Zakariya from somewhere below.

'You stupid black fucker!' he screamed. 'If I weren't so bleeding soft, I'd have you strung up on the flesh hooks and branded.' I heard the repeated sound of a stick on bare flesh and a slave's moans of despair. I pushed the window shut and pressed the catch into place. I needed to see Zakariya. I'd evaded his obvious questions the previous evening. The sooner I got hold of him now, the better it would be. I looked about for some clothes. There was a robe of white linen laid out for me on one of the chairs. It was one of those garments with many ties that call out for assistance. But I didn't need to impress anyone. For what I had in mind, respectability would be enough. With some groaning and wheezing, I pulled the robe over my head and tied it on me as well as I could. I stepped into a pair of slippers and made for the door.

The stairs led down to a corridor of humbler single rooms. At the end of this was a door that led into the main hall. From here, I turned left and made my way out into the garden. I bumped almost at once into Zakariya. His face had turned the colour of roof tiles, and he leaned heavily on his stick. He straightened up the moment he saw me, and pulled his face into the semblance of a welcoming smile.

'We have some business to discuss,' I said shortly. Trying not to look as curious as I felt, I ignored the black smoke that was coming from behind some bushes.

Now in his little office, Zakariya restrained himself just in time from biting one of the coins. Instead, he gave me a repeat of his welcoming oily smile. I let him refill my cup. I leaned back into my chair and looked a while at the closed window.

'What is that smell of burning?' I asked, not caring if it meant any loss of face.

'After his long decline, my father has finally died,' came the answer.

I thought of the vicious dotard who'd presided over things during my earlier stays in the house, and marvelled at the triumph of a good constitution over a bad heart and clouded mind. If he'd only just died, he must have made it almost to my age. I made a vague expression of sympathy and told myself not to ask if cremation had suddenly come back into fashion. I sniffed again. No, that wasn't quite human flesh. Besides, when had cremation *ever* been the fashion in Syria? Zakariya mistook my silence for something else, and smothered a giggle and bowed.

'My father was to the end an obstinate Cross Worshipper,' he explained. 'I have now ordered his collection of books to be destroyed. Where they contradict the true Word of God, they are blasphemous. Where they support it, they are superfluous. In either case, let them be consumed.' He bowed again, then looked up, obviously pleased at his attempted witticism. I acknowledged it with a wave of my cup.

'But, surely,' I said mildly – not that I imagined the world would lose much from the burning of a few dozen ranting supports of the Monophysite heresy – 'that is not a Saracen position. Did not the Caliph Omar himself order the preservation of all Christian and Jewish writings that came into the hands of the Faithful?' I might have looked into the eyes of a dead fish.

But Zakariya stared again at the three coins I'd set out on the table. He gave me another of his smiles. 'With all respect, My Lord . . .' Without asking leave, he sat down opposite me. I looked into my cup and said nothing. 'With all respect, My Lord, this is the beginning of times. God sent Jesus – peace be upon Him – to be His Prophet. His teachings were immediately corrupted by the Greeks. Now, God has sent Mohammed – peace be upon Him – as His last and greatest Prophet. His teachings cannot be corrupted. And they have wiped the slate of history. Those who accept them are no longer Syrians or Egyptians or Saracens – or even Greeks. They are the Faithful. All that went before is of no value. My sons shall learn the Holy Book by heart, and blend into the Community of the Faithful. I am the last of my blood whose first language must be Syriac, the last who was ever deceived by the muddy reason of the Greeks and of those who argued against the Greeks from within Greek premises. There is no God but Allah, and Mohammed is His Prophet,' he ended in a Saracen more piously than correctly voiced.

'Then the boy and I must change lodgings,' I said with mock earnestness, 'if we are to continue going to church.' Of course, I had no intention of visiting any place of worship. I'd wasted enough time already in these places, and had reached an age that gave me the perfect excuse for not wasting any more. But I'd hit just the right tone to get the man's face working.

'"Let there be no compulsion in matters of faith,"' he said hurriedly with another glance at the coins. 'Those are the words of the Prophet.'

And so they are. If he'd said nothing beyond that, I'd have thought better of the Saracen Prophet. However, you don't push someone too far when he's taken up a new religion. Those born in the Faith could take a relaxed view of its harder precepts. That didn't include Zakariya. If he'd gone out and spat on his father's grave, it wouldn't be much worse than he was now doing. And you don't argue with a man in that position – even when you are paying wildly over the going rate for his hospitality.

'Would it offend My Lord if I asked how long these miserable rooms should be reserved?' he asked. He now gave way to compulsion and picked up one of the coins. He rubbed it hard between forefinger and thumb, and his face took on its first genuinely peaceful look since I'd caught him finishing the holocaust of his father's library.

'Until further notice,' I said. I thought of adding some rider to this, but instead repeated myself: 'Until further notice. I will let you know of any change of plan. In the meantime, please attend on me every Tuesday morning to receive another advance payment of your rent.'

His mouth nearly fell open. He was on his feet again, bowing and bringing his right hand again and again against his forehead. It would be all as I asked, he assured me. Within that house, I might as well be the King of Beirut.

As the promises and boasts poured from his lips like water through a clock, I looked up at the ceiling and thought once more of the golden mass locked within the cupboard beside my bed. When Zakariya did finally shut up, I might think it worth ordering tuna fish baked in honey for dinner.

31

You may often have heard it proclaimed that money doesn't buy you happiness. I can understand that the rich have generally tried to impose, and the poor have too often taken comfort in, the belief that three meals a day, plus the chance of living past thirty-five, are to be pitied rather then envied. But I see no reason whatever for sharing the belief. Anyone who'd last seen poor, dirty old Brother Aelric brooding over a cup of beer in the cold wastes of Northumbria wouldn't have recognised the frail but hearty grandee carried about the streets of Beirut. Indeed, so long as the sun wasn't too close to the vertical, I was perfectly up to walking about the streets.

It was Friday, 26 April 687. I'd been here a month, and Jarrow was a fading dream. Its only active reminder came when Edward forgot himself and lapsed into English. The following day would be my ninety-seventh birthday – not a day I was planning to celebrate, or even mention to Edward. But the fact that I'd made it this far, in such good shape, and despite several thousand attempts during the better part of a century to keep me from living another day, was beginning no end to cheer me. If I could carry on like this till the full century, I'd have no reason to complain. Indeed, I had bugger all reason right now. The day had started well, and was growing progressively better.

Cup in hand, I was sitting in the back room of a bookshop just off the main square. The owner brushed more of the congealed papyrus dust from his face and bowed apologetically.

'The problem is, My Lord,' he said again, 'that nobody wants any of this stuff nowadays. I think I'm the only one left who sells anything but Syriac and Saracen – and that's my real business, you know.'

I ignored him and looked again at the walls, lined, as they were, with row upon row of crumbling leather volumes. I couldn't see the parchment labels on the spines, which meant I could hope they were other than still more worthless discourses on the Nature of Christ. I breathed in slowly to feed the hope, and savoured a smell that had given me comfort since I was barely older than Edward. It wasn't a pleasure he seemed inclined to share. Sitting on a low stool before me, he was trying, without much success, to wipe the brown dust from his hands. I breathed out and coughed, and waved at the crate that two sweating assistants had finally carried up from the basement.

'That one,' I said, pointing at one of the older and more stained rolls. 'Remember that papyrus rolls aren't like a modern book. Try not to break this one.'

Edward fumbled with the protective leather band. Once more, it was perished, and it came apart in his hands. I sniffed, but said nothing. He tugged on the protective outer sheet as if it had been a bale of cotton cloth.

'Oh, give it here,' I said, now with genuine impatience. 'Let me show you again how to read in the ancient manner.' I took the roll from him into my right hand. Holding it lightly in the middle, I pulled gently with my left hand on the outer sheet. As I rolled this neatly around the outer spindle of the book, I slowly let out more of the long papyrus strip with my right hand. 'Look, Edward, the secret is to keep your arms at a fixed distance from each other and from your body. You then keep up a light tension: too much, and you'll pull the gummed sheets apart, or break one; too little, and the sheet will buckle, and then you'll have trouble reading the text.' I unrolled the book all the way to the end. I then repeated myself in reverse. I gave the reclosed book back to Edward and watched as, clumsily, and with much swearing under his breath, he got it open again to the first two-inch column of text.

'Come on, then,' I encouraged. 'You don't expect me to bugger what's left of my sight on that worn-out script.' He screwed up his face into a vision of heroic concentration and read me the opening to the fourth volume of Simonides. I put up with his reading until he'd reached the end of the dedication to Hipparchus, then stopped him. 'Have I not repeatedly told you,' I sighed, 'that proper Greek makes a distinction between long and short syllables? Forget what others may do, especially in Syria. Have you ever heard *me* fail to mark the distinction? It is exactly the same as in Latin – and perhaps still more important, bearing in mind the probable change of the accent since ancient times. Listen to me recite the piece, and try to follow the text as I go.' I sat back and began on the long and graceful epigram I'd first read seventy-five years earlier in the University Library in Constantinople.

'But, My Lord, if you already know the piece, why must I read it to you?' Edward asked. For all he was trying, he couldn't keep the annoyance out of his voice. 'You remember everything you've ever read, and you've read everything.' I thought of explaining myself with a hard poke of my stick in his chest. But it wouldn't have done in front of the bookseller. Sadly, Edward *was* in need of more explanation. 'This Greek is even worse than Latin,' he said, now with open annoyance. 'It's nothing like the language that people speak. Don't they ever write anything except in a language last spoken thousands of years ago?'

'*One* thousand years ago,' I corrected him with even menace. 'The modern language has fallen away from its old perfection. But educated men try to keep both versions balanced yet separate in their minds. We, who come to both as outsiders, have an advantage here. Regardless of that, it is an effort worth making. What the Greeks achieved in their day of glory may not have been repeated. It is certainly not to be forgotten. Now, take up and read again. And do try, this time, to mark the distinctions of length.'

I was thinking of the great ode on the Panathenaic Festival that followed the one we'd just read, when I heard the first screams out in the street.

'Dear me, what is that?' I asked. 'I really thought Beirut was too small for a riot.'

The bookseller's face tightened, and he rubbed the papyrus dust from his hands with a dirty cloth. We listened to the rising volume of sound. It was a terrified screaming of women and adolescent boys. Among it all were manly bellows of rage, or perhaps also of fear. The bookseller ran into the front room of the shop and shouted at his assistants to get the stock inside and the shutters down. I pulled a face. This was a bloody nuisance. The day really had been going so well.

'Help me upstairs, Edward,' I commanded. 'There's a balcony from which we can look over the street.'

When we entered the shop, the street had been empty. The main square, though, had been crowded with Saracens and their local converts, all waiting to get into what had been the Church of Christ the Redeemer for the prayers of their holy day. The street was now a mass of running people.

'Is that blood on those men?' I asked, peering uncertainly at the rapidly moving blurs beneath where we stood.

Edward nodded. He took my arm and turned me to the right, in the direction of the mosque. We couldn't see the entrance. It was plain, though, that the crowds were trying to get away from the place.

I shut my eyes and rubbed them. I looked harder – and I wondered how thick the shutters were of this shop. 'Is that not a banner, hanging down,' I asked now, 'with a cross painted on it?'

Edward nodded again. 'Can you see the men standing on the roof above the banner, waving severed heads?' he asked.

Perhaps, if I'd looked harder, now I knew what was there, I'd have seen it all for myself. But the screaming grew suddenly more intense on our left. The crowds that had been running and pushing madly to get away were now jostling their way back towards the square.

'Christ is my Saviour! My Saviour is Christ!' came the repeated shout in Syriac. I saw the flash of steel about thirty yards along the street. I couldn't see those who had the swords. But it wasn't hard to work out what was happening. Soon enough, there would be the soft clatter of hooves on paving stones, as the Saracen guards made their way in to restore order. Any prisoners they took would come smartly enough out of their hashish fit once they felt the hooked gloves dragged through their flesh. In the meantime, it was bloody murder in the streets.

'It's people from the mountain tribes,' I said, speaking partly to myself. 'When there's a war on, we smuggle weapons to them and small amounts of money. For the outlay involved, you can sometimes get a big return. During the last war, we staged a big attack in Damascus. We took out twelve of the Saracen religious leaders as they were working themselves up to lead the Faithful into battle against us. The Caliph had his ambassadors straight off to Constantinople with offers of a renewed tribute.

'I don't like this sort of thing myself. But it helps keep these people off the offensive. And, bearing in mind we can't match the armies they have to throw at us, our entire strategy is one of asymmetric warfare. It's a matter of sea power and of new weapons, and of terror attacks. You see, they rule over a mass of Christians in these territories – not all of them reconciled to the new order of things. Except for a few merchants we allow under licence, we've none of their people to worry about. We win – no, we avoid losing – by doing to them what they can't do back to us.'

But I was speaking wholly to myself. An ecstatic look on his face, Edward was staring intently down at the slaughter a few yards beneath our feet. An old man was embracing a boy and trying to divert those slashing blows on to his own body. He might as well have been trying to keep the wind at bay. He gave a final horrified scream as another blow smashed in his rib cage, and he was pulled aside to expose the boy. I shut my eyes and tried not to hear the boy's final cry. I opened them to look at the answering cry from some people in the balcony just across the narrow street. Even had it been wise to draw attention to ourselves, there was nothing any of us could do. Dressed in dark clothing that covered them head to foot, the killers were pressing forward into the main square. They left behind them piles of the fallen. Blood glistened on the paving stones. The groans of the dying, or just the gravely injured, were a sadness to hear. But to offer active assistance so soon would have risked suicide. Until those maniac, jerking figures were well into the square, no gate in the street would open, nor any shutters go up.

I looked into the square towards the mosque. There was now a column of black smoke rising up to the sky. A dull yellow in the sunshine, flames were already darting from the upper windows. There was still no sign of the authorities, and it was most likely the nutters themselves had set fire to the place. Oh, the Angels of the Lord had struck hard this day – and, through them, so had the Empire.

I looked again at Edward, I could see he'd have loved the Circus in Constantinople – though less, perhaps, for the chariot races than for the nastier punishments we inflicted between the races on captured barbarian raiders. As it was, he'd keep those whores busy, come the evening. Soon enough, I'd have another bill on my desk for the inevitable blacked eyes and lacerated flesh.

'I think we've seen quite enough up here,' I said, not hiding my disapproval. 'And I'm sure you wouldn't want to keep Simonides waiting downstairs. His evocation of the boys proceeding naked through the streets of Athens has a charm even your reading is unlikely to abolish.'

32

'If you don't mind my saying, I think you were mad to leave the bookseller's shop before guards could be found.' Edward gave me another dark stare and went back to looking nervously about the deserted street.

'I do mind, thank you very much,' I said primly. Perhaps we should have waited a little longer. The bookseller had objected strongly to letting his best customer leave through the back of his shop into that labyrinth of alleys. Even so, Edward had put me right out by the revelation of his inability to scan, or even hear, the difference between Sapphic and Phalaecean hendecasyllables. It had always struck me as a perfectly clear difference. If it gave him trouble, it was surely a return of the wilfulness for which I'd often flogged him in Jarrow. On the whole, I'd thought it better for my temper if we were away from the sight of books. 'And do put that knife away,' I snapped, wondering if we hadn't passed this broken gate post once already. 'The only trouble we're likely to meet will be if the Saracen militia takes against you for it.'

He ignored me and we pressed on through the centre of Beirut. Of course, my chair had vanished at the first whiff of trouble, and I was now reduced to creeping along with my stick in one hand and Edward's free arm in the other. Except where they were still holed up in the burning mosque, the Angels of the Lord had finished their business and been chased off by the militia. The massacre outside the bookseller's shop had been nasty enough. But it had been a localised attack. I was hungry, and I wanted a lie down before the books I'd bought would be sent over. I needed to be rested for those. At least one of them I'd never seen before, and I'd work that secretary late into the night with reading it to me.

'I'd like to know what we're doing in this city,' Edward announced in his attempt at a manly voice. He stopped and kicked at a severed hand that lay in the road before us. I poked it with my stick and bent down to see it more clearly. Hacked off at the wrist, it was a man's right hand. Most likely, it had been holding a weapon. Its owner and the weapon were nowhere to be seen. I observed that it might have been left by one of the retreating Angels. Edward ignored me and kicked the hand into the gutter that ran down the centre of the street.

'It must be a very recent loss,' I added. 'I'm surprised the dogs haven't found it.' Still silent, Edward pulled me back into a slow walk. I looked up at the sky. 'We're headed in the right direction,' I said brightly. 'I'm sure home is just round another corner.'

Edward stopped and looked at me. 'Why do you persist in calling that place home?' he demanded fiercely. 'It's a vulgar lodging house. Everyone else who was staying there when we arrived has now moved on. Can't you see the owner is just waiting for you to die so he can lay hands on your movables?'

I laughed and struggled free of Edward's grip. 'Ha!' I cried happily. 'You won't learn the middle voice in Greek, or the optative. You don't avoid hanging nominatives. You frequently confuse the two aorists. You've still turned into a proper little snob. "Vulgar lodging house" indeed! I'm having a glorious time at Zakariya's. I even managed to fuck that little dancing girl the other afternoon.' I smiled into the scowling face. 'But surely you aren't worried, my dear boy – worried I'll get her with child? I know old men can dote on their last sons. But I promise, you'll still get place of honour in my will!' I thought he'd start another of his arguments, and how to evade the main issue of what exactly we were doing in Beirut.

Just then, however, we turned a corner and found ourselves in a wider street. I'd have said it was lined with dwellings of the humbler merchants and craftsmen – single-storey buildings, that is, usually without courtyards. It would normally have bustled with all the usual activity of making and selling. It was now still as the alleys we had just left behind. The whole street, right down to where it terminated against the wall of a church, was littered with corpses. Mostly women and children, there must have been a hundred of the dead – possibly more. They lay among broken furniture and bedding that had been pulled out of the houses. In a few cases, the women were still clutching little cloth bundles that I didn't care to inspect too closely. So far as I could tell, the policy had been to rape the younger women before slitting their throats. The others had been killed less systematically. The few unslit bellies were already swollen with the gases released by decay, and there was an endless buzzing of the flies who'd come to feast on the rotting flesh.

'I've told you, Edward,' I said wearily. 'Do put that knife away.' I waved my stick towards the men dressed in loose black robes who were silently flitting from corpse to corpse. 'The killers are long since moved on. Those are only the tooth gatherers.' I stood and watched the skilled use of pincers in the younger mouths. I felt Edward's hand take hold of mine. I gave it what I hoped was a reassuring squeeze, and tried to draw his attention from the baby that had had its brains dashed out against a drain cover. 'The roots filed off and welded into gold plates,' I explained with a nod at the hushed, furtive creatures, who scurried about just as if they'd been crabs on a beach at low tide, 'those teeth are worth their weight in silver. When my own first began to go, I did experiment with having new teeth pushed into the sockets. It wasn't the success I'd hoped, and I eventually designed a replacement set entirely of gold and ivory.' I poked my stick at the nearest of the corpses. It was an adolescent boy, perhaps a little older than Edward. He'd been castrated. It wasn't his dying scream, though, that had pulled his jaws nine inches apart. Except for one broken incisor, all the teeth were out already. The body had been looted and abandoned, the eyes still open, the limbs stiff in their dying position.

'It's – it's horrible!' Edward breathed.

I looked at him again. I really thought he was about to vomit. He was a strange child – happy enough to watch the infliction of death, fussy only about the treatment of the dead. I sniffed very hard.

'My last and dearest of sons,' I said, trying for a nonchalance I didn't feel, 'my dear, dear boy. Dead is dead, I've told you many times. What happens after death is of no more importance to the dead than what happened before birth. The one objection a reasonable man can have even to eating the flesh of the dead is that it would encourage still worse behaviour to the living.' I smiled and pointed at one of the tooth gatherers, who was looking up at us. It was now that I noticed the dogs peering warily at us from within some of the violated houses. They'd have their turn soon enough, and there would be good pickings for all of them.

'Who did all this?' I asked in Syriac. The man shrugged and went back to pulling one last tooth from the jaws of another adolescent boy. He wiped it clean and dropped it into the appropriate leather pouch. I unhooked the purse from my belt and tossed a couple of silver coins on to the paving stones. These were dark and sticky with blood. I looked hurriedly at my feet. I hadn't moved far enough into the street to ruin my velvet shoes.

'Word is,' he said, pulling himself slowly upright, 'it's orders from the Governor of Syria. Apparently Meekal heard that their priest was preaching against the Established Faith. His agents couldn't find the priest, so they made the next best example. The bodies have to lie here till the dogs have finished with them.' He gave me a closer look and stepped forward. He reached into one of his pouches and took out a large, white incisor. He held it out to me cupped in his stained right hand.

I avoided the urge to shrink back from him and shook my head. Once I could find the right workmen, I had other ideas for my mouth. He shrugged again and put the tooth away. I had a sudden flash of imagination. I could hear the tread of soldiers marching into the street, and see the glint of suddenly drawn swords. I could hear the terrified shrieks of the dying, and the vain pleading of the women for their children. I could see the men roped together and led off for public execution. I'd seen the like any number of times. I'd just seen an actual massacre. But these visions of horror are best not encouraged. I gave Edward's hand another squeeze and asked about the Golden Spear Inn.

'Well,' one of his colleagues interrupted with an oily smile, 'if that's where you're headed, you shouldn't be starting from here.' He stood up and looked at me from within the folds of his black hood. The pinched face was glowing with some loathsome skin disease. I looked upwards and pretended not to hear Edward's obscene mutter beside me. He'd understood enough from the name of the inn and from the tone of the reply.

'There were men here not long ago,' the first tooth gatherer said. He took the coins from the tooth pouch where he'd put them and looked closely at them. I ignored the hint and waited for further and better particulars. 'They were armed,' he added at last, 'and they said they were looking for an old man and a blond boy.' He pointed at the golden curls that showed beneath Edward's hat. 'They had a Greek look about them. If they lay hands on you, they'll have your heads up on poles before you can say "knife".' He laughed again and went back about his work.

I tried not to stiffen. At once, the street had lost all its post-massacre sadness. I looked at the row of silent buildings, and at the high, blank wall of the church. How far was it back to the inn? I could hear nothing. But Edward's ears were sharper than mine, and he was looking intently along the street. I could see he was feeling again for his knife. I put on a friendly smile and was glad I'd come out in my best silk. I held my purse up and let the coins within jingle slightly.

'Would it trouble you, O bearer of interesting news,' I asked, 'if I were to beg you to hurry to the nearest main street and engage a closed carrying chair?' He gave me a dubious look. I opened my purse and took out a half solidus. The gold gleamed bright in the sunshine.

'It is outrageous!' Zakariya wailed as his people helped me from the carrying chair. 'Is there no excess beyond these dogs of infidels?' There was a splash of blood on the lower part of his tunic, and his left arm was grazed up to the elbow. But he suddenly remembered himself, and trailed off into a long mutter about how it all reflected badly on the respectable Christians who counted among his very best friends. Without troubling myself to ask, I gathered he was referring to the later massacre outside the bookseller.

I turned and looked at the inn's heavy gate. Though shut and barred now, it couldn't keep out the sound of renewed shouting in the streets. Zakariya saw the questioning look on my face.

'But didn't My Lord hear the proclamation?' he asked with a nasty smile.

I listened with my good ear to the undoubted screams that drifted through the gap at the bottom of the gate.

'Well, My Lord,' Zakariya said, 'the news is that His Highness the Governor of Syria has decreed that any more terror attacks in Beirut are to be punished with the execution of all the Greeks. Yes, men, women, children – dragged from their homes and slaughtered in the street!' He giggled and looked heavenwards. 'You can be sure I've already done my duty.' He pointed at the blood on his tunic. 'That Greek filth down the road won't be undercutting me again,' he said proudly. 'These Greeks, I can tell you, have met their match in Governor Meekal,' he added in the voice he normally reserved for his sermons. 'And it's about time they learned their place in the new Syria. Alexander's dead. The Romans are gone. The Empire is nothing. We talk to the tax collectors in Greek, and that's it.

'Yes, Governor Meekal doesn't put up with no crap. He's just the man to drive through change – but then, My Lord will surely know all about that!' he ended with a repeat of his nasty smile.

I ignored him and looked at Edward. I could see he'd heard the commotion outside clearer than I had. But, not knowing more than a few words of Syriac, he'd have no excuse to run upstairs for another balcony inspection of the bloodshed.

'My Lord will forgive me, though,' Zakariya said, pulling himself completely back into order. 'You have a visitor. He's been waiting in your audience room since shortly after you went out this morning.'

I nodded. I'd already seen the horse and grooms being hurried through the side entrance. I left Edward to pay off the chairmen. My stick made a slow tapping on the tiles as I went on alone towards my suite. I'd manage the stairs by myself.

The young man rose politely as I walked into the room.

'Peace be upon you, My Lord,' he said, bowing low. 'I am Karim, son of Malik.'

A most well-proportioned young man – perhaps barely into his twenties – he spoke Saracen with the graceful fluency of a native. I thought quickly, trying to recall who Malik might have been. But I'd known too many of them. Still, the emblem on his gold headband told me who had sent Karim.

'And may the blessing of our Common Father descend upon you,' I replied in his own language. He'd stretched a point by addressing me as another of the Faithful – unless my ancient dealings with Omar were now being taken more seriously than I'd ever intended them to be. Just to be on the safe side, I'd meet him more than halfway. I sat down and rebalanced my going-out wig. I waved him back into his own chair. He smiled at me, his teeth a dazzling white against the brown of his face. He smiled – and, at the same time, was looking very oddly at me. I wondered for a moment if I'd put my wig on the wrong way again. But Edward would surely have pointed that one out to me.

'I trust My Lord was not inconvenienced by the troubles that afflicted our streets this afternoon,' he asked, now in a stilted Greek.

I tried to work out his position from the cut of his clothes. However, while the better class of Saracens hadn't yet given up on their desert clothing, they were moving increasingly to the same grade of white silk and the same close fitting. I smiled my thanks for his enquiry as to my safety.

'Not at all,' I said, still in Saracen. 'It was a regrettable incident that I do not look forward to witnessing again. But you may be assured of my own safety throughout.' I fell silent as the door opened, and trays of refreshments were brought in. It was all quickly arranged, and we were alone again. I sat forward.

'I hope you will not think it an unpardonable departure from the custom of your people,' I said, 'if I rely on you to pour out two cups of that deliciously hot kava juice.'

The young man smiled back at me, and reached forward for the little brass pot. I took up my own cup and sipped delicately.

'I trust His Majestic Holiness the Caliph is well,' I opened again. 'I hardly need say how honoured I am to receive one so eminent among his servants.'

'Nor we,' came the reply, 'to have as our guest the Great and Matchless Alaric. You will perhaps forgive the length of time it has taken us to learn of your presence. His Highness Meekal sent me over the moment he received the news.'

I smiled again. I sipped again. A shame, really, my stay here was ended. I'd just got these rooms as I wanted them to be.

33

White and solid in the sunshine, the walls of Damascus loomed before us. I leaned forward and tapped the shoulders of the head bearer. When he turned, I motioned him to line up my chair beside Edward's. His mouth slightly open, he was already taking in the scale of the wealth and power of this new Imperial capital. And it was an impressive sight. Apart from the obvious defence, one of the things you buy from fortification architects is that sense of awe that is in itself a form of defence. I wondered if Edward had even seen the three plumes of smoke drifting upwards from a hundred yards or so inside the gate we were approaching. Probably, he hadn't.

'I was last here just after the Persian collapse,' I said, breaking a long silence that had followed a protracted round of questions about what magnificence might lie within those walls. 'It was a sorry place back then. The Persians had thrown down its walls. They'd even carried off all the able-bodied inhabitants to repopulate their capital Ctesiphon. The only undamaged buildings amid the silent ruins of what had been an immense metropolis was the big Church of Saint John the Baptist. I spent a day here. Even without the summons to Jerusalem, that was quite sufficient for me.'

'What happened to the Persians?' Edward asked. 'Where did they go?'

'The short answer, my dear, is nowhere,' I said. This was the end of our three-day journey from Beirut – and most interesting it had been for anyone seeking a general view of how Syria had fared under the caliphs. But I pulled myself properly back into the past. 'On and off, we'd been at war with the Persians for centuries. Usually, we were stronger – sometimes they. But the quiet understanding was that neither side would push too hard. We both had our barbarian problems. Then, about ninety years ago, we drifted into a big war. Internal weakness – plus incompetence at the top – brought on a collapse of our defences. Before we could regroup, they'd taken Syria and Egypt and Asia Minor, and were even knocking on the gates of Constantinople.

'At last, I got together with Sergius – he was the Greek Patriarch at the time – and we forced that useless slob Heraclius off his arse and into the field. While I handled the politics and money, and his generals did the fighting, he jogged along in front of some ridiculously small armies that shattered the Persians. We ignored trying to retake anything we'd lost. Instead, we struck deep into Persia. Everything sent against us we annihilated. We took Ctesiphon, and then stood back while the Persians fell apart in civil war. The peace we made with the winners of that civil war was quite generous, so far as we made no new territorial demands. Though we could have demanded more, all I specified was the old borders. But it was the end of our only serious threat.' I broke off and pulled myself back into the present as Karim's chair came suddenly alongside.

'Am I right to assume,' he asked in Greek, 'that you have been telling your young companion in the Latin tongue of the glories the Caliph has directed within these walls?' I smiled and nodded. 'Then let it be known,' he said, raising his voice and sitting up to look straight at Edward, 'that this queen of cities now holds four hundred thousand people. It has twelve thousand baths. The churches of the Cross Worshippers that His Majestic Holiness, Commander of the Faithful, has allowed to be repaired are without number. The Great Mosque he has commanded to be built is already grander than anything outside the two holy cities of our homeland.' He prosed on about what struck me – a man of the one truly great City of the world – as the decidedly provincial glories of Damascus.

Before he could run out of superlatives, though, some runtish creature in an expensive robe hurried out of the gate and over the last hundred yards of the road that led from Damascus. There was a whispered conversation. Then Karim's brown face turned several shades darker. He opened and shut his mouth, and looked desperately round for guidance. The runtish creature whispered again, now pointing at the paved road that led round the outside of the whole city.

'I am advised that the minor gate through which we were supposed to proceed has been deemed unfitting for My Lord's first view of our capital,' Karim said hurriedly. He called to the officers of the small army that had accompanied us all the way from Beirut – a most useful small army, it had turned out, bearing in mind how we'd been harried by a mostly unseen enemy – and directed them to stop their continued tramp towards the Beirut gate. With a few shouts of command and one trumpet blast, the hundred men once again formed about us, as we began our brisk journey towards some more fitting point of entrance.

'What I was going from Damascus to attend in Jerusalem,' I continued once we were properly on our new course, 'was our Great Day of Triumph. There was Heraclius, seated on a golden throne within the Holy Sepulchre Church. Before him stood four of the five patriarchs – and Rome had sent out a senior bishop to stand in for the Pope. There were the leaders of various heretical Churches: even Heraclius didn't object to a spot of tolerance on that day. There was a Persian ambassador, and representatives of Christian communities from outside the Empire. There must have been forty thousand people in the church or lining the streets. During a service that I thought would never end, Heraclius himself stood and lifted a long case covered all over in gold and set with precious stones. This contained what everyone agreed to be the remains of the True Cross. It had been found in Jerusalem three hundred years earlier by the mother of the Great Constantine. Here it had been venerated as the most holy relic of the Faith. Then, the Persians had carried it off. Now, we'd regained it, and Heraclius was formally putting it back in its rightful place. As he set hands on that golden case, and the veins in his face bulged with its weight until I thought he'd have another seizure, all four patriarchs went down on their bellies to adore its contents. They were joined by the other dignitaries. Even the Pope's man went on his knees. It was all unbelievably grand and triumphant. You should have seen the coins we struck to commemorate the event.'

You should have seen them, indeed. Big, heavy things, they'd been; our purpose had been to show the whole world who was back in charge. But Edward was now more interested again in looking at the walls. They ran seemingly for miles in the hot sun. If they didn't match the vast and impregnable defences with which Constantinople had anciently been endowed, they still showed what a fight it would take for a besieging army to break through. There was a time when I'd have made more than a casual note of this last fact.

I was about to drift into an explanation of how Sergius and I had used the prestige of our victory to settle the Monophysite dispute with every appearance of finality. I'd already reached into my memory and pulled out the main arguments – about the Single as opposed to the Dual Nature of Christ, and our compromise of His Single Directing Will – when we came all of a sudden on one of the capital's external places of execution. We'd missed the morning action, but it was plain that the authorities had laid on quite a show for the onlookers. Men had been roasted alive, hanged upside down over smoking straw till they were smothered; castrated, broken with stones and scourged. There was a cluster of crosses, where the victims still feebly moved in the sun. Behind these, I could just make out the corpses of impaled men and children, their flesh being torn at by packs of yapping dogs.

I looked at Edward, wondering if he'd be cheered by a spectacle that only the civilised can manage. He swallowed and stared down at the unspoiled silk of his shoes. I shrugged. Perhaps the heat was getting to him.

At last, we came to the other gate that Karim had mentioned. This led from the desert. I shouldn't have been, but I was surprised by the volume of traffic on that road: heavy-laden camels and other beasts of burden, wagons piled high with produce, slaves and merchants of every colour bringing goods to market. By comparison, the Beirut road had been empty. In the old days, it had been the roads up from the sea ports that carried most trade with inland cities. Roads into a desert had military uses only. But the Saracen familiarity with the desert, plus our own hold on the sea, had worked another revolution in the conditions of everyday life.

We were now passing through the main gateway into the city. Above us, in gold letters set into the granite, the one inscription anywhere to be seen said in Saracen: 'There is no God but Allah, and Mohammed is His Prophet.' Inside the gateway was one of the remnants of much older work that had survived the Persians. This had recesses set into it and was covered with plaques. But the statues had all been removed. So far as I could tell, the inscriptions had been cemented over or otherwise obliterated. All that was left and that I could read was a partially obscured notice of a tax remission granted by some emperor whose name was now missing. We passed into a large courtyard, surrounded by very high walls. At the far end of this was another gate that led into the city. Here, the little people who'd been going in or out had been lined up to bow down before the three chairs and all their army of guards as they went by.

I had assumed a very short pause in this holding courtyard before we went through the other gateway into the city. People of our quality are not to be delayed by local guards. But the far gate was shut, and no one seemed inclined to get it open. Now, some other commander of the gates – this one of normal size, but with a false beard – crept out through a side door into the city, and began a whispered conversation with Karim. The brown face tightened again. He gave me a long and thoughtful look. Above the gate into the city, I could see what had been three plumes of smoke now as a single rising cloud.

'Your Magnificence will forgive us,' said Karim with false jollity, 'if we await the restoration of order on the city streets.' He got down from his chair and clapped his hands. Attendants hurried out of a low building, in their hands cups of honeyed ginger cooled with snow from the mountains. I took and drank, and ignored the smell of burning that drifted from behind the far gate as often as the breeze lined up. I uttered some non-committal politeness to Karim. But he was listening again to a low and urgent commentary from the man with the false beard. It was too fast and low for me to follow. So I sipped again and dug round in the front pouch of the carrying chair for my fan. Before I could find the thing, Edward was flapping his own at me. I smiled graciously and settled back. Someone behind me arranged the cushions into a more convenient softness. Karim went over to the doorway of the building to continue his conversation.

'So what went wrong, My Lord?' Edward asked.

I sniffed at the thin smoke that was now about us like a mist, then realised the boy hadn't got his tenses wrong. He was still asking about the past. I tried to think of a neutral answer. But if Karim could just about make himself understood in Greek, neither he nor anyone else within hearing distance could be supposed to know a word of Latin. Though I'd keep my voice low, we were safe enough. We could discuss the Victories of the Just from whatever point of view we pleased.

'Two days later after that triumphant celebration of world empire restored,' I said, 'we got a letter in comically bad Greek. It was brought to us by someone who was passing by Jerusalem with a train of camels. While we were otherwise occupied, some merchant who claimed an acquaintance with the Archangel Gabriel had unified all the Saracens under his own rule. He'd ever since been preaching them out of their less constructively barbarian ways. Now, he was inviting Heraclius, Lord of the Earth, to bow down before him. Of course, the letter went unanswered. Shortly after, the merchant died. That should have been the end of the matter. But this new faith didn't die with its founder. His followers waited a couple of years, then burst out of their desert homes.

'At first, we thought it was just an opportunistic raid. The Saracens had been an occasional pest for centuries. Then, after our efforts at reinforcement failed, we found that what had been taken back from the Persians was lost again for good.'

I laughed bleakly. 'When he gave his victory speech in the Circus in Constantinople, Heraclius departed from the text I'd written for him and referred to some prophecy a monk had jabbered down from atop a column: that before his reign ended, the Euphrates would no longer be the frontier between two empires. The man was spot-on, it turned out. Sadly, that river does now run through a single empire – it just isn't now *our* Empire! Still, it might have been worse.' I thought of those desperate holding battles we'd fought along the southern borders of our Asian Provinces. In Syria, and then Egypt, we'd lost our two richest provinces to these people. But we'd kept the rest. It might have been worse. And worse it might still be.

But the inner gate was now opening, and fingers of black smoke drifted through. I stared a question at Karim, who looked back, trying to keep the embarrassment from his face. He got back into his chair, and the carrying slaves took hold again of the long poles to front and back.

'You might ask,' I added quickly, 'why we didn't put up a better fight. But, you see, the all-conquering armies of Heraclius had been paid off, and we had no money to raise more. It didn't help that Heraclius had flooded the regained provinces with tax gatherers – though worse than that were the priests he sent in to bully everyone into the Monothelite Compromise.' Yes, the Monothelite Compromise. Sergius and I had been very proud of that. Properly sold, that could have ended two centuries of dispute over the Nature of Christ. Trust Heraclius to try imposing it at sword point. We'd simply got three verbal farts for the theologians to cry at each other, instead of two. But I put the sad recollection from mind and carried on with the matter in hand. 'The Saracens caught us off balance. If Heraclius had died of a seizure in that Jerusalem ceremony, I'd certainly have got young Constans to take the right action.

'On the other hand, Heraclius may for once have been right when he buggered up what little resistance we could offer. When they were attacked, the Persians didn't have our choice in the matter. For prestige reasons, they had to stand and fight. They threw everything we'd left to them at the Saracens when they invaded. They were utterly defeated, and their whole empire was swallowed up. We at least were left with the Asian Provinces, where even the common people are Greeks. It may – it really may – have been for the best.'

The lesson was over – rather, my part of the lesson was over. The inner gate swung fully open, and we were carried swiftly forward into the capital of an empire five times larger than the one now ruled from Constantinople.

'We cannot proceed along the Avenue of the Righteous War,' Karim said hurriedly. Directly before us, the street had been blocked with large cloth screens. These were held steady by men whose bearded faces my tired eyes weren't up to seeing in detail, but whose posture indicated nothing happy. I didn't for a moment doubt that all this was for my benefit. I gave a friendly wave. 'I am informed that the street has been closed for essential repairs,' Karim went on. 'But the Baths of Omar will surely impress My Lord. They can accommodate more people than all the public baths of Constantinople combined. If we go this way, we shall approach them from behind.'

'Let it be as you wish, my dear young friend,' I cried happily. If I cocked my good ear in the right position, I could just make out bursts of wild shouting, and perhaps a clash of arms, far behind those fluttering cloth screens. If Edward could hear anything out of the ordinary, his face said nothing. I directed his attention to the remains of a triumphal column put up in ancient times. The statue that had once topped it was long gone – perhaps it hadn't survived the Persian occupation. The column itself was now surrounded by scaffolding, and was coming down a section at a time.

34

'On behalf of His Majestic Holiness the Caliph, Commander of the Faithful,' the Grand Eunuch trilled in very dramatic Greek, 'I must announce that Your Magnificence is our most honoured guest. All that you may require, it shall be our pleasure to give.'

I looked out of the window at the bronze pipe that was loosely held in hoops six feet apart. These, in turn, were clamped to the outer wall. I didn't need the demonstration he'd failed to arrange. I could see that, if the animals on the ground moved fast enough, it would rotate, and water would be carried up by its internal screw to the vast copper tank that took up most of this floor of the tower. I wanted to ask how the screw would be turned that carried water from this tank to the one that must have been set into the roof of the tower. I also wondered how much noise all this would make as it grated round and round in those weather-roughened hoops. But I suspected I'd get no sense out of the creature. Better to wait and see for myself.

'It is to free you from the polluted air of the city that I have given you rooms in the Tower of Heavenly Peace,' he explained, just a hint in his voice to give the true motive. 'You are free to come and go as you please. You merely need to have the carrying slaves summoned with your internal chair to be moved up and down, and to be taken where you will within the great space of a palace adorned by His Majestic Holiness. The servant quarters, be assured, are on the floor beneath your own. The most loving and eager slaves of His Majestic Holiness have been assigned to obey – indeed, to pre-empt – your every request.'

I grunted and asked about my books. Looking on the bright side, the smoke of Constantinople had increasingly got on my chest. And it would be interesting to have a good view over Damascus.

'They have not yet arrived,' the answer came. 'There was – ah – trouble on the road that has blocked communications with Beirut for anyone not guarded so well as My Lord was on his journey. But I can promise that everything will have been collected from your lodgings and sent over.' He ushered me out of the empty room and got us all back into our carrying chairs, then set the panting slaves to continue about their business of carrying us up the long and airless, winding ramp that filled the innermost column of the tower. Except it didn't rotate, it was a larger version of the water screw. The only light here came from bronze lamps that hung, at regular intervals, from the underside of the next upward turn of the screw. If there was a little staircase somewhere, it wasn't evident on my first inspection.

Our journey finished right at the top of the tower. The Grand Eunuch beckoned to one of his assistants, who produced a golden key. With a push and a gentle click, this opened a door of cedar wood set flush into the wall. I passed into a corridor lit by glazed windows in the ceiling. There's no point giving my first impressions of the layout of my suite within the palace. After a comically tortuous route through the city, and then the interminable magnificence of my reception in the great entrance hall, I was too tired, and too bursting for another piss, to pay that much attention to my surroundings. So I'll tell it plain. We were housed at the top of the eastern tower of what had, when we ruled, been the Governor's residence. Now, repaired and much enlarged, and all pagan and Christian imagery doubtless removed or painted over, it was the palace from which a depressing and constantly growing fraction of mankind was ruled.

Our rooms were wholly contained on the top floor of the tower's big outer rim. Some of these rooms were connected to each other by doors. All could be reached by an inner corridor that hugged the cylinder of approach ramps. Though not of equal size, each room had the same depth of about thirty feet – this being the broken radius from the outer wall of the tower to the inner corridor – and, of course, had the general shape of a fan. In every room, the arc of the outer wall allowed for plenty of window space. This, plus more of those glazed ceilings, meant the whole suite was bathed in light.

I say we were on the top floor. Beneath us were another five, and the third housed the break in the water-raising system. With the exception of this third floor, and the one directly beneath us, which housed the slaves and all the other ministers to my wants, the others had been locked, their doors secured by red seals.

Leaving aside that we were sixty feet up, and the only access was through a door two inches thick with an outer lock, an emperor himself would have had trouble to complain about the arrangement and the furnishing of our accommodation. Indeed, bearing in mind that the present Caliph kept up the show of simple living that Muawiya had used as legitimising propaganda after murdering his way to the top, I may have been given the most luxurious quarters in the whole palace. And if it was ultimately a prison, what else had I expected?

After a long and thoughtful interlude in the facilities – no shortage of running water, I could see; and there must have been a separate firehouse for us somewhere up on the roof to heat us in winter and the water all year round – I rejoined the Grand Eunuch, who'd been waiting in one of the public rooms of the suite. I knew Edward well enough now to see the rising alarm behind the impassive mask of his face. I made a feeble pleasantry about the lack of need for any of the silver lamp brackets that hung from the ceiling of every room. He smiled briefly, then went back to examining the two-foot panels of glass that were fitted together to stop up all the windows.

The Grand Eunuch coughed slightly to regain my attention, then beamed and struck a pose of obsequious love. He pointed at a small ebony box that occupied a table all by itself near the window. I stared as the box was brought ceremoniously forward. What was this? Some piece of jewellery – more of those endless little gifts that were supposed to put me in a good mood?

'It was decided a long time ago – and by no less than His

Majestic Holiness,' the creature now squawked – 'that My Lord should be made to feel as much at home as could possibly be achieved. Beyond all else, you will surely appreciate the trouble taken by our agents at the very edge of the universe to locate this particular object.'

It would never do for me to hurry forward for an inspection. So I motioned Edward forward to take the little box and open it. For the first time on my first day in Damascus, I gave way to completely unfeigned astonishment.

'How on earth did you lay hands on those?' I gasped. That eunuch had finally got me, and I couldn't be bothered to hide the fact. I looked incredulously at the false teeth. I took them into shaking hands. Yes, they were mine, sure enough. One of the front ivories had been somehow chipped – as if someone had tried using them to chew on a bone. But this had been carefully filed smooth. Otherwise, the cleaning aside, they were exactly the same as when I'd reluctantly pulled them out for that bastard ship master to get me across the Channel. I pressed them lightly together, noting the tension of the springs that held them apart. I opened my mouth and slipped them in. The loss of two further upper teeth left little gaps that a goldsmith's attention would be needed to repair. But the gold plates still fitted perfectly on to my gums. I snapped my jaws together with a gratifying click, then turned to Edward and recited two of the more complex verses from a Callimachus ode. He looked back at me, horrified fear now plain on his face. I laughed and tried out further sentences in Latin and Saracen. A shame sound has no mirror. It would have been good to hear the difference these objects made to my apparent age. Never mind the slight soreness I'd feel for a day or two – nor the endless drooling of excess saliva – as I got used to them again. It was a glorious meeting with an old friend I'd missed almost every day, and never thought I'd see again.

I showed off my teeth with a smile at no one in particular and pretended to pay attention to the vague superlatives the Grand Eunuch gave in place of an explanation. In truth, I had no need of the details. I'd already discovered how small the world can be, given limitless money and intelligent determination. Without feeling the need to pretend helplessness, I left my stick where I'd put it and walked over to the largest of the windows. A blur of domes and minarets and scaffolding and the cheerful brown of roof tiles, Damascus lay before me. I tried to see if the largest building – it occupied the far side of the square fronted by the palace – still had a cross on its central dome. Even in the good light of the afternoon, that was beyond me. But I licked the upper plate of my falsies, and thought happily of some experiment I'd had to break off in Constantinople when I heard the Emperor's guards were hurrying across the City for me.

'I cannot begin to express the joy that His Majestic Holiness has brought me,' I declaimed. 'I cannot begin to express the love that your own goodness of heart has kindled within me.' The Grand Eunuch simpered and looked at his fingernails. His main assistant went into a fit of polite giggles that he hid behind both hands. 'One thing only I ask to make this the most perfect day of my entire life.' I paused. He leaned forward, ready to anticipate my smallest wish. 'I beseech you to send into my presence – tomorrow morning, if possible – three of the finest glassmakers in Damascus, together with three of the finest shapers and polishers of precious stones.'

The Grand Eunuch now looked puzzled. But after all that bleating about hospitality, it wouldn't have done even to ask a question. He turned to the smallest of his assistants, who took out a waxed tablet and scratched importantly away.

'Do ask them to bring their tools,' I added, 'and do ensure that they are men of good general intelligence.'

35

I splashed happily in the sun-heated pool. Once again, I wriggled free of the anxious slaves, who'd doubtless been charged, on loss of their lives, not to let an old man drown his silly self. I came up coughing and spluttering a few feet from the edge where Edward glowered down at me. I'd avoided him the night before by ordering him off to an early bed, and then withdrawing into my office with a clerk and a technical draughtsman to take my various dictations. Now, unless I wanted to spend all morning swimming up and down or playing water ball with the slaves, there was no avoiding him.

'Don't bother me with questions,' I said firmly in English. 'Either I can't answer them, or I won't.' He hadn't liked being shut into a gilded birdcage. But it was those teeth of mine – white and glittering in the afternoon sun – that had really set him off. Until then, he'd taken almost everything since my killing of those northerners for granted. He'd been awed by the superb self-assurance with which I'd brushed aside every difficulty and had got everyone dancing attendance on me. He'd been repeatedly overcome by the glories of the civilised world. Caesarea, Beirut, now Damascus: he'd no sooner got used to one apparently great city, than he'd been shown something greater still. And, like a child at night in the forest, clutching for safety at his father's hand, he'd been ever beside the Great and Magnificent Alaric. At last, he'd been brought to something near a full realisation of where we stood. He might have sworn obedience to me in all things back on the Tipasa beach. That didn't abolish his right to ask questions. I avoided the slaves again and struck out for the far side of the pool. In the warm buoyancy of the water, I might have been twenty years younger. With frantic, if silent, concern, the slaves waded after me.

Edward was already there when I arrived. I peered at the buffed gleam of his toenails and at the blur of yellow silk that began at his knees and went up to his neck.

'You told me it was the Emperor who directed your kidnapping from Jarrow,' he snapped.

I laughed at the hurt and faintly scared tone he couldn't keep from his voice. 'Correction, my dearest and most beautiful adopted son,' I mocked back at him. 'Since you were in no position to tell me otherwise, I assumed it was the Master of the Offices in Constantinople. Rather than vex an old man with questions now, you really should have made better enquiries of poor Hrothgar while he was in a position to enlighten you.'

Edward knelt down and looked me steadily in the eye. 'It must have taken months – perhaps years – to find those teeth,' he snapped again. He was no fool. He'd seen their implication almost before I'd popped them into my mouth. 'If it's the Caliph who employed Hrothgar, what was Brother Joseph doing in Jarrow?'

'Oh, come now, dear boy,' I said lightly. I stood up in the pool and raised my arms. Two strong and panting slaves took hold of me and lifted me out. Muttering away in Syriac, they towelled me off and carried me to a little couch. Edward came and stood beside me while someone fussed with an overhead canopy to keep the main force of the sun off my shrivelled, age-spotted body. 'Come now, my dear. Doesn't at least Joseph make sense to you now? He was sent out from Constantinople to make sure that this Saracen plot – and you don't keep much from the Intelligence Bureau – didn't come to anything. Once you'd ensured his failure by that brilliant pretence of stupidity, his job was changed to making sure I never completed the voyage.

'The one question I haven't been able to answer is what our mutual friend Cuthbert was about. We both agree that he was involved in the first siege of the monastery – his eagerness to have the gate opened went beyond any common desire for martyrdom. But that's all I can presently say. Did you never think, during those sessions of moral uplift he arranged, to take his cock out of your mouth and engage him in a little conversation?' I'd gone too far with that sally. I had promised him that the past was blotted out. Now, I'd thrown it straight in his face. He looked away, hurt. 'I'm sorry,' I said gently. 'But let me ask in a more reasonable manner – did you learn *anything* of Cuthbert that might indicate what he was about in the monastery?'

Edward shook his head. 'If Joseph was there to keep you from falling into Saracen hands,' he asked, now moving on to the next obvious point, 'why did he not simply kill you when he had the chance?' I shrugged. I reached out for my teeth, put them in and flashed him a brilliant smile. I got a black look in return. 'You might also tell me, My Lord, *why* the Saracens should devote years of effort to getting you here, and *why* the Empire should devote nearly the same – plus half its navy – to trying to stop this.'

I rolled over on to my back and stretched out my arms for a good oiling. 'I might tell you many things,' I answered, now serious, 'if I could, or if I wanted to.'

Edward breathed heavily. He began another question, but his breaking voice cut in, and all that came out was a boyish squawk. I smiled again, and got another black look for the effort. I closed my eyes and wriggled pleasurably under the firm hands of the masseur.

'Will you tell me, at least, why you saved me from the northerners?' he asked despairingly.

I opened my eyes and focused. I conveyed every pretence of having thought he'd gone away.

'You can surely answer that for yourself,' I said. 'Wilfred and I weren't up to the job. I needed someone to row that boat once I'd disposed of its oarsmen.'

With a gasp of rage, Edward was up and walking stiffly over to a table that held a jug of spiced honey juice.

'Edward,' I called sharply. 'Edward, come back here.' I waited, then spoke firmly but patiently. 'Back on the Tipasa beach, you were at perfect liberty not to offer that oath of fealty. I was certainly at liberty to laugh in your face. We went through with the ceremony because there was already a bond between us. Now, your oath was of unquestioning obedience. For my part, I assumed responsibility for your long-term interests. If I don't share with you whatever surmises may lurk in the undergrowth of my mind, it really is for your benefit. There really are certain things I cannot share with you. Please try to understand this.

'Let us, then, leave this conversation where it so far lies, and let us not come back to it. Do you see that black man over there – the one with the beard dyed orange? Well, take a half-solidus from your purse and give it to him. If we understood each other aright this morning, he will have smuggled in a whole skin of Syria's finest. If you are nice to him, he should give you some of it. You can mix mine with an equal volume of snow from the mountains.'

I woke from my doze just as the light was fading. There was a slip of parchment beside the bed. The messenger who'd delivered it stood wordlessly and bowed. I took it up and peered at the gold writing. Black on the yellow parchment would have taxed me in that light. Gold was quite beyond me. I'd speak to the messenger in due course. I called him over with my stick, and got up with stiff weariness. At my age, there's a limit to what massage can do. And I had strained myself in that pool. But the smell of charcoal from the glass furnace had reminded me of the works in progress. I hobbled expectantly out of the room and along the corridor.

In the large room beside my office – I noticed the books had now arrived, by the way, and were already out of their crates and arranged in the dark racks – the workmen were still hard at their jobs.

'Let's see how far we've got,' I said in Syriac. I picked up the glass discs, each one about five inches in diameter, and held them to my face. I swapped them round, then was about to reverse them, when the bearded craftsman gently took them back and handed them over again in the right order. I held them an inch from my face and looked through them at the golden writing. I moved them closer and focused hard.

'Excellent,' I said softly. The man breathed a sigh of relief. I'd not been happy with his colleague's explanation that glass as clear and hard as I'd directed would need to be specially made, and that

I'd need, until then, to put up with a bluish tinge. Nor had I been impressed with the crumbling about the edges of his own first effort with his polishing tools. But they'd worked like maniacs while I slept, and the results were nearly as good as where I'd been forced to leave off in Constantinople.

'I suggest you polish this left one a little thinner in the centre,' I added. I raised my voice and spoke generally. 'I am pleased, my dear friends, with the speed and accuracy of your work. Though what I want you have never before thought to attempt, you have followed my directions nearly to the letter. For tomorrow, I want the work repeated – this time with both discs a sixteenth of an inch thicker all over. We can then polish them down with less enthusiasm. For the moment, I am pleased with this first effort, and I want the discs set immediately in a gold framework with a long handle. I suggest you measure my face, so that the centre of each disc corresponds with the centre of each eye.'

The men bowed, and one reached for his measuring rod.

'Isn't civilisation a wonderful thing?' I asked Edward. I sat down opposite him and reached for his wine cup. When I'd nodded off, he was lost in his game of chasing a ball down the winding ramps to the ground, and then running back up with it. Now, he appeared to have been sitting here for some while by the open window to observe the progress of my works. He gave me a sulky look. I pretended it was all a matter of the stolen cup. I pushed it back across the table, and stretched my still tired limbs. He'd retreated back into blankness. I leaned on clasped hands and looked at him. I'd still not tell him what we were about. But I could at least tell him what I was doing here and now.

'According to Epicurus and his followers,' I began slowly in Latin – English being wholly insufficient for the summary I had in mind – 'every visible object is continually shedding its outermost layer of atoms. When these strike on the eye, they produce an impression of that object in the mind. That is the cause of what we call vision. If the eye is damaged, these impressions are produced imperfectly or not at all. It seems that the conscious focusing of the eye on an object is at best a minor adjustment. The basic perception depends on an unconscious focusing of the atoms from what may be a large or a distant object into the small part of the brain that deals with vision. In the case of the aged, the eyes lose some of that unconscious focusing ability. It has long been known that water or glass can distort objects viewed through them. This may be because the atoms cast off by objects are diverted from their straight course by the dense packing of atoms in the medium through which they pass.' I was speaking as simply as I could, and I was glad to see that Edward understood this lesson.

'All this being so, I have decided that these accidental distortions can be refined to the point where they offset the lost ability of the eyes to do their job. I have been thinking for some years of a set of mathematical formulae that could be applied to the shape of lenses so that every defect of vision could be exactly offset. These formulae have so far eluded my understanding – on account, I am sure, of a lack of precise empirical knowledge. However, I found, shortly before leaving Constantinople, that some degree of offset can be achieved by trial and error. I am now taking advantage of the Caliph's hospitality to push these efforts further. Perhaps, it is by such trial and error that the knowledge will grow on which some abstract, all-explaining theory can be based. But it is enough for me at the moment that I shall, before evening, be able to read for myself again.'

I snapped my fingers and called to the workman who was holding my lenses. I took them back and held them up to see out of the window. 'No,' I went on, 'I'm not able to see Damascus at all through these. The shape of the city is more blurred than with nothing at all. To see distant objects, we shall need to work on some other convexity of the glass. But if I hold these lenses in the right position, I can easily read the lettering on this letter from His Highness the Governor of Syria.

'It says, by the way, that His Majestic Holiness the Caliph has been called away by the needs of war with the Empire. In his place, the Governor of Syria invites us to a banquet to be held in my honour tomorrow evening.' As I spoke, one of the slaves wandered in and gave me a despairing look. Keeping the door shut had confined the dust of all that I'd commanded. But I could see the charcoal smoke had caused some resentment. I wrinkled my nose at his dustpan and brush and waved him from the room. He slammed the door as he went. I turned back to Edward.

'So, made young again by artificial hair and artificial teeth – and now, I hope, by artificial eyes,' I said, 'I plan to see how closely we are held prisoner in this most glorious of palaces. If possible, we shall tour the shops of Damascus tomorrow morning, and spend more of my gold on silken robes finer than the tailors of Beirut can imagine.' Edward nodded. I could see he was still upset with me. But that would have to be. I handed the lenses back, and wondered if my demand for 'immediate' work would allow me to spend all evening among my books. I'd picked up a Saracen chronicle of the last big war with the Empire that might repay my attention.

'As for you, Edward,' I continued, 'I have not forgotten your own bodily needs. At dusk, a deputy of the eunuch we met yesterday will attend on you in your bedchamber. As in Beirut, I advise you to be honest about your tastes. You have arrived at an age where the physical pleasures can be enjoyed at their fullest. Do not waste this time.'

I got up and went over to the glass cutter to suggest a refinement that had just come to mind. Suddenly, I remembered the messenger. Squatting on his haunches, he'd been waiting politely beside one of the larger cutting wheels. His master deserved nothing at all – from me or anyone else. The messenger, though, deserved an answer.

36

And Yazid wrote unto his father Muawiya, saying: The Greeks take fright and starve behind the walls of their great city on the two waters. With all the new might you have sent me, I will storm their walls. By the grace of God, O Father, before you read these words, the capital of the world will be yours. As it was prophesied, so you will sit upon the Throne of the Caesars, and the Message of God shall be spread through all the nations of the world.

But the Old One al-Arik readied himself once more to snatch victory from the Faithful. To the generals of Caesar he said: Degenerate, unworthy seed of the Greeks, bearded women who never speak but to counsel rendering up our city to the Men of the Desert; yea, let me take this war into mine own hands. Old as I am, yet shall I deliver us.

And al-Arik sought out one al-Inkus, a man of Syria, and gave him money, saying: Give as thou hast promised, and I will reward thee an hundredfold more. And al-Inkus gave as his father had found among the learning of the Egyptians.

And the day of battle dawned, and three score and ten thousand of the Faithful prepared themselves, and the sound of their battle cry reached unto the Infidels of the North, whose own numbers were as the grains of the desert sand, and who stood on the far shore to wait the command of Yazid; and the Infidel King said: The Men of the Desert shall know victory this day; let us prepare ourselves to take the Greeks from behind, and ours too shall be the mountains of gold and precious jewels and the fair virgins that are sheltered by the walls of the City.

But al-Arik stood on the walls of the City on the Two Waters, and gave orders that the great chain of defence be lifted; and from behind this there came five ships, and these five ships were as al-Inkus had been commanded to fit them.

And among the numberless ships of the Faithful the five ships of al-Arik sailed; and—

I looked up. I'd come across a Saracen word I didn't recognise. And, even with my two lenses to sharpen that elaborate, flowing script, the wavering lamplight wasn't enough for my old eyes to continue drinking in the narrative. But I'd read enough. Back in Beirut, I'd been assured that this was the standard history of the late war. It had little analysis, and the collapsing of two vast, opposed enterprises into a series of personal exchanges was a sure sign of barbarism. Even so, the writer had got his facts more or less as I'd myself let them seep out into the world. I thought back to that night meeting of the Imperial Council, where I alone had faced down those useless generals. The walls of Constantinople – 'incapable of holding'? I'd never heard such nonsense! They'd looked down once too often over that double sea of campfires, and their hearts had died within them. Constantine himself had attended the meeting got up by his eunuchs as a common fisherman, bag of gold tied to his waist.

The Saracen chronicler was right enough that it had all been down to me. But for me, Constantinople would now be the seat of the caliphs. Scrubbed and whitewashed, the Great Church would echo to the mournful wail of the *muezzin.* The Danube and Rhine would already have been crossed, and, one by one, the Germanic kingdoms would be going down before that terrible cry of *God is Great.* Instead of all that, we controlled the seas. Instead of that, the Greek provinces of the Empire had been made impregnable. Instead of that, the Saracens had been forced into the second best alternative of expansion towards the rivers of India.

I smiled and rubbed my eyes. I'd rather have been famous as the man who'd cut taxes and controls, and humanised justice, and given land to the ordinary people and let them keep and bear arms. Perhaps I might be that after another hundred years, when my reforms had fully renewed the Empire. For the moment, there was worse than being called 'the Old One al-Arik'.

'You can take me to bed in a moment,' I said in Syriac. I'd

caught the faint scraping again of sandals on the tiled floor, and felt ashamed of how angry I'd been earlier. It was very late. The last time I'd got up for a piss, I'd looked out of the window. There hadn't been a single light burning in Damascus. The moon might have shone above a deserted city. So far as I could tell, the palace itself was in complete silence. Edward must have finished with his whores and drunk himself blotto. Only I was still awake, rejoicing in the partial restoration of sight – I and some poor slave who might have been on his feet since the previous dawn. He'd only been doing his duty with those regular coughs and coded offers of boiled fruit juice. I slid a bone marker over the sheet where I'd finished, and rolled the papyrus book shut. I took up a pen and made a note for myself about my lens makers. The glass discs immediately available had all been five inches across. But the results were unmanageably large. We'd see how it went with three or even two inches. I wondered if that would make them harder to work. Unless I'd been given inferior workmen, Syrian glass didn't seem anywhere near so good as Greek. Perhaps I should order a dig in one of the ruined palaces I'd been hurried past by Karim. If cloudy with age, old glass might not have so many bubbles in it.

'You can let me sleep until I wake by myself,' I said as the sandals came closer still and stopped just behind me. 'I've made a list of books on this papyrus sheet. Have the goodness to give it to one of the clerks when they come in. I want—'

I did see the dark cord as it was slipped over my head. But I barely had time to register the fact when I felt the knot against my throat and it being pulled tight. There was a sudden flash of coloured lights in my head as I felt myself pulled up and backwards. I heard the scrape and crash of my chair as it went over. I heard the sharp, excited breathing of the man behind me.

Unless the cord is so thin that it cuts your head off, strangulation is – compared with most other forms of murder – a pretty slow death. But, supposing the noose is properly arranged, you black out almost at once, and there's not much to be done in the way of self-defence. That doesn't make you completely helpless, however. I still had the pen in my hand. Almost without thinking,

I swung my right arm upwards and behind me. I hit something hard, and the pen glanced off. I struck out again and again, until I got lucky. I felt the sharp reed sink into something soft. With a cry of pain, the man moved left out of my reach, stooping down until I felt his head just behind mine. The knot loosened just long enough for me to take in a ragged lungful of air. Then it was tight again. I threw my whole upper body forward, and swung back. The hardest part of my head smashed like a club into his face. There was a shocked scream, and I dropped loose on to the floor.

You really have just moments in this sort of fighting. I knew that I had to be up on my feet and reaching for any weapon at hand. But I rolled, gasping and shaking, on the floor. I couldn't see past the white flashes still bursting in front of my eyes. Except for the wild thudding of my own heart, I was effectively deaf. I fought desperately to pull myself together. I got hold of the noose that was still about my neck and tore it free. I threw it behind me. As I heaved myself slowly on to hands and knees, I felt my walking stick where it had fallen. I grabbed it, and, wheezing and shuddering, pulled myself to my feet.

I leaned on my desk for support and looked round. At first, I thought I'd chased the attacker off. But, no – he was on the far side of the room. He wasn't a big man, but was young and wiry. Leaning with one hand against the wall, he was doubled over. I'd got him hard on the nose, and he was too busy with blood and tears to come after me. I looked round for a weapon. The penknife was useless. Still holding on to the desk with my left hand, I raised the stick in my right. Watching it tremble and shake as I held it before me would have been comical if I hadn't been in so much danger. I opened my mouth and tried to call for support. But, if my windpipe hadn't been crushed by that first tug of the noose, nothing came out but a rattled croak.

The killer was now upright again. He had no knife in his hands, and didn't seem to have come out with any other weapon beside his noose. He too was looking about for a weapon. Like me, he didn't find much ready to hand.

'Christ is my Saviour,' he called in a low, triumphant Syriac.

'My Saviour is Christ.' There was no chance of seeing his eyes. Even so, I had the impression that he was high on the usual hashish. He smiled and went into a wrestler's pose. He moved slowly towards me. I swung round with my stick and began rapping it hard on the desk. I hit out at my cup, and, with a loud noise, it shattered on the floor. I clutched harder at the desk and held the stick out as if it had been a sword.

'Help!' I was now able to gasp in the feeble voice of the very old. 'Help – murder!' I jabbed uncertainly at him with my stick as the killer came forward again, and pulled it back before he could take hold of it. I used the advantage as he jumped out of my way to snatch up the inkwell. I threw it at his head. I missed, and it smashed on the floor, leaving a pool of blackness under his feet.

Perhaps the penknife might be some use after all, I thought. Unlike with the oarsman, I had no advantage of surprise, and this wasn't the murderous little instrument that Joseph had given me. But I might be able to get in a lucky cut before those strong outstretched arms got to me and closed too tight round me. The killer saw what I had in mind. He put his arms into a semblance of the praying position.

'Christ is my Saviour!' he cried, now exultant. 'My Saviour is Christ!' He stepped towards me across the office. In just that one step, he'd covered half the distance that separated us. He stopped and giggled, and spun round and round, his arms trailing outward beside him. 'Christ is my Saviour! My Saviour is Christ! Blessed are the pure in heart: for they shall see God. Christ is my Saviour! My Saviour is Christ!'

His little sermon over, he took another step towards me. I tested the weight of my stick and held it up before me. I held it as if it had been half sword, half truncheon. It was neither, and neither would have been much good in these trembling hands. I told myself not to whimper, and stood up straight.

As I looked, now steady, into his eyes, and thought I could see only death reflected back at me, the door of the office flew open. Standing in the doorway, stark naked, was Edward.

37

Edward was silently taking in what he'd seen. His hair was untied, and it floated about him in the lamplight like a golden haze. The killer turned to face him. He laughed again and moved towards the door.

'An old man,' he grated, still in Syriac, 'and a boy to guard him!'

Edward's response was a mouthful of obscenities in English, and then a lunge forward into the room. He set about the killer with the sort of cane you use for beating uppity slaves. Surprised, the man retreated at first, protecting his face with outstretched arms. He kicked another chair over, and it looked for a moment as if he might pull an entire book rack down on himself. But, if not very big, he was twice Edward's size and weight. Surprise is everything when dealing with a superior opponent, and Edward had worn his out too fast to make it count.

The killer reached out and snatched the cane. He took it clean out of Edward's hands, almost as if he'd been taking a rattle from an annoying child. He held it in both hands and put his head back for a low, chilling laugh.

'I am sent to kill an old man,' he called, speaking a sort of Greek, 'and now a boy as well!' He laughed again, and went on the attack. He slashed out at Edward and caught him about the shoulders. He beat out again and again. It was a cruel and thoroughly experienced beating. I heard the continual hiss of thin wood and its impact on bare flesh. Edward dodged behind the fallen chair and tried to push it towards the killer. It was too heavy. He succeeded only in exposing himself to more of those terrible blows. Once more, the killer laughed. He looked at me. I was still propped, useless, against the desk. He shouted loud in a burst of wild, drug-inspired pleasure, and turned his full attention on the boy.

Not once, under that beating, did Edward cry out. He held up his arms for protection. He did his best to shield his face. But, all the time, he lunged at the killer, trying to land a blow – hoping perhaps to regain possession of the cane. I watched until the killer turned and began driving Edward towards the office door. It was now that I went into action. I stepped forward and got him from behind with a blow of my own, much heavier stick. I missed his head, but got him a hard blow on the collarbone. There was a howl of pain, and he wheeled round to face me. I stabbed at his throat, and got him on the cheek. I raised the stick and swung hard. I felt the impact as I hit his left wrist. He howled again and made a grab for the stick.

Edward was on his feet again. He jumped on to the man's back and tried to pull him down to the floor. He was too light. But the man was clutching with his good hand at the hold on his neck. He pitched forward and back, and from side to side. I heard the thud of the boy's thigh against one of the book racks. But there was no breaking his grip. Edward tried to get his fingers up the man's nose and to pull. He scratched at the eyes. He ignored the still punishing backward slashes of the cane. I moved in closer with a hard jab into the genitals, and then another poke in the face. Using the stick in place of a stabbing sword, I went at every soft part of the body I could reach, concentrating on face and stomach. All the time, Edward stayed clamped on his back, pulling and shoving. I cursed my weakness and the hard thumping in my chest that almost seemed to knock me off what little balance I had. But I got the genitals again. This time, I must have got one of his balls. With a loud shriek of pain, he lunged backwards. Edward managed to swing himself sideways just in time to avoid being caught under the killer as he hit the floor. I took my stick in both hands and threw myself forward, landing with my stick across the lower part of his throat. I pushed hard.

There was a time when I'd have crushed his windpipe as if it were a foot of leather hose, and got up to watch him choke. But I'd lost both weight and strength over the years, and I might as well have been pressing against solid bone. The man was dazed from the fall backwards, and I was on top of him. But the killing blow

I'd had in mind was out of the question. So I raised the stick again. Still gripping it in both hands, I turned it vertical and brought it down hard. I missed his right eye, and carved a gash two inches long under his hairline. He squealed, and I felt his arms come up from behind to flutter about my throat. I held the stick aloft once more and struck with more precision. This time, its half inch went straight in. It grated against the socket, and there was a momentary pressure on the softness of the eye. Then, it crunched into the bone at the base of the socket.

The screams were deafening. As if I'd thrown him on to those burning coals beside Saint Flatularis, the killer went into a frenzy. He curled into a ball. He clutched at his eyes, trying to pull the stick out of his ruined socket. The merest touch increased the agony, and he stretched out on his belly – as if trying to find some resting position in which the pain might at least stabilise. There was none. Sounding barely human, he howled. He beat frantically on the tiled floor. Again and again, he smashed both knuckles down until the bones must have broken. But there was nothing to relieve that all-devouring pain. And, surely beside the physical pain, must have been the horrified realisation of what I'd done to him. He curled into a ball again. He straightened out and arched his back, and screamed till his breath failed him. He clutched at his beard with both hands and pulled. He threw his arms wide and let out another long, bubbling scream.

But, still, he wasn't finished. With an angry roar that seemed to fill the room, he heaved himself to a sitting position and was reaching about for me. With a scream that was even louder, he tugged the stick from his eye and threw it aside. I grabbed at the fallen stick and, with all my remaining force, got myself to my feet. I swung another blow at him, and knocked him to the floor. I could have stood there, panting and clutching at my chest, to watch the man writhe in the only hell he'd ever know. But he was high on hashish and high on God. Astonishingly, he was scrabbling with his arms to roll over and get up again. I knocked at his other eye, and missed. I caught him a blow on the forehead with the handle of the stick, and knocked him flat again.

'Take hold of his shoulders,' I gasped at Edward. 'Put all your weight on his chest. Try to keep him on his back.' I stood at right angles to the killer, his head at my feet. I watched a moment, trying to predict his convulsive, still shrieking movements. Then I lifted the stick again. As if spearing a fish in the sea, I rammed it with all my aged force into his open mouth. I felt his front teeth shave the polished wood, and the softness of his palate. I felt the momentary resistance of his tongue, as, rammed like wadding into a blocked latrine pipe, it went downwards into his throat. I felt the grating resistance of bones beyond the back of his throat. Edward still gripping like mad on to the shoulders, I stepped back for a better position. Using it as a lever, I pulled the stick towards me. The man's upper body arched. His arms went up in a last, despairing flail. Then his screams turned suddenly to a dull, frothing choke. If there was the click of snapping bones in his neck, I didn't hear. But the good eye opened wide and the whole body went limp.

I flopped down on the dead man's chest and clutched at myself. My heart was going like the drum at the end of an erotic dance, and I couldn't catch my breath. I shut my eyes and tried to ignore the renewed white flashes. I let myself go loose and rolled off the man on the hard floor. I could feel a burning pressure in my nose and a spurting wetness all over my upper lip. Given a little more time to think, I might have reflected on an end that my barbarian ancestors would have thoroughly approved. But this wasn't the end – not yet. I did catch my breath, and, slowly, my heart returned to a bearable, if uncertain pounding.

I grabbed at the dead man's clothing and pulled myself into a sitting position. I shook my head and opened my eyes and looked round. At first, I thought Edward had been badly injured. Gasping and shaking, he was on all fours, his head pressed against the cold tiles. He looked to be in a spasm of unbearable agony. I raised a hand uselessly towards him, and tried to cry his name. But it was only an orgasm. The hard flogging, and then the thrill of violent death had been too much for the boy. He sobbed uncontrollably as he reached the point of total crisis, and bit hard on his forearm until blood mingled with saliva. By the time he was done, and he lay quivering, face down on the floor, I was well out of danger. I still was in no condition to try standing. But I reached forward, and let a hand fall on his chilly, sweating back. He lifted his head on to his forearm and looked back at me with a dreamy smile.

'My dear boy,' I said, keeping my voice as steady as I could, 'you really need to control these urges. One day, I promise, they'll put you at a serious disadvantage.'

Not moving his head, he raised his free hand and brushed a lock of damp hair from his eyes. 'We killed the fucker,' he said in English. 'We did it together.' He squeezed his eyes shut and repeated himself, now exultant: 'We did it together.'

'We did indeed,' I said. 'And you fought like a lion.' I paused and chose my words. 'I'm proud of you,' I ended simply. I thought of reaching for that fallen chair and using it to pull myself to my feet. But that effort could wait until I was in better breath. 'Now, be a good lad,' I went on in a more businesslike tone. 'Go and pull on that cord over there. The sooner we get help from downstairs, the better. We don't know if this man was the only one sent.'

Edward smiled again and sat up. 'There's a dead slave outside the door,' he said. 'Other than that, we're alone.'

I was no judge of that. It seemed still and silent all around. But, with my hearing, there might have been a riot in progress a few doors round that inner corridor.

'And your own night company?' I asked with unusual delicacy.

He smiled brightly and pointed at the now abandoned cane. 'I beat her unconscious,' he said. 'She didn't even wake up when the noise started.' He jumped up, whole patches of his body marked and bloody in the lamplight.

'You'd better get some clothes on,' I said flatly. 'I suppose we might also wait for your – your signs of excitement to pass off.' He looked down and laughed. He moved his feet apart and stretched his arms. He stamped on the floor and laughed again.

'Oh, that won't go down in a hurry,' he cried, again exultant. 'After this, I don't think it will *ever* go down.' He put his head back and laughed louder, and arched his entire body. Then, silent, he looked down at me, his face now taking on a strange, doubtful expression. He came and sat between me and the twisted body of the man we'd just killed. He swallowed and leaned forward. He put a hand on my shoulder. I took his hand and slapped it softly. I laughed weakly until I thought I'd have my first coughing fit in ages. I took the hem of my robe and wiped away some of the blood from around my nose.

'My dear young man,' I said. 'All else aside, this is hardly the time or place for such things. Our wisest course of action, I do suggest . . .' I trailed off. The boy wasn't listening. And when did I ever behave wisely? If I'd behaved with an ounce of wisdom, Edward would by now be spending some of Ezra's money in Spain, and I'd be hidden away in some desert monastery, waiting for death. Instead, we were sitting in the heart of the Caliph's empire as his guests, with the body of some drugged-out religious assassin freshly dead beside us.

And, now the killing was over, it really was very still and quiet.

38

'But I'd never have thought it possible!' Karim shouted, all trace of the cautious diplomat erased from his voice. 'I cannot express how proud . . .' He paused and remembered his calling. He turned back for another look at the twisted, now stiff corpse at his feet. 'Dog of an unbeliever!' he snarled. He kicked hard at the body, then bent down for another inspection of the congealed blackness of the right eye and the congealed brown mass within the open, sagging mouth. I had another rueful look at my walking stick. Covered in muck, its bottom length ruined, someone had pulled this out, and it lay unregarded beside the body. He stood up and grinned at me. 'Nice work, My Lord. I can tell you that few survive an encounter with the Angels of the Lord. Yes – very nice work!'

I got to my feet and winced at the pain that flooded in from every joint. I leaned on the broom handle one of the slaves had given me as an improvised new stick, and pointed at the body.

'I wouldn't dream of telling you your business, Karim,' I said. 'However, before you dictate the arrest order for all my workmen, I would ask you to look at these stains on the dead man's clothing.' I poked my stick between the parted legs. 'I suggest that, rather than having come in with the others yesterday, and then hiding somewhere, it seems more likely that he climbed up the outside water screw. The window beside it was left open to bring in fresh air, and Edward found it pushed wide open. I have no doubt an investigation from the outside will confirm my belief. I do beg you not to put some very competent workmen on the rack, but instead to have bars fitted on all windows that can be reached from the outside. You might also make some enquiries within the palace to find out how the man got past the outer security, and how it was he knew where I was and how to get at me. You will agree that trousers are not commonly worn in Syria, and that those leather patches on the knees seem to make light work of climbing high metal pipes.'

Karim's face tightened for a moment. Then again, I was turning his easy case into a long and possibly embarrassing enquiry. But he smiled and nodded back obediently. It would all be as I asked, he assured me with florid courtesy. I took the cup of something dull that a slave was pressing on me, and wondered if my workmen were getting over the shock of hearing Karim scream threats at them. He got up, his smile now broader.

'My Lord will forgive me if I take my leave of this company,' he said gravely. 'I have my report to complete for His Highness the Governor of Syria. I will assure you of the great interest he takes in your comfort and security. I am sure that, in view of last night's most regrettable incident, he will wish to receive you even in advance of this evening's banquet.' He looked again at the corpse and frowned.

'Something I shall need to cover in my report,' he went on, 'is the apparent delay between the time you sent this piece of meat to Hell and your call for help. Everything points to a death no later than the midnight hour. Your call was just before dawn.'

I pulled a face. 'I'm an old man,' I said. 'It took me time to recover from the ordeal. The boy and I then sat awhile looking at the smoke from the fires that were breaking out all across the city. They reminded me of riots in Constantinople.'

Karim scowled and muttered something about Christian ingratitude for all the benefits of the Caliph's rule.

'But you really must pardon me, Karim,' I broke in, 'for not at first recognising you. When you told me you were the son of Malik, I thought you were related to His Present Majestic Holiness. Am I right, however, in believing that you are in fact the son of Malik al-Ashtar, companion of the Caliph Ali and his Governor of Egypt?'

He nodded and sat down again. This time, he sat on the little sofa where – unable to follow a word of the conversation – Edward had been sitting very still.

'You are indeed a master of all wisdom,' he said. 'Know then that my father may have died in the civil war that the Empire did so much to foment. Know also that Muawiya delighted in the removal of his rival's main support. I am, even so, a loyal servant of the Caliph. Abd al-Malik is eager to move on from those regrettable disputes over policy. My main family in Medina has long since accepted the hand of friendship, and I rejoice in the Caliph's fullest trust.'

'I'd never have thought otherwise,' I said with an easy wave. 'But I did once meet your father. It was after your people had taken Syria from us. We were both part of the negotiation after the main battle for the exchange of prisoners. I found him a most brave and generous opponent. I was sorry to hear about his death.'

Karim nodded again. He got up and crossed over to the door. As he bowed, I caught the unguarded look on his face. 'Loyal servant of the Caliph', my foot. The unifying bond of the Desert Faith was one matter. The bond of blood was something else. I kept a bleary, tired look on my face until the door was shut and we were alone. I reached behind one of the heavier bound volumes that was propped against the wall, and pulled out the wine jug.

'That was a good meeting,' I said, now in English.

Edward looked up and made an effort to focus on me. He'd started to hurt rather badly once his bruises came out. In retrospect, the two drops of Jacob's opium juice might have been more than strictly needed. He opened his mouth to speak. He shut his eyes and squeezed his fingernails hard into his palms.

'Why is everyone trying to kill you?' he asked with an effort. His face broke into a sweat and he leaned back into the soft cushions of the sofa.

'I have already explained, my dear boy,' I said patiently, 'that these are not things for you to worry about. Besides, not *everyone* is trying to kill me.' Drugged as he was, I could see the beginnings of a dark look. There was a knock on the door. I put the two brimming cups on my desk and stood in front of them. Three slaves entered with a large cloth sack. Another couple followed behind with mops and buckets of water.

'Ah, come to clean up the mess, I see,' I called briskly. 'Well, so long as it doesn't start to smell too bad, I can put up with a body in the library. So you take this poor boy and put him to bed. Gently with the clothes. Gentle with the sheets. Let him sleep until—' Edward heaved himself up. He'd understood what I had in mind from my tone, and his displeasure was now obvious.

'Very well,' I said evenly. I pointed at the body and let the slaves set about their business without further interruption. I made sure to drop a large sheet of papyrus over the cups, then took Edward very gently by the shoulder. If its effects had been bleached away by the drug, the pain itself was still there. 'Let us go next door,' I said, 'and see how my works progress. Indeed, since Karim has advised us not to leave the palace until further notice, there can be no shopping today. That leaves you with a choice between the long sleep that I do most urgently suggest and watching me improve my vision.' I helped him into the corridor, and guided him through the entrance to the room where the smell of charcoal and the low fluttering of a polishing wheel spoke of much hard work.

'I told you yesterday,' I said as I got him through the door and handed him to someone just inside, 'about the theory of vision taught by Epicurus. I find it more reasonable than the claim made by Plato that we all have an invisible light behind our eyes that illuminates objects for us alone. However, I'm still not entirely happy with Epicurus, great man though he was. I think a theory more consistent with the facts of vision is that light itself is a stream of atoms, and that vision arises from the differential absorption into or reflection from objects of this light. This explains darkness as a simple absence of light – though it does less well to explain why the perceived size of objects varies with their distance. But it still clarifies how shaped glass can deflect whatever atoms carry an image from their normal course.'

But Edward had turned pale, and was beginning to sag between the arms of the two workmen who'd taken him from me. I had him laid on to the only sofa not covered in papyrus sheets, and waited for the slaves to come and take him to bed. I then turned to the much clearer, small lenses I'd ordered. There were still problems with the curvature of everything I tried. There really is a difference between using Apollonius to suggest varying degrees of convexity, and getting these reproduced in glass. And that leaves aside the question of what degree of convexity might be needed to correct the defects of my own vision. Nevertheless, I was now able to pick out lenses that showed writing much better than the day before, and even lenses that let me take in something of the view from the window.

I distributed gold purses all round, and turned to a discussion of what I wanted next.

A slight hangover coming on, I sat in one of the smaller gardens of the palace. My own Tower of Heavenly Peace was about fifty yards over on my left. While I still felt up to walking about, I'd gone over to look at the unmistakable signs of climbing on the water pipe. They started a few feet above the rotating mechanism, and went up as far as I could see with one of my pairs of lenses. There was still no guard at the foot of the tower, and I'd seen no evidence from within that bars were being fitted. But a palace is a notoriously slow medium for the transmission of orders. I had no doubt something would be arranged before evening.

I handed my lenses back to the attendant who'd come out with me. Even when you haven't seen properly in years, there is a limit to how much you want to inspect of leaves and flowers. Besides, the hangover was bringing on a headache. If it hadn't been such a pleasant late morning, I'd already have had myself dipped into a cool bath and then put to bed until it was time to get ready for the Governor's banquet.

The Governor's banquet! I groaned inwardly at the thought. It would combine the Greek inconvenience of lying on a couch all evening with the Saracen prohibition of wine. I didn't even have the excuse that travelling through Damascus might be unsafe. This being the joint capital of Empire and Province, the Governor had his residence inside the palace. It would be a matter of being carried by chair through half a mile of crowded rooms to a stuffy hall where I'd be lucky to catch one word in two of any conversation. I took my lenses back and looked through them at the unrealistically sharp and enlarged gravel at my feet.

It was now that I saw the double dot of intense brightness within the shadow of my lenses. The moment I saw it, I realised it shouldn't have been any surprise. If these things could concentrate the atoms cast off – or reflected – from objects before they reached my own eyes, they could also concentrate light from the sun before it reached other objects. And it was light in itself that I was now discussing. The Epicurean theory was ingenious. But the theory of autonomous light was far more convincing. But, as said, this double light had an intensity I'd never seen before. Moving the lenses back and forth could make the size and intensity of the dots vary inversely. At the smallest, the dots were not merely bright – they could also focus heat. I watched a fallen petal smoke as a hole was burned straight through it. With shaking hand, I moved one of the lenses over a bug I saw crawling across the gravel. At first, it tried to hurry away from that intense light. But I moved with it. Finally, the thing stopped moving. Then with a loud *pop* and a little puff of smoke, it exploded.

'Quickly,' I said to the attendant, 'help me down on to my knees. No – put my cloak down to cushion me. I'll sit on the ground.' The man came out of his reverie and looked at me as if I'd gone mad. 'Do as you're told!' I snapped. 'And tear off a strip from that book.'

'*Haven't you lived long enough already?*' that fool Cuthbert had asked me back in Jarrow. The answer now was a most emphatic No! Ninety-seven years I'd been alive, and only now had I realised something I'd always been in a position to know. I'd seen the evidence almost every day. There was the reflection of concentrated sunlight from slightly irregular mirrors. There was the concentration of light through glass vases filled with water. There was even that tall story I'd read, and ignored, of how Archimedes had concentrated sunlight in a big mirror to burn the sails of a besieging fleet off Syracuse. In a flash brighter than those two dots I'd created, I saw the collected evidence of a lifetime's unthinking observation. And, behind this, I saw the dim outlines of a theory that involved more than correcting my own dodgy eyes.

I can't tell how long I sat there, playing with my lenses. But the sun had started on my left. The next time I took conscious note of its position, it was far over on my right. My legs were stiff with the strain. My cloak was ruined from the endless fires I'd started on it. I was thinking to have myself taken back up to my office, so I could start writing all this out in a way that would prompt further reflections and ideas for experiment, when a sudden shadow took all the light from my lenses. Even then, I made a fresh discovery. If I moved the lenses to the right distance from my cloak, I could see an upside-down image of a man standing over me. No – I could see two men. I looked up. One of them was Karim.

'In view of your great age, My Lord,' he said, 'it would not be appropriate to ask you to stand for His Highness the Governor.'

I tried to heave myself up on to the bench, but an attack of pins and needles kept me rooted to the ground. As Karim leaned forward to help me, I peered through my lenses at the man beside him. Dressed in black, his face covered in a luxuriant growth of brown hair, the Governor stood with both hands outstretched in a gesture of respect.

'Oh, it's you!' I said, not bothering to keep the disgust from my voice. I flopped on to the bench and tried to move my legs. 'I should have recognised your foul stench the moment your men got into that monastery. Don't preen yourself, though. I'd got a pretty clear whiff of it long before young Karim rolled up at my lodgings in Beirut.' I winced and tried to rub some life into my left leg.

The Governor smiled and dropped his hands back to his side. 'So, we meet again,' he said in Greek. I ignored him. He struck a pose and raised his voice. 'At last, the circle is complete. When we last met, you were the initiator, I the initiate. Now, I am the master.'

I looked him in the face and grimaced. 'To see you standing there, dressed up like a bloody Saracen,' I replied, 'why, it would have broken your poor father's heart.'

39

Meekal the Merciless – once Michael, son of Maximin, now Governor of Syria – looked back at his aged grandfather and laughed.

'Leave us,' he said to Karim. He repeated himself in Syriac for my attendant. When we were completely alone, he sat down beside me.

'Do I get a kiss?' he asked in Latin.

I looked back at him. He'd aged in fifteen years. The beard was probably dyed. What might remain of the hair was hidden under the close-fitting turban of the Saracens. Between turban and beard, I saw a face now deeply lined. Only the eyes were the same as ever. Of a blue so dark it might have passed for black, they burned as if they were another of my lens experiments. I stared straight into them, unafraid.

'Those teeth you had the kindness to recover,' I said with a sniff, 'they've a habit of playing up unexpectedly. You're welcome to try for a kiss. But don't complain if I accidentally bite off your nose.'

He shrugged. 'I knew you'd survive the journey,' he said, starting over. Though still in Latin, he dropped his voice for added safety. 'The Caliph wouldn't believe me at first. It took a lot, even of my persuading, to get him to allow the incredibly long chain of cause and effect that has resulted in this meeting. But here you are. And all the reports assure me you are no less the man that you were when I rode out of Constantinople.'

'The Intelligence Bureau got wind of your scheme,' I said.

He bared his darkened teeth in a grin. 'So I hear,' he said. 'That ship we commissioned at such ruinous expense was taken by the Imperial Navy last month. Apparently, the survivors had kept alive by drinking each other's blood. You may be pleased to know that they were blinded and stuffed down the first convenient lead mine. You will also be sure that I was ever so concerned by the news. I didn't sleep well again until we heard that your accounts had been reactivated.

'Oh, and I don't doubt the Intelligence Bureau got wind of that also. We do go through the motions of keeping things under wraps. But the Empire has its agents everywhere. And, talking of these, look at that bastard Christian you had to finish off last night. It was a neat job you did on him – Karim has just shown me the body. But, to answer some of the questions you set for Karim, the man knew exactly where and how to find you because the Empire told him. And who told the Empire is a matter that I shall soon discover.'

'I could have got you made Exarch of Italy,' I said. 'As it is, your brother was forced into the Church. I and my own blood only survived by reminding everyone that your father had been my son by adoption.' There was no point in putting on a show of bitterness. But, adoptive or blood, the man had shat all over his family.

'I know that my father worshipped you,' Meekal replied with what may have been genuine sadness. 'Your name was the last word he ever said. But then he was such a very good man. Without you to watch over him, he'd surely have died penniless and despised. Such a shame you had to be in Africa when the Lord Death came knocking at his door.'

One of the nice things about false teeth is that, even when they are, smiles never look natural. Mine wasn't. We fell silent.

'But your talk of adoption reminds me that I have a new uncle,' Meekal said with another of his grins. 'I can't say where you picked him up. But Karim tells me he's quite a stunner.'

I stared back in open hostility. To say that I feared any corruption of Edward's morals would have been a joke. Even so, this was a family get-together I'd put off as long as I could.

Meekal leaned forward and dropped his voice still lower. 'I say, Grandfather, would you fancy coming inside for a drink?'

I raised my eyebrows. 'I thought that was one of the few vices you had to give up on conversion,' I jeered.

He smiled again. 'Not really,' he said. 'So long as you don't do it in public, no one important really cares. Besides, I'm the man who broke the last stand of the rebel fire-worshippers in Persia. And in a land far beyond the knowledge of your geographers, I offered conversion or the sword to seventy-two thousand men whose brown faces were tattooed white. If the Great Meekal wants a drink after all that, no one dares object.'

'Better to reign in Hell than serve in Heaven,' I said in Greek, quoting Euripides.

'Not Hell,' he answered with a laugh, now back in Greek. 'It's anything but Hell. As for reigning – well, we shall see.' He got up and held out his hands. 'Now, do come inside. You look quite fagged out after a day in the sun.' I took his hands and let him help me up.

'Come in, dear boy,' I said without looking up. Edward came quietly into the office and sat down on the sofa. I continued reading back the notes I'd just dictated. I finished them and put them down behind me on the desk. I put my lenses on top to keep them in order. 'You can go,' I said to the secretary. He got up with a bow and left the room. I stared at Edward. He looked recovered from his opium. Sadly, the weals had come up over every part of his exposed body, and he winced at every move. His lower thighs were covered in a patchwork of bruises. It would be days before he felt better. He got up and came over to kiss me on the forehead. I nodded vaguely and motioned him back into his place.

'You are angry with me,' he said with an anxious look.

I thought of the wine jug still in its hiding place. Edward was in no state to fish about behind the big book. I'd get up in a moment.

'Not angry with you,' I said. I twisted painfully round and looked again at the notes. 'I am angry, I'll confess, but not with you – nor over anything you might think important.' He twisted carefully in his place and crossed his legs. I sighed. 'Look, Edward, I've been fixed for years on a project of sight improvement that I've now come close to making effective. I made further interesting discoveries while you were asleep. Now, by yet another happy accident, I've discovered this.' I reached round once more and took up a piece of parchment two inches by six. I'd dyed it black with ink, and had got one of my workmen to glue some one-inch leather studs on to it. At each end of the strip was a hole with a six-inch length of ribbon. I reached behind and tied it round my head, arranging it at the proper distance. 'You may not see the pattern of holes where this covers my eyes. But, so long as the light continues good, I can see you almost perfectly. So long as there is any sunlight, I can read better than with those lenses.' I pulled the thing off my head and dropped it on the floor.

'But surely, this is good news?' the boy asked. He looked confused. He'd plainly fixed it into his mind that I was angry with him. 'If you can see better with this than having to carry those heavy glass discs about, why are you not happy?'

Good question. I collected my thoughts to explain myself clearly in Latin.

'Because, Edward, I don't understand how letting the light into my eyes through a series of dots achieves the same effect as those lenses. I can imagine the deflection of atoms through a curved medium. These pinpricks are a mystery that destroys every theory of vision I've ever encountered. And because, Edward, I should have noticed something so simple as this before your grandparents were born. And because, Edward, I needlessly spent years in Jarrow – and, before then, years in Constantinople – barely able to read words chalked large on a board, let alone in a book. And because, Edward, right at the end of my life, I feel like a traveller who climbs over a ridge on what he thinks is an island and sees spread out before him a vast and limitless continent. Try to imagine the horror – or, at least, the sheer annoyance – of what I have discovered.'

'But if you can see to read,' he said, looking still more confused, 'does it matter if you don't know the reason? So long as you can read now, does it matter if you couldn't read yesterday?'

I sighed. Fair questions. And there was, even if the boy didn't realise, a good philosophical theory behind them. But drinks with Meekal, and then this, had soured me no end. I got up and, with much grunting, managed to lay hands on the wine jug. I poured two full cups and handed one to Edward.

'This should dull some of the pain,' I said. I didn't bother specifying whose. 'If you don't feel up to the banquet, His Highness the Governor will excuse you with all wishes for a better tomorrow. I, unfortunately, am judged fit to put in some kind of an appearance.' I sat down again with a heavy thump that reminded me of my own bruised bones. 'Do you know why I brought you here with me?' I asked. He sat up and leaned carefully forward. 'I brought you because I thought you might be of some use to me, and because I couldn't think what else to do with you. On reflection, I think it would have been better to pack you off to Spain.'

'They want something big of you?' he asked. 'Is it secrets of how to take Constantinople?'

'Sort of,' I answered. 'My grandson Meekal' – I ignored the further question in his eyes – 'was too polite to come straight out with it this afternoon. But he wants me to help complete the destruction of the Empire. I have no doubt you will be some of the pressure he loads on me to go along with him. I won't tell you when I guessed this much. But I do most humbly apologise for what I've semi-knowingly brought you into.' I finished my cup and reached ineffectually forward for the jug. The light was now fading, and someone would come in soon to light the lamps.

Edward got up and refilled my cup. He stood over me and looked down into my face. 'Then do what they want,' he said. 'What's one empire against another? No – these people have welcomed you with honour. All the Greeks want is to kill you. I can accept you're upset about the cure for your eyes. I can't see what the bother is about who rules in Constantinople.'

I smiled bleakly and took a fold of the boy's tunic between my forefinger and thumb. It was made of the thick-woven silk that costs its weight in gold. It suited him well. I tried to remember him as he'd been back in Jarrow, with that silly hairstyle and those dirty rags he used to wear. Even with every reason to treat me well, Meekal would have trouble not to rape him on the spot. There was a gentle knock at the door. One slave came in with a lighted taper for the lamps, another to remind me of my bath and the fine clothes that had been sent up to adorn me. Pulling on Edward's arm, I got up.

'I've given instructions,' I said, 'for you to be put to bed with one drop of opium in warm honey juice. Please make sure not to ask for more than that.'

Edward stopped at the door. 'Do you think we'll get out of this alive?' he asked.

I grinned. 'I'll work on that,' I said.

40

'As my esteemed grandfather,' Meekal whispered as he passed by, 'you are, of course, exempt from the obligation to present me with a gift.'

I smiled and kept my place at the head of the queue. 'My dearest kinsman,' I said back to him, 'you represent the Caliph, in whose most generous hospitality I bask. I should be mortified to be treated differently from any other guest.'

He turned his mouth down and continued on his slow, ceremonial path to the high point of the banqueting hall. Dressed from head to toe in his usual black silk, he took his place before a vast tapestry that, in its chaotic representation of birds and flowers, was obviously Egyptian, and stood, with Karim on his left and, on his right, a much older man whom I recognised as the great Abbas – Deputy Commander of the Faithful and Admiral of the fleet that I'd watched burn to the waterline from my place on the walls of Constantinople. He looked grimly back at me, then, with a resigned gesture, nodded his greeting.

The hall was a square about two hundred feet on each side. Its roof, supported on four great internal columns, was a dome of glass bricks that glowed with the last rays of the setting sun. In preparation for the long evening ahead, great rings of lamps had already been suspended from iron hooks sunk into the glass bricks. Attached like acrobats by ropes to other hooks, slaves waited on ledges far overhead to swing silently out as required to attend to the lamps.

The floor was of polished black granite. Like the waters of a Kentish pond, it gleamed in the dying light of the day and the growing relative brightness of the lamps. Where the tapestries broke off, the walls were covered with mosaics from an older time of hunting and feasting scenes.

'It is an honour that I shall describe to my sons,' someone behind me said softly, 'to stand so close to the Magnificent al-Arik, Shield of the Greeks. One of my wives is niece to a man whom you caused to be instructed in the learning of the ancients. Her family, though now of the Faithful, still rejoices to have known your generosity of heart.'

'I shall be honoured to know his name,' I said gravely. The converted name of Hamid meant nothing to me. But I spoke well of his willingness to remember favours from the days when he still ranked among the Cross Worshippers.

But now the herald had taken his place just before Meekal. With two blasts on a silver trumpet, the gathering was called to order. He stood forward and raised his arms for attention.

'His Highness Meekal, Governor of Syria, trusted companion of His Majestic Holiness,' he cried in a loud voice that echoed from the back of the hall, 'Meekal, whose piety is known from a thousand battlefields and in innumerable works of charity, bids greeting to you, beloved guests and friends. Peace be upon you all. May you recall the words of the Prophet, upon whom be there peace.' There was a general mutter throughout the hall of 'Peace be upon Him.' The herald smiled, and took in another lungful of air. 'When asked what was the greatest good in the Faith, know that the Prophet replied, "Feeding others and giving the greeting of peace to those whom you know and those whom you do not know." '

So the man went on and on, while the guests shouted out the appropriate responses. I didn't think it would end, and that I'd have to pull the rank that age and achievements had earned me, and be taken off to my couch. But it did end, and we shuffled forward. With a flick of my tongue, I had my teeth in place. I opened my mouth and took a deep breath.

'Mighty Meekal,' I cried in a voice that was somewhere between a quaver and a shout, 'trusted and beloved friend of the Caliph' – I thought it best not to dwell on the family connection, even if it was a matter of common knowledge – 'accept this humble gift of a book that, nevertheless, contains the wisdom of the ancients.' I nudged the attendant who stood beside me. He stepped forward and presented the scientific work of Aristotle I'd picked up in Beirut. I'd made sure to have the pages taken out and cleaned and then rebound in white vellum with gold and silver inlays. Young Michael had been a crap student: his own taste in the ancients had never run beyond military history. Meekal the Merciless would never notice the gross corruption in two of the middle chapters – assuming it wasn't Edward's own reading that wasn't at fault. But it was a pretty book.

He glanced at it and smiled graciously. 'It shall, O Magnificent One, be placed among my most valuable treasures,' he called out in a great voice, 'and shown to my most honoured guests.' He dropped his voice and fell into Greek. 'And do have this, my darling Alaric.' Someone reached forward with a small golden box. 'You've already had your teeth back. I trust this, your recovered cock piercing, will be of equal use.'

We hurried through the formal kiss, and I was carried off to my dining couch. This, sadly, was placed right beside Meekal's. With the changes necessary for the difference of religion, this was a banquet that reproduced all the heavy formality of the Imperial court. Age would get me out of staying to the grisly end. But I reclined in the raised area of the hall, a couple of hundred other couches spread out beyond like the blocks on a polished wooden floor. My every gesture could and would be observed.

I maintained a diplomatic immobility during the reading from the Prophet's sayings, smiled benignly through the endless speeches and shouts of greeting to the Old One al-Arik, and finally took in one hand the loaf that Meekal held out to me. We broke it together and shared a drink from a goblet that was more impressive than its contents. The banquet had begun. It was the standard civilised food – fresh salads, pickled cucumbers, hummus eaten with unleavened bread. Some of this I could eat, some not. Beyond some goat that had been boiled down to a sort of jelly, Meekal didn't press the meat dishes on me. My teeth placed discreetly in their ebony box, I ate with a nice balance of the cautious and the grateful. I even managed not to drool too much on to my new banqueting robe.

One of the differences between Greek and Saracen dining is that the latter tend to eat in silence. It's one of the customs they brought with them from a desert where food is so rare that it isn't to be spoiled by the chatter of conversation. That saved me from the ordeal of having to be pleasant to Meekal. But, regardless of custom, he was hard at work with his secretaries. It was, so far as I could tell, the usual work of the powerful – petitions, diplomatic letters, internal administration. He drank steadily from a cup of what may have been ginger broth, and chewed morsels of food between dictating brief answers and instructions. Every so often, he'd dart a look of wolfish triumph in my direction. I countered these by ignoring him.

Once, after a long and very gloaty inspection, I called for the potty men. While one held the silver pot for my – genuine – call of nature, the other held the screens about me. It was, in every sense, a moment of bliss. As the screen was taken down, though, I saw Meekal was on his feet. Breathing hard, his beard thrust out straight in front of him, he was looking exultantly about the hall. Several hundred hands had stopped their steady scooping up of food, and everyone was looking nervously in his direction. Then, he pointed at one of the serving boys. I looked hard at the lad. He seemed well-made, and perhaps a few years older than Edward. I couldn't say more, as all that playing with lenses and dotty parchment had left my unaided vision worse than it had been. But I heard the quiet mutter of approval that ran about the room.

I shrugged as my own attendant rearranged my banqueting wig. This sort of thing would never have done in the Imperial court – not even under Constans. But this wasn't Michael the Greek. Meekal the Saracen could probably have taken the boy straight outside for a spot of bum fun. For my own reason, I rather wished he had. But the first courses were now being cleared away, and we had a most welcome break. I put my teeth back in for a desultory conversation with someone who came up and asked about the mosque I'd caused to be endowed in Constantinople. At last, he drifted off to bore someone else, and a small man with a boy walked into the one clear space within the hall. Now, the buzz of chatter fell silent. With a bow to Meekal and to me as guest of honour, he looked round. His mouth opened, his teeth a brilliant white against the brown of his face. He began.

'Once upon a time there dwelt in Egypt a confectioner who had a wife famed for beauty and loveliness; and a parrot which, as occasion required, did the office of watchman and guard, bell and spy, and flapped her wings did she but hear a fly buzzing about the sugar. This parrot caused abundant trouble to the wife, always telling her husband what took place in his absence. Now one evening, before going out to visit certain friends, the confectioner gave the bird strict injunctions to watch all night and bade his wife make all fast, as he should not return until morning. Hardly had he left the door than the woman went for her old lover, who returned with her and they passed the night together in mirth and merriment, while the parrot observed all . . .'

It wasn't a long story, but the repeated cheers and calls for the wittier passages to be recited over, dragged it out to what seemed a great length. It was made still longer by the flute accompaniments. I listened carefully, trying to keep the detachment of a philosopher and of a spy. The easiest part of spying is to find out how many soldiers the enemy has, and what use is to be made of them. You can't fault this for the purely military aspects of victory. Far harder is getting inside the enemy's head – to learn the causes that shape his manners and beliefs. So far as I was any kind of spy tonight, I was depressed in exact proportion to the entertainment. These people might be regarded in Constantinople as a race of barbarians just like my own ancestors. But this was a false assumption, based on recollections of how the Western Provinces had been lost. These people hadn't come out of their desert with little of their own. It wasn't a matter of waiting until they had adopted the superior ways of their subjects, and could then be evangelised and absorbed into our own civilisation. There would be no shadowy *imperium* extended here through the Church, aided by the occasional reconquest. If they copied from us, it was only to incorporate into a civilisation that could, in its own way, become equal to our own. Their literature stood on its own and needed nothing from us. Behind this rose their own Desert Faith – silly enough in its details, but without the terrible mess of Persons and Substances the Greeks had immovably fastened on the Christian Faith. We could, with our superiority in the sciences and with grim determination, hold their Empire from rolling forward into the Greek Provinces of our own. But these were not the Goths and Angles and Saxons. They were not even the Persians, as corrupt as they were alien. In time, they might appreciate Aristotle and Apollonius. They'd neither feel nor have any need for Homer and Herodotus. Least of all would they need Christ.

None of this was a new revelation. I'd been putting it forward for years in the councils of an arrogant, if increasingly down-at-heel, Empire. But, sitting here, watching those bearded faces shine with joy at a recitation that had nothing Greek in its substance or content, was a chill reminder that the victories in the East of Alexander and the Caesars were already one with those of the Assyrians and the Persians.

The story finished with a great burst of cheering, and the boy ran about the room, collecting the silver shaken out from some very large purses. There was an encore of flute playing from the boy while he danced about, followed by more silver. At last, he and his master went to the back of the room, where food would be set out for them, and we all settled back for the next round of courses.

'Is it true that al-Inkus was buried alive after communicating his secret to the Emperor?' someone asked behind me.

I perked and twisted round to see who was speaking. It was the Admiral Abbas. For the first time, I noticed that his left arm hung lifeless at his side. Another victim in the catastrophic defeat I'd seen from the walls of Constantinople? Perhaps.

'Callinicus was a man of great abilities,' I said, trying not to sound guarded. 'I believe he was an architect from Heliopolis – whether in Egypt or in Syria, the accounts differ. There is also some dispute over the manner of his achievement. Did he learn from an ancient manuscript, as some declare? Or did he make an original discovery? Since the man disappeared immediately after delivering his secret into the hands of the Emperor, no one can say. The manner of his death – if, indeed, he is dead – must ever stay a mystery.'

Abbas might have asked more. Just then, however, Meekal sat upright on his couch and looked straight at the pair of us.

'Can you smell fire?' he asked. I dropped my own proposed question whether the fried river fish now being brought round had the bones left in, and sniffed the air.

'Surely, my dear, it's the lamps,' I said, looking vaguely upwards. My sense of smell hadn't been that good in years. Now he mentioned it, though, there was a faint smell of burning. More to the point, others in the hall had noticed. Several men were off their couches and running over to the door to give instructions to the attendants. Then, far over to the left, there was a panicky shout of 'Fire!'. There was a mass scraping of couches and a clatter of dishes. Someone came up and whispered in Meekal's ear. With a roar of anger, he was on his feet.

'Get up!' he shouted at me. 'Keep hold of me while we get out. The fucking Empire's set fire to us.'

41

Panic abolishes most distinctions of rank, and Meekal had to use his right fist to get us across that shouting mob to the door. As we got there, we were nearly knocked over by a sudden reverse in the tide of escaping humanity. With Meekal to hold me upright, I stood a moment in the doorway and looked out into the darkness of the great garden in the palace. It was only a moment. But that was enough to see a bright ball of fire coming at us through the air. The earthenware jar shattered about three yards from us, sending up splashes of burning liquid to cling to anything it touched. I felt something catch the shoulder of my robe. It spun me round, and I nearly went over. As Meekal caught me and covered me with his own body, I saw a man go down. He landed a foot or so away, writhing and choking, an arrow in his throat.

Out of the darkness came a cheer of triumph and a shouted 'I know that my Redeemer liveth!'

Back inside the hall, Meekal pushed me into the arms of Karim and bawled an order that I was too busy looking about me to follow. It was a desperate, furious stream of instructions. I caught one look of his face. It had about it the cold ghastliness of the dead. Then he turned to put some kind of order into the dinner guests.

'Get that gate shut!' he shouted above the cries of confusion and of fear. 'Line up, men, line up,' he now bellowed. 'Swords at the ready.' There was a martial sound from the trumpet, and the familiar commands gradually brought order into the hall.

'I must get you out of here, My Lord,' Karim shouted into my bad ear. Fighting a sudden fit of the trembles, he clutched at me to stay upright. 'I am charged on my own life to keep you safe.' He shivered again, and nearly had me on the floor.

I shook my head. We were in a building of solid stone. It couldn't be burned down. If Abbas had been anywhere close in that chaotic hall, I'd have tried for a witticism about the use of fire in battle. But, if Meekal was bringing order out of chaos, it was hard to say that chaos didn't still have the upper hand. Whatever the case, running away with a jittery Karim didn't sound at all a wise choice. It would be safest to press against the wall to avoid being knocked over by the crush of men. But even as I thought how to explain this, there was a smash of glass, and more of those burning pots came flying through one of the high windows. These weren't hand-held projectiles. Somehow or other, the Angels of the Lord had not only got within the palace grounds – they'd also brought in some kind of artillery. There was a regular hail of fire into the hall. Men screamed and ran about as the burning oil stuck to clothes and flesh. Already, I could see that a couple of the men who'd taken direct hits would soon be dead if no one thought to put out the fires all over them. One of the tapestries was already on fire. It or the fuel that had carried the fire was giving off clouds of smoke that would finish someone like me off in no time at all.

But Karim was recovered from his fit. He had me up on his back and was carrying me through the increasingly orderly crowds towards the little door at the back of the hall used by the serving men. He rattled the door, then shouted a command at the trembling slave to get it open. We passed through into the sudden chill and silence of the darkness, and I heard the bolts drawn hard shut behind me. I felt the crunch of gravel under Karim's feet as he ran away from the building, and then the softer pad of his feet on grass as he dodged to avoid the men I could hear shouting and rejoicing somewhere close by. He put me down against a wall, and stood gasping smoke out of his lungs. I looked uselessly around. I knew the Tower of Heavenly Peace was on the far side of the palace. But there must be buildings nearby that would be guarded. If only there was a single light burning in the upper windows to let us see where these were. If only I could see anything other than a dark blur. Even the moon was out of sight.

'There's two over here,' someone shouted in Syriac. The voice wasn't above six yards away. Karim clutched at me again, and began the effort of pulling me back to my feet.

'No!' I said, now calm. 'You'll never outrun these men, or those who come to help them. Keep your mouth shut and leave this to me.' There was a sudden blaze of light from one of the wooden huts outside the hall used for keeping food hot in the winter months. With a tremendous effort, I got up and tried to look active.

'God be praised,' I cried in Syriac – and luck be praised I'd kept my teeth in. 'This is a blow for truth I never thought I'd live to witness.'

'What are you doing here?' someone snarled back at me. 'This is a job for the fit.'

I croaked a variant on 'Lord, now lettest Thou Thy servant depart in peace according to Thy word,' and giggled.

'Get the old fool out of here,' the voice snarled again, now at Karim. Plainly, he was taken in by my words, if not impressed by my presence. 'We're holding the eastern gate.'

That should have been it. We could have sloped off deeper into the palace grounds, and waited for the Palace Guard to get its act together. But as Karim was pulling me back on to his shoulders, we almost fell over about half a dozen other men.

'Get these wankers out of here!' the voice now commanded. 'We can't lose another Elder.'

And that was it. Pulled and shoved to keep on course, Karim was hurried off to the eastern gate. I thought of pretending a heart attack to slow him down enough to be left alone. But I could feel that Karim was in no state to play along with me. With the panting sobs of a man terrified out of his wits, he had his head down and was keeping pace. Swaying about over his back, I could see the bright mass of torches coming closer as we approached the eastern gate. I could pass as anything I cared to be. What to do, though, about that brown face and his Saracen clothes?

'Let us through,' I cried as we came level with the gate. I noted the fallen bodies of the guards. 'Let us through. My servant is wounded.' The torches parted. No one could see Karim's face. No one paid attention to his clothes. We hurried through into streets alive with people and more torches.

'Is the palace burned?' someone asked. 'Is the tyrant dead?' There was a ragged cheer at the very thought – though whether Caliph or Governor was in mind no one bothered to make clear. I clapped Karim on the back to keep going. Now staggering under my weight, he carried me into a side street and dropped me hard on the packed earth that served here in place of paving.

'How many Saracens are there in Damascus?' I asked. He leaned against a wall, wheezing and coughing. There was a blast of trumpets in the main road and the unmistakable tread of military boots. 'We can't stay here,' I added. 'Soldiers don't know friend from foe in the dark.' I repeated myself: 'Is there a Saracen district nearby where we can get shelter?'

He shook his head despairingly. Even now, Damascus was overwhelmingly Christian. The Faithful lived in encampments outside the walls or inside the palace. The only converts were local trash – persons of very low degree, he emphasised.

'Then let's just get away and hide somewhere quiet till morning,' I said.

Karim tried to protest. But I wasn't going back anywhere close to that palace while there was a riot in progress. Whatever his father had been, Karim wasn't a military Saracen. But if I wasn't much of a soldier either, I'd seen dozens of riots in Constantinople, and I knew exactly what to expect. Not waiting for him to pick me up again, I started off away from the noise. A sword would have been useful. These fine clothes made us walking targets. But the first rule of street fighting is to get away from it, regardless of what further trouble may lurk round the corner.

'So, where are we?' I asked after half a mile. 'You were happy enough the day before yesterday to show me the sights of Damascus. Shall we take this opportunity to see a few of them now?'

Karim stopped and took my arm off his shoulder. The clouds had parted, showing the nearly full moon. In its light, he guided me towards a bench. There was a heap of rubbish behind it and on both sides. If even I could smell it, there must have been quite a large dead animal rotting somewhere close by. The bench looked clean enough in the moonlight, however. Karim sat down and looked ahead in silence.

'We're lost,' he said at last without turning.

No shock there, I thought. My reply was a sniff. I looked at the high, blank walls of the houses that, here and there, pressed almost together overhead.

'At all times of the day and night,' he went on, 'these streets around the palace are crowded with Cross Worshippers of the lowest and most desperate kind. Once order is restored, we shall be lost among them. They will surely tear us apart. I have failed His Highness the Governor in allowing you to sit here, waiting for death. I have failed you, My Lord – and failed so ignobly. May my family curse the day that I was born!' His voice shook. It was as if I heard the tears rolling down into his beard. The Saracens were maturing fast into their exalted position: some of them weren't only non-military; they also weren't particularly brave.

'Then I suggest we get up and keep moving,' I said firmly. The last thing you want in a coward is a fit of the shakes. We'd never move anywhere with that. I looked along the street in the direction we'd been going. After a dozen yards, it twisted sharp right. Left or right, all the streets had been doing that since we left the palace. According to the moon, we were going west. Just a while earlier, it had been east. I sniffed again. No hint of a nosebleed was my first good news since I'd seen Meekal projected through my lenses. 'If only you lot might listen,' I said, 'you'd learn a lot from the Greeks about town planning. A grid arrangement of at least the central districts of a city can bring so many benefits. So, while we're on the subject, can a touch of street lighting. We can only hope that continued progress along this dried-up riverbed of a street will bring us somewhere safer than we are now.'

As I was about to push myself upright, there was a sound of running footsteps from where we'd come. I looked round. The sodding moon was full out – not a cloud in sight. There was nowhere to hide. Even if Karim was up to lifting me again, he'd never outrun whoever was coming our way. I thought of telling Karim to take to his heels. There was no reason for both of us to be butchered. But what I'd feared in his case had come to pass. He was clutching at himself and leaning forward. He began droning some edifying gibberish from his Holy Book. I sighed and tried to make myself comfortable on the bench.

'What the fuck are you doing there?' a man shouted in Syriac. 'We've got the whole Palace Guard after us, and you just sit there, waiting to be cut down!'

'I told you there was an Elder went off this way,' someone whined at him. 'You tell me now I was wrong.'

Panting from the run, a big man with a bushy beard stood before me. He turned and waved at the three other men with him. 'Get him up into your arms,' he said. 'He'll never get away by himself.' He knelt down and kissed the hem of my robe. 'Forgive me, Father, my profane words, but we cannot afford to lose another Elder to the darkies.'

I patted his head uncertainly, then uttered a benediction. No one bothered with Karim. If he wanted to get away, now was his moment. But, as I was lifted off the bench and perched between two of the Angels of the Lord, I saw that he was getting ready to tag along beside us. Oh, well, I thought, explaining him as well wouldn't be much harder than explaining myself.

As we moved off, I thought I heard the thud of hooves on the packed earth of the streets. It really wasn't my evening.

42

If I'd so far thought little of Damascus as a capital, the vast labyrinth of stinking alleys into which we now plunged confirmed my opinion of the place. Except that most of it was newly built, and it had never been other than it was, it reminded me of the Egyptian quarter in Alexandria. But that had been a very long time ago, and I'd always then been able to protect myself from the human trash who lived there, or been able to run away. Here, I might as well have been a sacrificial animal, bound and carried towards the altar. The only consolation was that I didn't have to spoil my nice velvet boots on those now filthy streets.

We came to a stop at the end of a little street that had snaked round and round on itself. I was set down against the wall that terminated the street, while the men who'd been carrying me put their backs into moving a broken-down cart that seemed to have been left where the wheels had come off it. Beneath was the stone cover of what I could see at once had, before the troubles brought on Damascus by the Persians, been the sewers. Because the city had been rebuilt without regard to the ancient street patterns, these were no longer used for their original purpose. As I was handed down through the narrow entrance, I breathed in cautiously through my nose. It wouldn't have been hard, but the smell down here was somewhat better than in the streets above. The paved central channel was now dry, and we were able to make better time than we had been above.

We hurried along the straight tunnels, the torch of the man before us flaring and roaring with the speed of our progress. I could hear the increasingly laboured breath of the men who were carrying me, and the echo of their heavy tread on the stone channels. Here and there, we turned into another tunnel. Here and there, I could just make out signs of frequent use as a thoroughfare: recently dead torches fixed in their brackets, heaps of weapons, even the dismantled parts of an artillery catapult. Of course, I can't say in which general direction we were heading. It might have been further in to the centre. It might have been away. At length, however, we came to a doorway crudely hacked into the ancient brickwork. Piles of rubble from the work almost blocked the continued way ahead. Some narrow passageway however had been left through the rubble. In the brief glance that I managed down this passageway, I could see that there was a regular junction a few yards ahead of perhaps three other tunnels. No one without a good knowledge of these tunnels would easily seal off all the approaches.

There were more torches within the doorway, and a man came out to see if we represented danger. He looked briefly at me in my fine, if now soiled, robe, and bowed low before me. I gave him another of my benedictions. Karim walking beside me with palpable terror, I was carried through an arched cellar towards a flight of stairs. These were worn down by age, and I felt them crumble still more beneath our weight. At the top of these was a stout wooden door. With a pattern of knocks that were repeated on the other side and then renewed, the door was unbolted from within, and we passed into a room that seemed as brightly lit as the banqueting hall had been.

We were in the nave of an old church – no, I could see from its shape and the remaining decoration to the walls that we were in what had once been a temple. From its size, it must have been somewhere close to the ancient centre of Damascus. Before the establishment here of the last Faith but one, the temples of several dozen gods and demi-gods would have jostled for prominence, and been thronged with singing, garlanded worshippers, come to make sacrifice. This must have been one of the larger temples. Given daylight and more time, I might have been able to tell for whose cult it had been built. Then again, I might not. The windows that had been cut into the walls on its conversion to a church were now bricked up again, and I could have no idea whether there was still any direct access to the streets outside. There was a strange kind of service in progress. Over in what served as the chancel, a priest was chanting a *Te Deum* in Greek. Around him, a few dozen worshippers made their unscripted responses. Here in the nave, perhaps a hundred men lounged about, drinking and looking pleased with themselves. Mostly young, they had the pinched, wiry look of the urban lower classes. They weren't the mountain fanatics we'd helped organise into the Angels of the Lord. Even so, it was plain they were gathered together to fight and, if need be, die for the Orthodox Faith.

My carriers put me down beside one of the walls. This was covered with the usual paintings of saints and Gospel happenings. The paint was now chipped and rubbed away in places. Most importantly, all the large, staring eyes of the anciently clothed figures had been scratched out, in some places leaving deep holes in the plaster. Every representation I could see of a cross had also been defaced.

It might have been interesting to see more of the building, and to speculate on its recent history. But now, every head in that nave was turned in our direction. Whatever assumptions had been made about us in the unlit streets evaporated the moment we were pushed inside the first pool of lamplight. All else aside, Karim's brown face stood out in that gathering like a rotten tooth. Over in the chancel, the priest let up his chanting. The exultant chatter about him died away. Wherever I cared to look in that church, I saw hard, unsmiling eyes.

'Who are you?' one of the older men asked. 'And' – he looked straight at Karim – 'what is *this*?'

'Greetings, my dear Brothers in Christ,' I said, stepping with my best effort at a firm tread away from the wall. I leaned on the back of a chair and looked benignly about. I felt the sudden need of a piss. But I held myself steady and continued speaking in the hesitant, softened Syriac of a Greek.

'I am Seraphinus,' I said, reusing my assumed name from Caesarea. 'A Greek from Smyrna, I am travelling in this now benighted realm to bring comfort to my relatives. This boy beside me is my servant. Though dark of face, he is as true in the Orthodox Faith as I am myself.'

'There is no God but Allah, and Mohammed is His Prophet,' Karim said, breaking the silence that followed my own words.

I groaned inwardly. What a time the stupid boy had chosen to find an ounce of courage. But I shuffled left and trod hard on one of his feet. He yelped. Given luck, that might be the end of his contribution.

'It was a glorious blow that you all struck this evening against the dark hordes who feed like lice on the fair body of Syria,' I said in a jolly tone. 'Let us join together in prayer for our eventual deliverance.' I wondered if my cock piercing might still be somewhere about me. It was pure gold, and might turn a few heads.

'It is the Old One himself,' someone squealed. 'He lives and is among us!' There was a loud groan all about, and much shuffling and scraping of boots on the unswept floor. I saw the glint of a sword held in the shaking hands of a boy who might have been about the same age as Edward. Not a good beginning, I supposed. On the other hand, it saved the trouble of introductions. Now that standing wouldn't make much difference to what happened next, I hurried round and sat on the chair. It increased the itching in my bladder, but took the weight off my shaking legs.

'This is surely a sign from God!' the priest called. He hurried over and raised a hand as if to strike me. I frowned at him until he dropped his hand. I could do nothing, though, about the lunatic glint in his eye. 'Behold, my sons, how futile are the hands of man. So long as you relied on your own weapons, the Old One escaped your every effort. With Satanic spells, did he not evade you in Beirut? Was not your attack on the road to Damascus a miserable failure? Now it is plain for all to see that your attack on the palace, where he feasted and caroused with the brown filth of the desert, has come to nothing. Yet, here he is – directed hither not by the hands of man, but of God!'

I did think of reminding him of the previous night's failure. But he seemed in no mood for interruption. His last sentence he howled in a Syriac that showed long residence in Constantinople. Sure enough, I didn't have to wait for confirmation.

'It was in the Imperial City itself, where I was but a deacon, that I heard of his speech to the Emperor's Council. "Let us not take back the Orthodox of Syria into the bosom of the Empire," he said with poisoned tongue. "Let us rather leave the bounds of Empire to embrace only those whose native language is Greek. Let Orthodoxy become no more than part of the glue that binds Greek to Greek. Let us only trade and fight and stand strong in the world as a nation of Greeks. Let the Orthodox of other tongues be confounded with the Jews and the heretics, to make their peace with the Saracens." '

It all showed how news gets around. Proceedings of the Imperial Council are supposed to be confidential. If this man had been in the Council Chamber, taking minutes of the session, he'd not have quoted me with greater accuracy. Even before he'd finished his report, there were screams of less well-informed denunciation. 'Death to the Old One! Damnation be upon him!' someone bellowed close beside my bad ear. 'God wills it!' an old man quavered behind me. Someone too young for a proper beard lurched at me, knife in hand. I waved him back as well. Curled up like one of my roasted bugs, Karim huddled at my feet.

I sat forward in the chair and looked coldly about the room. I might have been in the audience room of my own palace in Constantinople, looking over the crowds of supplicants I'd usually allowed in after breakfast. And I took the chance to continue racking my brains for some reason why the pair of us shouldn't be torn limb from limb. In that ship off Cartenna, I'd been faced with one of those times when even I couldn't think of an excuse without *some* preparation. This, however, wasn't quite one of them. Since the priest had set the tone of the proceedings with a speech, I'd surely be given right of reply. If nothing else, I might be expected to plead for mercy before not getting any. I moved my tongue to flip my teeth back into position. I shut my eyes for a moment to gather what remained of my strength. I got up on my feet.

As I stood, I raised my arms for silence. It was like the killing blow to a wounded animal. At once, the room was still. I could now hear Karim reciting over and over: 'There is no God but Allah, and Mohammed is His Prophet.' And very useful that was to what I had in mind! But I ignored him and hoped everyone else would. I stepped forward and walked with commendable firmness towards the sanctuary. It was mostly very young men in my way, and, if no one actually bowed, the crowd parted before me. Without pausing, I walked through the broken, defaced remains of the iconostasis and stood before the altar table. For just a moment, I raised my arms to the cross that was still visible in outline on the painted wall in front of the altar. Then I turned to face the completely silent crowd. Breathing hard while I felt for my voice, I looked round the church.

It was now, over on the right, that I saw there was a little chapel. Its doorway had obviously been cut into the old temple wall at the time of consecration. I couldn't see fully in from where I stood. But there was a lamp burning inside, and it all had a pleasingly mysterious look about it. But I stopped the useless effort of trying to focus and looked back over the hushed, expectant crowd.

43

'Great men of Syria, dear brothers,' I began in Syriac, dropping all pretence of a Greek accent. 'It is said that God Himself has brought me here tonight. I will not deny the obvious. How else could an old man in my condition bring himself from the Palace of the Tyrant to this ruined but still defiant House of Faith? But was it so you might kill me that I now stand before you? Was it for the sake of some vulgar display that Our Heavenly Father brought your best efforts to nothing, and then – in His own miraculous way – conveyed me here to address you?

'No – a thousand times, no!' I cried with raised hand. I paused and let my voice produce some faint echo from the hard walls. 'I come here not as sacrifice, but as messenger. If I cannot be killed, it is because God watches over me.' There was a scared murmur from somewhere in the room. I paused again and let it gather strength. Then I lifted both hands for silence and continued. 'Know you this, dear Brothers in Christ. I am returned from a land on the edge of the world. I come from what was anciently a province of the mighty Empire established by the arms of the Romans and long sustained by the hand of God. I come to a land that is now under the judgement of God. Because of the manifest sins of your countrymen who rejected the Truth laid down at the Council of Chalcedon for the heresy of the Monophysites, the Persians were sent among you – to smite all of Syria with fire and the sword. Did the Syrians repent? No! They waited passively for the Greeks to liberate them and bring them back within the bosom of the Empire. Did the Syrians then show gratitude for the deliverance granted at the hands of the Greeks? They did not! They persisted in the darkness of heresy. Therefore, while the Persians had been suffered to chastise you with whips, the Saracens were raised up to chastise you with scorpions.

'O men of Syria! I say unto you that the Jews and heretics sinned who welcomed the Saracens as deliverers from the True Faith of Chalcedon. But did the Orthodox themselves do other than bow their heads beneath the new yoke of darkness?' I stopped to gather breath and to let the babble of sobs and self-pity rise in volume. I glanced briefly at the priest. He wasn't looking happy. I hadn't directly answered his point about my wanting to leave his people to shift for themselves. Nor would I. But I was, I could guess, preaching a far better sermon than he'd ever managed. Karim was looking up from the floor. How much of my Syriac he was following was anyone's guess. It was close enough to his own language. But, if the wooden Greek he spoke was any indication, his linguistic abilities were limited. Fortunately, he wasn't my audience. I waited again for silence, then continued.

'But surely all is changed. I stand now not before sheep, but men – and men who have never been other than steady in the love of Christ. Your courage and your resolution have softened the heart of God. By your exertions, you have saved your own souls. By your example, you will save all of Syria. And that is why now I stand before you. With my help, you are to strike a blow against the darkness that shall never be forgotten. I am the Herald of your deliverance. How that deliverance shall be achieved is not yet to be given to you. But be assured – I am the Herald of the One God, the One God manifest in Three Persons.

'Hear my message, O men of Syria. And let me depart in peace.'

I was rather hoping for a burst of applause, and then to be carried in triumph round the church. However, if I didn't get that, no one seemed inclined to butcher me at the altar. In dead silence, I stepped down from my place and walked back to my chair. Once more, the crowd parted, and, unmolested, I sat again beside Karim. I was glad he'd now had the sense to shut up about his Allah and Prophet.

After a long silence that I'd faced with the immobility of a statue, someone got up and announced a 'conference of the Elders'. This was to take place in the chapel. More lamps carried before them, about a dozen of the older men now walked inside, and the nave fell silent again.

It was a long wait, and I heard repeated bursts of shouting – though less the antiphonies of debate than the reading and responses of a liturgy. I couldn't make out the responses, but they were angry. I thought at one point the discussion was over. But it was only someone come out with a cup and a jug of beer for me. I'd have preferred wine. Beer, after all, was for common people in Syria – and it reminded me too much of Jarrow. But a cup of beer is always preferable to a knife in the guts, and I took the cup with a graceful nod. I drained it and handed it back for a refill. Throughout the nave, there was a slight easing of tension. I leaned back into the chair and thought hard about the movement of light atoms through a pinhole. Perhaps, within that narrow space, the atoms of air were somehow concentrated to make a kind of lens. But that made no sense. Because they had to be unhooked from each other, air atoms were always evenly distributed. Any bunching in one place would be corrected as atoms moved into the relative void around them. I wondered if the effect might somehow be produced within the eye itself. That was a possibility. I might even live long enough to refine the hypothesis and think of an experiment for testing it.

I smiled at a young man who was gawping at me, and held my cup out expectantly. The beer did bring back memories. Caught between two groups of ruthless, fanatical God-botherers, the quiet calm that had mostly been in order at Jarrow suddenly didn't seem so very unattractive. But I'd not be left for ever to my own speculations. The Elders were now filing out of their chapel, and I was to know my fate.

'God is with us,' said the man with the biggest and greyest beard. I gave him a display of my ivory teeth and waved my cup in his direction. That was it for the moment. The Elders were getting into position about the altar. I thought of the relative darkness within the chapel, even if there was a lamp burning, and made a mental note to investigate how colours and light intensities appeared to vary according to the eye's own expectation. But now the Chief Elder had his arms up for attention.

'With God on our side,' he opened with grim reluctance, 'we shall never be defeated. Instead, we shall destroy the followers of the Desert Impostor – sweep them straight into Hell. Then we shall have our reckoning with those who passed by on the other side when confronted with ungodliness. There is a time, soon coming, when Syria shall again be free and Orthodox.'

'Amen to that!' I cried softly, trying not to look as sceptical as I felt about the means to achieve this impossible and probably undesirable deliverance. But the words had been spoken, and I wasn't to be killed. There was suddenly a whole crowd of jabbering Syrians about me, all boasting of their past and future service to an empire that had long since given up on them as other than a useful irritant. I'd never have guessed it from the Elder's brief statement. But I'd swung them round. One of the other Elders pushed his way through the crowd and took my hands in his, holding them for a long and almost respectful kiss.

'You are leaving at once,' he said. 'There will be a chair to carry you to the Fountain of Omar. From there, you can make your own way back to the palace.' As he spoke, two men came round from behind to stand before me. They bowed low and then reached forward. I handed my cup to Karim and spread my arms so I could be lifted out of the chair.

'You go alone,' the man corrected me. He looked evilly down at Karim. 'The darkie goes nowhere but Hell.'

I put my arms down again and ignored the men who were hoping to lift me. 'We came here together,' I said with a smile. 'We leave together.' There was an embarrassed silence. The Elder who stood before me shifted his position and looked nervously round. I forced myself to lean forward and place my hands over Karim. 'If you want to kill him,' I said, 'you'll have to kill me first.'

'My Lord,' the man said with slow desperation, 'if we allow him to live, he will surely bring men back here. His life is forfeit. He knows the deal.'

Karim certainly understood that. He whimpered and clamped his arms around my knees.

'The deal is,' I said with my coldest command, 'that the boy comes with me. I'll vouch for his silence.' I sat back and took no further part in the shouted discussions. I really needed a piss.

The Fountain of Omar gleamed new and black in the moonlight. It filled the centre of the square that contained what had once been the Church of Saint John the Baptist. As in Beirut, this had now been converted to the use of another religion, and shone an undifferentiated white. From my earlier visit of so long before, I recalled a forest of statues in the square, some of these going back to the early successors of Alexander. All that now remained were the empty plinths, their inscriptions covered by a thick wash of rendering. I might have seen a pile of broken statuary heaped up in one of the side streets. Or I might have seen nothing of the sort. But I was in no mood for looking at the sights of the new Damascus. I'd been set down on a wooden bench to look straight over at the mosque, and left there with no one for company but Karim.

'The Night Watch will be coming past at midnight,' he said, not looking at me. Though he wasn't to be killed, the Angels of the Lord had still given him a difficult time. He'd not been kicked about too hard. Even so, he'd been spat on and roundly abused. His response had been less than might have been expected from a son of the fearless Malik al-Ashtar.

'I must say, dear boy, that we've had a most lucky escape,' I said. I reached up and carefully scratched the back of my scalp. Karim was looking hard at the mosque. 'Did you see if there was anyone watching us from that little side room in the church?' I asked. In a moment, Karim would surely start playing along. For now, he continued looking stiffly ahead.

'His Highness the Governor told me to guard your life with my own,' he said at last. 'Would it be a lot to ask if you were to say nothing of what has happened this evening? I mean – is it possible to replace all that happened after we left the banqueting hall with something different?' He stammered and squirmed at the unspoken recollection of how, once I'd saved his life, he'd been made to kiss an icon and abjure his Prophet.

I smiled at him with an audible click of ivory, and placed a hand on his shoulder. I really ought to have been on the edge of collapse from exhaustion and strain. In fact, I felt like a young man of barely seventy.

'Of course,' I said comfortingly. 'I can think of many reasons for managing perceptions of our little adventure. I might suggest, however, that Meekal is no fool, and it would be best if the slight deviation from the truth that you mention didn't include a role too creditable to yourself.' He nodded vigorously and let out a breath of relief. 'Excellent!' I said, now brisk. 'Then I suggest we incorporate your undeniable ignorance of Damascene geography and be rather vague about our movements. These will include a long shelter in one of the many derelict churches I have noticed, and a long and uncertain progress to where we shall, no doubt, soon be discovered. Of course, since every wall in a palace has ears, I do also suggest that we never refer to any of this even when we think we are alone.' He nodded again. We lapsed into silence, and I strained to see if the clump of broken whiteness I'd seen earlier really was broken statuary, or something entirely different.

'I hate them!' Karim suddenly hissed. 'I hate them all!' He doubled up and clutched at himself. I began some desultory comment about 'People of the Book', and how our captors had been a minority within a minority. But he ignored me, and carried on speaking more to himself than to me. 'Why must we use Imperial money?' he spat. 'Haven't we gold enough of our own? Why must we use the Empire's language? Isn't our own good enough? My people conquered Syria. Why are we now expected to fit ourselves in to Greek ways? I hate them all. I'd see them all put to the sword!'

'My dear Karim,' I observed mildly, 'you surely forget that I am a Greek myself.' He looked at me, a strange confusion in his eyes. I thought quickly, then laughed. I patted him gently on the shoulder and searched for a change of subject. I remembered the jug of beer that had been left with me. I had to threaten my poor joints with actual dislocation to reach down and get it. But it was still half full. I took a long swig and then looked again at Karim.

'I know that wine is not allowed to the Faithful,' I said pleasantly. 'Does that include beer?'

Karim stared at the jug held under his nose. He sighed and took the offered bait. 'I think it does,' he said in a tone of firm piety. 'The prohibition should be taken to mean anything that disturbs the mind. This being so, wine should be taken as a specific instance of the general class.'

Good lad! I thought. One day, he might have enough Greek to appreciate Aristotle in the original. Or perhaps the old windbag might find himself decked out in Saracen clothing. A shame it wouldn't be Epicurus instead. Or perhaps not.

'That being so,' I asked again, 'where does it leave kava and hashish and opium? These also disturb the mind, but I've never known them to be regarded as unlawful among the Faithful. And what of the verses I heard interpolated in this evening's recitation:

> Joyless in this world is he that lives sober,
> And he that dies not drunk will miss the path of wisdom?

At last, Karim laughed. The tension relaxed and he sat properly up. He took the jug and sniffed its contents. Luckily for his morals, it was one of those beers that tastes better than it smells. He handed it back and watched me drink deep.

'You don't know what you're missing, my dear boy,' I said. 'Plural marriage may have its moments, but doesn't beat a good piss-up.' We passed to reminiscences of his father, who might well have pulled things round for Ali in the civil wars, if only Muawiya's assassins hadn't got to him when they did. Looking carefully into the young man's face, I mentioned how, with Ali left in charge, the realms of the Caliph might today be no smaller, but have a very different shape.

But now there was the heavy tread of military boots on old Greek pavements. It was time for the Old One al-Arik to show once more his legendary management of perception.

44

I woke in my own bed with a splitting headache. Worse, Meekal was glaring down at me. He grunted and scowled as I opened my eyes and looked at him. I pointed feebly at the jug on the table. He poured a cup of lemon water and carefully raised me up so I could drink.

'So you survived even that!' he said in Greek, sitting back down. He waved the doctor forward.

I shut my eyes again and thought of nothing in particular as the man passed his chilly hands over me, checking pulse, poking and prodding, muttering away to himself over what he was finding. I opened my eyes when he was done and tried to sit up.

'No, my beloved grandfather,' Meekal said, 'you just stay where you are for the moment.' He turned to the doctor, who nodded and then shrugged. He was a typical doctor. I might be at death's door. I might be ready to train for a torch race. His manner was all the same.

'So I really am still alive?' I croaked. From the shadows the sun was casting in the room, we were already late into the afternoon. I closed my eyes once again and tried to stretch my weary, over-strained limbs. I thought of my reception back into the palace: the hugs and tears from a scared Edward, the loud prayers from Meekal, still reeking of smoke, but now got up in armour and covered in blood, the silent and terrified Karim. I must already have been out cold when I was carried back here. Certainly, I had no recollection of anything once the palace gates had thudded shut and I'd been thrust into a carrying chair. I'd slept the morning through. With a sudden thought, I forced myself into a half-sitting position. The doctor got some pillows behind me, and I was able to lean back.

'How long have I been asleep?' I asked. Meekal got up and paced over to the window. He stood with his back to me. 'What day is this?'

'If I set a task for that fool Karim beyond his abilities,' he said without turning, 'I am willing to blame myself. But I expected better of you than to get caught up in an Imperial terror attack – especially when this attack party had been sent specifically to murder you. That you survived last night is less down to anything you did than to the fact that God is on our side.' He stopped and continued looking out of the window. Was that a prayer he was muttering under his breath? I couldn't tell. If it was, though, this wasn't the Michael I used to know. I suddenly realised that, but for him, the whole suite seemed absolutely quiet. 'It's Thursday,' he said, now redundantly. 'You've lost only one morning of your remaining time before you must stand before God.'

'Where is everyone?' I asked.

Meekal turned to face me. His beard had been waxed and pressed into something that resembled a pair of sharpened ox horns. He came back over and sat down again. He pulled his chair closer and stared at me with his freezing, dark eyes.

'Get out,' he said to the doctor, still in Greek. 'But I correct myself,' he added, sliding at once into the ceremonious politeness of the powerful, 'let me show you out.' He got up and pushed the man from the room.

Once alone, I lifted my arms and held them out before me. I bent my knees up and tried to touch them with my chin. With a bit of strain in my upper back, I just about managed. Still tired, and now conscious of aching all over, I settled back, reasonably content. If I really had fatally overstrained myself the night before, it didn't show up on my own examination. I'd see what I could find on Meekal's face when he eventually returned from his conversation with the doctor.

I sat watching the movement of a shadow cast by a chair. It moved steadily towards the edge of one of the larger floor tiles. The whole suite was creepily silent. The shadow had just crossed over to the next tile when Meekal came back in. He dumped the golden key to the whole suite on the table beside me and sat down.

'I kicked all your shouting, messy workmen out when they downed tools for lunch,' he said quietly in Latin. 'How they didn't wake you this morning is a small miracle. I cleared everyone else out with them. I understand that my pretty new uncle went off earlier in the day with Karim to watch the public executions. Had I known of this in time, I would most certainly have prevented your boy from leaving the safety of the palace. Because of his family connections, I am sadly unable to discipline Karim. But I will speak with him about this. In the meantime, your boy is safe enough. And letting him see the public executions may serve a useful purpose. We didn't take many prisoners last night. But I think the boy will be impressed by the show we can put on here in Damascus.'

'And now we're alone,' I said, trying to smile. I looked about for my teeth. But my gums were sore, and I didn't need to stand on ceremony with Meekal. 'I don't suppose there's any wine left in my office?'

'It was my intention to let you settle into your rooms here in the palace,' he went on, ignoring my question. 'I was to take you on a tour of the city tomorrow, so you could see the Faithful at prayer. The day after that, we'd get down to business. However, in view of last night's attack – coming so soon after the earlier attempt on your life, I think it appropriate to come straight to the point.' He paused and looked at the golden key. He got noiselessly up and crossed the room to the door. He pulled it suddenly open and looked up and down the corridor outside. He closed the door and went over to the window. He shut the glazed frame, and then pulled down the silken blind. Light now came from the glazed window overhead, but this was of double glass and was already fastened. He sat down again.

'You do know why I had you brought here, don't you?' he asked. 'You know why we had you lifted from under the very noses of the Intelligence Bureau. You know why we brought you all the way back here, right through Imperial waters. I'm sure you appreciate the diplomatic triumph required to get the northern barbarians to do as we wanted. And I'm sure you appreciate how much it cost us to get that ship designed and built. So, must I spell out why you are now here, and received with such lavish honour? Why is it that we have even decided to overlook your apostasy from the conversion you made in front of the Caliph Omar himself? As you ought to know well, the punishment for apostasy is death.'

'You tell me, my dear,' I said, patting my nose with a corner of the white bed covering. I looked down to see if I'd been bleeding again. I hadn't. 'You might also tell me why you'd arranged a meeting for me at Kasos. How you'd have got a fleet there is beyond me – especially since you don't even control the sea approaches to Beirut.'

Meekal smiled grimly. He got up and went over to a sofa that was turned to catch the light from the window. He took up a scroll and unwound it to a place already marked, then stood in a pool of sunlight that came from above.

'I found this on your desk this morning,' he said. 'I didn't expect you'd overlook anything so flattering to your own place in history – and this does flatter you, as you will agree.' He cleared his throat, and, in a remarkably melodious Saracen, went over the passage I'd been reading the night before last. He reached the hard word that had stopped me, and went straight on:

And among the numberless ships of the Faithful sailed the five ships of al-Arik; and lo, al-Arik raised his golden sword from his place upon the walls, and the morning sun glittered on the armour of the Old One as it does upon the waters where mingle Tigris and Euphrates; and there was a sound of drums and many trumpets; and fire spat from the mouths of five pipes that were within the five ships.

And a roar of thunder was in the fire spat forth from the five ships; and like unto a spear shaft that is set alight, the fires leapt five and even seven hundred cubits across the waters of the sea, and fell upon the ships of the Faithful, and these were burned utterly to the water.

And behold, the fires shot upwards and downwards upon the water as directed; and yea, the fires were unquenched by the waters poured upon them, but burned even on the water; and the sea was set alight, and countless ships of the Faithful were caught and burned even as they fled the shafts of fire from the five ships of al-Arik; and there was great slaughter among the ships of the Faithful.

And the Greeks sent ambassadors among the Infidels of the North, and gave much gold, saying, O good men of the north, take now this money and depart from the City upon the Two Waters, lest the fire that jumps and is not quenched shall be also rained upon you; and the Infidels of the North lost heart and went from the place with much astonishment and fear.

And other ships of the Greeks now came forth and spat fire even at the Faithful who waited in armour upon the shore; and the slaughter was wicked even as the breath of the Angel that of old blasted the men of Sakkenah as they rejoiced in their moment of triumph.

And Yazid looked upon the many fires and the smoke of the fires, and cried out in a loud voice . . .

Meekal stopped reading and tossed the book unclosed back on to the sofa. The sun overhead fell on him from behind, and his face was hidden in shadow.

'Your chronicler writes like a man who was there to see the catastrophe,' I said.

Meekal pursed his lips and sat down again. 'It was the greatest combined operation across those waters since Xerxes,' he said, back in Latin. 'We lost more men under the City walls than we sent out for the conquest of the whole Persian Empire. It had taken us five years to build that massive fleet. You burned it to the waterline in a single morning. Add to all that your harrying of the retreat. Of the armies we sent out – the flower of the Saracen youth – not three hundred broken, half-starved men made it back to Damascus. The shock killed Muawiya. Oh, he carried on another few years. But you should have seen him. No one who'd known him before could leave his presence without weeping.'

'And I'll bet it made you feel sick, my dear,' I broke in. 'You said in your parting letter to Constantine that the Empire was finished, and that you'd soon be back in the City at the head of a Saracen army. If you'll pardon an old man's vulgarity, you thought you'd come to piss on our corpse. Instead, we sat up and fucked you with a broom handle.' I laughed so much at the look on his face that I went into my first coughing fit in months. It had been their first proper defeat – and it had changed the whole balance of power in the world. 'You should have seen the service we laid on in the Great Church,' I spluttered. 'It went on all bloody day!'

'We brought you here, Grandfather,' Meekal said through gritted teeth, 'and are loading you with honour and protecting you from the Empire, for one obvious reason.' I smiled up at him and thought of teasing him with a pretence of senility. But he was going into one of his fierce moods, and I didn't fancy a slap round the face. 'We brought you here,' he hissed, 'so you could give us the secret of the Greek fire. Our next attempt on the City shall not be a failure. I want to know the secret of the Greek fire.'

I laughed again – not worrying if I coughed my guts out, or what tears ran down my face, nor even if he boxed my ears. I laughed and gasped and pointed at the cup of lemon water. Now alarmed, Meekal grabbed it and held it to my lips.

'Oh, dear me, Michael,' I wheezed. 'You've got the wrong man here. If you want to know anything about Greek fire, it's surely Callinicus you should be speaking to. All I did was recognise its potential and put up the money the man demanded. You want Callinicus for the secret itself – him or the reigning Emperor. No one else knows it.

'But I suppose that means you'll have to put me to death now,' I said with a mocking parody of fear. 'It also means you'll need a fucking good story for when the Caliph gets back. From what you tell me, you could have gathered another siege army for the money you spent on getting me out of Jarrow.'

Meekal said nothing. He went over to the sofa once more and took up a bent strip of dark enamelled gold. It was in the shape of a hair band. He put it over his face and arranged it to cover his eyes. I saw the afternoon sun sparkle on the dozens of small perforations where the eyes would look on to the inside. He came and sat down again.

'I took this from one of your workmen,' he breathed very softly.

'It is a wonderfully simple cure for bad eyes. Once you get used to looking through the many holes, reading becomes so much less of a strain. Why it wasn't discovered many ages ago adds only to the genius of the man who at last commanded it to be made.' He paused and took the thing off. He gave me another of his unblinking stares. 'Now, my dear grandfather, you can stop playing with me. I know perfectly well that there is no Callinicus. There never was a Callinicus. Nor was there any body of ancient writings he may have found in Egypt. You – and you alone – are the man who made fire for the Greeks. And you are the man who will make it for us. You were the only shield Constantinople had. You will now be our own Sword of Damascus.'

45

There were limits to how far even I could push Meekal. Rather than deny the obvious, I hugged myself and looked happily up. He stared silently back, his face a mask of greed and triumph – and also of a kind of pleading that took me back to when he was a boy and, scared of another beating from his tutors, needed help with a lesson.

'My darling Michael,' I cried, 'did you work that one out all for yourself? Or did you get someone to do it for you?'

He ignored the insult, noting only the confession. His face relaxed as if after an orgasm. His lips moved in some renewed and voiceless prayer of thanks.

'I knew on the first reports it had all been your work,' he said. 'Everyone else was taken in by your story of this Callinicus. But I'd spent too much of my life hearing you talk of matter and its combinations, and the benefits of its artificial combination. I only wondered why it had taken you till the last moment to save the Greeks. Was it your sense of drama?'

'Not really,' I said. 'Its discovery was one of those happy accidents. I'd been looking for some while into a combination of elements that would have enough explosive force to propel a thousand arrows at a time. What I found lacked the full explosive force I needed, but had all the other properties described in your chronicle. We did try it out on some barbarians who were attempting to raid a city on the Black Sea coast. That revealed one or two errors that nearly spoiled its effect. But we'd corrected those well enough by the time Yazid ordered his big assault on the walls. Ah . . . !' Meekal had fished once again on to that sofa, and now had a jug in his hands and two cups. 'You always were a good lad,' I quavered, 'or you were whenever you weren't being a complete bastard,' I added more firmly. I took the offered cup and sniffed its heady contents.

Meekal leaned over me. 'You will, of course, reproduce the Greek fire for us,' he said. 'You will help ensure that our next attack on the Empire will be victorious – that we can counter their fire with our fire, and that our great numerical advantage will count in full.'

I put the cup down and looked about for my teeth. One of the springs was coming loose, and now was as good a time as any for fiddling with it.

'I'd have thought, my dear boy,' I replied without looking up, 'that, with all the resources of the Caliph at your disposal, preparing a very simple compound would all be in a morning's work.' I waited until I knew there'd be no response. 'Well, well,' I gently mocked, 'the new masters of the world – and still they can't think for themselves. Even with Syrians and Egyptians in the harem, the Saracens still can't match the science of the West.'

'We have been trying ever since it was first used against us to reproduce your compound,' Meekal said. 'Every attempt has been a failure. Our most hopeful effort, some while ago, resulted in the death of five hundred irreplaceable craftsmen. It's only because of God's most infinite mercy that we didn't lose the whole programme.' He put a hand on the bedclothes over my knees. 'Grandfather,' he asked earnestly, 'Great and Mighty Alaric, we need your help. Will you help us?'

'And what reason can you give me,' I asked, 'for doing as you ask?' I moved my knees from under his hand.

'I could remind you that you are an honoured guest of the Caliph,' came the reply.

'And I could remind you that I was abducted by agents of the Caliph,' I said.

'That doesn't count,' said Meekal. 'You escaped and then came here of your own free will.'

'The only reason I'm not snug in my English monastery,' I snapped, 'is because you abducted me in the first place. Besides, I went to Beirut, and was living there quite happily on my own means. I'm in Damascus simply because you sent Karim with an invitation it would have been unwise to reject. Don't deny that I'm your prisoner. And don't wave your supposed hospitality in my face when you want me to commit treason.' I took hold of the bed sheet with both hands and pulled it up to my neck. I looked at Meekal and sucked my lips over the toothless areas of my gums.

He looked back, the prongs of his beard quivering with suppressed emotion. Then, he relaxed and smiled.

'You speak of treason, O Great and Magnificent Alaric,' he said. 'You have been condemned already as a traitor in the Empire. You are an outlaw there. Its agents have tried to murder you twice in the past few days. Can you still think yourself bound by any duty towards the Empire?'

'Possibly,' I said, 'possibly not. I am mindful, however, that, with or without me, the Empire is the only power in the world able to look you people in the face. Destroy the Empire, and there will be no stopping you from going west, and taking your religion with you.'

'I never thought religion mattered so much to you,' Meekal replied with icy control. He got up and went to the window. He looked out for a long time, then turned back to face me. 'If I could persuade you that an age would come when no one even believed in God, you'd jump out of that bed and dance about the room.' He returned to my bedside and stretched out his hands. 'Now, stop playing the old fool with me,' he said. 'Get out of bed and come over here.' I took his hands and pulled myself up. He draped a sheet about me and helped me as, with much grunting and creaking, I walked slowly over to the window, and stood in a shaft of the warm afternoon sunshine. He helped fix my dotted visor in place and waved at the skyline of Damascus.

It was like seeing through a mesh grating, and the uneven glass of the window made things more confusing. Everything was broken up into blocks. Some of these were repeated. Most didn't fit together into a continuous whole. But this was the first time I'd really tried my invention; the brief inspections at dusk the previous day hardly counted. In time, I had no doubt, the ordinary eye could adjust. Even now, though, the invention worked. For the first time, I could see Damascus as other than a vague blur. I stared over the low huddle of mostly flat roofs – with a few splashes of dark red tiles – to the main buildings of the centre. And, through the thin clouds of dust and of wood smoke, I could see the line of the outer wall, and over that to the brown bleakness of the mountains beyond. All could be seen with astonishing, if discontinuous sharpness. But Meekal now had me by the shoulders, and was directing me to the sights in and about the centre.

'Do you see that squat building over there with the roof of green copper?' he asked. 'That is the Spice Market. It was built by Muawiya for the reception and sale of goods brought from the outermost limits of China. Can you see the building just to the left – the one with the blue dome? That is where silk from the Empire is worked into cloth of gold and exported to the Faithful in Scythia. I can show you banks and factories. I can show you mosques and churches and synagogues. I can show you crowded markets and camel trains a mile long. Our empire is one of trade and toleration. No one asks what another man believes. The only question anyone thinks it worth asking is whether a man is solvent. Everything you preached for seventy years in Constantinople about low taxes and toleration is a reality in the domains of the Caliph.'

It was a good speech. Its effect might have been improved had there not been columns of smoke rising above two of the biggest churches in the city. But there was no point in mentioning these. Already, he was clutching at me again and jabbering hard.

'Alaric – Alaric, turn about and compare yourself with me.' He stood back and spread his arms. 'I came here as a renegade Greek. I might have been a baseless criminal on the run. I might have been a spy. Yet, by the repetition of one sentence and the loss of a foreskin, I became the free and equal companion even of those whose fathers had known the Prophet. How long were you in the Empire? What repeated services did you render it? How often did you save it from its own drivelling senility? Was there ever a moment when the very trash in the streets didn't sneer at your barbarian origins?

'Yes, I want the secret of that Greek fire so we can try once more to take Constantinople. But we don't want Constantinople as another Alexandria or Ctesiphon, as yet another provincial city. We want it as the capital of a renewed world empire – an empire combining the discipline and regularity of the Greek mind with the enthusiasm and nobility of our Desert Faith. All is ready for us to step into the shoes of Caesar. And, yes, we do bring a new religion. But hasn't the Empire changed religion once already? The turn to Christianity was much more of a break than we offer. That was the destruction of polytheism by an Eastern mystery cult. What we offer is a purified worship of the One God, in which Christ continues to be honoured, but not as some quasi-divinity that requires all the resources of Greek philosophy to explain.

'Join us, Alaric. Renew the Empire. Free the world. You have been pulled out of retirement for one final achievement. Let that achievement be the creation of a free and prosperous world ruled by the caliphs of Constantinople. Surely, you can see how God has sent you here to be our Sword of Damascus?'

I watched Meekal work himself into another frenzy of eloquence. As his voice rose, and he switched between Greek and Latin and Saracen, I shuffled carefully round to where I could flop back on to the sofa beside that discarded chronicle. I looked at Meekal and pulled off my dotted visor. It showed me too many copies, in too great clarity, of the roots of his dyed beard and the increasingly wild look in his eyes.

'Oh, please, Meekal, please!' I cried, holding up my hands for silence. 'You've made your speech. Don't spoil the effect with repetition. You tell me that, if only I join you in shitting on the Empire, we'll have a better world out of it. If that's your meaning, I think I've heard enough. You might care now to say what I can expect from a refusal to join you in this venture. Does it involve an escort back to my lodgings in Beirut?'

That brought him back to his senses. 'Refuse my offer,' he said, his face pushed close to mine, 'and I'll kill you with my own hands. I'll kill you as an apostate.' He spoke slowly and with controlled fury. 'And, before you start whining that life is nothing much to lose for a man of your age, just reflect that I know you better than any man alive. And let's not also forget my pretty young uncle. I might – given proper reason – choose to regard him as my kinsman, and share with him under your will. Or I might spurn him as your last barbarian catamite. I could then find him a place among the Caliph's dancing boys. Or I could have his looks prolonged with a little nip of the gelding knife, and set him to combing hair in my own harem. I might even have him taught to sing most fetchingly to my wives.

'So, what is it to be, my darling grandfather? Will you join with the Faithful in spreading light over the world? Or will you die cursing the day my agents found your refuge in the West?'

'My time is upon me,' I said. 'In other words, I need a shit. Will you have the kindness to call some slaves up to attend to me?' I grinned and rubbed my belly. 'Or must Meekal the Merciless soil his hands with other than blood?'

46

'You'll need to push your finger in to get me properly clean,' I said, still leaning forward. 'Mind you, be very careful. I didn't like the look of those fingernails.'

Grunting and now farting himself from the strain, Meekal reached down to open the valve that sent a stream of water to carry my little offering into the downpipe from the Tower of Heavenly Peace. The shitty stain in the channel beneath the ebony seat he'd leave for someone else to clean.

'Ooh!' I cried in a voice that echoed about the room, 'you've a way with that oily sponge. What a bath slave the world lost when I rescued your father from outside that church in Constantinople.' I twisted round to look up into the stony face, and wondered if he was reflecting on the deficiencies of my argument. It was hard to tell if he was thinking anything at all.

Meekal helped me into one of the smaller sitting rooms. This looked over one of the less grand prospects of Damascus. But there was a table set with food. He took off the napkin that covered a dish of bread pulled from the inner part of a loaf, and waved at a dish of pitted olives and soft cheese. He went back along to my bedchamber and returned with the wine and the Saracen chronicle. I pulled my dotted visor down again over my eyes and looked through it. With plenty of sunlight falling on it from above, the chronicle was so clear before me that I could see small strands of papyrus where the copyist's pen had snagged the sheet. I scrolled idly backwards, looking out for the passage where Meekal had first stood before the Caliph and called out in a great voice his profession of faith. Perhaps, after all, the writer had the makings of an historian. I looked up and smiled into the sweaty, now desperate face.

'Look at this again,' I said, holding out the visor. 'Take it and look at it closely. When you snatched it from the hands of the man who was still finishing its ornamentation, you saw almost at once what its purpose was. And if you couldn't by yourself reproduce the elegant workmanship that lets it balance so lightly on the face, you could easily make a functioning copy for yourself.

'With the weapon I invented, it's an entirely different matter. The combustible mixture itself is made of specific ingredients that must be combined in exactly the right proportions. It must then be matured like wine – use it too early or too late, and it will not ignite. There is then what may be called the delivery system. The bronze kettles that hold the two mixtures – yes, there are *two* mixtures – must be of a certain hardness. The fire that heats the kettles must do so to a precise temperature: too low, and the mixture will not boil, too high, and it will explode. The spouts through which the mixtures are forced must, for the same reason, be neither too wide nor too narrow; and the steel must be hard enough to survive the repeated variations of temperature. The fire at the end of these spouts has rules for its heat and placement.

'What I'm saying, dear boy, is that the manufacture and use of Greek fire do not suggest themselves to the casual observer – though you know that already. Moreover, the business of reproducing the secret would need a cluster of skills that are beyond the abilities of any one man. If you want to make people see again, you could turn these things out by the thousand in no time – and do so without my further assistance. Or you could lock me in here and have me turn them out for you. If you want Greek fire, you need skills that I do not myself possess. And it seems that you need skills that are not possessed in Syria. You are asking me to oversee a project that would involve not so much reproduction as reinvention.'

I turned my attention to the food, and made sure to slobber as much down my naked front as I could. All the time, Meekal stood before me breathing hard.

'So you will do as the Caliph begs?' he asked during a lull in my noisy, unmannered eating.

'I thought it was you who was asking, dear boy,' I said. 'If it's the Commander of the Faithful himself who begs my assistance, perhaps I should await his return from whatever war he is fighting.'

Meekal crashed a hairy fist on to the table. There was a splash of cheesy water all over his black outer tunic.

'Will you do as I ask?' he now roared. 'Or must I bring that fucking child in and castrate him under your eyes?'

'Do that,' I said, 'and you can fuck yourself for the secret.' I took a sip of wine. I raised my arms and looked at Meekal. He looked back awhile, then reached for a fresh napkin and began wiping me clean. How much had this project cost so far? How much had getting me here cost? If you're a little person looking in, a government has unlimited resources for getting its way. But I'd been an insider too long to know other than the truth. It didn't matter how much of his subjects' gold the Caliph could steal from them: it always had more than one possible use. How much of this had Meekal lavished on the project? And how much of his prestige rested on the project's complete success?

'Now,' I said, getting up and walking out of the room. I left my sheet where it had fallen off me. He picked it up and followed me into my office. I pointed him into a chair and leaned on my desk in much the same position as I'd taken with the assassin. He waved the sheet in my direction. I wrinkled my nose at the spoiled silk and looked at him. He'd seen me naked having my shit. He could carry on seeing me naked. 'My darling Michael – or Meekal, or whatever else I'm supposed to call you nowadays – I have been made an offer I might not be able to refuse. You can bet your life I'll not accept it, though, until I have some proper guarantees of the boy's safety. Oh, and when I say "proper guarantees", I don't have your personal word in mind. The whole world knows how little that is worth.' I stopped and pushed my visor back down to see if I could read the titles of the books shelved against the far wall.

'I could adopt the boy,' Meekal suggested with a faint smile.

I couldn't read the titles. But I could see my old walking stick. Still bloody, it was propped between two blocks of the shelves. I walked forward and recovered it. A shame it was ruined. I'd been so pleased when I took delivery of it in Beirut.

'Michael,' I cried in a soft, menacing tone as I moved towards him. I leaned over him, lifted my visor and stared into his eyes. 'Do you remember that time when you were a boy, and I caught you torturing a puppy? Do you also remember how I set about you with a slave whip? You may give yourself airs and graces among the darkies and anyone else who's scared of your dungeons. So far as I'm concerned, you're still the little shitbag I was sorry almost at once I hadn't beaten to death.

'No, shut up and listen.' I moved my face closer to his. 'I have read the tiresome utterances of your new Prophet. I have had their deeper obscurities explained to me by a learned Saracen. Adoption, I have no doubt you are aware, is not allowed among the Faithful. And under the Greek law that applies to me and mine within the Caliph's dominions, Edward is already your uncle. You can no more adopt him than you can sodomise yourself.'

Meekal had been recoiling further and further into his chair – perhaps to get away from my less than wholesome breath. I now suddenly stepped back and hit him hard on the chest with my stick. He fell backwards, and only that fancy turban he was wearing prevented his head from cracking open on the tiles. I stood over his fallen body, holding my stick like a teacher's cane. What would the world not have given to see Meekal the Merciless reduced to tears by a silly old man? What would he have not given for it not to have happened?

'Now, get out of my sight,' I snarled. 'Come back when you have something better to offer than a puff of oral smegma.' I walked past him out of the room. As I was opening a window in the room next door to look properly over Damascus, I heard the main door to my suite crash shut.

'It might have been the opium,' Edward agreed.

I nodded sympathetically. While I was asleep, the slaves had come back in. It was useful that I was woken in more clothes than I'd been wearing when I dropped off. The light was going down fast over Damascus, and, through the still open window, I could smell the palace kitchens hard at work. We sat, a concerned Karim beside Edward, in the small sitting room where I'd earlier dined. Edward tried to look brave again, but went pale instead.

'You might wish to bear in mind,' I said, 'that to see a man flayed, after he's been made to watch all his children roasted alive, can sometimes be too much even for the hardened spectator at these events.' Karim raised an eyebrow, as if this were the first time he'd ever heard the point made. Edward went back to looking ashamed. Executions are a morning attraction in most cities, but I didn't feel inclined to ask where they'd been for the rest of the day. I only hoped Karim had given Edward a better tour of Damascus than he'd so far managed for me.

'So what are you both doing this evening?' I asked. 'You seem to have had a jolly enough day together. I imagine you'll want to round it off with a visit to a brothel or some other place of public recourse. If so, I regret to say that Meekal has probably given orders for Edward not to be allowed again through the palace gates.' Both faces dropped. Then Karim looked angry. I raised a hand to silence whatever outburst was coming. 'No,' I said, 'you should know that you cannot possibly hope to cross a man like Meekal directly. But I am sure the palace itself affords endless opportunities for entertainment.

'However, in young Edward's case, I do suggest a break from enjoyment. The Saracen tutor I employed the other day made his first visit this morning, but was sent away. I believe he will return with the dusk. For obvious reasons, Greek will be the language of instruction.' I saw Edward's face cloud over. 'Come now, my little son,' I mocked. 'Unlike our own English, Saracen does not allow clusters of more than two consonants. This helps give it – in the right mouth, that is – a most beautiful sound. You should learn it for its own sake, and because it is the language of your new friend Karim – and because I have never come across a language that did not turn out sooner or later to be of use. Go, then, and prepare yourself to receive your tutor. Karim, I am sure, will be happy to sit in on the lesson.'

I sat back and looked out of the window. The day was almost over, and, if I'd seen off that turd of a grandson, I could record no other worthwhile activity. So much still to do. So little time left in which to do it. I glanced at Edward and Karim. Their combined ages probably didn't go far beyond thirty-five. I sighed and looked again out of the window.

'You look sad, My Lord,' Edward said. 'Shall we not sit with you awhile?'

'Thank you, but no,' I said firmly. 'You go and get ready for that lesson. Don't bother looking in on me afterwards. I think I will spend the evening alone with some opium. The strain of the past few nights is heavy upon me. And I have yet to recover myself from the journey to Damascus.' I reached for my stick – no replacement had yet been supplied, so I'd washed most of the blood off the old one in the latrine – and began my weary progression back to bed.

Karim stood up. 'My Lord,' he said, now in Saracen. I stopped. There was something both urgent and scared in his voice. 'My Lord, if I could beg one more evening of you, it would be most gratefully received in certain quarters.'

As I wondered what he could possibly mean, I heard a movement in the corridor outside. Karim coughed loudly. Without any knock, the door opened, and an elaborately dressed eunuch entered.

'I come, My Lord,' he trilled in Syriac, 'from a person of the highest quality.' He was followed into the room by one of the household slaves, who set up an immediate babble about my not being disturbed. Karim stood forward with a small purse. He pressed it into the slave's hand and pushed the man from the room. The eunuch, his lead-ravaged face painted a fashionable green, smiled and bowed low. 'I am instructed to ask that My Lord should come at once,' he said with one of those thrilling descents of the voice that only a eunuch can manage. 'The secrecy of my mission has required a most delicate calculation of times with the changing of the guard outside this tower. If there is any delay, the mission must be cancelled.'

I looked at Edward, whose face was its usual blank. The conversation had been in a language he didn't understand, and it was plain that Karim had told him nothing. Karim's own face, if a little red, was a diplomatic blank.

'Are you in a position to tell me what all this is about?' I asked. He shook his head. I groaned, and thought of my soft bed and the still softer opium that would carry me into a night of blackness. 'Get me ready,' I said wearily. 'And get me a cloak. There was a chill breeze last night that I'd not wish to expose myself to again.'

47

Surrounded by a wall nearly as high as that of the main city, the palace must take up about a fifth of Damascus in size. As I'd suggested to Edward, it was a world in itself. I hadn't been able to explore very much of it. But my own experience of the Imperial Palace in Constantinople – of which this was largely a copy – had told me what to expect. The curtained chair that carried me out of the Tower of Heavenly Peace moved briskly across the surrounding lawns and into one of the larger buildings. Through the silken meshes that allowed no one to see into the darkened interior, I peered out at my surroundings. Now at a pace deliberately slow and stately, so as not to attract notice, we passed through a set of halls, each of the most lavish magnificence. The lighting was so brilliant, I had no trouble using my visor to see around.

In perhaps the largest and most lavish of these halls, there was an erotic dance in its early stages. A blonde girl stood naked on a raised platform. Arms and legs wide outstretched, face upturned with eyes closed, she jerked and twitched in time to the music of drums and wailing flutes that came from below. I saw the glitter of nipple rings on her large, erect breasts. On each side of her, naked boys, their bodies painted gold, hopped and gyrated in time, though with less restraint, to the music. Before her, covered all over in silver scales, a black girl knelt. I watched fascinated as, tail first, and inch by inch, she fed a live snake into the blonde girl. In and in, the thing went – a good five feet of it. Anatomically impossible! you may cry? Well, I saw it happen, and in good light. Before my chair had carried me too far past to see more, she'd got virtually the whole thing in. Now, her flat belly distended, the blonde girl moved more freely to the music. The snake's head poked out like some dark, mobile penis. The boys capered and strutted, their own dance punctuated by bursts of rapid wanking. About the platform, large, bearded men sat in a semicircle. Beside each was another naked girl. I had the impression they were all drinking wine. Certainly, their growls of appreciation sounded drunken. At times, they drowned out all but the higher squeals of the flutes. Before my chair had passed completely through a gateway of polished granite, I heard a still louder roar from the men, and heard the scraping of sandals on the marble floor as if everyone was getting up to press closer about the platform. But I could now see nothing through the curtains of my chair, and we were soon passing through other, much smaller rooms.

I saw men sitting around gambling. I saw men and girls and boys huddled together in groups, clouds all about them of smoke that smelled of burning opium. I saw conjurers and acrobats. In one room, I even saw an old man, dressed in a Greek cloak and demonstrating one of the proofs from Euclid on an immense board that filled the entire far wall. His lecture was followed by a crowd of men and boys, who scratched silently away on waxed tablets.

Now, we were in the open again, and could move more quickly. I felt the carrying slaves jog over lawns and gravel paths and, more often, along paved routes. We skirted several large buildings on which bright torches had been fixed. We passed through another building that was internally in darkness, though, from the echo of the footsteps of the carrying slaves, was no less magnificent than the first building. I felt the rise and fall from level, and heard the dull sound of leather on wood as we passed over a long bridge. There was the sudden chill and darkness of a tunnel, then more grass and gravel. It had rained briefly while I was under cover, or there had been late watering of the gardens. I could smell the wet marble as it mingled with the shrubs and flowers about me. Though always distant, I heard competing strains of music and loud cheers. On one occasion, I heard the shrill, continuing screams as of tortured boys or women.

At last, with a smell of aromatic wood smoke, and the sound of heavy bolts drawn shut behind us, we were in yet another building. We stopped in what I thought was a large entrance hall, though the light was too dim for me to see out with or without my visor. Except for the loud breathing of the slaves, there was no sound. After some time spent waiting, the eunuch who'd collected me poked his green face between the curtains.

'If My Lord will consent to be helped down,' he whispered, 'there are strong arms to carry you into the Presence.'

I nodded, and made sure to climb slowly from the chair all by myself. There were a few lamps carried by black girls that allowed me to see for a few yards around. Two black eunuchs, both naked but for their jewelled loincloths, bowed together and reached out their arms to take me. I waved them away and leaned hard on my stick. There was a tongueless murmuring of protest, then the green eunuch gave a halting order in some language I didn't know. Walking slowly for my benefit, he led the way to a small latticed door at the end of the hall. As he got there and waited a moment, the door swung silently open, and we passed into a small and dimly lit antechamber with two doors in the far wall. One of these doors opened, and we were now in a small sitting room. Decorated with an almost smothering heaviness of tapestries and cushions, two chairs were set to a table where I could see and smell the pot of spiced kava. I was beckoned into one of the silk-padded chairs, and the room emptied.

I sat in silence. I poked my tongue against the left spring of my teeth. It was beginning to annoy. Worse, it was causing me another burst of salivation. As I pushed the teeth out of contact with the sorest points on my gums, I wished I'd remembered to bring some more of the gum steeped in opium that had always served to take away the pain.

Suddenly, I heard the door open again. I was now sitting with my back to it. I got up to turn round.

'Please, My Lord,' a woman said in Saracen, 'there is no need to stand on my account.'

Already on my feet, I pretended not to hear. I leaned on my stick and turned. It was a woman covered all over in black in the Eastern manner. It's hard to tell much about a woman when she's swathed like a corpse at a funeral. But I could see she was both fat and unusually tall. She spoke the elegant language of her nation's higher classes, and with the unstressed firmness of one accustomed to command. But for the voice, I'd have taken her figure for a man. She hurried forward and took my hand. She raised it to the heavy black veil that covered her face, and I felt a brush of lips against my fingers.

'Do, please, be seated, My Lord,' she said softly but urgently. There being no one else to do the honours, she poured two cups of the steaming liquid with her own hands. 'Will My Lord take sugar?' she asked, uncovering a dish of the shining, black crystals.

I shook my head. I'd once found it a pleasing luxury. Nowadays, though, it tended to set my gums off still worse when they were sore. We sipped awhile in silence. This was good kava – not the already powdered stuff you mostly see in Constantinople, now direct trade with the Red Sea coasts has been cut, but freshly roasted and ground. It was spiced with cinnamon and something dark that I could sense, from the slight racing of my heart, was a stimulant.

'Since we have both passed the age of any reasonable temptation,' she said, 'and because we may be seen as related, you will surely not consider it a breach of manners if I choose to make myself comfortable.' She reached up and pulled at her veil and head covering. I saw a mass of black hair and, below that, a faintly brown face. Though pockmarked and a little bloated, it was a good face – very regular features, and well-proportioned. She saw the look of polite confusion on my own face and laughed.

'I suppose that silly boy Karim simply packed you off here without telling you anything at all,' she said. 'Well, let us get over the matter of introductions. You are the Senator Alaric, trusted adviser to Caesar since long before the Prophet was other than a despised preacher in Mecca. I am Khadija, widow of Malik al-Ashtar. Please accept my most respectful greetings.'

'Madam,' I said, 'I am delighted to make your acquaintance. And, if I may be so bold as to mention it, your own fame in the world is not forgotten. Who, indeed, will ever forget the woman who, on horseback, rallied the fainting Saracens at the Battle of

Ctesiphon, and led them in a charge that shattered the last regular army of the Persians? There is even an epigram in Greek on the event. I can see that Karim is blessed on both sides of his family. I must, however, wonder . . .' I ran out of words. How on earth could we be related? Had she been remarried to Meekal? If so, poor woman. But she was laughing at my inability to disguise the confusion.

'Dear Alaric,' she said, 'though I should be proud if he were, Karim is not my son. He was got by Malik on one of his secondary wives. Most sadly, she died giving birth, and I was given charge of the baby. Now, she had been a dancing girl in Jerusalem before my husband took her to his bed, and she said she had been assured that His Magnificence the Senator Alaric was her grandfather.'

I thought back over the fifty-odd years since I'd been in Jerusalem. That had been for the Restoration of the True Cross. There was no point asking if I might have got someone with child there. I'd spent all of my five days in the city – that is, all the time I hadn't spent telling Heraclius what to say and do – in a blur of drug-maddened sex. There was no point asking if I'd got anyone with child. The only question was which of the two or three dozen women I'd gone through had been Karim's great-grandmother. Free? Slave? Prisoner? Wife or daughter of someone important? That was beyond me.

'Of course,' Khadija went on, 'I was never sure how much credit to give the story. The girl was not entirely balanced, and she was given to pretending more of herself than was justified. Though Karim was told the story as a child, I also cautioned him against spreading it. I now see you in the flesh, however, and I can have no doubt but the girl was telling the truth.'

I thought of Karim. Could I see anything of myself in him? Now I thought about it, perhaps the ears. But there was no proper resemblance that I could see. Then again, we mostly spend very little time looking at ourselves, and never see ourselves as others do. If Khadija could see a resemblance, I wasn't ashamed to admit the relationship. But she was speaking again.

'When he was chosen by Meekal to collect you in Beirut, he was convinced the mission was a sign from Heaven. He has spoken nothing to me but your praise since his return to Damascus. I will not embarrass you with what he thinks of how you killed that assassin. But his father always spoke well of you. Among much else, he said you were the only one of the Greek negotiators whose word could be trusted. And, if he never doubted it was other than in the interests of the Empire, he was mindful of the support you rendered the followers of Ali in the civil wars. If only your warning had not been intercepted, my husband would never have made his last visit to Egypt.'

I smiled sadly. And it had been a sad loss. I'd backed Ali to the hilt. Without Malik by his side, he was no match for Muawiya, and had been swept aside in the consolidation of Saracen rule over the East. But there was no reflecting on what might have been. The question was, what did this woman want now? Anyone who believes that Saracen women are political eunuchs has never come across women of the higher classes. Come to think of it, he's never paid much attention to eunuchs. The last thing Khadija had in mind was an evening of gossip over the kava with her stepson's great-grandfather.

48

I finished my kava. There was a time when I'd have sucked in the residue at the bottom of the cup. This I'd have crunched and sucked until there was no more of the nutty goodness to extract. I was now more concerned about abrasions to my already sore gums. I emptied the grounds into a silver bowl set before us for that purpose, and replaced the cup on the small, polished table. Khadija raised the pot and looked a question at me. I smiled and watched as she poured again.

What did the woman want? I'd have my answer, soon enough – though not before every other subject had been exhausted. This was a diplomatic meeting. There was nothing here of the perfunctory courtesies, followed by hard bargaining, I'd known with her husband. This observed all the usual courtesy of the East. We used up the whole pot of kava on long accounts of our mutual relatives by marriage. It seemed I was connected, through Karim, to all the leading families who'd stood around the Saracen Prophet, and who now were the background government of all that the caliphs had taken. I spoke at length of the son from my second marriage, who was now Bishop of Athens, and of my son-in-law, who'd scored such a notable success in fighting the wild tribes on the northern shores of the Black Sea. Thanks to him, I'd been able to make up fully for the loss of the Egyptian grain tribute with a more natural set of trading arrangements. I watched closely as she paid attention to this. I took a risk, and spoke more of the last news I'd had of the Empire's gradual and silent victories in pacifying the northern frontiers.

'Is it necessary for you to withdraw for a few moments?' she asked delicately as I finished my last cup of the hot beverage. I smiled politely. I'd come out with an empty bladder, and I could go quite a while longer yet. She got up and went over to the door. She opened it and clapped her hands loudly. Even before she was back in her place, one of her black girls was already coming through the door with another tray of refreshments.

'Do honour me by trying one of the figs,' she urged. 'They are grown in the most sheltered garden of the palace, and they are now at their most succulent.'

It wouldn't do to take my teeth out in front of her, so I put one in my mouth and, trying not to let the seeds get under my plates, pulverised it with my tongue. I washed it down with another sip of hot kava. Unless my taste was now messed up, this new pot had left out the stimulant. I sipped again less cautiously. Nevertheless, my mind was beginning to work faster, and I could feel a cold sweat in my armpits.

'We have long been aware of the Empire's recovering strength,' she said with a change of subject and tone. 'When the generation before my own encountered the Greek and Persian Empires, the Soldiers of the Faith advanced as if into a desert. They swept aside armies without soldiers and took cities without people. Even before the disaster of our attack on Constantinople, however, we knew well that those days were past. At first, it seemed a question of brilliant holding actions by the Empire's generals. We thought that, if only we could throw in army after army, those hard but shallow defences would collapse. But, every time we broke through the defences, we found that provinces, devastated only shortly before, were resettled and newly prosperous. And, always, we were pushed back out by the people themselves. We were facing an empire with better ships, better military discipline, and increasingly better internal conditions than our own. Our advantages of wealth and of numbers meant nothing.'

Khadija spoke on with coolness and general understanding that wouldn't have been out of place in an Imperial Council at its best. What she said I mostly knew already: how the collapse of every empire and kingdom in the East was bringing problems of over-extension, with armies stretched thin and local rebellions and disloyal governors. Even without the civil war, there could be no serious renewed attack on the Empire. But it was interesting to hear it all confirmed.

'Do you remember,' she suddenly asked, 'what you said to my husband at your last meeting?'

She'd got me again. We'd spent days aboard a Saracen galley – it was when we still balanced each other at sea – arguing about joint control of Cyprus.

But she was continuing. 'You told him that, like all other barbarians, we'd have one generation of conquest, and another of greatness. By the third generation, corrupt and disorganised, we'd sink into feebleness. We are now heading towards that generation, and what you said to Malik is now something often discussed.'

I nodded and thought of trying another of the figs. Otherwise, the soft biscuits looked interesting. Sadly, even soft biscuits had hard crumbs. There was a knock on the door and the green eunuch entered. He bowed to me and presented Khadija with a slip of parchment, folded over and sealed with wax. She broke the seal with her thumbnail and glanced at the contents. Her face tightened and she looked more closely. She looked up and smiled an apology. She rose and took the slip over to the main ring of lamps. She held it over one of the flames until it was all but a cinder, then dropped what remained into a tray of sand.

'If the messenger expects an answer,' she said coldly, 'tell him there is none.' The eunuch bowed to her and again to me. As he pulled the door noiselessly shut, Khadija sat back down opposite me. She composed herself with a visible effort.

'Alaric, because he is a renegade,' she resumed, 'there are those who doubt Meekal's loyalty to the True Faith. I do not share this vulgar prejudice. I believe his conversion was genuine. I believe that his zeal is no cover for a second treason. His conduct in holding Syria together, after Muawiya had slid into his long senility, is proof enough of that – as has been his military conduct in the East. I also trust his judgement, that the Empire must be destroyed now or perhaps never. Steadily, with every year, the balance of advantage swings against us.'

She paused and took a long sip from her cup. She sat back and looked steadily at me through narrowed eyes. I made sure to clear my face of all expression. She continued looking at me. I broke the tension as, with a polite murmur, I finally removed my teeth and began sucking at one of the biscuits. It had a taste of nutmeg, though perhaps more of hashish.

'Do you agree that Greek fire is the key to Constantinople?' she asked suddenly. 'Do you agree that possession of the secret will allow us to destroy the Empire?'

I finished my biscuit. I rinsed a mouthful of kava over my gums. I replaced my teeth and smiled.

'If the reforms I put to Constans had been carried fully into effect,' I said, 'the question would now be whether the Empire could be restrained from an offensive of its own. However, even the partial implementation of my reforms has repaired the worst damage. Give the Empire another generation, and we shall see what tribute payments are then demanded of you and enforced. For the moment, the Empire reposes in the relative calm that your civil war has imposed on you. Another attack, with all your forces, might get you once again to the gates of Constantinople. Without a Greek monopoly of the weapon you mention, you might not be so easily driven away. That being said, I still fail to see how you can get through the gates. You've said yourself that the Empire's weapons are better in general than your own.'

She smiled and leaned forward. She put a gentle touch on my right hand. 'That is all very well,' she said. 'However, let me also ask how close do you think Meekal is to reproducing the Greek fire here in Damascus? He has been working on it now for eight years. The cost of the work has at times been crushing. It might have been still more if, after his last failure, steps had not been taken to limit his access to people and materials.'

I sucked on my upper plate and thought. I'd been right that Meekal was being pressed on the financial side. And that was one of the reasons I'd been lifted from Jarrow. Whatever the cost, it had been easier than breaking through that wall of resistance from the old families who stood about the Caliph. I sucked harder on my upper plate. I got my tongue under it and licked out a crumb that wouldn't dissolve.

'How close is Meekal to success?' she asked again.

I shrugged and pretended not to be looking closely into her face. 'Since I still haven't agreed to help him,' I said, 'I can't say anything at all about his progress. Surely, you'd have access to his reports.'

Khadija smiled again and shook her head. 'There are no written reports,' she said. 'As for direct inspection, Meekal has concentrated work out in the desert, twenty miles from Damascus. There, he conceals everything behind a cordon of impenetrable security. None of us knows what he is doing out there. We know about the big explosion there – indeed, we *heard* it here in the palace. We know the broad costs. We really know nothing else. I was rather hoping that you would be able to enlighten me.'

'My dear Khadija,' I said with a little smile, 'until – rather *unless* – I agree to help him, I shall be in no position to enlighten anyone.' A most interesting turn things were taking; all this talk of 'we' and 'us' was hardly accidental.

'You will not be aware, My Lord,' she said with another change of tone, 'of the earthquake of three years ago that levelled part of the sea wall of Constantinople. I only heard of it myself from a Syrian monk who was there for this year's Easter festival. This was a breach easily repaired. However, in the course of repair, it was discovered that much of the land wall was also on the point of collapse. Two entire miles of the wall must be taken down in sections and rebuilt. Though every monk in the City was pressed into the work, the Empire has neither money nor labour to complete the rebuilding to the quality needed until next year. This surely puts your confidence about the Empire's security in a different light.'

It certainly did. If Meekal got his way, nothing would keep him from riding into Constantinople. I took my teeth out again and looked at the chip in the ivory. It was beginning to annoy my tongue. I'd have it repaired sooner than planned.

'Madam,' I said, 'I think you are now asking me to set to work on a project that is more assured of success than I had thought. What makes you think I will assist in the destruction of the Empire that I served for so long?'

'Because it is the will of God that you help us,' she said, with another interesting emphasis on the 'us'. 'It is our destiny to replace all other kingdoms and empires with our own, and to replace all other faiths with our own. And you must realise how God has brought you here to help in the work. When Meekal suggested his plan to the Caliph, there were those who laughed even to his face. Yet here you are. The Imperial Navy could not stop you. The Angels of the Lord tried twice to kill you, and failed. In all the adventures of your journey, God has preserved your life. God has preserved you in health and strength. You surely must see the reason.'

'Perhaps I do see the reason,' I said with an attempt at a weariness I wasn't for the moment feeling. 'The problem is that I am but an old man. My best work is all behind me.' I would have said more. But Khadija was smiling again. She waited while I finished playing with my teeth.

'If it is the blond boy,' she said, now very gently, 'we can arrange guarantees that Meekal himself would not dare break.'

I took off my wig and scratched the crown of my head. It gave me time, and diverted attention from my face, while I thought about that one. It needn't have been a surprise that she too didn't believe the story about Callinicus. How she knew about the threat to Edward raised a number of possibilities – all of them interesting and perhaps useful.

'And I do appreciate the regard you pay to family matters.' She paused and gave me another slow look. 'I am told you have no posterity now within the Empire,' she said.

I couldn't keep my eyebrows from arching just a fraction of an inch. All that chatter of families, and she'd known my situation pretty well. Doubtless, I'd fathered bastards throughout the known world. But, aside from my son the Bishop – who was too pious to break his vows – all I had left that was certainly of my own blood was Karim. But I wrinkled my nose and smiled.

'Karim is a fine boy,' she said. 'And he thinks himself all the better for being yours. I have said that this family matter has been kept within the family. To be sure, it is not something anyone has brought to Meekal's notice. Even today, he prides himself on the adoptive connection.' She paused again.

Fucking old bitch! I thought. She hadn't entirely got there yet, but she was well on the way. And she was starting – in her ever so delicate Eastern way – with a threat: help reproduce the Greek fire, and see Edward and Karim outlive me; refuse, and see my blood spilled from two bodies, and kiss goodbye to Edward. I resisted the temptation to say bluntly what I felt – after all, there was more coming yet from her – and smiled again.

'But Khadija, my dearest kinswoman,' I purred, 'I appreciate your sense of religious destiny. I will certainly not argue with it. However, what you are asking surely increases the standing that Meekal has with the Caliph and in his councils. And let us be plain – for all you desire a final victory over the Empire, do you really want it *today*? And do you want it in the manner in which it is most likely to happen?' Her face went a darker shade as I spoke. That was the implication of all she'd been saying. Even so, I was breaking the rules of our conversation, and she had to work hard on that composure. 'Oh, come now,' I went on, 'let us agree that Meekal's idea of co-opting the Greeks and ruling the combined Empire from Constantinople is a sound one. But where would it leave the old families? Most of you still have your hearts in Medina. You live in Damascus only because that's where Muawiya decided to have his capital. You feel lost among the arts and luxury of the Syrians – and they, let me tell you, have always been regarded by the Greeks as a decidedly inferior race. Move the capital to Constantinople, and you certainly will spread your faith over parts of the world currently beyond your reach. But will it any more be *your* faith?'

I had just trampled like a battlefield elephant over all the diplomatic courtesies, and Khadija sat awhile in silence, her face politely frozen. Then, unexpectedly, she laughed. She pushed her chair back and reached up to scratch her head.

'Dearest Alaric,' she said at last, 'we do understand each other so very well.' I smiled and took another of her drugged biscuits. 'I will come directly to the point. We want the Greek fire, and I will promise and do whatever is needed to get you to work on supplying it. At the same time, I shall be grateful if you could ensure no breakthrough in Meekal's project until such time as the Caliph and all his Council are back in Damascus from the civil war. Above all, it would not be in the interests of the True Faith for Meekal to have the secret entirely to himself. It is our intention to conquer the remaining territories of the Empire – but not within the time that Meekal has in mind, and certainly not for the purpose that he has in mind. We cannot wait too long. But we can wait a little longer. Given our destiny, we have no need to strike while the walls of Constantinople are being repaired.'

I took my teeth out again and made proper work of the biscuit. I followed this with another of the figs. For the first time that day, I'd found myself with a reasonable incentive to call Meekal back into my presence and grant his request for my help. And I could look forward to the sight of his face when, on final completion of his project, it was handed straight over to Admiral Abbas or someone else who hated his guts.

There was another knock on the door. The green eunuch came in with a second slip of parchment. Khadija's face hardened again. Her mouth opened as if for some impatient comment. Instead, she nodded. The eunuch went back out. She turned to me, her face arranged into a smile that was almost charming. No one dismisses Alaric: he takes his leave. I pushed my teeth back in and gripped the table so that it shook. I stood up.

'My dear friend,' I said with as much ivory as I could show, 'this has been a most interesting conversation. But the hour is late, and I am, I must repeat, an old man. You will forgive me if I take my leave of your delightful company.' I looked again at the wall behind her. It wasn't a trick of the light. The tapestry that hung from ceiling to floor was swaying in some very gentle breeze. There might be a window open behind this. More likely, we were in a curtained-off area of a larger room. Behind that heavy silk, who could tell what secretaries were taking careful notes of all we'd discussed?

Beginning her own spray of gracious comments, Khadija took my arm as I walked back to the door, and made sure to give me into the hands of her green eunuch.

'Remember, Alaric,' she said, still inside the room, 'God has appointed all of us to work to a certain fate. Yours is to ensure that, even in Rome, the Faithful shall be called to prayer. We shall be victorious all over the world, and remodel it according to the will of God. It is your destiny to sweep aside the last barrier to our victory. The life of no one individual can be suffered to stand in its way.' Her eyes shone with holiness – or perhaps with whatever drug we'd been taking. 'God wills it,' she added. 'God wills it.'

'Though God may not will it for those who presently think it their right,' I said drily.

She suppressed a smile as, with little squeaks and much fluttering of hands, the eunuch led me back towards my chair.

49

For a man of my age, and in my situation, you will surely agree, my most sensible course of action involved bed until noon the following day, or such time as Meekal presented himself again. But, with those stimulants roaring away in my head, I wasn't feeling that sensible. And there had been something curious about the shadowy creature who was doing so much to stay out of my sight as I emerged back into the palace grounds. It had been a brief motion of greater darkness within the shadows on my left – that, plus some furtive looking about by the eunuch. But that would have been enough for Alaric in his prime. And it was enough for Alaric now.

I waited until we'd gone round the wall of a neighbouring building. I reached forward with my stick and tapped the shoulder of the head carrier.

'Stop here,' I said. I let another of the carriers help me down from the chair and walked up and down on the grass. Though sweating in the cool breeze of the night, I felt decidedly jaunty. I pointed at the tallest of the carriers. 'Take off your outer garments,' I said. I laughed softly at his look of confusion. I reached into the front compartment of the chair and took out my purse. I opened it and produced enough gold to buy all their freedom twice over. 'Help me into your clothes,' I commanded, 'and keep yourselves out of sight under those trees.' I went over to the chair and dumped my blond wig on the seat. Off came my visor, and then the eyebrows shaped from the lightest mouse hide. Out came my teeth. Now came off the artful mingling of white and red paint from my face, and finally the shaped leather jerkin that gave the appearance of muscle to my upper body. When put on me, the general slave livery of the palace hung from a thin, shrivelled body none but those who knew him well would ever have associated with the Magnificent Alaric. I thought about my stick. But, even damaged, it wouldn't have given the impression I needed. I could probably do without the thing for a while.

'Keep an eye on that gate over there,' I said firmly. 'Be ready to snatch me for a quick getaway.' The head carrier nodded nervously. I could probably trust them. In any event, I was committed to trusting them.

I walked with moderate briskness into the main hall of Khadija's apartments. I had a sheet of papyrus in my hands, and what I hoped was a credible story. But I was now a bald, drooling old creature. No one pays attention to that sort of slave when he looks to be about his business. The two guards sitting just inside the hall gave me the inspection you give to a falling leaf and went back to their conversation. I walked towards the latticed door. As I'd expected, there was one of the slave girls sitting in the antechamber. Evidently bored and half asleep, she looked up at me. I waved my papyrus at her and nodded at the other of the two far doors. She slumped back in her chair and paid no further attention.

I'd expected a larger room. In fact, it was little more than a cupboard. But I was right in my general surmise. This was divided from Khadija's sitting room by a curtain, and there was a table and chair next to the curtain, for notes to be taken of her conversations. Since the room was empty, I had no need of the story I'd been turning over in my head. There was a lamp in a bracket attached to the wall. Either this was turned right down, or it was running out of oil. Whatever the case, its flame waved feebly in the breeze from the shuttered windows. There was a stack of clean papyrus on the table. One of these was covered in writing that I was in no position to try reading. I took up the pens one after the other. They were all dry. The conversation I'd just had with Khadija was obviously one that she preferred to keep in her own mind. No sound of conversation came through the curtain. I thought to risk pulling the curtain a few inches where it brushed the far wall of the room. As I reached out, though, to take the silk hem between forefinger and thumb, I heard the door open from Khadija's main quarters.

'Your impatience for a meeting does not suit my convenience,' she said coldly.

I dropped my hand. I was glad I'd crept into this room, and that the door had one of those locks that doesn't make any sound. I looked at the chair. But moving it would probably make a noise. I held my breath and sat myself slowly down on the carpeted floor. I pushed my good ear as close as I dared against the curtain and concentrated hard. If anyone came into this room, I was already in what might pass for a sleeping position. It was a risk I'd need to take.

'I watched as his chair was carried off into the night,' I heard Joseph say. I smiled complacently at the sound of his voice, and it was only luck that I didn't brush against the curtain with my instinctive self-hug. He might have followed me to Jarrow and then to Africa and now to Damascus. He might – surely, must – nowadays be the brightest and best of the Intelligence Bureau. But no one gets much past old Alaric. One look in his direction, and I'd seen him skulking in those shadows. He was now speaking Saracen fluently and without any noticeable accent. They spoke briefly about matters that were of no relevance to me. Then Joseph asked abruptly, 'So, what did you think of him?'

'He's an old man,' she said. 'He's completely broken down by age, and the veins on his nose indicate much indulgence in the wine of the infidels. I'd never have supposed from looking at him how hard it's been to kill him.'

Joseph's response was somewhere between a laugh and an unpleasant growl.

'I can't say your people have been trying to much effect,' he jeered softly. 'They tracked him down well enough to his place of confinement. I understand they got their agent in place around the same time as Meekal got his. Your agent, though, seems to have done his job with singular incompetence. Alaric thought he was safe in Britain – safe beyond all civilised reach. It should have been easiness itself to kill him while he slept. Engaging the same race of northerners as Meekal had, and expecting them to be let into the monastery was unnecessarily complex. Whatever happened there, your agent failed miserably. Meekal's plan was rather more successful, and so Alaric was brought back into our world.'

'And, once you'd discovered he was back,' Khadija broke in defensively, 'I don't see that the Empire's own efforts were crowned with greater success. I've had a full report of what happened last night. Your people never so much as saw him once he was out of the banqueting hall.'

'That is unfortunate,' came the mocking reply. 'Our problem, however, was catching up with him. Meekal commissioned a ship that was too fast for our own ships of that weight. Last night, he had Karim to lead him to safety. You, my dear Khadija, had him locked in his own rooms. He still dispatched your best agent – and, if I hear right, with his walking stick!'

The conversation fell apart in mutual recriminations that were enjoyable to hear, but aren't worth reporting. That Hrothgar had been working for Meekal was old news – I could barely recall when the first suspicion had crawled into my mind. But it was definitely news that Cuthbert had been working for a different interest group among the Saracens. I should have guessed this from what Khadija had already told me. Perhaps, had I gone straight back to bed, it would have come to me. But it was useful to have the information directly, and with no reasonable doubt of its truth. I wondered if Cuthbert had known whom he was serving. If he had, he'd have been shitting on the Faith for a pittance. It really would have been interesting to get that document pouch open. It went to show that you should never pass up the opportunity to read another's correspondence. But I filed all this away for some future use. It had none at present. More useful was to know it had been Khadija and her friends behind the murder attempt of the night before last. That explained the assassin's knowledge of all relevant details. It also explained why the real Angels of the Lord had omitted the attempt from their own list of failures.

'But, unless you managed to poison him earlier this evening,' Joseph started again, 'I see you've given up on your plan of murder.

Does that mean you think you've made a deal with him?' I think Khadija nodded in the resulting silence. Joseph laughed again. 'You really do think you've made a deal with him,' he said in a tone of mild contempt. 'I suppose the deal is that he helps Meekal turn that money pit of his into a knock-out weapon against us. He then helps you stitch up Meekal so the weapon belongs to you and your friends. You can then escape this gentle prison among those you despise, and your friends can take back control of this Empire from those who want to provide it with stability and permanency.' Joseph was no fool. I hadn't trained him. But I could take pride that I'd probably recruited his trainers.

'Come, My dear Lady,' he prompted, 'isn't that what you think you've done?'

'And what would be so wrong about that?' Khadija asked sharply. 'Would that not also be in Caesar's interests?'

'It might,' said Joseph. 'But I would remind you of our earlier agreement – so much more welcome to the Emperor – that we should, at the earliest opportunity, help Alaric into the next world. None of us wishes Meekal to have in his own possession the most devastating weapon ever developed. But we do not wish any of the Saracens to have this. We may have little belief in the ability of anyone but Meekal to use it to proper effect. But a weapon of that nature is not to be trusted in any hands but our own. Let me ask, though, what reason you have to suppose Alaric will turn on Meekal.'

'Because,' Khadija replied, 'he has an adopted son whom only we can protect.'

That set Joseph off into another of his sneering laughs. And I had trouble not joining in with laughter of my own. This was glorious stuff. I hadn't spied with so much enjoyment since – court intrigues, of course, don't count – since I'd overheard a Lombard king versifying his next siege of Rome. Here was every apparently ill-fitting piece of the puzzle pushed into place. And here were two people subtly lying to each other in the hearing of someone who could recognise every lie and every suppression of the truth. It was better than a play.

'I do assure you, My Lady,' Joseph said when he'd given up on laughter, 'that the boy is of no value. According to my reports, he is a vicious, unintelligent creature. I have seen him myself, masturbating at some public spectacle of the obscene. If you think he can be used as a hostage to force anything out of a man like Alaric, you will be disappointed.'

'My own reports tell me otherwise,' Khadija said quietly. 'Let me assure you that we shall, within the next five years, reorganise your Bureau in Constantinople. Would you like to be its Director?'

More laughter – this time polite. 'And if he does give you the weapon on which you pin all your hopes of conquest, do you suppose it will be sufficient? Even without Alaric, our own programme has moved on. Greek fire, as he gave it to us, was always a variety of different weapons. We have now developed some of these in directions that would surprise him. What he developed could burn on water. What we have now can be ignited by water. You will not have heard, I am sure, of the victory we gained early last year over a race of yellow men on horseback. They raided deep into Thrace and refused all bribes to withdraw. And so we led them across a field strewn with cloth bags of our latest weapon, and waited for the rain to fall. When it was safe for us to approach, we counted twenty-five thousand charred corpses. Do not imagine that, in the development of weapons, you can ever match the advantage we have gained to compensate for our weakness in numbers.'

Oh, this was glorious stuff indeed! The only meaning of that news was that Leontius had talked his way off Constantine's rack. I'd been thinking about him on and off ever since setting out for the West. But who else could have picked up on my idea of using quicklime as a primer? I crouched behind that curtain, sweating and trembling, my mind soaring like some enthusiast who thinks he's heard the voice of God.

'I must tell you then,' Khadija said, 'that our arrangement is at an end. It is now in our interest to keep Alaric alive. There will be no more palace gates left open for your people. If you persist in your own assassination efforts, we will, for the moment, join forces with Meekal to resist you.'

'It is as you wish, My Lady,' Joseph replied in a tone of gentle mockery. 'Even so, that need not mean an end to cooperation with the Emperor in other respects. Your allowance will continue to find its way into your Medina accounts. Though imprisoned here, you need not worry that your voice will fall silent in the nativist councils of His Majestic Holiness.'

I could have sat listening to this all night. But the meeting was now at an end. I heard the scrape of Joseph's chair, and the beginning of their elaborate partings. Time to get myself out of here. Who could say that Khadija wouldn't walk straight through the curtain to make her own record of the meeting? That meant I had to get myself out into the antechamber before they did. I heaved myself up as noiselessly as I was able. I opened the door and pulled it to behind me. The slave girl was now sleeping. I hurried past her into the main hall.

50

Out in the hall, I bumped straight into the green eunuch. He'd been hovering just beyond the door with a tray in his hands. I cringed before him and made sure to look down at the ground.

'Why is it that I'm always the last one to bed?' he snarled. This wasn't the obsequious creature who'd fawned before the Magnificent Alaric. I was lucky he had a tray in his hand, and not a stick. I bowed lower and mumbled something respectful. 'If you think I'm here to fetch and carry at all hours of the night, you're mistaken. Here' – he thrust the tray towards me – 'take the Mistress her sleeping draught. If she wants me, you can find me in the kitchens, fixing myself a late supper.'

As he flounced off towards another door, I looked at the tray. It had on it a lead bottle and a tiny glass cup. Was it worth getting the slave girl awake? Should I just put the tray down and shuffle away? As I stood there dithering, the latticed door opened again, and Khadija and Joseph came out into the hall.

'*Oh fuck!*' I thought. Trying not to shake, I held the tray up and bowed low before Khadija. She ignored me and walked right past with Joseph. They spoke softly for a moment beside the gate. Then Joseph was off into the night, and Khadija was coming back towards me. I stepped back into a shadow and bowed as low before her as my aged back allowed.

'When I'm ready,' she snapped, 'you can have that brought to me in my bedchamber.' With that, she was through the door again and disappearing into her private quarters. So long as the face under it isn't particularly attractive, there's so much to be said for the full Saracen veil. It restricts the vision most wonderfully. I don't suppose, however, it was needed on this occasion. As I've said, no one notices a slave – not unless he's a good deal younger and better looking than I was.

I counted to twenty and went through the door after Khadija. I left the tray beside the now snoring slave girl. Khadija had vanished deep into those parts of this building where even aged male slaves would not be allowed to follow. I'd done a brilliant job for one night. Time to get back to bed.

As I reached for the door handle, I heard Karim's voice raised in annoyance.

'Then get her up,' he snapped in reply to some objection I wasn't able to hear through the door. 'I'm hardly an unwelcome guest in this place!'

His voice was getting louder as he approached the other side of the door. The slave girl behind me was stirring at the sudden noise. In a moment, she'd be awake and brushing the creases from her dress. I looked at the door in front of me – no going through that, not with Karim on the other side. I looked at the door to Khadija's sitting room – no going through that either. I hurried across the floor and back into the spying room. If no one had been here to take a record of what I or Joseph had said, I was safe enough for any meeting with Karim. I flopped down again beside the curtain and controlled my wheezing as I prepared to listen. I'd rather not have been here at all. Since I had no choice, I might as well make the best of things.

I heard Karim let himself into the sitting room. I heard someone – presumably the green eunuch – go off into Khadija's private quarters. I heard the gentle pulling of a chair as Karim sat and made himself comfortable. After this, there was a longish time of silence. I could hear my heart banging away inside my chest, and the suppressed rasp of my own breath. At last, I could feel a piss coming on. I looked round. The only container in the room was an inkwell. I'd have to contain. So long as it didn't mean too lengthy a wait, I surely could contain.

As I sat there, my back against the wall, my good ear to the curtain, debating on how long before my bladder muscles went limp on me, I heard the usual door open. It was Khadija. I heard Karim jump up, and what may have been an embrace.

'I spoke with him at some length,' she said in answer to an unspoken question. 'You can be proud of descent from such a man. If our Faith had more men of his quality – even though aged – we could rule the whole world from Medina.'

'What did he tell you?' Karim asked eagerly. There was a mumbled reply that I couldn't catch. Perhaps Khadija was speaking with her face turned away. Sharper ears would have picked up her words. Sadly, I was reduced to straining and trying to guess. But Karim spoke again: 'You're saying he will help us?' he asked.

'Of course, Alaric will help us,' she said, now clearly. 'He has agreed to be our Sword of Damascus against the Greeks and all their friends. He will help us because he hates Meekal. Also, he will help us because I have persuaded him that we have no immediate intention of turning against the Empire. He and the Greeks in general have no faith in our ability to use their weapons against the Empire in the way that Meekal probably can. He believes that we shall only use the unquenchable fire against each other; that it will, in our own hands, be as much a weapon against us as for us. Because of that, he will work with all signs of willingness for Meekal, but ensure that the secret is handed straight over to us.'

'But we will use it at once against the Greeks!' Karim cried exultantly. 'We shall pray in the churches of both Constantinople and Rome, and it will be our language and our ways – and our blood – that triumph in the world.'

'Yes, O last and dearest son of my late husband,' came the gloating reply. 'Our empire will not use Greek money or the Greek language. The Greek party among us – the party that Muawiya led to victory in the civil wars – shall be destroyed.'

There was a long pause while they both doubtless thought of the approaching glories of their people. Yes – 'their' people! Was Karim not forgetting the little matter of his own ancestry?

'And the Old One will be kept safe?' he asked with a tone of concern gratifying to the Old One's vanity. 'We know that Meekal would kill him once the secret was in his hands – him and the boy. But we will spare them, won't we?'

'You have my word, my dear Karim, that they will both be

spared,' came the immediate and smooth assurance. 'You need to accept that, whatever the case, Alaric is old and cannot live that much longer. But he will be left to live out the remainder of his years in honourable retirement. As for the blond boy, we will force Meekal to an oath that even he cannot break. And we will ourselves be fully bound by that oath. After all, so long as we get the weapon of the Greeks, what reason could we have for harming a boy who can do no harm to us?'

They turned to the details of how to tie Meekal to his word until such time as he could be removed from all positions of authority. This done, they moved to another rhapsody about the coming Victory of the Faithful – or of the Faithful born and bred in the Faith. I paid little attention to this. Far more relevant was which account, of the three I'd had this evening from Khadija, was likely to reflect her true wishes. Did she want the Greek fire so she and her friends could settle with Meekal and the Greek Party before – eventually – turning on the Empire? Did she want it so they could make a coexistence deal with the Empire? Did she want it for an attack on the Empire almost as immediate as the one Meekal had in mind? Whether she was telling the truth to anyone about keeping me and Edward alive was a worthless speculation. She didn't sound the sort who killed for enjoyment. She'd kill or spare strictly on the basis of how well either suited her interests.

You don't like a woman like Khadija. But you do have to admire her. In her youth, she'd led the Faithful into battle. Now, a gentle prisoner in the Caliph's palace, she'd do battle for the same cause with bribery and fraud. The only criticism I might have of the woman was her crap security. But wasn't that really how Muawiya had done over her husband and his boss Ali in the civil wars? Wasn't that how the Empire was doing the Saracens over in general? My reforms of the Intelligence Bureau had been one of the best uses I'd made of the Imperial taxpayers' money. No wonder we were always a step ahead of these people. It was a matter of learning their language and its various nuances – and then of waiting for them to sit back and spill the contents of their minds as if they'd been so many drunks with overfilled cups. For all we'd destroyed them utterly, the Persians had never been this careless.

I had no idea what time it was. I hadn't seen a water clock all evening. I hadn't seen the sky in ages. Those stimulants had taken away all internal sense of time. It must have been approaching the midnight hour. It might easily have been some while later. The single lamp in the room had long since gone out, and there was no light but a dim reflection of the moon from somewhere beyond the shuttered window. I was too pleased with myself, and still too drugged to feel tired. Still, how long could I be away from my bed before someone raised the alarm?

But Khadija and Karim were prosing on endlessly about matters of no concern to me. It was all a matter of names and of household expenses that were irrelevant. I kept my good ear against the curtain just in case. But there was nothing more for me. I waited patiently for the conversation to run out of force, and for those long internals of silence that you find between close friends or relatives to grow longer still. At last, they slid into the conventional phrases that indicated a farewell. I stretched my arms and legs in the darkness, reasonably sure that the clicking of aged cartilage wouldn't carry through the curtain. I heard Khadija get up and go – I hoped for the last time – through the door into her private quarters. Shortly after, there was the sound of Karim's getting up. I heard the gentle click of the door into the antechamber. Another moment, and I could try another getaway of my own. All was silence about me. I stretched my arms and legs again and prepared for the effort of climbing to my feet.

Then the door opened, and a pool of lamplight splashed into the room. Framed in the doorway was Karim – one arm clutching the still sleepy slave girl, his outer robe hitched up in his other hand. For what seemed a very long time, we looked at each other. With a whispered command, he dropped the girl behind him, and came fully into the room.

'What are you doing here?' he whispered, his voice shaking with the shock of discovery. I smiled back at him, and held out my arms for him to lift me.

'You should know the answer to that one, my dear,' I whispered with much firmer voice. 'You caused me to be brought here. Are you surprised if I chose to stick around to seek what else I might learn?' I closed and opened my outstretched hands. As if automatically, he bent forward and helped me to my feet.

'If she finds out you've been spying on her, she'll kill you,' he moaned. He looked back at the slave girl. So far as I could tell, she was still sprawled on the floor where he'd dropped her.

'Well, my dearest and only posterity,' I said with a smile, 'it's up to you to make sure she doesn't find out. Can you help me back to my chair? It should still be waiting outside.'

'What did you overhear?' he asked.

'Oh, everything – yes, *everything*!' I said, now with a gentle laugh. 'And what I didn't hear I was able to guess. Now, are you going to raise the alarm – and this would not be in anyone's interest? Or are you going to get me out of here? And are you going to keep your mouth as tightly shut about this as I've kept mine about your less than glorious performance of last night?'

The slave girl had vanished from the antechamber, and the main hall was now empty. Finally, the guards had had the sense to shut and bolt the gate. But that was no problem with Karim beside me. He kicked some life into the guards, and I followed him with apparent meekness out into the chilly night air. My carriers were verging on moral collapse when we found them. Ignoring me, they threw themselves down before Karim in the sort of prostration an emperor would have thought flattering, and listened to his instruction to take me straight back to the Tower of Heavenly Peace.

'I don't think she got round to telling you,' I whispered slowly in Greek. 'But Khadija will now let you firm up my security.' He nodded with plain relief, and with some embarrassment. 'And you can be assured that, so long as young Edward is guaranteed safe, Khadija will get everything she wants. Your own children will learn many things, I have no doubt – but Greek will not be on their syllabus.'

By now, I'd been packed into the chair, and the carriers were in position front and back. With a nervous order from Karim, they had me aloft.

'I don't know how you've managed to stay alive this long with your behaviour,' he muttered with a faint return to his diplomatic manner. 'But I pray to Allah that He will continue to watch over you.'

'I have not the slightest doubt, my darling great-grandson,' I mumbled as I tried to get my teeth back into position, 'that Allah will continue the same watch on me as He has always kept.'

Without bothering to reply, Karim slapped the shoulder of the head carrier and watched as I was carried rapidly out of sight.

51

That really should have been the evening's work. Even a younger man, by now, should have been wilting. But good opportunities hardly ever present themselves singly. It was as we were passing again over the long wooden bridge that I saw Meekal. It was too dark for playing with my visor. But I'd pulled the curtain aside to cool my sweating face, and I'd have known that long stride anywhere. I watched with idle attention as he approached from the right. At our current speeds, I guessed, he'd pass the far end of the bridge shortly before I arrived there. Interesting that, for all his exalted position, the Governor of Syria and effective deputy of the Caliph himself still went about the palace on his own two feet. Khadija's stimulants were still at full blast in my head, and I felt little inclination to go back off to bed. The idea may have been in my mind the moment I saw Meekal. Certainly, it wasn't long after that when the idea was fully formed.

'Follow that man,' I hissed. The head bearer twisted round with a muttered protest: hadn't I made them risk enough already? I ignored the protest. 'That man over there,' I said, pointing. Our relative speeds had changed, and Meekal would pass the bridge some while before we were off it. 'I'm sure you recognise the Lord Governor of Syria.' In the moonlight, the face staring back at me seemed a mask of sudden fear. 'You heard me,' I hissed again. I paid no attention to the reply – half protest, half terrified plea. 'I said follow that man. Do it, and there's five solidi extra for each of you.' That decided them. With a few soft words of command from their leader, the slaves were padding faster down the planks of the bridge. Meekal was now about twenty yards over on our left, and was ready to vanish round a corner. 'Careful, careful!' I called softly. 'Follow at a distance. Try not to appear eager to keep the man in sight.'

So, with cautious haste, I swayed along in the chair. Back in the main buildings of the palace, the evening may still have been in full swing. This far out, there was nothing but the occasional covered chair and the ubiquitous slaves, all carrying boxes of food and drink and the obvious implements of pleasure. If Meekal had looked round more than once, he'd have found reason to pause and come back for enquiries. But he turned round not at all. He did stop at one point, but that was only to look up awhile as the moon dodged in and out of the clouds. The carriers stopped behind a deserted pavilion and, shaking with fear, waited for the chase to begin again. And it did. We passed now within some streets of derelict buildings that had, before the palace walls extended so far, been houses for the middling people of Damascus. These would, sooner or later, be demolished, the ground on which they stood given over to some more exalted purpose. For now, they remained as evidence – if such was needed – that the world in which I was living had nothing about it of the immemorial. There were five of these streets, dark and quiet beneath the fitful moon. As scared now of their surroundings as of Meekal, the carriers prayed softly as they picked their way through the overgrown streets.

At last, perhaps three hundred yards from the light outer rim of the walls, we came to a dense grove of trees. Every palace has one. In Constantinople, of course, the hunting ground covered an area at least three times larger. Being several hundred years older, the Emperor's little forest was graced with much higher trees and a much more convincing appearance of natural growth. But, against the day when Damascus was besieged, or the palace itself was besieged by the people of Damascus, the caliphs had taken care that all the normal pleasures of life might continue, if on a smaller scale than usual. At a pinch, you'd go into there on horseback – though you'd have a better appearance on foot of boundless, overgrown solitude. Into this grove, Meekal now vanished.

'We daren't go in after him, My Lord,' the head carrier gasped.

I nodded. Even on a gravelled path, anyone would have to be stone deaf not to hear us. I peered over at the walls. The grove seemed to run right up to them, though probably stopped ten or so yards short for security. Was there an unfrequented gate in that stretch of wall? Was Meekal only going through the grove so he could get out, unobserved, into the city?

'Wait over by that tree,' I said, trying to sound surer than I now felt about matters. 'I will give further instructions when I am ready.' Obediently, the carriers trotted over to the shade of the low apple tree. 'Put me down here,' I said, 'and sit as if you are all at rest.' I sat for what seemed an age. I sat until I began to feel stupid. The moon was now fully out from behind the clouds, and its mysterious light bleached out all that wasn't in shadow. A gentle breeze ruffled the chair curtains. Somewhere in the distance – perhaps outside the palace grounds – a dog barked without letting up. The sky told me it was rather earlier than I'd assumed. We were still approaching the midnight hour. Even so, this vigil was dragging on and on.

Then, just as I was about to order the retreat, there was a sound deep within the grove. What it was I couldn't tell with my hearing – but the carriers heard it. I saw them sit up and listen. At once, though, their own response was overwhelmed by the dry clatter of several hundred wings as what may have been every bird in the grove left its perch for the night. That, plus the cries of animals on the ground, brought the night suddenly to life. Just as suddenly, though, it faded again. The carriers looked at each other in the returning silence, and then to Heaven. I steadied them with a distribution of gold. So far as I could, I scanned the still blackness of the grove for any sign of movement.

I can't say how much longer we waited. I had one of the chair curtains pulled down so I could wrap it about my own chilled body. There were faint bursts of sound as, back towards the centre of the palace, the bands of revellers began to break up for the night. The birds were almost set off again by a procession of several dozen blacks that passed by close to where we sat out of sight. Accompanied by drums, though in mournful voice, they shouted out what may once have been their battle cry as, chained neck to neck, they were hurried past by a pair of eunuchs who didn't seem to care what skin they broke with their discipline rods. As if on some night exercise, they were driven from deep within the palace grounds, only to be turned and driven back.

And that was it. The drums and chanting faded into the night. The bursts of revelry became fainter and further apart. That dog barked endlessly, and the moon rose ever higher above the high wall of the palace and the trees that, young as they were, already topped the palace wall. Once again, I began to wonder if it was time to order the carriers out of their cautious doze and have myself taken off to bed.

Then, suddenly, a small, dark figure darted out from the trees. It stopped in the moonlight and looked frantically about. I sat up and stared hard. Was it a deer or some other small animal? Was it just a trick of the light? I strained and focused. I stood up and rubbed my eyes, and looked again. *How the bloody hell . . . ?* I thought. I stepped forward and poked my stick into the back of one of the huddled carriers.

'Catch that boy!' I said urgently. 'All of you – after him. Bring him back here. And try not to make any noise.'

As the carriers caught up with him and noiselessly surrounded him, I saw Edward pull out a knife. He turned round and round, stabbing frantically, his knife glittering dark in the moonlight. Without giving him space to break free and run, the slaves darted back. Still perky from the stimulants, I hurried over the thirty yards or so that separated us.

'Edward, Edward!' I gasped softly in English. I doubled up with a coughing fit, but was up again in moments. 'It's me. Come over here before we all get seen.' The boy looked in my direction, then went back to stabbing at the air. I hurried closer and called again. This time, he looked properly at me. I caught a blurred glimpse of his face in the moonlight, and wanted to step away. Then, he dropped down and covered his eyes. His body shook with a wild sobbing. 'Get him up,' I called to the carrying slaves. 'Get him into the chair with me, and get us both back to the Tower of Heavenly Peace. Be quick about it. There's double gold all round.'

I looked at the dark, menacing stillness of the grove. Even I might have thought twice before stepping into that, come the dusk – certainly if I knew Meekal was lurking somewhere inside.

52

'I think you're a bloody fool,' I said, still in English. 'If any of the agents I used to employ had confessed to half your incompetence, I'd have sacked him on the spot – and cancelled his pension too.' I looked at Edward over the top of my visor. I pulled off my wig and dropped it on the desk. Now we were out of the open, the night heat was turning sticky. I took a deep breath and looked hard at him. 'But I want you to tell me again,' I said gently, 'and this time, try to give me a connected account, *exactly what you saw and heard*. I don't care what you think you saw, or what you think any of it might indicate. I want the facts as you witnessed them, and nothing more.'

The boy gulped down another mouthful of wine, and looked for reassurance at the bookshelves of my office. We'd got back here without trouble. The guards Karim had already taken care to double outside were all too busy sniffing their bowls of smoking hashish to pay that much attention. A distribution of what gold I'd not lavished on the carrying slaves had shut their mouths, and might keep them shut; besides, if they were already in her pay, I didn't suppose anyone would be comparing the time I'd left Khadija with the time of my return. I'd helped get Edward out of his pissy, vomit-stained clothes, and he'd sat an age shuddering in the warm bath I'd drawn for him with my own hands. I noted how the weals were already healing on that marvellous skin. But, if the bruises and remaining cuts still hurt, he wasn't calm enough to pay attention to the pain. Now, I stood over him, pouring wine into his cup, and hoping he wouldn't pass out before I got enough of those tearful and discontinuous fragments to reconstruct the whole story.

'Did you recognise any of the other men?' I asked. That was in itself a useless question. But it served to draw the main attention away from Meekal. Karim hadn't stayed around to share in the boy's lesson, and, once I was dressed up and ready to go, Edward had got himself ready to tag along behind. As I might have expected, he'd stopped a little too long to feast his eyes on the snake woman. By the time he'd pulled himself away, my chair was nowhere in sight. Instead, he'd wandered lost for a while, hoping he'd see us all again by chance.

'Very well,' I sighed. I hurried him to the main events. 'You are sure it was Brother Joseph?' I asked. 'It isn't easy to disguise yourself as a eunuch – especially when you have a beard like his. What makes you so completely sure it was him?' You might think it a silly question. But I wasn't telling Edward anything of what I'd been up to that evening. And, supposing he hadn't seen or guessed that Joseph had followed us to Caesarea, his last sight of the man had been far off in the western seas of the Mediterranean.

'He spoke Latin,' came the answer through chattering teeth.

I thought of a dab of opium in the wine cup. But you can't be sure of the effect that will have on the very young.

'But you weren't close enough to hear what was said,' I prompted. The boy nodded. But he'd heard the other man addressed as Meekal, and guessed that he was the Governor of Syria. They'd spoken together a long time outside the hall where the geometry lesson was still in progress. Apparently, Joseph had spoken in cutting tones about the teacher's ability. Then the pair had moved just outside Edward's hearing. Meekal had laughed much and shaken his head at some repeated urging. Beyond that, Edward had got nothing from the conversation. Joseph had eventually melted into a crowd, and the choice had been come back here to bed or follow Meekal about. He'd done the latter – and much he'd got from it with his total lack of Saracen. Meekal had gone to a meeting of the palace guards, where he'd been greeted with much cheering. He'd then spent a long time in some low building without lights. He might have been in conversation with one or with many men. Edward had tried listening at a window, but the shutters had been pulled to, and it was impossible to make sense of the faint noises from within.

At last, he'd followed Meekal into the grove. I groaned as he said again that he'd not once noticed my chair. Since he'd been flitting about in the shadows, and my own lack of night vision was to be expected, there was no disgrace in my not having seen him. But he'd never make a spy with that degree of attention to his surroundings. I didn't mention that Joseph had seen him; that would only have sent him into another sobbing fit.

'So you followed Meekal along some narrow, winding path to a clearing,' I said, trying to sound matter-of-fact. 'There were six men already waiting there. Beardless and with pale faces, they were all dressed in black, with high, pointed hats. They danced about him for a while, chanting. They then helped him out of all his clothes, and, naked in the moonlight, Meekal fucked a corpse. Is that what happened?' Edward said nothing, but covered his eyes in recollection of the horror. I did manage to sound matter-of-fact. This was, however, a new departure for Meekal. If much had been alleged by the stupid monks he'd never gone out of his way to conciliate, not even the Emperor Constans in all his shocking glory had ever actually tried necrophilia. 'The boy was dead,' I asked in the same flat voice, 'you were sure of that?' He nodded. He said again how the stiff, naked body had been unrolled from the black shroud in which it had been lying on the ground when Meekal arrived. Edward had been close enough behind his bush to see the heavy cord still tied about the neck, and to see the ferocious delight with which the body had been enjoyed. And all the while, the moon had shone through the softly sighing branches, and owls had flapped and hooted overhead. I thought of the serving boy at the previous night's feast. He'd been such a jolly young creature. But I was far too grown-up to join Edward in shocked tears. I also thought better than to remind him of his own tastes in love. I waited for the new shivering fit to pass.

'Let us go back to the men in pointy hats,' I prompted once more. 'They had light, shaven faces. But you don't think they were eunuchs?' He nodded. I took that as a negative. 'And there were six of them – you counted six of them for sure?' He had. 'The faces could have been painted white,' I went on. 'That would be fairly standard with the sort of proceedings you witnessed. Now, as Meekal fucked the corpse a second time, they danced about again, chanting in what you think was Saracen. It was after this, when they cut off the dead boy's head, that all the birds woke up. You say that Meekal got up and joined them in shouting and waving their arms – though the noise was too great for you to hear anything.' He nodded. 'Very well. Once everything was quiet again, Meekal took up the severed head and danced with it held aloft. It was now that the others set up a regular chant – the same words over and over.' I waited for the nod. 'Can you repeat for me what sounds their words had?' Edward opened his mouth. I leaned forward, hoping against hope. He squeezed his eyes shut and thought hard. Then he opened them and shook his head.

I could have beaten the stupid boy. I'd just got for myself a stick to wave over Khadija's head if required. I could now have had a sharp little knife to shove into Meekal's guts. As it was, though, I had enough. I patted Edward's shoulder and reminded him of my words earlier that evening, about the usefulness of learning foreign languages.

'It seems that you caught your nephew in some act of sorcery,' I explained. 'But you knew that already, I'm sure. I want you to tell yourself – and to keep telling yourself – that there is no magic. Leave aside whatever nonsense was clogging Meekal's mind, all you witnessed was an act of physical grossness, following what I cannot regard as other than a brutal murder. However, the Saracens do believe in magic. If possible, they take an even dimmer view of it than the Christians do.

'You're bleeding lucky, young man, that no one saw you. By now, you'd be ripening somewhere for Meekal to shove a knife up your arse till it too could accommodate his massively engorged member.' I cursed those stimulants Khadija had poured down my throat. They'd kept me going. But I thought for a moment Edward would puke up again. I got the wastepaper basket ready. But he controlled himself and drew himself up on the sofa to hug his knees.

'What did it all mean?' he asked. He squeezed his eyes tight shut.

I laughed softly. 'The corpse-fucking we can take as an act of superstitious blasphemy,' I said. 'It's the sort of thing people did on the quiet, back in the days of the Old Faith, before committing an act of the most desperate treason. There are varying explanations of its meaning. But the most reasonable is that it's an act of ritual defilement, followed by cleansing. You say Meekal wheeled round and round at the end of his dance, then tossed the head into some bushes. I think you'll find that he threw it in exactly the direction of the rising sun. The idea is that the thing takes on all the sins and general worthlessness of the killer's life to date. All this is then communicated to the first person who touches the head when the sun is risen. The body can be dismembered and buried wherever may be convenient. I don't suppose any of the parts will be discovered. In any event, one more body in a place like this won't raise many eyebrows.' Oddly enough, Edward seemed to find some comfort in my conjectural explanation. But, if this wasn't the first time I'd tried lecturing him out of belief in it, he'd grown up – rather as I had – in a world where magic and divination were taken for granted.

'That being said,' I mused, 'while you really can fuck anything once, twice indicates a disturbing partiality.' I thought briefly how, just that afternoon, one of Meekal's fingers had been pushed up my bum. I shuddered. I'd not be repeating that experience in a hurry. But it was time to draw Edward's attention from horror back to simple mystery. 'I wonder,' I continued, 'what Meekal could have been doing with Joseph – in full view, and inside the palace. That is worth considering, don't you think? I'll bet you thought you'd seen the last of him when he was trussed up back in Jarrow. You never thought he'd follow us all over the world.' I tried for a laugh. Just then, though, as if some invisible attendant had withdrawn his supporting arms, the stimulants suddenly wore off. I sat down heavily in my chair and fought off a fainting attack. I put up a hand to my nose, and looked at the dark stickiness on my fingers.

'Whatever the case,' I said with much labour, 'we are where we are. If you find everything over your head, that's just too bad. All else aside, your life now hangs on my cooperation.' Edward looked up. I did now manage a laugh, even if it wasn't a very pleasant one. 'Oh, it's all wickedly ironic,' I said with a tired wave. 'You forced me out of that monastery by threatening to slice up poor Wilfred. Now he's dead, you've taken his place with Meekal. One day, I'll get round to reciting the whole of one of those sicko plays Seneca wrote as entertainments for the court of Nero. I can think of one passage in particular that fits our situation. For the moment, we pretend none of this happened. We must simply hope that no one saw either of us.'

I got up and tried to stretch. It wasn't my most successful move of the day. I let my arms fall limp. Was that more blood I could feel running down my chin? I pulled myself together. I leaned hard on my stick and moved towards the door.

'I'll see you to bed,' I told the boy. I picked up the key to the main door as I passed the table on which I'd dropped it. 'Yes, I'll unlock,' I said firmly. 'If Meekal wants to send men in to throttle us while we sleep, some silly lock won't keep them out. It will simply mean no one can get in to serve breakfast. Just as if nothing had happened, I'll leave the door unlocked and the key in the outside lock. That's what Karim bribed the slaves into accepting.'

'Then, please, Master – don't make me sleep alone,' Edward asked. He jumped off the sofa and almost knocked me over with his scared embrace. I felt his warm body next to mine. I was so knocked out, it might have been a bag of warmed bricks. I put a hand on one of the unmarked areas of his back.

'I suppose it has been a difficult couple of days,' I said in what I hoped was a reassuring tone. 'Oh, come with me,' I said, dropping all pretence of emotion. 'It's not as if there was a shortage of space in the bed.'

53

I woke in Jarrow from another of my dozes. I looked up into the leaden greyness of the sky. It was coming on to rain again. I'd have to drag myself back inside if I were to avoid getting wet as well as cold. I looked over at the gate that led back into the monastery. While I slept, a layer of oak planks had been nailed over it, hiding the weathered cross. I tried to think and to remember. But there was nothing clear in my head. It was as if I'd finally had the stroke people had been warning me against for years. I stopped and began counting slowly backwards in Greek, trying desperately to remember anything at all. I managed the counting. But each time I thought I'd grasped something solid among the contents of my mind, it seemed to shrivel then vanish in my hand.

I said I'd have to drag myself inside. But was I up to doing anything for myself? More jumbled fragments of memories. I gave up on thinking and looked down. I was sitting on a wooden chair with arms each side. Hadn't this once been Abbot Benedict's chair? If so, all the biblical imagery that had once covered the arms was now cut away or rubbed smooth. My legs were buried under a loose packing of blankets against the chill. I tried to move my right foot. There was a slight tingling, I thought. Perhaps there was a slight movement. It was hard to say.

I looked over to my left. I was sure this had once been the patch of grass where the boys would kick a ball about between lessons. But it all seemed so long ago. Again, the curtain came down between me and what I knew had once been a perfect memory. I shouted at everyone to go inside. No one looked round. No one got up from his place. Seated on the damp grass, the boys looked steadily forward. I tried to focus on the teacher. For some reason, this was a regular lesson – but in the open of a Northumbrian spring or autumn or summer. I willed myself to hear their chanted responses to the teacher's lesson. But my hearing was no longer even what it had once been. It all sounded like a vague mumbling. But I tried harder. Now, I could hear something. Yes – it really was quite clear after all:

La ilah illa Allah: Mohammed Rasul Allah.
Allahu Akbaru. Allahu Akbar.

This they chanted over and again in their flat northern voices. I thought that I might once have been able to understand the words. But understanding even of words was also long since gone. At every pause in the chanting, however, Meekal – yes, he was there at the head of the class, scowling and pointing at the boys – would repeat his interpretation into English:

'*La*, "no", "not", "none", "neither"; *ilah*, a "god", "deity", "object of worship"; *illa*, "but", "except" (the word is a contraction of *in-la*, meaning "if not"); *Allah*, "Allah". You, boy – yes, you – come to my office after the lesson . . .'

I opened my mouth to shout that a whole storm was coming on, and everyone would get soaked. But, even as I took in the breath, I was interrupted by the call from above. It came from the now white-painted bell tower:

Allahu Akbar, Allahu Akbar
Allahu Akbar, Allahu Akbar
Ashadu an la ilaha Allah
Ashadu an la ilaha Allah
Ashadu anna Mohammedan rasulah . . .

Where the bell had been, there was now a platform. There, in the highest place of what had, in ancient times, been the monastery, sat Brother Cuthbert. The once shaven face was now covered with a beard of red and grey. The tonsure was hidden beneath a turban. Arms upheld, he summoned the Faithful to prayer in a menacing drone. Twenty feet below him, Wilfred scurried about like a lizard on the wall. I think he was trying to reach the platform. But

Cuthbert's words seemed to present a barrier to further progress up the wall. Despairingly, the boy looked down at me. As in Cartenna, the teeth were long and white. They projected far over the full, dark lips. All this I could somehow see very clearly. I could even see the pattern of the tower's stonework as it showed through the insubstantial body.

I could sense that Cuthbert was approaching the end of his call. He looked down at Wilfred. He looked down long and gloatingly in my direction.

'*Allahu Akbar, Allahu Akbar*,' he called. '*La ilah illa Allah. Deus uult! Deus uult!*' As he ended, and everyone down on the grass got ready for prayer, Wilfred's whole body began to drift apart like the last mist of the dawn . . .

I woke in my bed in Damascus. I was covered in sweat. I looked up at the glazed ceiling panel. No light but distortions of the brighter stars came down. All about me was silence. The main window was shut and the blind pulled down. I tried to move. But Edward had his arms clamped tight around me. His face was pressed hard into my chest. I tried to reach behind to unclamp his hands, but couldn't make it. Instead, I stretched down to tickle the small of his back. That got him loose. As he groaned and rolled over, I wriggled away and put my feet down to the cool tiles of the floor. I sat silent and very still, waiting for the sweat to evaporate from my body.

I reached for the water jug and drank, realising for the first time how thirsty I'd become. We were now coming deep into the summer. When there was no cloud or wind coming off the mountains, these nights could only get hotter.

I got to my feet and peered about for my slippers. Because the slaves hadn't yet come back in, nothing was where it should be. I walked slowly with bare feet across to the door and let myself out into the circular corridor. I looked uncertainly left and right into the darkness. I decided to go right. I went as far as I could from the bedchamber and into one of the larger audience rooms. It wasn't a room I'd yet bothered using, and the furniture lay before me in a jumbled, shadowy blur. I felt my way to a sofa and sat down. I looked up to the glazed panel in the ceiling. It was perceptibly lighter than it had been. We must be approaching the dawn. I pulled my feet up and lay on the sofa, looking up at the brightening sky.

I thought for a while I might nod off. But there was now a cold, dim light all about me in the room, and I could see the outlines of the heavy furniture put there to impress visitors without giving them much comfort. I got up again and drifted over to the window. I realised that this was the window nearest the bronze pipe that brought water up to the roof. It was also the window through which Khadija's assassin had climbed. There were still no bars on it. Probably, there was no need of any. After all, I was now Khadija's devoted servant. I smiled weakly and fumbled with the catch. I pulled the window open and breathed in the cool air of the outside and listened to the gentle but gathering roar of a Syrian dawn. I thought of the many descriptions of the dawn in Homer. All very beautiful, they were too cheerful for my present mood. I opened my mouth and recited from the much darker Virgil:

Postera Phoebea lustrabat lampade terras,
umentemque Aurora polo dimoverat umbram . . .

Yes, poor stupid Dido had hoped to build her Carthage and reign in peace. She hadn't considered the somewhat different interests of her Trojan guest. Already, his mind had been taken over by the rival and infinitely grander vision of the Rome he was to build. Virgil had looked back on this from a Rome that was at the zenith of its glory. The Rome where I'd briefly lived, six hundred years later, was a stinking ruin. I remembered how I'd stood one day on the crumbling steps of the Temple of Jupiter, and had looked down from the Capitoline Hill over the bleak ruins of the Forum. But, even if the glory of the merely corporeal Rome was now fallen, the idea of Rome was transferred to what the Saracen chronicler had called the City on the Two Waters. In time, the idea might move from Constantinople. Wherever it might move, it was worth fighting to preserve.

I looked out at the first rays of the rising sun. If I waited just a little longer, I'd see those first rays as they struck the higher minarets of the city, and then as they moved steadily down this tower to where I stood. Gradually, Damascus would awake. There would be those calls to prayer. The shops would open for business. The streets would fill with those who had money to spend, and with those who had to be up to earn their money. Some while before then, the night would have passed, and I could say that I'd lived to see another day.

Was that the main door opening, far back along the corridor? This was about the time the slaves came in to attend to their business. They could feed me while I bathed, I decided. Edward, I decided further, could be left to sleep until he woke by himself. I'd have him watched, so I could be with him when his eyes did open. I'd then pack him off to Karim for the day. Sooner or later, after all, Meekal would drop by for another little chat.

'Bugger me!' I whispered at the bronze pipe. 'Sod, bugger, damn! I wish I were at home.'

Through more than ninety years, the sound of my own voice had generally brought comfort. Now, it only brought me to the matter of where home might really be.

54

There are hotter places and times on earth than a Syrian August. But you try reminding yourself of that after a whole morning of swaying, jingling progress through the desert that stretches eastward from Damascus. I took another sip of beer cooled with ice from the mountains, and – not for the first time that journey – wondered how the black slaves carrying my chair didn't fall down dead in the sun.

To be precise about the timing, it was Thursday, 1 August 687, and we were just into the second month of Meekal's accelerated project. This was my eighth personal inspection. It should have been my ninth, but the Angels of the Lord had intensified their attacks, and the desert road had been judged too dangerous for me to risk the journey. Meekal, though, had diverted more soldiers from the desultory war with the Empire, and, flanked by a whole brigade of mounted Saracens, we'd made a slow, nervous progress out of Damascus. I handed my beer cup to the slave who walked beside the chair. I adjusted my visor and tried to turn back to the volume of mathematical writings open on my knees.

'We'll soon be there,' said Meekal. I'd heard his slow approach on horseback, but didn't look round at him. 'I said,' he repeated in a louder voice, 'we'll soon be there.' I made a fuss with the speaking trumpet I'd recently had made. He now shouted into it, nearly blowing my head off with the power of his voice.

'There's no need to shout!' I whined back at him. 'I can hear perfectly well so long as people don't mumble.' I rejoiced at the scared look that came over his face whenever I gave cause to think I was entering some decline. If I was his prisoner, he was just as much mine. If he'd given me no chance of slipping my own leash,

I could at least tug on his. He was right about our location. Glancing up through my visor, I'd been able for some time now to see the low, sand-coloured mass of where we were going. I thought of giving further practice to my querulous tone, with a comment about the flies. Just then, though, I caught sight of the cloud of dust ahead of me to the right.

'I was about to wonder if the boys would catch up with us,' I said, now in my normal voice. 'I see instead that they've overtaken us.' I looked hard through the pattern of little holes in my visor – a pattern long since corrected out of my notice by some adjustment of the mind – and wondered at the speed that Karim and Edward could get out of those desert mounts. Even in my long prime, I'd never been much of a horseman. If I so much as spoke of climbing on to another saddle, it would only be to confirm Meekal's worries about the decay of my faculties. But there was no hint of envy, or even regret, as I watched the pair of friends chase each other back and forth across the firm sand. If I worried about their safety, there was no point mentioning it. To be sure, Edward's guards were even faster on horseback, and were up to seeing off anything but a regular ambush. If they kept modestly behind in the races, and if they joined in the congratulations of the winner, there was no doubt of their purpose.

'Greetings, My Lords,' Karim called out as he came alongside. 'We made it from the palace to here in a single gallop.'

I thought of the poor horses, but smiled my approval.

'And this time,' Edward broke in, 'I rode faster!' I smiled again. He'd spoken Saracen. He spoke that with Karim. He spoke it with all his other friends. If he still sometimes spoke with me in Latin – though more often in English – his Greek was fading like the heat of a kettle removed from its fire. 'But it's a despised language,' he'd explained over dinner the other evening. 'Nobody wants to learn it any more. Besides, those writers you keep speaking about – they've all been dead for centuries. And their language too.' So he'd turned that formidable, if undisciplined, intellect of his to a study of the East's rising language. Now, he was well inside its logic. Apart from obvious insufficiencies of vocabulary, his main problem was the limited range of cases compared with English, Greek and Latin, and – of course – the somewhat defective writing system of the Saracens. Even I'd once had trouble with that. Dressed as a Saracen, his beardless face browned by exposure to the sun, he might have been chasing about the desert from his birth.

'All is well with you?' Meekal asked when the boys had raced back off into the desert.

I nodded. Playing the old fool is fun only in little bursts. And, if I wanted to scare him, I had no wish to prod Meekal into anything more hostile than he already had in mind.

'Halt and state your business,' the guard called across the remaining distance between us and the one unblocked gate of the old monastery.

'I am Meekal, Governor of Syria,' came the obvious answer.

'And I am Alaric, Chief Weapons Adviser to His Majestic Holiness the Caliph,' I added.

From twenty feet up, on the parapet of that stone wall, the guard looked coldly at us. We held up our ivory identification passes. He looked down at them. Another guard came briefly forward, then went back to his job of lounging against the new brick wall behind that stopped anyone from looking down into the monastery.

'I want the old man out of his carrying chair and everyone else off horseback,' he snapped down at us. 'Before I give orders for the gate to be opened, I want to see you all with your arms in the air. I must warn you of the standing orders for any disobedience of the rules.'

I groaned and got up. I stepped out from beneath the shelter of the overhead canopy and took my place with everyone else under the baking sun. This was, after all, my eighth visit, and enforcement of the rules never varied. At least I was allowed to step into the shadow of the walls before the modesty screen was placed round me and I had to strip naked for the inspection of my clothes and body.

'What are these?' the unsmiling official asked, holding up the polished lenses he'd pulled out of their box.

'Those are none of your business,' I said sharply. 'They aren't on the contraband list. Let that be enough. If you drop or so much as scratch one of them, I'll have you demoted and flogged.'

The official hurriedly pushed the lenses back inside their protective covering and looked at his superior. He in turn looked at Meekal, who was passing his inner tunic over the modesty screen. Meekal nodded and my inspection was at an end. I waited under the shade of the massive gate for the more thorough strip searching of the carrying slaves to be completed.

'You know we can take no chances,' Meekal said as he joined me in the shade. 'Only the day before yesterday, someone tried to lie his way in as a supply carrier. Fortunately, we already knew the man he was impersonating had died in one of the previous attacks. I had tight cords put round his knees and elbows, and then watched while the limbs below were sawn off. You'll be pleased to hear it was a completely successful experiment. He lived. Indeed, he sobbed most affectingly when he saw his limbs heaped before him. Unless he's died of thirst in the meantime, I might show him to my dear young uncle.'

'I didn't know the boys were allowed inside the walls,' I said, cutting off the leer.

'I rejoice in your retention of all your faculties,' came the reply. I got an ironic bow. 'As it happens, I have decided to exclude them. They'll have to wait outside with the guards. Now we've tightened the security again, even the Commander of the Faithful will need to prove identity and then right to enter.' I pricked up my ears at the use of the indicative future. Meekal noticed and smiled. 'Oh, yes,' he whispered, 'Abd al-Malik will be putting in an appearance within, I think, the next ten days.'

'His Majestic Holiness has, I suppose, been victorious in the civil war?' I asked with polite irony of my own. I watched as my carrying slaves put their skimpy loincloths back on. In a moment, the gates would swing shut, and the guards would go back to their paranoid inspection of all about the walls.

'The Caliph is *always* victorious,' Meekal answered without irony.

'But don't you find it rather hurtful,' I asked again, 'that you weren't beside him? Isn't it a little odd that you're thought good enough for smashing up the lesser breeds to the East, but not for turning on other Saracens – on *real* Saracens, that is?'

I'd got the bastard there. His face went white with anger, and his hands shook as he refastened my cloak. He began some stammered excuse about his duties in Damascus. But now the gates did swing shut, and we were sealed within what had, before the Saracen conquest, been the Monastery of Saint Theodore the Uneating.

The monastery buildings themselves had been mostly demolished, leaving plenty of space within the high surrounding wall. This had now been separated by new walls into four separate zones, each with its own solid gate and its own complement of silent guards. The first of these zones was just inside the main gate. Here were the living quarters of the workmen and the administrative buildings. We were met by Silas, a Syrian with the usual dark beard. He was the site manager, with overall control of the project in my own absence. If he too was kept in the dark about how everything done there fitted together, he was, I suppose, the nearest I had to an assistant. He bowed low before us, and – just to show he was doing his job – spent a longish time looking at our passes and entering our details in the relevant ledger that one of his secretaries had brought forth from his office.

'I want to begin with the preparation vats,' I said.

He bowed again, and led us through the huddle of low buildings and piles of material that filled up much of this first zone. As he unlocked the gate, his secretary made another entry in the ledger and presented this for my inspection and Meekal's, and then our countersignatures. We now had to wait again in the increasingly pitiless sun as my carrying slaves were all blindfolded. Silas himself would guide the head carrier through the next stages of the visit.

We passed through into an almost empty expanse of packed sand. In the middle was a high building, though of one storey, about the size and shape of a steam room in the house of a rich man. Of new brickwork – most of one wall of very new brickwork – this was secured by another stout door. We crossed the thirty yards of open ground and paused at the door.

'My Lords have their keys ready?' Silas asked. We nodded. He'd left his secretary on the other side of the gate, and so had carried the ledger himself. He now opened this and made yet another of his entries. Meekal walked round the whole outside of the building, and made a close inspection of the door and its locks. He nodded to me and signed again. I countersigned, and watched as Silas recorded that I had made no inspection of my own. I then reached inside my tunic and pulled out the large iron key that was fastened to a golden chain about my neck. I held this up for the other two men to see. They produced their own keys. With a 'May it please your Lordship' from Silas, I climbed from the chair and put my key into the first lock. Silas and Meekal put in their own. I gave the signal, and we pushed in hard and pulled out again. My hands shook slightly from all the beer I'd downed on the journey, and I missed the elaborate mechanism behind the key plates. We all took our keys back out and prepared to repeat ourselves. On the next attempt, we all hit the right spot together, and, with a slithering of bolts, the lock contracted within itself. Silas waved us back. He put a cloth over his nose and mouth, and pulled the door open. I turned away and held my breath as I smelled the noxious fumes. I walked carefully away from the door and listened to the rhythmical fall and rise of the bellows that Silas was working inside to replace all the air. At last, he was done. Now without his protective cloth, he stood in the doorway. He'd already unshuttered the window, and enough light was coming through the narrow iron grille to let us see what was within once our eyes were adjusted.

55

'But it's moving by itself,' Meekal said in Greek once Silas had withdrawn to the far wall of the compound and we'd unlocked the wooden cover that hid the vats from inspection by anyone else. 'It's as if some invisible spirit were stirring the liquid.'

I looked at the seething mass within the first of the three-hundred-gallon containers. Except for the dark, oily sheen, it looked like nothing so much as beer in its first couple of days after brewing. Taking care not to breathe in while I leaned over it, I cautiously pushed in one of the wooden stirring rods. The disturbance set the mixture into a frenzy of bubbling and plopping. I drew the wooden shaft out, and noted how it smoked as if it had just been inside a furnace.

'How often must I tell you, my darling little grandson, that there are no invisible beings at work around us?' I asked in a resigned tone. 'There are no conscious forces beyond our own. Everything that happens has a natural explanation. It is by understanding the world that we can control it. Oh, you can disagree, but that's how it is. Denounce me as an atheist if you want – but I know you wouldn't dare. Whatever the general case, though, be assured the whole process now before you is a natural phenomenon. It's a matter of breaking down common substances into their constituent atoms, and then recombining these into one new substance that does not of itself exist in nature. The seething shows that the breaking down is complete, but that the recombination has a few days to go yet before the new substance is stable. I have given you a full verbal description of the process. There will also be written instructions when we are sure that this attempt is a success.'

'And it will be a success this time?' Meekal asked. His voice had taken on that pleading tone again.

I thought of sneering about his need to impress the Caliph when the man came to see what had been achieved with such horrifying amounts of his cash. Instead, I shrugged.

'The problem,' I explained, 'is that the oil seeping from the ground in Syria is of a different kind from that along the Empire's Black Sea coast. It's much thinner and much lighter. This means we can cut out many of the refining processes. At the same time, the results are more volatile. We haven't lost this batch yet to spontaneous combustion. I don't think we shall. It remains to be seen, however, whether it can be made to explode in a predictable manner when combined with the combustant.' I prodded him with my stick as he reached forward to dip a finger into the vat. 'If you're willing to give up fourteen days of work, you might get some entertainment from this in one of your public executions. I really wouldn't let that stuff on my own skin.' He pulled his hand back and laughed. I climbed carefully down my own stepladder and followed him along the line of other vats. These we didn't bother unlocking. With my hearing trumpet in my good ear, I simply listened for the sound of what is best described as fermentation. If each had been slightly varied in ways that only I as yet knew, all but one sounded at roughly the same stage of completion.

'In this one,' I said as Meekal got the cover open, 'I more than doubled the amount of resin. It may be that this will start up again in the next few days. But I think I've worked out how to damp the process without entirely smothering it.' I leaned on the rim of the earthenware vat. As I'd expected, it was warm to the touch. The basics of all this could be explained in terms of Epicurean physics. Even so, I still couldn't reconcile the details. A thousand years before, the Master had obviously found the right path to understanding the nature of things. But he really had taken only the first few steps along what I'd learned for myself was a very long path. A shame he himself had intended his physics as nothing more than a support for his ethical teachings. Where might a whole thousand years of conjecture and experiment have taken humanity? No point in trying to answer that one. None either in thinking what might have happened, even granting the ethical bias of his teachings, if he rather than Plato and Aristotle had won the battle of the books for the human mind.

'Quickly – come out with me!' Meekal gasped. He clutched at my arm and hurried me into the bright, fresh air. I blinked in the sun and breathed in and out as the clouds that had, so insidiously, gathered about, drifted from my head.

'Thank you, my dearest,' I said, leaning against the side of my carrying chair. 'You do have to be careful about those fumes. And they will be gathering faster before the process stabilises. Now, do be a love and fish out some more of that beer. As Silas is standing with his face to the wall, and these slaves can't see a thing and don't know Greek, I suppose you might care to join me in some refreshments.'

We drank. I rested. I watched the vultures overhead; doubtless Meekal's latest victim had parched or suppurated to death. I thought about his reference to 'supplies'. Did this mean he'd found another place where oil oozed from the ground? If so, the cellars that stretched far beneath us would be filling up with more of the basic materials. I turned and explained again to Meekal the need to filter the oil twice before it was finally sealed into the large earthenware containers to settle. He nodded impatiently. That much, at least, I had impressed on him.

The sun was now at its highest point, and I cast barely a shadow on the ground. Even with half a pint of coolish beer to keep me going, I didn't fancy hanging about too long in the open. I nodded to Meekal. He pushed the door shut and called Silas over. We locked. We signed. We countersigned. Meekal now applied his Governor's seal. We passed back through the gate into the first zone.

I'll not bother with describing my inspection of the combustant. There never had been any problems with making this. It was simply a matter of unstopping one of the big jars and sniffing to make sure all remained well. The attendant security measures took far longer than the inspection. At last, we were back into the first zone, where Silas had ordered a most welcome lunch for me of bread in milk and olive paste. While I ate, Meekal gnawed at a crust and went with Silas through all the many ledger entries made since our last visit. All was in order. Still, he sniffed about – questioning bread consumption, asking about the burial of the workmen who'd not survived the last explosion, testing to make sure he knew the names and faces of every single guard.

Now, the break was over, and it was time to inspect the fourth zone, this entered through a gate at the far end of the third zone.

'If not in writing, I gave precise instructions about the size of these openings,' I said with rising impatience. I had my visor up and was looking through my lenses at the double valve that the straining workmen held before me. 'It must fit exactly over the two spouts of the joined kettles, and the opening of each valve must allow the correct quantities of vapour into the mixing chamber. Again, the single exit spout must be of a certain diameter. It needs to fit precisely over the final bronze projection pipe. I'll not fault the hardness of the steel – after all, this is Damascus. But this thing as it stands will simply produce another explosion.' I replaced my visor and stood back to see the abortion that had emerged from fourteen days of labour in another of the sealed zones. It was a ball with about the same volume as a large cooking pot. The two feeding spouts were probably the right size and distance apart – we'd see about that in a moment. But it was plain, even without a measuring rod, that they weren't long enough to fit safely within threaded sleeves on to the kettles. The exit spout was also too short. And it was too narrow. The bronze projection pipe really would pop straight off – that, if we didn't have an explosion from the backed-up mixture. It really would all have to be redone.

'Oh, never mind!' I said with a sly look at Meekal's face. No doubt, once my back was turned, there'd be an explosion of his own all over those useless buggers in the valve workshop. For the moment, the valve wasn't critical. 'I suppose you've fixed up a demonstration already for His Majestic Holiness when he rolls in,'

I added. 'This being so, you'll need to work those Syrians double shifts to get the job done properly in time.'

I turned my attention now to the big double kettle. This was a huge contraption. It would have filled one of the larger rooms in the Tower of Heavenly Peace. At least this time – and I was looking at a third attempt – my instructions did seem to have been followed to the smallest detail.

'There's no gap,' Meekal said hurriedly, 'between the inner bronze chambers and the outer casings of iron.'

I looked again and grunted. We'd see very shortly how well they'd been fitted together. I held up my lenses again and looked closely at the welded joints where the cylinders had been sealed at each end with five-inch thicknesses of iron. Those were the real weak points. We'd see what extra strength the brass retaining bands would give. I looked at the repaired and now reinforced wall that would protect us during the experiment. It was a miracle we were both still alive after the fiasco of our July experiment. Now, I was glad of the sandbags that would spread the force if there were another disaster.

While the valve was fitted to the double spout – yes, there wasn't quite enough thread for the sleeves to get a proper hold – I tapped both kettles with the silver head of my walking stick. They sounded as if they'd do. Once it was fixed in place, I tapped the steel mixing valve. The ratio of wall thickness to volume didn't let me tell much at all from the sound. Nevertheless, I did test the basic security of its fitting to the kettles.

I took my seat beside the kettles and nodded at Meekal. He gave an order to the workmen, who then lit the fire. With air from the bellows, the charcoal was soon an intense white even in that scorching sunshine.

'I didn't think to ask you,' I said with sudden alarm, 'if both kettles are filled half with water. It needs to be neither more nor less than half.' Meekal nodded. Relieved, I sat back and waited. I had another headache coming on. It might have been the fumes. Just as likely, it was all the beer. Meekal stood beside me. Neither of us spoke as we watched the nervous pumping of the workmen on the bellows. I put up my ear trumpet and leaned forward again. 'I think it's boiling,' I said in Syriac. One of the workmen nodded. 'Then do please screw on the lids.' He bowed and began fumbling with the eight-inch brass discs that would seal both kettles. I got up and let Meekal carry my chair behind the protective wall. As the workmen hurried round to stand behind us, Meekal bent down and pulled out the stopper on the water clock.

'But tell me again, my dearest kinsman,' he asked, now speaking Latin for added security, 'why the kettles are only to be filled halfway.'

I sniffed and looked at the dribble of water from the clock. It had already reached the first marker in the collecting bowl. I'd decided we had to wait until it reached the fifth.

'Your lack of attention to these matters disturbs me,' I replied. 'The purpose of dividing the work as we have is to ensure that no one person – indeed, no group of persons working together – shall be able to reproduce the Greek fire. The plan is that you, and only you, will have the overall knowledge needed to make everything work. Now, that really does mean you need to understand what is happening.' I held up a hand for my cup, and waited while it was filled with iced lemon juice. 'The idea that Greek fire is a burning liquid is an error that I have deliberately cultivated. In fact, if these kettles were to discharge their contents as a liquid, I don't see how the flame jet would be longer than a few dozen yards, and it would all be used up in a single burst. The truth is that all materials exist in three forms: as solids, as liquids, and as vapours. Each state depends on the amount of heat applied to the atoms. The greater the heat, the looser the atomic structure.'

'So you've said,' Meekal sneered. 'But this does conflict with what I've read in Aristotle.' He smiled at the involuntary tightening of my face. 'He says that fire is heat and dryness. Water is cold and wetness. Steam is made by combining the heat of fire and the wetness of water. The product is air and earth. All my teachers in Constantinople were of that opinion. And I have read the same in that book you so kindly gave me.'

I breathed in and out very heavily. I took off my visor and looked at the questioning face. Was the man taking the piss? Of course he was. I forced myself to relax and drank more of my lemon juice.

'If you don't wish for a public beating,' I said coldly, 'you'll keep your mouth shut about that man and his equally deluded followers. According to Aristotle, none of this is even conceivable – unless you call in the "intellectual" support of magic. Now, unless you have something sensible to add, I suggest you shut up and wait.' I took off my hat and wig and mopped my sweaty scalp. I looked again at the clock. Another two markers to go. I dropped the wig into my lap and replaced the hat.

'Epicurus was wrong when he said that there are atoms of heat,' I said, breaking the silence that had resulted from my last comments. 'I think it more likely that heat is a kind of motion, the communication of which causes atoms to vibrate within their structures. Whatever the case, the furnace under those kettles converts their liquids to vapour. These two vapours then mix together in the bulb of the double valve and become explosive. When they are lit, it is burning vapour that shoots out. Because Greek fire is a vapour and not a liquid, these kettles can be used and reused throughout an entire battle without any need for recharging.'

I fell silent again and watched the clock. We were almost at the fifth marker. I was now sweating heavily. I was also beginning to shake with the tension. The valve excepted, all had gone perfectly this time. I didn't want another anticlimax. The water level had risen to the fifth marker in the bowl. It was now or never. I took up my walking stick and got slowly to my feet. I peered cautiously round the wall to the double kettle. It was beginning to shake, but I could hear none of the bright hissing that would indicate a failed joint. I turned back and smiled at the head workman. He swallowed and clutched at the silver relic case about his neck. I continued looking round the wall as he walked forward and began tapping with his long crowbar at the brass plug screwed into the exit spout of the mixing valve. I could hear Meekal groaning away behind me in some stupid prayer. Incongruously, the other workmen beside him were calling desperately on Christ and the Virgin; surely, if they had any say in the matter, we'd have a catastrophic explosion that took us and all our achievement straight to Hell. But I put the human noise out of mind. I pushed in my hearing trumpet and listened intently. Yes, I could now hear the high whistle as the plug reached the last turn of its thread. I rapped the wall smartly with my stick and called out a word of encouragement to the workman. With a last cry of fear and pleading, he brought his bar down with a firm tap on the spout, then threw himself down. I pushed sweaty palms against the wall and took a deep breath.

56

With a deafening 'whoosh!' the combined jets of invisible vapour shot across the hundred yards of clear space in front of the kettles. I saw the wooden screen placed by the wall go back, and heard its dull clatter against the stones of the wall. I breathed out and pushed my head further round the wall to see the kettles. They hadn't exploded, but the first charge of vapour was spent, and it was now steam and water shooting forward. As I looked, the kettles began to shake and rattle about in their housing. As I pulled myself back behind the wall, I heard the cracking of support beams within the stuttered scream of the discharged steam and water. I felt the impact of the kettles as they flew backward into the sandbags, and then the warm spattering of water that rained down on us.

As the scream died away to a gentle hissing, I hobbled out from behind the wall as fast as my stick would push me, and looked at the result. Meekal grabbed at me and tried to pull me back. But I evaded him and stood before the upturned kettles. They'd burst several of the sandbags on their impact, and were now lodged there, spout pointing straight up. I laughed and waved my stick. I poked Meekal away and watched him vanish back behind the wall to try to force the workmen up from where they'd prostrated themselves on the packed sand. I wouldn't bother with dragging myself over to the wall. But I could see that the wooden screen had been shattered by the blast, and that the wall behind it was dark from the soaking. I looked up. The noise of the explosion had frightened the carrion birds into flight. They flapped about overhead with tuneless calls.

'But, surely, the kettles have burst?' Meekal asked with a shaking voice.

I walked forward and struck the largest of them with my stick. It rang like a misshapen bell. I wheeled round and faced him. 'On the contrary, my dear,' I said triumphantly, 'it was a complete success.' I went back to my inspection of the kettles. They had eventually flown back with tremendous force. But for the sandbags, they'd have smashed themselves and the wall to smithereens. 'Oh, don't worry about the recoil,' I said with a dismissive wave. 'I fully expected that. You see, every time there is motion in one direction, there is another motion in the opposite direction. And this was water we were using. The real mixture is much heavier. It doesn't expand like water does. Instead, it seethes away within the kettles, producing vapour in a steady, controllable casting off of atoms. Mounted aboard a ship, you'll need to reinforce the timbers. But there will be no expulsion of heavy liquids to produce that extreme opposite motion.'

I sat down in the chair that had been placed behind me, and felt very weary. Meekal strutted about the kettles, looking at them, testing their still great heat with the tip of a finger.

'Congratulations, then, my Sword of Damascus,' he said, now in Saracen. 'God has brought your labours to a fine conclusion.' He dropped his voice and went back into Latin. 'Does it not disappoint you, though?' he crooned. 'You spent my childhood lecturing me how the application of reason to the natural world could improve human life without limit. Yet your greatest demonstration of this reason has only been to destroy life – to create a weapon of massive destructive power. I wasn't there to see it used outside Constantinople. But I saw the burns on some of the few who survived.'

I looked about for my wig. It must have fallen to the ground behind the wall when I'd got up.

'When I used the words "complete success",' I said, 'I meant complete success this far. We still haven't seen a demonstration of the main weapon. The mixture we're brewing needs much more pressure. We still don't know how the kettle joints will stand up to that. Still, I do rather think you'll have a fine show to put on for the Commander of the Faithful.' I paused. 'I must ask myself, though, how he'll take it when you tell him that you are to be the only person, outside the Imperial Palace in Constantinople, who has the secret of the Greek fire.' I hid behind my visor and watched his face carefully. He smothered a smile and muttered something about revealing the secret when the time was right.

I would have pushed my luck a little further. At this moment, though, the gate opened over on my left, and one of the guards came slowly towards us back first. He turned as he reached us and looked steadily at the ground. Two men on horseback had been sighted, he told Meekal. They'd been watching the monastery for some while from a little hill a quarter of a mile to the north.

'They'll see fuck all from out there!' Meekal said, still in Latin. He laughed. 'No action for now,' he said to the guard in Saracen. 'My compliments to General Hakim, though. Ask him to get his men quietly ready to face an attack.

'We're safe enough,' he explained to me once the man had withdrawn. 'Those Cross-Worshipping bandits aren't up to regular fighting. Besides, I've left orders in Damascus that, if we aren't back by tomorrow morning, an army of ten thousand is to be sent out to relieve us.'

'It seems the Mighty Meekal thinks of everything,' I said drily. 'Your real grandfather might have been impressed – assuming, that is, he could have overlooked your treason. Old Priscus was capable of many things. But, if always in his own manner, he was loyal to the Empire.' That wiped the smile from his face. Yes – dear old Priscus! If he'd lived to see it, he'd have died of envy at what I eventually did to the Persians. Given half a chance, he'd have bullied Heraclius into a last desperate stand against the Saracens when they took Syria, and we'd have folded like the Persians. But, if he wasn't ultimately the second Alexander he always fancied himself to be, he never betrayed the Empire. I looked over at my own work, still embedded in the sandbags. I got up and stretched my legs.

'Get that lot sorted,' I said to the workmen. 'I want those kettles better secured for my next visit.' To Meekal: 'I've seen enough for today.' I glanced over at my carriers. Still blindfolded, they'd now got themselves off the ground, and were coming out of their shaking fits from the noise of the experiment. Their bodies had turned white where dust had stuck to the sweat.

'Get them properly rested and fed,' I ordered no one in particular. 'It's a long trek back to Damascus in this heat.' I turned back to Meekal. 'I need to spend much of the afternoon in the records building,' I said. 'As ever, I suppose, I'll have to write up my own notes. This time, though, I want to go again over the records of the works before the big explosion. I doubt I shall copy the mistakes made then. But, if you're now forcing the pace, I need to make sure of certain things. You're welcome to sit in there with me. You might even be useful for reading some of the more charred records. But, if you'd rather be off and torture someone, I'll not hold it against you.' I dug my stick into the sand and began to move towards the gate into another of the zones.

Karim said nothing, but looked like a man who tries not to show that he's recently shat himself from terror. Edward was shouting away in fluent Saracen to anyone who'd listen.

'They scarpered like wild pigs in the hunt,' he said. He took out his little sword and waved it in the sun. 'As we came closer, I thought they'd stand and fight like men.' He paused, then spat melodramatically. 'But, like all the other unbelievers, they were just cowardly pigs!'

I looked at Meekal with raised eyebrows. He shrugged. I wondered if Edward wasn't growing a little too close to his new friends. But there could be no doubt he was their young hero. The other Saracens stood round him, calling out his praises and giving him little hugs.

'While he is your hostage,' I said quietly, 'you really should consider keeping him safer than you do.'

Meekal scowled and said he'd speak with General Hakim about the breach of his orders.

'You can tell me the whole story over dinner,' I said in English. 'I don't suppose you'll be passing up yet awhile on the wine.'

'It will be as My Lord wills,' Edward replied in Saracen. His face shone with the happiness of the fool who's just nearly got himself killed for nothing. He helped unfold the seat of the carrying chair into a daybed before racing back within the mass of grinning, bearded faces. How long, I wondered, before even his Latin went? How long before his English? Did the boy so much as dream nowadays about the soaking mists of Northumbria? If I were his age now, though, would I be any different?

I rested back against the cushions. I fished into the luggage compartment for my lead box of opium. I removed my teeth and sucked thoughtfully on the resin.

Dreaming of my mother, and of my father, whose face I barely remembered, I slept right through the attack on us that left fifty men dead on the road and another hundred injured. Karim told me about it afterwards. Through chattering teeth, he described the wild rush of the mountain tribesmen as we passed a high ridge of sand. They'd swept down with a battle roar that almost knocked him off his horse. The horsemen weren't up to making any impression on the Saracen guards. It was the hail of arrows that caused the real damage. Meekal had gone wild with alarm, and had darted about, screaming at the guards to cover me with their shields. No prisoners had been taken this time. It had been a matter of getting me and my remaining carriers as fast along that exposed road as men could run. Even so, an arrow had embedded itself in the carrying chair not a quarter-inch from my throat.

I came to as the light was fading in my bedchamber. I'd been put into a cool bath to stabilise my temperature from the heat of the day and from the opium, and then wrapped up in bed like an infant. Before I opened my eyes, I heard Edward's anxious voice, asking again and again if I would ever wake up again. Karim was beside him, urging that I'd surely be fine. I could tell that the hand feeling about my wrist belonged to a doctor. I opened my eyes and waited for the riot of fading colours to resolve into a picture of my surroundings. Meekal was looking out of the window, hands clasped tight behind his back. The boys sat together, looking earnestly into my face. I stared back and smiled.

'Not dead yet?' I croaked. The doctor held a cup to my lips, and I gagged at the extreme bitterness of its contents. I waved it away. I struggled to sit up, but the combination of opium and immense weariness kept me on my back. 'Any chance of some of the local red?' I asked feebly.

A thoroughly nasty look on his face, Meekal turned and came to lean over me. 'The doctor says – and I agree – that you should give up that shitty opium,' he said. 'And the wine too. If you carry on like this, you won't see another spring.'

'I'm a free man,' I snarled back at him. 'I'll put what I like into my body and cry "fuck off!" at anyone who dares tell me otherwise. And don't any of you ever forget that!' I made a better effort and now did sit up. The doctor fussed about with pillows. Edward stuck a cool sponge on my forehead.

'What's that bandage doing on your arm?' I asked. Edward opened his mouth to speak, but was nudged silent by Karim. 'Did you come off that bleeding horse?' I asked again.

There was a noise in Meekal's throat that might have been a laugh, or might just have been another of his prayers to the Almighty. He took hold of Edward's good arm and pushed the boy closer to me.

'The deal is,' he snarled, 'that you give me what I want, and the boy comes to no harm. Will you threaten me with a lawyer if I choose to regard your sudden death as a breach of contract?'

'Fuck you!' I snarled. I struggled out of the cushions and sat fully upright. Everyone stood back. 'I'm hungry,' I added in a more reasonable tone. 'More to the point, I need a piss – I need one badly.' I looked defiantly about the room. 'Well, go on,' I said loudly, 'get out of here. Since Edward's right arm is otherwise occupied, the doctor can stay and do me the honours.' I reached over to get at my water cup. I overbalanced and nearly came off the bed. Meekal kept me from hitting the tiles. He lifted me as if I'd been a bag of twigs – had I lost weight in the past few months? I wondered – and sat me on the side of the bed. I scowled everyone else out of the room, and prepared myself for a consultation with the doctor.

57

'The world must be seen as it is,' I said, 'not as we'd like it to be. One of these days, I shall fall down dead. Or perhaps I just shan't wake up one morning. Until then, I plan to carry on as normal.'

I sucked on a boiled chicken leg and washed the meat down with a cup of water into which Edward had dropped wine with all the stingy care of an apothecary. Karim muttered some piety about how God would deal justly with me. I decided against the obvious witty riposte. It would only make Edward unstopper those tears again. Meekal had gone off about his official business, and I'd told the doctor where to take his pessimistic ambiguities. Now, we were at dinner. Since the most convenient language was Saracen, I'd had the slaves all cleared out and the main door locked from our own side.

'But do tell me again, Edward,' I said brightly. 'Do you really think you cut off that man's nose as he came at you?' He did. So did Karim. I lifted my cup in a toast that left plenty of room for a refill more to my taste. I was about to reach for my teeth so I could begin a long anecdote about Karim's father after the Battle of Antioch. But Edward interrupted.

'I was looking at your clothes this morning,' he said, pulling the conversation back on his chosen track. 'They are all too big for you.'

'Listen, boy,' I sighed, 'I agree that I'm not getting any younger. Even so, I have, for the past few months, been working like a maniac for Meekal. Have you noticed any advance of senility? Do I walk about any the less easily? I've lost some weight. That's all. Now, do you recall that tomb we passed on the road to Caesarea? It was the one put up for a man who died at a hundred and ten. If you can think of one reason why I shouldn't match that, do tell me now. Otherwise, don't spoil dinner.' I managed to reach the wine jug. That cheered me no end.

'Did either of you hear the demonstration?' I asked with a final change of subject. Edward hadn't – he'd been too wrapped up in shouting at the retreating spies. Karim, though, had heard the explosion, and looked back in time to see the fountain of steam and water that, however briefly, had risen high over the walls of the monastery.

'Was all the work before you came for nothing?' he asked.

I looked at Karim. There was a depth of knowledge behind the question. But this didn't surprise me. Did it merit an answer? Probably not. Still, I wanted that tearful look off Edward's face, and the wine was lifting my spirits by the moment.

'Not really,' I said. 'Eight years of lavish funding by the richest power in the world were unlikely to get nowhere. If it might have taken another eight years of trial and error to reproduce the mixture itself, the basic problems of casting and welding had been settled. Indeed, some of the work your people did on the containment of extreme pressure was news to me. The real problem was the big explosion of two – no, three – years ago. Someone got it into his head that the mixture was a powder, not a liquid. What he then produced was highly unstable, and should never have been heated, let alone heated under pressure. The result was an explosion that killed just about everyone who'd got the project going. But for that, I'd have been more useful than critical. As it is, the research notes survived; and it really would have been another few years at most before all the lost ground was recovered. Still, I can't deny that bringing me in to supervise them has brought things very quickly to the edge of success.'

'Then, we shall destroy the Greeks?' Edward asked.

I smiled at his sudden fierceness. 'Yes,' I said quietly, 'I suppose you will. Am I right to suppose that you'll be attending Friday prayers tomorrow?' The boy didn't answer, but looked down. 'Well, it's none of my business if you do. And, if it helps keep you safe from that fucking nephew of yours, I can't say you're making a poor choice. Yes – you stick with your great-nephew, Karim.

He'll see you right. Isn't that so?' Karim nodded. Of course, the moment Edward got up in that mosque and uttered the irrevocable words, the relationship that Greek law had created between the pair of us would fall to the ground. The bond of fealty, of course, nothing could break. But he'd now be Karim's brother in the Faith, and there would be none of that joking insistence on being called 'Great-Uncle Edward'.

'Will everything be ready for demonstration to the Caliph?' Karim asked with another revelation of knowledge.

I nodded. 'You'll understand that a complete prior demonstration would be helpful,' I explained. 'I still don't know if the kettles will stand up to the full pressure, and it would never do for the Commander of the Faithful to lose his eardrums. But I don't think we'll have time. We must all hope that today's experiment was the success I declared it to be.

'Oh,' I said with a sudden change of tone, 'do tell Meekal when you see him tomorrow that I'll need another visit to the monastery before the next demonstration. I want another look at those research notes. There was something there that might be useful. Also, I'll need authority to be taken into every one of the closed zones. When the Caliph does go out to inspect our efforts, we can't afford any mistakes.' Karim nodded again.

'And' – I wasn't finished: I looked about for a sheet of papyrus on which I'd been working before dinner – 'I'll need all these things brought in here.' Karim looked at the sheet and frowned. 'Oh, you'll get everything here in Damascus,' I said with airy reassurance. 'I've seen the observatory from one of the windows here that looks over the main city. I would go there myself, if it didn't mean travelling outside the palace. As Edward can tell you, my researches into the theory of light have reached the point where I need proper instruments. You get me everything on that list, and I'll see to its positioning up on the roof.' I finished my wine and looked about the table to see if there was anything left that didn't require teeth. I reached forward for some olive paste and took up a spoon. I put it down again. I still wasn't finished.

'Now,' I said firmly, 'while I have no intention of dying in the near future, I do think the time has come for me to finalise a few arrangements that have been in the making for some while.' I motioned Edward to a wooden box over by the window. I waited for him to open it and take out the two sealed sheets of parchment. 'I made a new will in Beirut. I see, however, that circumstances have changed. In light of these, I have decided to make over the bulk of my estate while I am still alive. These deeds make the pair of you very rich men.' While I waited for both seals to be broken, I put my teeth back in and prepared to flatten all objections by clothing myself in the formality of His Magnificence the Senator Alaric. 'The transfer deeds are made under Imperial law. Regardless of my somewhat doubtful religious status, I remain a citizen of the Empire, and my intentions will be recognised by the Syrian courts under the Ordinance of Omar. They are drawn in a form that makes them irrevocable by any third party – short, that is, of gross despotism. You will both need to add your signatures of acceptance. These can be witnessed when I call in my Greek secretary. Because of his evident youth, there is a rider to Edward's deed, in which he must certify that he has reached both puberty and the age of fourteen. While he is not entirely sure when he was born, no one is in any position to object if I declare, as his adoptive father, that Edward was fourteen on the 20th April.

'No' – I raised a hand to cut off the protests I could see rising – 'this is my considered intention, and I shall think hard of anyone who objects to it. I fail to see how, for a man of my age, such wealth can be other than an inconvenience. I retain a seventh part of my estate for my own uses. This should be more than adequate. I have given instructions for its disposal in another will that I signed yesterday. You are named as joint executors, and I do ask you to comply with the requirements of the trust I have created. The money is to be used for the purchase and release of slave secretaries who have reached the age of fifty. I have always accepted that an institution so deeply embedded in the life of men as slavery cannot be abolished by positive legislation. Even so, the procedural changes I persuaded Heraclius to make after the Persian War have moved the Empire a reasonable distance towards its effective extinction. I can have no such influence on the laws of the caliphs – especially when their conquests have given such life to the slave markets. But I can hope that a fortune often acquired by dubious means will be put to the service of humanity when I am dead, and that my act can serve as an example to the faithful of every religion.'

I sat back and took my teeth out again. I was finished, and I was weary. Fuck Meekal! In a sense, he was right. My life's work had been crowned by the development of the most horrid weapons. But, if woefully inadequate, this was my response to the fact. I closed my eyes and pretended to sleep. When I opened them again, I saw the boys still looking at me in silence. I laughed and made some feeble joke about the virtue of gratitude. I reached for my stick and got myself over to the window. I pulled at the glazed frame and let air into the room and all the distant sounds of the palace and of Damascus. There was the general sound of the outside at twilight. Mingled with this was the sound of a distant drum and of flute music. For several days now, the palace had been filling up with new arrivals. Tomorrow, or the day after, the Caliph would be making his entry, and the relative silence of the palace since our arrival would be at an end. For the moment, the night sounds of revelry were within their accustomed limits.

I gripped the frame to keep myself steady and breathed in deeply. I looked over towards the hills behind which the sun was fast setting. Its departing rays had turned the sky to pink. In a moment, it would be darkness, and we'd have to call the slaves in to fuss with the lamps. It was then I'd have to put off my visor and give myself eyestrain with my lenses. For the moment, we were alone with just enough light for me to turn round, if I were so minded, and look at the worthless luxury of my living quarters.

I felt a hand on my shoulder. It was Edward.

'Brother Aelric,' he said in oddly accented English, 'the hour is late, and you should rest.'

I turned and smiled at him. Karim stood a few paces behind him, a worried look on his face.

'Yes, it is late,' I said in Greek. 'But you won't believe the amount of work that has still to be done, and that only I can do. Do please go and call the slaves back in. Don't forget about my Greek secretary. Once you've gone out, I will sleep until the midnight hour. I'm then to be woken and helped to my office.

'Karim,' I said, back in Saracen, 'I need those astronomical instruments on the roof at the earliest moment. I shall also need the Director of the Caliph's observatory to explain their use to me. I imagine the man is a Greek. Certainly, it will be faster if we can work in Greek.'

58

I was woken late the following morning by a sound of trumpets. I got myself to the window and looked out. I could see a few men running about below in plate armour. One of them was carrying a large green banner with something white painted on it that I couldn't make out.

'His Majestic Holiness will make his entry before the day is out,' said the slave who'd been sitting beside me as I slept.

I grunted and went back to sit on my bed. The man pulled a cord for the bath slaves to come up, and lifted a cloth off a tray filled with the usual soft foods. I looked at the peeled eggs and the bread that had been carefully extracted from the centre of a loaf. I was about to ask if the books I'd ordered late the previous night had been delivered yet from the Caliph's library when I saw the sheet of folded parchment on the bedside table. I was about to reach for this when I heard noises overhead. There were footsteps and a heavy bump. I looked up at the glazed ceiling panels, and saw a bearded face looking down at me. I smiled and the face vanished again.

'Is young Edward around?' I asked. The words were no sooner out than I saw him just outside the door. 'Come in,' I cried with some attempt at vigour. I stopped and drank from the cup of water held to my lips. I looked vaguely about for my slippers. 'Come in and sit down,' I said to the boy. 'I'm sure you can fill me in on all the news.'

Once Edward was done with all he had to relate of any importance, I turned my attention to the letter. It was a summons to a banquet arranged for five evenings away. Meekal had added a note in his own hand that I was to attend both sober and undrugged

– but that I'd not be expected this time to play any active part. My job was to smile and bow. He'd then pat me on the head and send me off with an early goodnight kiss.

Sadly, the message didn't end there. I was being allowed an early night, it explained, because I'd be expected the following morning to go out with Meekal and give my final touches to the project. The day following that, the Caliph would be turning up there some while before noon. He'd watch a full demonstration of the Greek fire, and then ride back to Damascus for Friday prayers. '*For all our sakes*,' the message ended in an underlined scrawl, '*let nothing go wrong!*'

'That gives me six sodding days,' I grumbled. I thought of my seething vats. 'Telling me to work those round the Caliph's schedule makes as much sense as telling me to arrange the phases of the moon. The stuff will be ready or not. If not, the Caliph will have to be content with a jet of steam. Doubtless, Meekal can enliven proceedings by sticking a few convicts in front of the jet. Whatever the case, there can be no demonstration of fire until the mix is stable.'

I might have been speaking a new foreign language for all the comprehension I saw on Edward's face. I grunted and tossed the letter at him. He screwed up his eyes to concentrate on the Saracen script. He could just follow the main invite. That was in a good secretarial hand that avoided contractions. Meekal's scrawl, however, was still beyond him. I took it back and read, making sure to comment on the unusual sequence of tenses, and how the placing of an adjective in one sentence plainly governed the meaning of the next.

'I don't suppose the Angels of the Lord will be putting in an appearance at the banquet or any other proceedings,' I said. 'If no one else is, the Commander of the Faithful should be safe from their attentions.' I laughed and put a whole egg into my mouth. Edward reached forward with a napkin just in time to stop the soft yolk from bursting in his direction. I did my best to suppress the choking fit with another gulp of water, and did still more to look grand again. 'Unless you've had your own invitation,' I wheezed,

'I propose to bring you along as my page. Even if you are one of the Faithful by then, I doubt anyone will think ill of that.'

Edward bowed and went back to his description of the ceremonies he'd gone out with Karim to witness. They'd been told the Caliph was already in the palace; he'd apparently made a quiet entry just before dawn, and would put in his first official appearance in Damascus at Friday prayers in the big mosque. Would I be there? he asked with a change of subject. Though separated from the women, I could sit behind the grille and watch as Edward made his profession of faith.

'What name will you take?' I asked. 'I can't think of an easy equivalent for Edward.'

'I shall be known henceforth as Moslemah,' came the proud reply. I grunted again. It was a bold choice – not that it would make any difference with me. Since I still hadn't bothered to ask for his real name, I'd not be using this one. For our remaining time together – however long that might be – I'd call the boy Edward.

'You don't have to answer this,' I said, now in English. 'But do you believe a word of all that stuff about Mohammed as the Prophet of God?'

'And what future would there be for me as a Christian?' came the reply. It was a good answer.

I shrugged. Eighty years earlier in Canterbury, I'd made a similar decision for myself. In my case, it had been a sprinkle of water, followed by appointment as Father Maximin's English secretary. If you want to get anywhere in life, you need to identify what religious views are the long-term fashion and accommodate yourself to them. If they turn out to be utterly malign, or just absurd, that's the luck of the dice.

'Whatever people tell you,' I said after a slight pause, 'the operation hurts, and can put you out of action for a month.' Edward wrinkled his nose and sat back in his chair, a resigned look on his face. 'Still, it has to be done. So, take my advice – get it done by a Jewish doctor. The Saracens are more enthusiastic than skilled. And, while we're on the subject, you might as well get it *all* out of the way. Double cuts don't always mean double pain. Would you think it improper if I made you a gift of my own piercing bar? It served me well for longer than most people live. In an emergency, it has other uses too.'

The boy smiled. 'How serious was your own conversion?' he asked.

I took advantage of my own resulting silence to massage my gums with some of the bread. I tried to work out which of the untrue accounts might be most suitable. Of a sudden, I decided to tell the truth. He'd had that much on the Tipasa beach, I recalled. He might as well have it all now.

'It was entirely for the money,' I said in the safety of English. 'When the Saracens took Antioch, every bank in the city failed. This left my overall affairs embarrassed. I was tied up with a mass of temporarily worthless land in Constantinople, and was badly in need of ready cash. Luckily, I was on hand not far from Antioch. I was able to hurry over and strike a deal with Omar, who had come out of the desert to see the wonders of his conquests in Syria. I got full compensation – in gold, mind you. In return, I became the first known Western convert.

'You can be sure I sent Omar my letter of apostasy the moment he was looking the other way. Back in Constantinople, Heraclius had no choice but to believe my story. No one else did, though. The best I could do about the penance was to have the Great Church closed for an afternoon to the unwashed of the city. Still, I had to crawl on my belly – and under the gloating eyes of the entire Imperial Council – across the nave, to where the Patriarch waited with a birching rod.' I shuddered at the recollection. 'Omar took the apostasy rather well. I think the Religious Council advised him that my conversion was void on the grounds that I manifestly lacked conviction. I even left much of the gold on deposit in Antioch – a useful move as it turned out. I must say, I thought everyone had long since forgotten the whole business. It was never brought up in any of my subsequent dealings with the Saracens. I'm surprised – and annoyed – it's now become common knowledge.'

Edward gave me an uncertain look, then changed the subject. That's the problem with truth much of the time. Lies are often so much more credible.

'I think you need to get the circumcision done within one Saracen month,' I said, turning the subject back. 'Get it out of the way. But make sure first that even you are sated.' I got another uncertain look. Oh, the happy days of youth! I thought with a pang of envy. I looked at the remains of my breakfast. They could wait. Better than that, they could wait long enough for the bread to go slightly hard. I could then insist on soaking it in wine. I looked up at the rising noise of bangs and heavy treads. 'Be a good man,' I said to the slave, who'd stood patiently by throughout my conversation with Edward, 'and have my bath made ready. After that, I can be taken up on to the roof. I want to supervise the placing of the instruments. Do also ask my Saracen secretary to attend me in the bathroom. I have letters to dictate.'

While I was still dithering over the choice of hot or hotter water in the bath, Karim decided on a call. A pleased look on his face, he perched himself on the ledge of the marble tub.

'If you pluck them all out,' I said to the attendant, 'I'll have none left at all. But do rid me of enough purely white eyebrows to give me a younger appearance.' I peered into the steaming water at my legs. Depilation was off the menu for someone of my age. But another shave all over would see me right up until the day of the banquet. If I stewed here long enough, the few patches of body hair that the years had left me would come off without too much scraping . . .

'Would My Lord be offended if I dismissed the attendants?' Karim asked with firm politeness. I looked at the age spots on my right hand and nodded permission for the attendants to withdraw. Karim followed them out and closed the door. He came back and sat again on the marble rim of the tub.

'Be a dear,' I said, 'and pull that lever over there. I don't want a flood of hot, but a slight trickle might do my heart no damage.' My arms resting lightly on the rim, I sat back in the bath so that the water came up to my chin. I looked blearily through the steam at Karim.

'I hear that Meekal wants the Caliph to see the project,' he began.

I nodded and lifted my right foot above the water. Something I'd discovered with my visor was that it improved my vision even when I wasn't using it. I explained this in terms of the focusing muscles. For some reason, I didn't seem to get the same result with any of the lenses I'd now perfected. Light and vision were funny things. Would even I live long enough to arrive at any understanding of their working?

'I think I see a line of dirt under my big toenail,' I said. 'Since there's no one else to attend to it, would you do your dear great-grandfather the honours with that pointed scraper on a ledge over by the window?' I gripped the sides of the bath and slid down another two inches to get an easier position for my foot. I spluttered a moment as I breathed in an accidental mouthful of bathwater.

'Meekal is coming here later today,' he added. 'He had a wretched meeting with the Caliph. Khadija has raised most of the Council against him.' I shrugged. 'She tells me we need to discuss the demonstration. Do you suppose everything will be ready in time?' I squirted a fountain of water between pursed lips and followed this with a toothless grin. Karim nodded. 'It might be useful,' he said, 'if not everything worked perfectly on the day.' I lifted my left foot above the water and let him inspect the nails for more dirt I might have picked up the previous day. 'What I mean,' he went on, a slight pleading tone in his voice, 'is that we don't want a complete failure – not the sort of thing that will get everything cancelled. What we have in mind is a partial success. We'd like it made plain that the weapon can be made to work, but only after more time, and more money – perhaps quite a lot of money.

'Can you hold off giving Meekal the final details of how everything works?' he asked, changing the subject. 'There will be a full meeting of the Council once everyone is back in the palace. The Lord Treasurer will present a long report. Our friends will make their move in the discussions arising. Once Meekal has been sent off to inspect the garrisons against the Yellow Barbarians, Khadija will have an offer made of private funding to complete the project. We are thinking of another successful demonstration in the early autumn. Can you play along with this?'

'When Edward becomes one of the Faithful,' I asked with another of my toothless grins, 'I suppose he will pass under your complete protection? And that will mean the full protection of Khadija and all her friends?'

Karim nodded, giving me something from his people's Holy Book about the Brotherhood of the Faith.

'Then it will all be as you ask,' I said. 'I am curious, though, why Khadija is so confident that she can finally get Meekal put out of the way. Are finances really as tight as you indicate? Does this mean the civil war is going worse than the palace heralds keep saying? Have there been more reverses in the war with the Empire?'

'You'll need to speak with Khadija about that,' came the evasive reply. I lifted my arms in front of me and sank under the water. I felt Karim's hands close on my shoulders and pull me back up. I rubbed water from my eyes and smiled into his scared face. 'Don't do that again – please,' he begged. He looked at the wet sleeves now clinging to his forearms.

'What you're asking me,' I said, 'involves risks in which none of you people will share. If I don't give Meekal the show he's expecting, it may be enough to discredit him. On the other hand, he may tough out the Council meeting. If he does that, he'll not be pleased with me or mine. Can you oblige me with the names of Khadija's friends in the Council? I need to be sure this is a regular conspiracy and not some half-baked palace intrigue got up by women and eunuchs.' I looked closely into the now plainly terrified face. 'I want the full names and offices of the conspirators. And don't trouble me with making up the details. Over the past three generations, I've developed a crap-detection sense that many judges might envy.' I gripped the sides of the bath and kicked my feet up and down. I listened with lazy contentment as water gurgled down the lead overflow pipe.

'And do open that cold lever a little. I'm beginning to feel as a lobster must.'

59

'You know,' I said brightly, 'it looks so much different, even from another fourteen feet higher.' The foreman muttered something about the breeze and gently led me back from the edge of the roof. The sun was now fully up, and I could feel a trickle of sweat from under my wig. But if it was unlikely to carry me over the edge, the breeze was most welcome. 'I hadn't realised that the Spice Market had a double vault to its roof,' I said. 'I've been looking at it for months. But I suppose fourteen feet does make a difference.'

The foreman sighed and went back to his explanation of the roof – and he was in a position to lecture me on the thing, as he'd helped lay it the previous Ramadan. It was a marvel of two-inch-thick cedar boards, each cut into a gentle fan and laid with barely a gap from the centre of the tower to its outer edge. Over these was a layer of pitch, then of canvas, and then an outer covering of lead.

'Admirable, most admirable,' I said. 'However, even if the boards are supported along their lengths, I do still urge two further layers of ten-foot boards, each at a right angle to the other. That should spread the load without any further worry.' The foreman bowed and made some marks on his waxed tablet. It would all be as I desired. I looked again at the half ton of brass that sat before me, gleaming in the sun. The young man who'd so far stood silent before me, hands folded across his breast, would soon explain the use of those dials and levers.

I was thinking also of an awning to keep the sun off me. I'd be up here several days running, sometimes through the hottest hours. As I was deciding between silk and linen, the foreman and everyone else threw themselves down for a long grovel.

‘Ah, Meekal,’ I said without turning, ‘I was wondering when you’d put in an appearance.’ Even my defective hearing wasn’t enough to blot out the sound of his breathing: I might have had an angry bull behind me. I turned and made the feeblest pretence of a bow.

‘What is the meaning of this?’ he said with the sort of quiet menace that can swell very fast into hysterical screaming. He waved at the half-dozen large astronomical instruments.

‘I’m a newcomer myself to solar observations,’ I said with a bright smile. ‘Until that young man cowering at your feet enlightens me, it’s all a bit of a mystery. However, I do think that big machine over there with the electrum plates is used for finding the angle of separation between two stars. I’m sure I’ll find it useful for something.’

Meekal put his head down and walked a few paces along the roof.

‘Have you any idea,’ he said, turning back to me, ‘how much these devices cost?’

I held my arms wide out and pulled the appropriate face. ‘It isn’t my concern either,’ I added. ‘The deal is that I ask for whatever I need. The funding is your problem.’

Meekal pushed his face close to mine. ‘The deal is that you complete my project,’ he hissed, now in Latin. ‘From what little sense I’ve had from Karim, these are for your private researches.’

I sat down and stared at Meekal. I picked up a fly whisk and waved it vaguely about my head. Everyone else was still clutching the ground, as still as in death.

‘Then, if you’ll pardon me for saying,’ I sneered, still in Syriac, ‘you’re a right barbarian. We aren’t talking here about a recipe for fish sauce. I need complete freedom to research as I see fit. Do you want the Caliph to stand up and cheer when I set those kettles off? Or do you want to offer him an unusually vigorous steam bath?’

‘I have just finished a meeting with the Caliph,’ came the response in a voice that really did remind me of one of my kettles. ‘He was accosted on his return to the palace by the Director of the observatory you had just plundered. His Majestic Holiness was not pleased.'

I got up and laughed. I walked close to the edge of the roof and rapped hard with my stick on a bronze adjustment bar.

'So that's how it is,' I cried in a loud voice. The breeze had dropped down again, and my voice was flat but clear. I made sure to keep in Syriac. 'When the Commander of the Faithful is away, you're top dog. When he's back, you answer to his finance clerks. And to think you betrayed your family, your country, your religion for this. I could have got you made Exarch of Italy. Why, you'd have had more authority as Prefect of Cartenna!'

Meekal glanced down at the carpet of grovelling bodies. 'Get off this roof – all of you!' he snarled softly. He waited until everyone had darted through the hatchway in the centre of the roof that led down to the access ramps. He kicked the hatch closed and came back to me. I was back in my chair, and was pretending to inspect the handle of my fly whisk. He stood over me. His black robes heaved in time with his breathing. 'If you cannot do so in private, I do suggest, for your own good, that you show some respect in public.'

'Fuck you, Michael!' I answered in Greek. I looked up at the cloudless sky. My left leg was hurting, and I could feel the need for a piss coming on.

'Is there *one* reason,' he asked slowly and with much effort, 'why I shouldn't have these things collected at once and taken back to where they belong?'

As I was wondering how he'd react to my standing up and pissing close to his feet, I heard the first scrape of the water screw. It was over on the far side of the tower. But, without the insulation of walls and glazed windows, the laboured, squealing, grating sound was unpleasant on the ear. I clutched hold of a brass lever and pulled myself up. I held out my arm for Meekal to take. Together, we made our way across the roof to where the covered water tank was placed. For the moment, the noise came from below, as water was pushed up the rotating lower screw to the tank within the tower. Then, with a more continuous and still louder screech of bronze pipe within bronze hoops, the upper screw began to rotate. At first, it was just a shuddering movement of weather-corroded metal. Then, with a loud splutter, the first bright splash of water jumped on to the collection pan and was channelled into the lead tank. It was like watching a giant, if sluggish, ejaculation as the tank was slowly filled. Far below – perhaps right on the ground, perhaps within the tower itself – there came the higher sound of a whip and a suppressed cry. Someone laughed unpleasantly, and there was another crack of the whip.

'You know,' I said, speaking as best I could above the noise, 'I've been wondering ever since I came here if some arrangement of gears wouldn't cut out the need for a break into the pipe.' I waited for the puzzled look on Meekal's face to pass. I waited in vain. I shrugged and let him help me on to the low stool he'd carried across with us. Water was now running back down the pipe, and this was lubricating its movement within the hoops. The noise had changed to a dull, continuous grating of metal on metal. 'It's about seventy feet from here to the ground. There's no reason why a single pipe of that length can't be made. Each of the two existing lengths was cast in sections, then welded together. The two sections themselves could easily be joined. The limitation is that the highest rotation speed isn't enough to push water the whole distance. That's why the engineers broke the course with a supplemental tank. But if the rotation speed could be increased without limit, there might be no limit to how far water could be raised. That's why I thought of gears.

'Since yesterday, though, I've been thinking further. I used steam in our demonstration as a substitute for the real thing. But suppose you could match a steam kettle to the sort of wheel you see on a water mill. That, plus the gears, would give enormous force to any rotation. You'd be turning heat into motion. Has it ever struck you that all human might so far has been based on the power of human or animal muscles?' I ignored the lack of response. I was speaking now more for myself than for Meekal. If he'd gone and thrown himself off the roof, I might have got up for a dance of joy. Or I might have carried on with the lecture.

'Even when there is no limit to the quantity of muscle power, there are limits to its effective use. Yet heat can be generated wherever there are adequate supplies of fuel, and can be converted into both intense and rapid motion. Give me funding and a team of engineers and metal workers, and I'll give you a machine that will raise water seventy feet – and have it spurting ten feet beyond that. Indeed, once the basic point is realised, of the conversion of heat to motion, I can imagine ships that sail regardless of winds and tide, and vehicles that can travel on the roads day after day at the speed of a galloping horse.'

'You've been at that shitty opium again,' Meekal sneered.

I smiled and sat up. I took off my visor and waved it at him. 'Bearing in mind what I have already achieved,' I asked, 'must I make out the same case, in each and every other instance, for the benefits of understanding and controlling the world about us? Can you not at least see that the first civilisation to bow before the power of natural reason will conquer the world? Is not the weapon I am about to give you a feeble thing compared with what might one day be? Are not your own victories in the East as much an effect of chain mail and swords as of religious enthusiasm?'

Meekal gave one of his contemptuous laughs. He held out a hand to take my arm and led me over to the exit hatch from the roof. I stopped by one of the larger instruments. Its calibration marks told me it was of Alexandrian workmanship – possibly from before the Roman conquest of Egypt. For something of its age, it was in good shape. A pity, though, that seven hundred years hadn't rendered it as obsolete as the numerals that had to be learned before it could be made to work. I pulled free of Meekal's grip and carefully sat myself on the warmed lead within the shadow of the instrument.

'Do you remember that story told of Tiberius – the Emperor who succeeded Augustus in ancient times, not the one a hundred years back who came before the unfortunate Maurice?' Still nothing from Meekal. I got slowly up and looked over the rooftops of Damascus. The breeze was coming up again. 'He was approached one day by a craftsman who said he'd made a new sort of glass cup.

As the Emperor reached out to take the cup, the craftsman let it fall from his grasp. Tiberius stood back to avoid the smashing of glass on the floor of his palace. Instead of shattering, though, the cup bounced on the marble. The craftsman took it up and produced a little hammer, so he could knock out the slight dent of the impact. Impressed, Tiberius asked if anyone else knew how to make such glass. "No," came the answer. It was a secret known only to one man. Was he rewarded with a kiss of joy and a soft loan to build a bigger workshop? No, he had his head cut off. Let the secret of unbreakable glass be common knowledge, said Caesar, and no one would ever commission cups of gold and silver. After a while, no one would even buy new glass cups. The death of one man, he said, was essential, if thousands were not to lose their livelihoods.

'If you want to see the effects of that mode of reasoning, go and look at the heap of stinking ruins that Rome has since become. There is no limit to the work that can be done and needs to be done by human labour. Improvements that increase the force of human labour simply increase the wealth and power of the human race.'

Still no words from Meekal. But I could now see the look of pained resignation on his face. 'So I get to keep this lot for the next month,' I said rather than asked. Still no answer. 'Do be kind enough, then,' I said with bright cheer, 'to remind that foreman when you let him back up here, that this roof has a slight pitch, and that levelling wedges need to be placed under the planks.' This time, he nodded.

'Oh,' I added, 'if you want everything ready on time, I'll need to spend several days at the old Saint Theodore Monastery. I'll need to go into every one of the restricted zones, and pass and repass between them. This isn't negotiable. I need more than one day to get everything ready. So you can either drag yourself out of Damascus with me, or dispense me from some of your security rules.' I got a cold look for that. I ignored it. 'And you can replace those mangy guards you've been using for my protection. Now the Caliph is back, I want a brigade of proper fighting men about me every time I set foot outside the palace.'

Another cold look. But Meekal was walking towards the hatch. You may think I'd pushed my luck quite far enough. But I could feel the jolly tiredness of an early siesta coming on. I rapped the lead covering of the roof with my walking stick.

'And since you're going that way,' I croaked, 'do have some beer sent up for me. Yes – beer *and* a piss pot. It wouldn't do for me to piss over the edge of the roof. You never know at the moment who might be passing by underneath.'

60

Because it kept me in the palace at a time when I had work to do elsewhere, the banquet was as much a nuisance to a busy man as a burden on an old man. But if I'd twisted like an eel to get out of it, Meekal had held me firm. And so, dressed in heavy finery, my head freshly shaven and bewigged, I was led to my dining couch as if to some place of execution.

The banquet was in the same place as before. There was scorching to some of the columns that hadn't come off with scrubbing, and there was a small army camped all around the hall. This time, of course, there was no attack to cut short the proceedings. This time, also, I wasn't anything like guest of honour. My own dining couch was at the far end of the hall, and my only dealings with Meekal were a whispered lecture as he came to stand beside me on the use of gold in the transmutation of materials. I gathered that His Majestic Holiness would spend the following day on an auditing of the research budget, and there was some opposition within his Council to the extravagance of the demands I'd made. But this was a brief lecture. How much of it Meekal really took in wasn't my concern. He'd probably parrot the relevant points well enough. Besides, it had all been agreed long in advance that the Council wasn't to be told enough to compromise the security of the project.

'I'll join you out in the desert before you arrive at the monastery,' he'd said with one of his unpleasant glares. I had supposed Meekal would be stuck all day with the auditing. But, if I'd caused him further trouble with my demand for the additional gold bars, even that wouldn't keep him stuck all day in the Council. The several days of freedom I'd pulled out of him, to potter about in the monastery to my heart's content, would now be brought to an end. 'Then it must be Karim who has responsibility for my safety on the desert journey,' I'd replied. 'The additional men seem to have scared off the Angels of the Lord. Just make sure to send out someone with Karim who knows how to direct a fight if one is needed.'

Meekal had given me a last doubtful nod, before going off to take his place beside the huge, glowering figure of the Caliph. He sat on his throne, as rigid as in the best Imperial ritual. Before him stood the leaders of his Religious Council, together with both Orthodox and Heretical Patriarchs of Jerusalem. Between them – perhaps to give them someone they could both agree on hating – was one of the Jewish leaders. Because all the Saracens were dressed in plain white, it hadn't the full magnificence of Constantinople. But, if it might be lacking in the externals, this was – no one present could be in the slightest doubt – an event presided over by the richest and most powerful man in the world. The Saracens, of course, were let off with bows and acclamations. For everyone else, it was the full prostration. Even I was led forward at last, and helped on to hands and knees for the adoration of God's Chosen One.

'Greetings, O Alaric,' some eunuch chamberlain whispered in Greek as I finished tapping my forehead on the carpet. 'Your presence is pleasing to the Commander of the Faithful.'

I gave a quiet sniff. It didn't do to look up into the face of His Majestic Holiness. All else aside, it would have been a breach of manners for him to behave as other than a block of wood. I listened hard and counted the soft blows on the gong. In Constantinople, five blows during and after the prostration indicated a person of considerable quality. I thought Meekal had got five. I counted seven for myself.

'If you feel another fainting attack come on,' I muttered to Edward once I was arranged back in my place, 'do sit down at once. Your job is to pour the scented water over my hands at the beginning and end of each course. Otherwise, you just need to smile and look pretty. We can get away after the iced fruits have been served. Meekal can't say when they'll be served. But it's all agreed that no one will think the worse of us for leaving. I can then prepare a cup of something soothing. One dip in that of the afflicted member, and you won't notice the pain.' I grinned and pushed in my ear trumpet so I could hear more of the herald's pompous oration. It had been going on an age, and showed no signs of ending. There had been a gigantic slaughter in some place with an unmemorable name. The arms of the Caliph had prevailed after a day of this, and there was a long detailing of the prisoners and property thereby won. I listened hard, but heard no indication that the False Caliph had been killed or taken. Almost certainly, this would mean another campaign in the civil war. Sad, this, for everyone closely involved – but no bad thing for the Empire.

As if he'd read my thoughts, Edward leaned forward and nodded at the main couch beneath the Caliph's throne. I adjusted my visor and focused. Eusebius had already been watching me closely. I smiled. He noticed and looked away.

'That, my dear, is the Imperial Ambassador,' I said. 'It doesn't mean that the two empires are officially at peace. But it looks as if at least one side has run out of puff for the time being. I wonder if he'll be invited to the demonstration the day after tomorrow. You can be sure he's heard all about it.' I had another look at His Excellency. You could have fitted out a border fort with the price of that gold and purple robe. Such, however, are the costs of diplomacy. 'He's the last known descendant of the Great Constantine – the one, that is, who established Christianity as the Empire's official faith. One of his uncles was married to my youngest daughter,' I went on. 'It wasn't a happy or a productive union, I regret to say. The moment he'd got himself knocked on the head in a Circus riot, she joined the Sisters of Saint Drusilla and spent the rest of her life stitching head coverings for lepers. She never spoke to me again. Eusebius himself studied with Meekal. They were pretty close for a while. I wonder if efforts will be made to bring back the Prodigal Son.'

But the Ambassador's page was now holding up the gold ewer, ready to pour water over those fastidious, if quietly sticky, hands. I held up my own hands for Edward's attention, and wondered what might be in the covered dishes that were now appearing in the hall.

'The Caliph's beard is very big,' Edward whispered in English.

'Well, he *is* the Caliph,' I replied. 'Another thirty years, and yours might be no less grand.' This being said, I had a look as the Commander of the Faithful was carried past. 'That heavy gloss only comes from regular eating of arsenic. Having a food taster is a step too far as yet away from the simplicity of the desert. But – it depends how you count them – at least one caliph has been murdered in the past fifty years; and poisoning is endemic throughout the East.' I stopped as Edward did his business with the ewer and the cloth, then gave myself with modest attention to the jellied goat in honey.

'Will there be dancing girls?' Edward asked during a break in the eating. Someone was reading in an interminable drone from a book of religious jurisprudence that seemed wholly concerned with table manners. A screen in front of his face, the Caliph was being fed by a dwarf with three arms and a hump.

'Not until much later,' I said. 'The Caliph's Religious Council might find something allegorically pleasing in the display of bare flesh.' I glanced over at the grim, grey-bearded faces of the leading expounders of the Faith. Their looks could have curdled fresh milk. 'The patriarchs, on the other hand, would outdo each other all the way to the moon in their displeasure.' I gave him one of my best toothless grins. 'Besides, I really don't recommend the smallest excitement in your present circumstances. I think there might be acrobats before we must leave. If it's pleasure you want, I'll add a dab of opium to your dipping cup. Topical applications there can be most interesting.' It was an inconvenience that Meekal had insisted on the full conversion, and had then sat gloating as the Jewish doctor did his business. It had confined Edward to a carrying chair beside mine on our trips through the desert. Now, the boy stood by my couch, twitching and grimacing at every move.

The banquet ground on in all its boring magnificence. Just after the acrobats, another of the Caliph's attendants brought me a dish of dormice mashed into vinegar. A cup of the iced fruit would have been more welcome. But I swung myself into a sitting position on the couch and bowed respectfully. Through my visor, I might have caught the ghost of a smile on the stiff face. Where was Meekal? I looked hard at the couches placed about the throne. One of them was empty. And there was no Meekal. He'd been wolfing down meat as if he'd just come back from the wars. Between courses, he'd been sucking up horribly to the oldest and most forbidding member of the Religious Council. Now, he was off somewhere else.

'At this rate, we'll be here all bloody night,' I sighed. Pale in the lamplight, Edward was perched on the couch beside me. He tried not to move his mouth as he crunched on some nuts I'd put beside him. Back in my office, I had a mountain of work still to do. I'd never so far taken much interest in solar observations. But the hours I'd been able to snatch from those inspection trips to the Saint Theodore Monastery had been of surpassing interest. If only I'd been able to apply more of that time to the necessary calculations . . .

I turned to the man on the neighbouring couch. It was my old friend the Admiral, whose fleet I'd sunk under the walls of Constantinople. Now my sight was artificially improved, I could see that his left arm was black and shrivelled. More work of mine? Hard to say. I smiled at him and asked how things were going in the shipyards of Tyre and Sidon. All things considered, it wasn't the sort of question someone like me should have been asking of someone like him – especially not with Eusebius just a hundred yards away to remind us, should we forget, who we were or had been. But the poor man was plainly as bored as I was, and we were soon deep in a semi-hidden conversation as we refought the Battle of Cape Mogadonia. That kept me going till the next course: raisins pickled to twice their size in fish sauce. My hands shook as I tried to skewer these on the wooden sticks provided, and more went on the napkin tied to me than down my throat. I was thinking to give up on the effort and pretend to have fallen asleep, when Edward took up the job for me. The raisins were an improvement on the preceding dish of chopped cabbage sweetened with powdered lead – not that I'd bothered with more than a taste of that. But I'd sooner have been in my bed, cuddling a flask of wine, or knocked out on something more exotic.

'Time, I think, to claim the prerogatives of age,' I muttered to a now almost comatose Edward. 'We'll wait until the potty men come round with their screens, then make a quiet exit.'

He nodded vaguely, and went back to looking at the shoes of gold and silver thread that Karim had presented on his conversion.

'On the contrary, Brother Aelric,' someone from behind whispered in Latin, 'you will stay to the end if you know what is good for you and the boy. No – don't turn round. It will only spoil things. Bear in mind that I'm not really behind you. I've never been anywhere close to you. Just stay to the end. And do try to look as if you're enjoying yourself. The Caliph spoke highly of you to Eusebius.'

I waited until there was a noise of unfolding screens to my left, then turned to Edward.

'Have I gone senile?' I asked.

'No,' came the reassuring answer. 'He poked me in the back just as he used to in Jarrow when I fell asleep in his class.'

'Then your wish will come true,' I said. I nodded at the departing patriarchs. They left through the back entrance I'd taken with Karim on my last attendance here. They were barely through when a dozen heavily robed figures entered, with a couple of clean-shaven musicians close behind. As a great shout of relief rang through the hall, I noticed that Eusebius too was missing from his place. 'Don't say, though, I didn't warn you!' I added with another grin. Edward's reply was smothered by the opening peal of the drums.

I adjusted my visor. I'd been told to *look* as if I was enjoying myself. Tired as I was, I might do better than that.

61

'You can get everything sorted up there come morning,' I said to the twittering eunuch. 'Tonight, the boy and I will sleep downstairs in the slave quarters.' I looked again at the half ton of astrolabe. Its broken remains were distributed across the smashed tiles of the floor. My own bed had been flattened by the impact. Anyone on it, or within a foot of it in any direction, would have been crushed like a grape in the press. If I hadn't been so tired, I might have shared the general horror at this latest violation. As it was, I simply wanted somewhere to sleep for what remained of the night.

'My Lord will be aware,' came the nervous explanation, 'that a loud crash was heard shortly before the midnight hour. I have not myself been on to the roof. But I do know that the instruments placed on it were of exceeding heaviness. It is perhaps a surprise the roof did not give way sooner.'

I ignored the creature's increasingly shrill piping. I could guess easily enough what had happened. I was no engineer, but my arrangement of boards could have taken a dozen times its actual load. I'd also sited the astrolabe nowhere near above this room. The real questions were how anyone had got up there – and how whoever had got up there could have known that I generally wasn't in bed between midnight and dawn. I was about to ask a few relevant questions of the slaves when Karim burst into the room. Gibbering in his nightgown, his face like death, he looked about us, then dropped into the one chair that wasn't broken.

'God be praised!' he panted. 'I came at once when I heard the news. It is surely a sign from God you weren't both killed.'

I poked with my stick at a brass lever. Search me how much the thing had cost – not that it mattered: Meekal could add it to the overall bill. What did matter was that it had been so very pretty. I doubted there was another like it anywhere in the world. Still, now he was here, I'd have Karim look into the possibility of a replacement.

'My dear Karim,' I said wearily, 'since Edward is not in the habit of sharing my bed, I don't think he was in any danger.' I frowned. 'Any chance, by the way, of standing up for an old man?' He jumped up, now looking guilty. 'That's a good lad.' I flopped into the chair and looked up at the hole where half the ceiling had been. Against a background of utter blackness, hands clutching the broken edges of the roof, Edward stared down at us.

'The boards you told me would spread the weight are all taken up,' he said in English. 'Also, there are some cutting tools left here.'

I turned a disapproving stare on Karim. 'I don't like to question your competence, dear boy,' I said. 'But you are in charge of my security in the palace. And this is the second time intruders have got in here.' That might have set Karim straight into a moral collapse. Just as he put his hands up to his face, though, Meekal walked in. That set everyone about me into a round of bowing and scraping. He looked awhile in silence at the smashed astrolabe.

'I did hear that loading up that roof wasn't a good idea,' he said. He was keeping himself admirably in check. Meekal looked up at Edward, then again at the mass of detached and broken dials littering the floor. He kicked morosely at a brown stone about the size and shape of a turd. 'What's that?' he asked. He went and leaned by the window, scowling at everyone in sight.

'It's something I learned from the northerners you hired to abduct me,' I said with one of my ivory smiles. 'You put it into a wooden bowl, and float this within a larger bowl of water. It always points north. It cost thirty times its weight in gold,' I said with heavy emphasis. 'Don't worry, though – this can be rescued.'

Meekal ignored me. 'I suppose this *was* an accident?' he asked of Karim. That nearly sent the boy over the edge.

Luckily, Edward chose this moment to ignore the stairs leading to the central ramp of the tower, and to drop lightly down the twelve feet that separated him from the one clear patch of floor.

He spoiled the effect with a wince of pain just before hitting the floor. He landed on his bottom with a suppressed squeal. He scrambled up and nodded a bow at Meekal, and came and stood beside me. I looked at Karim and shrugged. What point in swimming against the tide?

'I think it best to assume an accident,' I said. I gave Edward a pre-emptive kick to shut him up. 'Fortunately, I was so entranced by the Caliph's hospitality that I broke my normal schedule.' I stood up. I felt my knees going, and sat down again. 'Now, my dear friends, I want someone to arrange a bed for me *now*. I also want this mess all cleared up and made good by this time tomorrow. While you're at it, you can get me a new astrolabe set up on the roof – and I don't want any disruption of my living quarters.' The eunuch began twittering away about the impossibility of my instructions. I clapped my hands in his face. His voice dropped to a whine about nothing relevant to my instructions. I sat back down and fanned myself with my wig. One of the slaves jumped forward and set about me with a proper fan. 'And will somebody bring me a cup of wine?' I snarled with recovering energy. 'Just because the rest of you have forsworn its use doesn't mean I have to suffer as well.'

'Do you suspect Karim?' Edward asked. I looked over at a sand dune that was held together with dead weeds and laughed. One of the carrying slaves turned and looked at me. I waited until he'd turned back about his business, and took another swig of beer.

'Where these matters are concerned,' I answered, 'long experience tells me to rule out no possible explanation, however weak it may seem.' I paused and smiled. I looked at a flight of birds overhead, and then at the dull expanse of sand ahead of us. 'But I don't suspect Karim of more than incompetence. He may be of my own blood. He may be your own dearest friend. But I do suggest that he is neither particularly bright, nor brave in the slightest.' Edward shrugged. Of course, he'd seen all that from the first. I didn't think it worth discussing. But I could see it was these qualities that had drawn Edward to him. When your entire life has been directed for you by men of ruthless and fearless determination, it can be a relief to find company in those who simply like you.

'You can rule out Karim,' I said firmly. Edward gave me a relieved look. The sun was now rising higher, and I could feel a prickly sweat under my wig. Damascus was far behind us, the monastery still far ahead. I thought again of the jagged hole we'd inspected together in the first light of dawn. 'It may have taken several dozen men to get everything up there and placed exactly where I wanted it,' I said. 'To cut through those timbers and pull the astrolabe into place might have needed half a dozen men at the most. I'll grant, however, the noise of the cutting would have sounded like a drum down below.'

'Then it was an inside job?' Edward asked.

I allowed myself another laugh, this one cynical. 'It took my great-grandson three days after the first attempt on me to get round to strengthening the guard,' I said. 'The guards he did post are as idle and negligent as he is. His policy of cycling slaves between our suite and the main palace is a sure recipe for breaches of security. Now the palace is filled to bursting with comparative strangers, there can be no security. Yes – dear Karim! If his father and uncles had been of his own sort, the Empire would still be ripping itself apart over the Monophysite heresy in Egypt and Syria . . .' I trailed off and waited for a couple of the mounted guards to ride slowly past our chairs.

'My dear boy, I would normally leave the matter of gathering information to you. I'd have you question all the slaves. Most obviously, we'd need to know who gave the orders for them to lock the suite and withdraw to their own quarters. We'd also need to know who was in charge of the guards, and whether the guards heard or saw anything before they'd knocked themselves completely out on their hashish. I really don't think you'd find anything worthwhile. But the effort would need to be made. If you did find anything, though, it would only lead you to dear Eusebius. The Imperial Ambassador may not have been here more than a few days. But trust me – he was conspiring before he could crawl.'

'But if it was the Empire,' Edward broke in, 'why did Brother

Joseph tip us off? I saw him only briefly in that ship off Cartenna. But I am convinced he was urging the fleet on to kill us all. He's been around Damascus for months. Now, he gets himself into the presence of the Caliph to warn us against coming back here to bed. It doesn't make sense.' I could have told Edward much else about our friend Joseph. But I hadn't done so yet, and I saw no point in doing so now. 'And,' he added, 'what was he doing in Jarrow?' The boy sat back in his chair and looked up at the deep blue of the sky. 'I still don't know where he fits into all this.'

I thought he'd ask more about Joseph. But we were now approaching one of the larger dunes, and I could see Karim waiting there as agreed. I wriggled into a more comfortable upright position and stared at Edward.

'These are all worthless questions,' I said. 'There will be no investigation of the murder attempt. There will be no further discussions of Joseph or of Jarrow.' I shut down the confused objection with a wave of my hand. 'I want you to know that your usefulness to Meekal will soon be at an end. Don't try reminding me of the oath he took in front of Karim and all those religious scholars. If he broke his public oath to an emperor, you can forget about any promises he might have made in private. Besides, Karim is also on his list. Meekal spoke to me last month of the statue I commissioned of myself back in my twenties. I had it done in the ancient style – all nudey and tarted-up realistic. He asked if Karim didn't remind me of the thing. Of course, I passed it all off with a joke. Even so, I've seen him staring thoughtfully at Karim. The moment I've given him the last secret of that weapon – and it can't be held back beyond tomorrow – he'll have me killed. He'll then kill you. He'll also kill Karim. He suspects the blood relationship, and he doesn't want a Saracen blood feud on his hands – not even from someone like Karim. Because he wants the matter to end there, he'll get Karim sentenced to death in the regular way. But it's certain death for us all.'

'But he can't kill Karim,' Edward broke in. 'He's Saracen nobility. He's too well connected.'

I laughed again. That wasn't how Karim had seen things when

I'd explained myself earlier. I'd almost had to offer him wine to bring him out of the resulting funk.

'He can and will kill the poor lad,' I replied. 'Except for a sort of stepmother who's little more than a prisoner in the palace, his connections are all far off in Medina. And they are all part of the losing side in the last civil war. It's a shame you didn't understand what Meekal was told in that obscene ceremony. But its meaning has always been clear enough to me. My grandson fancies himself as the next caliph. And he thinks he'll be that before the close of business tomorrow. I didn't look too closely. But, when I was there the day before yesterday, I saw that the fire kettles had been mounted on a new base that swivels. His first demonstration of the Greek fire will be against the Caliph and anyone sitting beside him. That will probably be the whole Council. He'll blow the Caliph and all his Council to charcoal. Then he'll do away with me. Then he'll finish things for the pair of you. Don't try telling me otherwise. I've known the fucker all his life. I know the workings of his mind. *Better to reign in Hell than serve in Heaven* just about sums up his entire approach to this long and expensive project.'

We were now almost level with Karim. He smiled uncertainly back at me and bowed. 'Edward, I want you to get on that horse and bolt for it with Karim. The commander of the guard has been bribed and will look the other way unless he's forced to notice what's happening. You have twelve pounds apiece of Meekal's gold. That should get you to Medina with plenty left over. Meekal can't last as caliph. He's not a Saracen. And, again, I know him. He'll grasp at power like at sand – the harder he grasps, the more it will slip between his fingers. He'll be gone within a few months – a year at most. You can then come back here if you want. Or you can go anywhere else within this vast but ramshackle empire.'

There was no point trying to restrain the babble of protests that now broke from Edward's lips. I let it pour out until the boy was short of breath.

'We haven't long now,' I said urgently. 'So don't waste my time with talk about taking me with you. One way or the other, my life will soon be over. Even Meekal won't be up to making the end specially painful. For you, blinding and castration will just be the start of things. I'll repeat myself. You got me out here using poor Wilfred as your hostage. You then stepped unwittingly straight into his shoes. Now, I'm giving you the chance to get away before it's too late. Take the chance and go. It's too late for elaborate farewells. Just go. If you want to thank me, do so by living better than you'd have managed in England. Live long as well – disprove what I sneered at you all those ages ago back in Jarrow. But go now. Take my last command as your lord – and go!'

Edward grabbed at my hand and kissed it. He wanted to say more, but he was shaking too hard with sobs, and Karim was making desperate clicking noises to keep the horses calm. They mounted together. I heard a long groan of agony from Edward as his own horse darted forward. They scrambled up the high bank to the top of a dune. They looked down a moment on me and on the long caravan of armed might surrounding my chair. I looked away and didn't watch them disappear over the other side of the dune. Assuming we took the usual time to get to the Saint Theodore Monastery, and assuming I could keep Meekal busy with our joint unlocking and registering, they'd have a thirty-mile start on any pursuit. That was the most they'd have, though. Meekal *would* eventually realise his hostage was gone, and would certainly lead the pursuit. And he was fast on horseback. But thirty miles, and no surety as to their direction of escape – that should be enough.

I drank deep from my beer jug. I focused on the merry jingle of the bells on my chair as I fought back the tears. It would have been glorious to be with them – speeding across the level sand towards the horizon, towards adventures that might give some minstrel a lifetime of unlikely tales. But, for all I could give myself new hair and teeth and ears and eyes, even I couldn't make the waters of time flow uphill.

62

'Did you catch up with them?' I asked in Greek. I splashed with every appearance of happiness in the bathwater – cool this time, and a great relief after a day of almost lunatic activity in the desert.

'Get out of here – all of you!' Meekal roared at the attendants. They dropped their instruments of cleansing and bolted from the room. Meekal pulled the door shut with a crash that made all the glass pieces in the window rattle. Still sweaty and covered in sand from the long and fruitless chase through the desert, he towered over me. 'What the fuck are you up to?' he demanded, back in Greek.

'Nothing, my dear – nothing at all,' I said. I took up a flask of scented oil and poured some of it over my scalp. 'I can only tell you that Karim rolled up late while we were somewhere outside Damascus and suggested another race across the sand. That's what I told you when we met up earlier. And that really is all I can tell you now. I can't imagine why you're making such a fuss about things. I fail to see why you had to dash straight off into the desert with your escort and leave me alone all day with dear Silas for company. If it hadn't been for the Caliph's inspection tomorrow, I'm sure I'd never have got him to break all your security rules, not to mention some of your locks. All that – and the boys will probably soon be back here for a late dinner. In a moment, I'm sure Edward will come through that door. What a silly man you are to get into such a lather. Was the auditing *so* stressful?'

With a shout of rage, Meekal plunged his arms into the bath and searched round for the plug.

'You'll find that it's all controlled by that lever just above my feet,' I said helpfully. He got hold of the lever and twisted it up until it came off in his hands. 'Oh dear!' I cried. 'Do you know the price of good plumbing repairs? That will be another bill for the auditors to wave under your nose.' I raised my arms and waited for Meekal to control himself sufficiently to help me out of the tub. He stood in grim silence as I rubbed the water off my body and got myself into a sleeved robe. Taking care not to slip on the tiles, I walked slowly over to the door. I led him into one of the sitting rooms and arranged myself on a sofa that faced towards the window. The sun had now gone entirely down. Fortunately, the lamps were already lit.

'Now do sit down and join me in a little drink,' I said in a reassuring tone. I pointed at a low armchair with its back to the window. 'Let's have a quiet rest and wait for some glimmer of common sense to light up your rage-blackened mind.' I pointed at a closed cupboard that had, the last time I opened it, contained a sealed jar of wine and some cups. I waited for Meekal to calm himself with a few cups. I did think of some fulsome praise for the palace maintenance people who'd done such an excellent job on the repairs. Except for some building dust that hadn't yet been swept away, you'd never have guessed what effort had been put in during the day. But Meekal *was* calming down, and it wouldn't do to set him off again with irrelevant chatter. I sat quietly with my cup of wine and the few private thoughts I permitted myself.

'Have I not played fair with you?' he asked eventually. 'I've played fair with you, and more than fair. Why are you shitting on me now?' I finished my own cup and lay back on the soft cushions of the sofa. I hadn't dried myself properly, and was beginning to feel slightly chilly. 'Since it's plain you won't tell me anything at all,' Meekal said, getting up, 'I see no point in prolonging this conversation. I'm going out into the desert to see that all really is arranged for tomorrow. If it isn't as I expect, I'll impale everyone in sight, and be back here before morning.' He pushed his face close to mine. 'Haven't I played fair with you?' he asked again.

'You've never played fair with anyone,' I sneered, now switching into Saracen. 'However, don't accuse me of shitting on you. If you promise to be a good boy, I'm inclined to do you a bigger favour than you deserve.' I waited till he'd controlled himself again, and pointed to the back of the window seat. 'I suggest you pull off the fine silk of that upholstery. Go on,' I urged, 'get over there and rip it all away. I'm sure it will make many things clear.'

Uncertainly, Meekal walked over to the seat and pulled at the silk backing. As it came away in his hands, the wood panelling of the wall showed – together with an eighteen inch by nine hole in the wood. Meekal looked at this a moment. Biting on suddenly white lips, he turned back to me.

'So far as I can tell,' I said, 'there's one of these in every room. I think you go two – or perhaps three floors down from here: it's a few months since I got myself down there, and I'm hazy about how many turns in that ramp I had to make. But one of the sealed doors shows evidence of regular tampering. Why don't you go down and take a look of your own?'

I stretched full out on the sofa and stared at the ring of lamps that hung from the ceiling. I counted to a hundred, then opened my mouth and recited in my loudest and most sarcastic voice: '*quo usque tandem abutere Catilina patientia nostra? quam diu etiam furor iste tuus nos eludet? quem ad finem sese effrenata iactabit audacia?*' I broke off with a laugh and called out in Saracen; 'Have you killed anyone yet, dearest Meekal?' I laughed again. Now choking back the laughter, I continued this most wonderfully apposite recitation of Cicero: '*nihilne te nocturnum praesidium Palati nihil urbis uigiliae nihil timor populi nihil concursus bonorum omnium nihil hic munitissimus habendi senatus locus nihil horum ora uoltusque mouerunt? patere tua consilia non sentis constrictam iam horum omnium scientia teneri coniurationem tuam non uides? quid proxima, quid superiore nocte egeris, ubi fueris quos conuocaueris quid consili ceperis quem nostrum ignorare arbitraris?*' I had my mouth open for the '*O tempora o mores!*' when Meekal came back into the room.

'So, those birds also were flown,' I said, still in Latin, with a nod at the unbloodied sword he carried in his hand. He threw the sword down with a clatter and sat back in the armchair. I got slowly up and poured him another drink. Silly of the man, when you think about it. After all, he'd spent much of his childhood in the Imperial Palace, which is riddled with these channels for carrying sound from one place to another. He should have taken it for granted that nowhere in this palace would be any more secure. But he sat there, utterly crushed. I refilled my own cup and sat back on the sofa. I picked up a cushion and threw it at the hole in the panelling. By a stroke of luck that looked exactly like a skill retained into old age, I got the thing right into the hole. I lifted my cup in a toast to myself and looked at Meekal.

'Who was listening?' he asked simply.

'That old bitch Khadija,' I said. 'Why must you trouble me with asking?'

'Because it saves me the trouble of asking her myself,' came the answer. 'So she's heard everything said within these walls. And that would explain the source of all the information the auditors had in their files earlier today.' He sat upright and reached for his sword. 'Since you've been good enough to tell me this much, I hope you will agree there is no point in holding back on the rest. Any chance of telling me what the fucking cow is up to now?'

'Gladly,' I said. 'Can you imagine that she tried to have me killed in these very rooms just a few months ago? I think that abolishes any duty of confidentiality. I'll tell you the lot – on *one* condition.' Meekal sat forward. 'I want the boys to go free,' I said. 'Call off your dogs.'

He laughed. 'Karim is no loss to anyone,' he said. 'Alone in that desert, he'd dry up in the sun like a slug. Your boy will probably get him to safety. As for the boy, would you believe me if I said I never had any intention of breaking my oath?' I smiled and shook my head. Perhaps he was telling the truth. The problem all villains face sooner or later, though, is that no one believes them when they do tell the truth. 'Whatever the case,' he said, 'you get your assurance. I have no "dogs" out looking for them. Now, tell me everything.'

And so I did tell him everything. I told him as much as I'd heard and guessed. Oh, very well – I didn't tell him *everything*. Except perhaps with you, dear Reader, I never do that. But I did tell him as much as I cared to let him know, which was quite a lot. 'Just you threaten that head eunuch of hers with the rack,' I ended, 'and he'll confirm the whole story. He'll confirm her dealings with the

Intelligence Bureau. I strongly suspect he'll also confirm her dealings with the rebels in the civil war.

'Now, do you need a list of the names I've given you? Personally, I'd rather keep it verbal.'

Meekal shook his head. He'd nearly burst with joy as I'd recited the names Karim had given me. Every one of them was his sworn enemy in the Council. Every one of them, he promised me, would be waiting his turn on the rack once he'd denounced them to the Caliph.

'It is surely redundant to ask,' he said with a nasty smile, 'whether you have taken up Karim's suggestion of a failure for tomorrow's demonstration.'

I shook my head. 'The demonstration, I promise, will be a complete success,' I said. 'It will be everything you could ever expect. I only ask you to remember your promise.

'But you'd better go,' I said wearily. 'You can imagine the sort of day I've had out in the desert. And I need somehow to get through tomorrow. Yes, go – just go.'

For the first time in ages, I didn't bother with opium that night. I let the slaves get me to bed. As ever, I said I'd have no one to sit beside me. While someone got up on a stool to put out the lamps, I looked up at the fresh plaster above my bed, and breathed in its damp smell. It reminded me of the house I'd once bought in Rome. I'd been only twenty then. I'd lived for months surrounded by that smell. It was something I'd ever since associated with hope and youth. I'd laughed at the suggestion of a move to some other room. I took a sip of water and wished a good night to the slaves. I then lay back and closed my eyes. It was like falling in darkness into a bath of exactly blood heat.

I was back on my diverted ship to Athens. The Captain had told me we were now just a day from Piraeus, and a shift in the autumn winds meant we'd be approaching through the Saronic Gulf from the west. That meant I'd be able to see the place where, over a thousand years before, the Athenians had surprised and sunk the Persian fleet.

'What do you suppose would have happened had the Athenians

lost?' I asked of Martin. He leaned beside me on the side of the ship, looking over the flat waters of an early morning. They had a surprisingly dark, oily sheen about them. 'I mean, suppose the Persians had brought all their superiority to bear, and the Athenian fleet had been routed. In the short term, the Persians would have finished conquering Greece. Xerxes would have gone home in triumph. And what would that have meant for the whole subsequent history of the world?'

I'd often had these 'what if?' conversations with Martin, and I expected him now to insist that the Athenian victory was the work of God. How otherwise would the Greeks have spread their language and ways over the world, and then had this fixed and preserved after their own conquest by Rome? Since the result was the stage on which was played out the drama of the Gospels, it *had* to happen. To suppose otherwise was inconceivable. However, he didn't rise to the bait. Instead, he let go of the rail, and, surprisingly stable for him, walked a few paces back along the deck.

'I've been waiting for you a very long time,' he said from behind me. I turned and frowned at him. 'Everyone else I knew, and so many I never knew, have gone before you. I have given up wondering when I shall really see you again.'

I wanted to ask what he was talking about. But there was a jumble of thoughts glowing feebly away at the back of my mind. As I was still trying to choose the right words, Martin turned away from me and walked steadily across the deck to the stairs that led down to our living quarters.

I was alone on the deck – not a sailor in sight. Even Priscus, with his vomiting and his bag of drugs, would have been preferable to the deep silence that lay about me in all directions. There were no seabirds crying out, no fluttering of sails in any breeze. I heard not so much as the lapping of water against the keel of the ship. I gripped the rail and looked hard in the direction of where Athens surely lay.

The sun was now lifting itself above the line of clouds that fringed the eastern horizon. I squinted as I looked into its growing brightness, and raised my arms to take in its first warmth.

So it had always been. So it would always be.

63

The day of testing had arrived. Locking the gates behind them, all the workmen and all the guards had come out from the monastery. They took their places on the sand before the high wooden platform that had only just been completed. Mounted and fully armed, my own little army of guards kept a quiet but intent watch over the sands that led to the distant hills.

'You've chosen a nice day for the demonstration,' I said with an irrelevant look at the sky. Meekal said nothing. He'd varied his normal black with a green and purple turban to show his own exalted office. 'So, when does the Caliph put in his appearance?' I asked. 'Any news yet that he's left Damascus?'

'What's in that box?' Meekal asked.

I looked down at the lead canister I'd been holding to my chest. I'd now put it down on the sand, and someone had put a jug of fruit squash on top of it. I sat down on my stool and waited for the slave to arrange the sunshade over my head.

'Oh, that's a token of my thanks to His Majestic Holiness,' I said easily. 'I've *so* enjoyed his hospitality these past few months. I hope to enjoy rather more of it in the coming months. I'm told Damascus can be delightful in the autumn.'

He grunted and took a slip of papyrus from an attendant who'd just come over beside him. He stared at it and frowned.

'You'll be interested to know,' he sneered in Latin, 'that Karim was spotted this morning in Damascus. He was buying bread.' I raised an eyebrow and gave him an artless smile. 'I said I wouldn't chase either of them. But if they now throw themselves into my hands, who am I to refuse any gift that God may send? You can watch the boy die in one of my dungeons. Karim I'll have punished as befits an enemy of God. Unless you appear set to outlive me, however, I'll allow you to live out your natural term. I think you'll find it interesting.'

'You really are too good to me, Michael,' I replied. With a scrape of boots on sand, he turned and was away. He took his place among a group of bowing secretaries and put his mind to dealing with official duties. I thought I could make out the word 'burning' a few times. To be sure, I heard one mention of beheading. There's nothing like clearing your accounts when out of sorts with the world. I leaned back and rested against the firm chest of a slave who knelt behind me.

It had been a busy morning, and the one stimulant draught Meekal had allowed me was wearing off. I looked up at the network of polished bone that kept the fabric of the shade in place. Where bone and fabric were joined with fine threads, little beads of sunshine gleamed like the lamps at a palace banquet. I listened idly to the droning voices of the secretaries a few yards away. I listened to the grating but quiet responses with which Meekal punctuated the droning. I didn't recognise any of the names I managed to catch. But it was obvious he'd been busy all night with foiling the Khadija conspiracy. Now, unless I'd lost track of the time, he was pronouncing an unusual number of death sentences. Did even persons of quality not get a trial nowadays in Syria? I hadn't bothered attending it, of course. But I'd at least been given one in Constantinople.

The best thing to do with tiredness in this heat is give way to it. The Caliph wasn't due for ages yet. Why Meekal had got everyone out so absurdly early, to swelter away in this sun, and without adequate shade, was anyone's guess. I pulled my visor properly down – less to see clearly than to block out some of that dazzling light – and leaned harder against the slave. I felt the blackness sweep over me now in earnest. Soon, I was deep into another dream. I had now arrived in the Athens of my youth. I was walking briskly past the roofless shell of Hadrian's Library, while Martin prattled on about nothing in particular. I think I'd made some money down in Piraeus or at dice, and I was looking for some way to get rid of Martin, so I could go about my proper business of celebrating in a brothel.

I woke with a sore neck and spent some while trying to work out where I was, and why I was beginning to feel my innards twitch with nervous strain.

'Who are those children?' I managed to ask eventually.

'They are from the Saracen school in Damascus, My Lord,' came the answer from just behind me. 'They are here to sing for His Majestic Holiness.'

'Well, I hope they won't be dragged in as well for the demonstration,' I muttered. The slave took hold of my head, which would otherwise have flopped completely to the side, and I let him sit me forward. Someone else poured me a cup of warmed fruit squash. As I drank it, I came properly back into this world. A larger crowd had assembled while I slept, and workmen were fitting a curved wooden screen together about twenty yards from the raised platform where the Caliph would be taking his seat. They ran about, calling softly to each other and arguing over how each part should be tied together. Arranged in a semicircle on each side of the platform, the lesser quality of Damascus were taking their places as if for some theatrical performance.

I got my stick and stood up. I moved my neck about to get out some of the stiffness and looked properly round. There must have been five thousand people here. The platform was still empty except for some slaves, who darted about with pans and brushes, or to pull on the cords that held the awning taut. Beyond the crowd, more soldiers had been placed. These were more of the big fighting men who'd come back from the war. To make any kind of successful attack on this event, it would need a regular army. You could forget the usual drugged-up suicide mission.

There was a cry from over on my left. I reached down to where my ear trumpet dangled at my chest and put it in to hear what was being said. It was a carrying chair that had fallen over. One of the slaves had tripped on a rope that was stretched tight at knee level, and the whole chair had gone down. Slaves bawled at each other as they fished within the disorganised heap of curtains for whatever grand personage would eventually emerge shaking and spluttering.

I now saw the long train of other chairs that were ferrying in from across the desert what looked to be the heads of the Religious Council and the Caliph's older ministers. They were arriving fast, and were being led to what I took to be temporary seating in the shade of the main platform.

I could smell food cooking somewhere. My mouth filled with saliva, and I remembered that I hadn't felt up to breakfast. I was certainly up for lunch! I wondered when this would be served. Perhaps I might get someone to bring me a dish of something a little in advance. After all, I was surely part of the coming entertainment. It wouldn't do to have me fainting from hunger.

I was thinking to turn and make a polite request of the slave who'd supported me while I slept, when I heard another cry.

'The Commander of the Faithful comes!' I heard someone call. The cry was repeated from somewhere out of my sight, and then again, until all distinctness of words was lost in the loud babble of many voices. I looked vaguely about. My slave took me by the shoulders and turned me to face into the sun. I pushed my visor close to my face and squinted. There was a cloud of dust several miles into the distance. I looked and looked, until I thought I could make out dark shapes within the cloud. They came on with the speed and regularity of a cavalry charge. There was a faint sound of galloping hooves, and now the cry of men who had seen where they were heading and were racing to see who would get there first. Behind me, I could hear men shouting their encouragement. I even heard someone lay odds on who would arrive first. There was a disapproving murmur, and he shut up. At least ten thousand eyes focused now in silence on the final charge towards us across the sand.

It was a massive white horse that got to us first – though only by the length of a horse. The rider pushed on with unbroken speed right into the open space before the platform, then came to a sudden halt. As grooms ran forward to take the horse, the rider swung off with an easy motion and stood, looking straight ahead.

The whole assembly got up and bowed. The men of the Religious Council shuffled forward, waving their sticks and calling out a coordinated greeting. A drum started up, and the schoolboys, all dressed now in long robes of white with green bands, began some elaborate, swirling dance.

While the Caliph stood, watching the dance, his companions came forward from where they'd dismounted and joined him. The meaning of the dance was lost on me. But it went on and on until I could feel my legs shaking and I thought I'd need yet again to claim the prerogatives of age. But it finished, and the boys lined up before the Caliph. He walked up and down the line, stopping now and again to smile at one of the boys, or to pinch a cheek. Now the schoolmaster was leading the boys away, and the old men were flocking round. I saw the Caliph stretch his arms and look up. I think I heard the cracking of tired joints. He finished his conversation and made for the steps up to the platform. He was followed by several dozen other men: the Religious Council, of course, and the ministers, and their attendants. Right at the end, and with much respectful bowing from everyone already up there – and even a helping hand from the Caliph – was Eusebius.

'So nothing has kept the Imperial Ambassador away,' I said to no one in particular.

'So it would seem,' came a displeased and slightly embittered voice from behind me. I turned. Meekal had now changed into the full regalia of the Governor of Syria. Dressed from head to toe in shimmering green satin, he looked like a piece of ship's timber in a presentation box. I caught a look at his face, and the giggle died on my lips. 'I did insist he be taken on a tour of the dye factories,' Meekal spat. 'He isn't supposed to be here.'

'You know Eusebius,' I said. 'Where there's food to be had, or bribes to be taken, or information to be gathered for the Empire – there he will be. But isn't that what he's paid for?'

Meekal wiped sweaty hands on a napkin he'd taken from a slave. Without looking down, he dropped it on to the ground and stepped closer to me.

'You know the drill,' he said in Greek. 'You keep close by me while I speak. At the appropriate moment, you get into the chair that will come over and lead the way to the gate. All the inner gates have been left open. You'll be carried straight into the fourth zone. I'll order the furnace to be lit. While the kettles heat up, you'll stand behind me to correct any defect in my explanation. Have chairs been set out for the Caliph and the others?' I nodded. It had been my last act before coming out with everyone else. 'Good! unless the Caliph asks, you don't need to say a word until we are inside the fourth zone. Until then, you sit or stand beside me as required, looking frail and submissive. Is that clear?'

I nodded. He grunted back at me, then took my right arm. He led me over in front of the curved wooden screen and waited while I was seated on a low canvas chair a couple of feet away on his left. The sun was overhead on my right. It wasn't yet noon, but was already blistering. I drank from the cup that had been placed in my hands, and looked back at the Caliph and the assembled thousands.

64

'O Mighty Commander of the Faithful, Learned Elders of the Faith,' Meekal cried in a great voice. I'd wondered how the wooden screen behind us would perform in the open expanse of the desert. I couldn't tell for sure without being in the crowd of listeners. But I could guess from the firm resonance of his voice that the thing was working more or less as planned. Looking straight at us, the Caliph moved a hand slightly. Meekal took a deep breath and continued.

'Whereas the perfidious Greeks of the Empire – alone of all the peoples of the universe – have resisted the arms of the Faithful, yet have they not done so on the fair field of battle, where the Faithful have been ever victorious, but with treacherous wiles. Recall ye not, O Majestic Holiness, how, arrayed in shining arms before the very walls of Constantinople, the Flower of the Faithful waited for the order of final assault? Recall ye not how, quaking behind their walls, the Greeks and their Emperor could barely have resisted one unarmed woman of the Faithful, had there not been those massy stones to shelter their useless bodies?'

There was a great laugh at this joke. Meekal took the applause like some aspiring actor in the Circus in Constantinople. When it showed no sign of dying away of its own, he held up his arms for silence, then went on with his laboured oration. Trying with reasonable, if not quite full success, to smother his foreign accent, he repeated the story as you already have it – the five ships, the tubes that spat fire that burned upon the waters and was quenched not by the pouring on of water, the panic and growing chaos among the attackers, and so forth. Over a chorus of lamentations and horrified cries, he described the retreat of the Faithful across the frozen ground of winter, and the repeated counter-attacks I'd sent out to keep them moving to the place of their final catastrophe. I thought he went over this in more detail than was entirely tasteful. However, this wasn't an oration in Greek, where the rules of Demosthenes – or even the Asianics – were to be strictly followed. It was a tale for a race that was still mostly barbarous. And, safe outside their own capital, the Saracens were thoroughly relishing the tale of horror and disgrace.

I looked up at the sun. If still not close to its noonday angle, it was moving in that direction. I was glad of the shade that was again over my head. Got up in that huge turban and what may have been an entire bolt of satin, Meekal must have been cooking alive. But if he was leaking sweat like a squeezed sponge, he was enjoying himself far too much even to pause for a drink.

'There are those,' he cried sarcastically, 'who say that the Greeks, alone of all the races of men, have been reserved for some other fate than defeat by the arms of the Faithful. They tell us to be content with the great and expanding realms of the Caliph to the east, where the sun and the soft greenness that is their shade of the sun have made men luxurious and weak. There are those who fear the sharp swords of the Greeks, or who just covet the gold dropped by the Greeks into their hands. These are the ones who speak of delay and consolidation, and of another attempt on the Greeks at some unspecified time in the future.' There was a hint of impersonation in this last sentence. It was greeted with a shout of denial from the main audience. On the platform, the denial was less enthusiastic. I thought I could see a few faces turn slightly to each other. Certainly, there were gaps in the huddle of ministers about the Caliph. So far as I could tell, not one of the persons Karim had named to me was present up there. Meekal waited again for the noise to go down, then was back at a speech that he must have been rehearsing for ever.

'But the attempt is not to be put off to "some unspecified time in the future". No! I say unto you, O Majestic Holiness, O Anointed Successor of the Prophet himself – I say unto you: hear not Meekal, humble servant of the Caliph, but hear the words of Abdullah, son of Amir, last survivor of those who heard the

Prophet speak.' Meekal stopped and held up his arms for continued silence. He turned left and nodded. I tried to see past him, but he was in the way, and I was unable to see the cause of the shuffling and scraping towards us across the sand.

'Behold the venerable and heroic Abdullah,' Meekal bellowed triumphantly. As he spoke, the chair came in sight. Carried by just four slaves, here was Abdullah himself. I'd never seen the man before. Then again, perhaps I had seen him – but he hadn't then been the drooling, paralytic wreck who sat gibbering and twitching in the sunshine. I leaned forward for a good look at the man. Rather as young women look at each other to see who might be fairest, so the very old look at each other to see who is more broken down and ready for the grave. No contest here, I can tell you! I counted back. The Prophet had been dead for fifty-five years. Assume this sad creature had been in his twenties back then: it made him much younger than me. He'd need to have been in his middle forties to match my age. Of course, at that age, he'd qualify now as a Companion of the Prophet, whether or not they'd ever exchanged a word. And he hadn't been called that. I tried not to give myself a complacent hug and sat back in my chair, waiting to hear whatever words of wisdom he might recall – or that might since have been spooned into his addled brain.

'While I was at meat with the Prophet,' he slurred after several false starts. He stopped for the hushed roar of the 'Peace be upon Him' from every quarter, and for a long coughing fit that couldn't have left him with much of his lungs by the time he stopped. I saw Meekal stiffen slightly. Was there another whispered prayer? But old Abdullah was now looking forward with a little more appearance of having recalled who and where he was. 'When I sat with the Prophet,' he said in a firmer but still weak voice, 'it was asked of him which of the two great cities would be opened first by the Faithful. Would it be Rome or Constantinople? Be it known that the Prophet answered: "The City of Heraclius shall be opened first." '

There was a sudden commotion among the audience. I saw definite looks of concern on the faces about the Caliph. Meekal held up his arms again for silence. He gestured at Abdullah to continue, even managing a respectful bow.

'The Prophet told me that the highest duty of the Faithful was to strive for the great city of Constantinople,' he said in a voice that was half drone, half whispered croak. ' "When the palace of the Caesars and the Great Church of the wondrous dome shall sound to the prayers of the Faithful," he said, "the Pope of the Romans shall not prevail another year. Then shall the arms of the Faithful be dipped in all the waters that flow about the disc of the earth, and the work of the Faithful shall be done." Such be the words of the Prophet – may Peace be upon Him!'

Well, that got everyone to their feet. They cheered and stamped. Men rushed towards the platform and called out at the Caliph for the right to be the first martyr in the renewed assault on the walls of Constantinople. There was a general chanting of 'Holy War! Holy War!' A polite smile on his face, Eusebius was listening carefully to the whispered interpretation of all this. If Meekal ever let him go, he'd have a fine report to make to young Justinian.

But old Abdullah had done his job. Now, shaking like a monkey against the bars of its cage, he was carried back under the shade, and Meekal was strutting about in readiness to get to his main point. And he was getting there – even if it was taking longer than I'd anticipated.

'Your Majestic Holiness,' he crowed, 'my greatest gift yet to the Faith of Mohammed – may Peace be ever upon Him – is the fire of the Greeks. Eight years have I laboured. Eight long years have I laboured in the face of doubt and plain opposition from those whose duty told them otherwise.' More nervous bobbing of heads beside the Caliph. 'But my efforts now have been crowned. Be it known that the horrid fire that the Greeks poured on the heads of the Faithful shall now be returned threefold. When next the armies of the Faithful shall beset the walls of Constantinople, there will be no second defeat.

'Yes! Yes, O Great and Mighty Commander of the Faithful – I have given victory to the Faith. And if anyone doubts, then let his tongue be stilled. We shall now proceed the quarter of a mile that separates this place of audience from the place of demonstration. Then shall the whole world know the power that I bring to the Faithful.' He darted a look at Eusebius, who was still looking polite. 'The world shall know the power that I bring, and the world shall tremble!'

There was another roar of enthusiasm. More men rushed forward and threw themselves down before the still figure of the Caliph. All about him, other faces were looking openly scared. Meekal bathed in the applause. He held up his arms and turned round and round. He pointed at me, and spread his arms wide. He put his head up and laughed – though the sound of his laughter was drowned out in the tide of shouted war cries that poured over us. He darted round and looked briefly at me. He raised his eyebrows as if for my own applause. He even smiled. Then he nodded me towards the waiting chair.

I looked up at the sun. I looked at the quarter-mile distance to be covered – it looked closer to half a mile. Meekal had gone on far longer than I'd thought to take into account. Plan A was off the agenda. There was nothing else for it but to go for Plan B. I sighed and got to my feet. Instead of dragging myself over to the chair, I turned to face the Caliph and raised my own arms for silence.

'Abd al-Malik,' I cried in my best approximation of a younger man's voice, 'Caliph of the Saracens, hear the words of Alaric, Senator of the Greeks and occasional correspondent with your Prophet.' There was complete silence from the crowd, though much looking and whispering between the men around the Caliph.

'Shut up, you old fool!' Meekal whispered loudly in Greek. He made to grab at my arm. I avoided him and, though making sure not to pass outside the collecting zone of the sound board, stepped towards where the Caliph sat.

'Abd al-Malik,' I cried again, 'have I your permission to speak?' I looked closely at his face. He stared blankly back. Then he nodded. Safe now from Meekal, I took up what I guessed to be the most effective point for the reflection of sound. 'You will be aware that, whatever Meekal boasts, I am the one who has produced the Greek fire. I was brought here under duress from my place of refuge, and set to work to achieve what none of you had been able to manage for yourselves. I will not ask you to condemn this abuse of an old man. Besides, it has been done. But I do inform you that, if its final purpose is use against the Empire, the first use of what I have given Meekal is to destroy you and all your ministers – rather, to destroy you and all those ministers he has not yet falsely accused of treason.'

There was a confused murmuring from all around. Meekal made another attempt to catch me. I gave him a hard poke with my stick and raised my free arm towards the Caliph. With a sudden lapse of all into silence, the Commander of the Faithful stood and pointed straight at me. I smiled at Meekal and watched as he shrank back from me. I looked into his angry, scared face and coughed politely in place of laughter.

'I accuse Meekal – formerly known among the Greeks as Michael, Commander of the Emperor's Personal Guard – of treason against you. I declare that his intention is to take you within that walled compound and to spray you with a jet of fire that can turn flesh and bone to ash in the blinking of one eye. I will show you the mechanism he caused to be placed there for this purpose.' There was another rising murmur. The Caliph remained on his feet. Eusebius was now asking urgent questions of his interpreter. All the time, Meekal stared at me, on his face a mixture of shock and plain confusion.

'Before then, however,' I continued once I had the general attention again, 'I accuse Meekal of sorcery. I accuse him of sacrificial murder and necromancy, all in the interests of making himself Caliph in your place.' I paused for the rising babble of shouts that I expected. Instead, there was complete silence. I heard the high splashing of blown sand against the wood behind me, and the call of a bird overhead. I glanced left to where Meekal was standing still. He had a hand to where his sword might be underneath his outer clothing. But he didn't seem likely to go at me while I had the Caliph's attention. I took a deep breath and continued with a slightly tarted-up description of what Edward had told me. I spoke quickly, wondering at every moment if Meekal would chance his luck with the Caliph by killing me before I'd come out with everything. But he seemed rooted to the spot.

'And as the traitor to both God and man violated the corpse,' I called out in a tone of horrified disgust, 'his satanic accomplices danced about him chanting, "O, my brother, you shall be Caliph"! Yes, O Caliph, this I heard from the traitor with my own ears: "O, my brother, you shall be Caliph"! With spells and ceremonies forbidden on pain of death among all the Peoples of the Book, he called on the Dark One to assist in his work of treason. "O, my brother, you shall be Caliph"! "O, my brother, you shall be Caliph"! he was told – and told on the authority of the Dark One, to whom the traitor's prayers are all truly directed.'

I'd got the story out. As I finished, I had to raise my voice – even if I stood in or near the best sound collecting zone – to speak above the gathering volume of terror and disgust. Eusebius was stretching forward in his seat, a look of near ecstasy on his face. The ministers and religious scholars were all pulling faces of exaggerated horror. At last, I was getting my reaction. Still impassive, though, the Caliph looked on in silence.

Trying not to behave like an old man, I moved with forced briskness back to where I'd been sitting. I ignored the grinding in my back and I leaned down and lifted the lead box. I turned back to the Caliph and held it triumphantly aloft.

'Let the renegade Greek Michael tell you I am senile and deluded,' I cried dramatically. 'But let him then explain how this could be part of my delusion.' I tugged at the lid that made for a perfect seal on the box. It came off with a gentle pop. I scooped off the top layer of the white powder with which it was tightly packed, and pulled out its main contents. I shook off the remaining powder, and – to what was now a collective and uncontrollable wail of fear – held aloft the severed head of the serving boy Meekal had chosen and throttled and then fucked.

65

Even when desiccated, heads can be rather heavy. My right arm shook as I continued holding this one up for all to see. It may have been my preserving powder. Or it may have been the bright sunshine. But the head had a greyish tinge. Still, it was very well preserved. I'll swear you could see the boy's final gasp of terror on those rigid lips.

'Behold the head of Meekal's victim,' I cried, still trying for a younger man's voice. 'I found it where it was thrown and have kept it safe all these months. Who, of those who were there, at the great feast of welcome for me, will deny that this is the head of the boy that Meekal took for himself.' There was a slow nodding among some of the men about the Caliph, and more shouts of horror from the crowd.

'And this is your "evidence", O Magnificent Alaric of ninety-eight summers?' Meekal now called. His voice, rediscovered, dripped scorn. 'You tell me that, without assistance, you followed me through the palace to the unfrequented hunting grounds, and that you closely observed me in this alleged act of sorcery?' He looked towards the Caliph. He turned suddenly and stared me in the face.

I smiled and stared back. I might have been lying through my teeth about what I'd seen him do. But I really had gone off there – and on foot, mind you – with Edward the following morning. While the boy had moped about, trying to look other than frightened of touching the accursed object, I'd spent ages poking round with my stick. It had then been straight into a leather bag, and back for quite a successful experiment in preserving. Meekal could sneer all he pleased at my faculties. The head really did speak for itself.

Or did it? Meekal was speaking again, and now with recovered confidence.

'The man asks me to call him senile and deluded,' he cried in his earlier manner. 'I readily grant his wish, Your Majestic Holiness. He is indeed senile and deluded. He tells you that he saw all this nearly three months ago. Surely an act so grave as this should have been reported at once to the relevant authorities. Instead, he expects you to believe that he witnessed it, and said nothing, and then worked obediently for me in what he claims to have known would culminate in a further grave act.' He paused and waited for his words to sink in. There was silence all around us. As ever, the Caliph looked on, still standing, his face drained of expression.

'Your Majestic Holiness,' he went on with a sneer, 'I put it to you that what the Old One describes, even had it happened – which I deny – could not have been witnessed by anyone in his condition. He needs special equipment to see in broad daylight. And he tells you what he saw in the moonlight?' Meekal laughed. Without looking again at the head, he walked straight past me. He went over to my chair and rummaged about in the luggage pouch. He pulled out a small glass bottle and a larger silver box. He held them up. 'The man is old. But I hardly need call him senile. I hardly need even remind you of his apostasy from the True Faith – and, therefore, of his unfitness to be heard in accusation against one of the True Faith. I need only say that he has spent too long shopping at the apothecary.' He held up the glass bottle and waved it above his head. 'The Old One is a notorious drunkard and opium eater. For seventy years, he's been fuddling himself every day – and boring everyone about him with accounts of his unbalanced dreams. Who can doubt he has now lost all sense of reality?

'Treason? Sorcery? Murder? The only question worth asking is where the fool got his body parts.' With a contemptuous snort, he dashed my opium bottle to the ground. I watched as it hit a stone and shattered, and the precious juice of the poppy drained into the sand. Meekal stepped closer towards the Caliph. 'Let us end this ridiculous interlude,' he cried in a louder voice than before.

'The Old One can be led off to a place where he can do no further harm to others or to himself. The rest of us can proceed about the business for which we are gathered.'

There was a perceptible draining away of tension. Someone laughed as I let my arm down just a little too fast, and the head fell to the ground, leaving me clutching a handful of hair. I stared down into the dead eyes. As if of its own motion, the head rolled down a slight dip in the sand and stopped beside the broken bottle. I stepped forward and bent to retrieve the head. Of a sudden, I overbalanced and fell on to my hands and knees. My stick was a few feet out of reach, and I struggled vainly to get back to my feet. Someone else in the crowd laughed. There was another laugh from somewhere else. I could now hear a soft giggling from many places within the crowd. Again, I tried to get up. Again, I failed. When I looked up from the ground, the Caliph was now sitting, a sour look on his face. One of his people was trying to whisper in his ear. As he leaned forward, the Caliph turned away. Meekal was strutting about, pointing at various slaves whose job it was to get things ready for the trek over to the demonstration.

'I'll kill you for this with my own hands,' he said softly as he passed me by. 'I'm sure I'll find a way to make it slow and painful – even for you.' I ignored him. The sun had now resumed its course and would soon be at the highest point. For what little it was still worth, I'd carry on. I forced myself back to my feet and stood forward again, and raised my stick for attention. I was ignored. I thought of turning and rapping my stick on the sounding board. But would anyone have paid attention then? Far over on my right, the carrying slaves were already on their feet, and were preparing to come forward to collect those who were to witness Meekal's crowning achievement.

As I wavered, there was a commotion at the back of the main crowd. It was a matter of complaints and the displacement of one body by another, and then of the corresponding movements and complaints by those about the initial points of disturbance. It was nothing much at first – I even thought it was more of what seemed a concerted attempt to deny me my attention. But the sound and movement increased as someone pushed his way through the crowd closer and closer to the front.

'The Old One speaks the truth!' I heard a voice cry from an unexpected point along the front row of the crowd. I shaded my eyes and twisted my head to see if there might be better vision through some other cluster of tiny holes in my visor. But, if I couldn't see him, there was no doubt it was Edward. 'The Old One speaks the truth,' he cried again. I saw him now. Dressed in the white riding costume of the Saracens, though with his short, blond hair uncovered, he crossed the sand that lay between me and the crowd and stood beside me. 'With my own eyes, I saw all that he describes. I, Moslemah, a convert to the True Faith of the Prophet, also accuse Meekal of treason and sorcery!'

'You're a fucking idiot,' I hissed at the boy in English as the chorus of shouts and argument swelled among the crowd. 'I told you to get out of here. Why have you come back?'

'I asked myself what you would have done in my place,' he replied in Saracen. He raised his arms again for attention. But now Meekal was back from making his arrangements. He pushed Edward roughly away from me and looked straight at the Caliph.

'This farce has been played out long enough,' he called impatiently. 'Whatever clothes he is wearing, this child is nothing more than a barbarian catamite. His conversion is as genuine as the Old One's. Now his original owner is too worn out to play the manly part, he's given his arse to the wanted traitor Karim – son of the traitor Malik, whose widow is, even now, awaiting questions about her own treasonable correspondence with the Empire and with the rebels.' He pointed at a couple of guards, who'd been lounging on the edge of the crowd. 'Arrest the Old One and his boy,' he said with angry contempt. 'Your Majestic Holiness, the demonstration awaits.'

I looked up at the sun. It was almost now at the zenith. It really was now or never. I stepped forward and took in a deeper breath than I thought my old lungs would ever accommodate.

'Abd al-Malik,' I shouted with firm urgency. 'Abd al-Malik. You will not hear the word of man. Prepare now to hear the Word of

Allah.' The Caliph turned back to me. He raised an arm for silence. The crowd and all about were suddenly stilled. I walked back within the sound collecting zone. 'The boy and I speak the truth,' I called. 'If you go within those walls, I swear that you will never come out alive. I watched all day yesterday as Meekal laid his trap for you. All this is the truth. And, as witness of the truth, I call on Allah, the Common Father of all men, to give a sign.' I stopped and pointed dramatically up at the sky.

And now my heart froze. All day, every day for months, the sun had shone from a sky of unbroken blue. For the first time, I saw a little cloud barely the sun's own diameter away from the sun. The shock drained all energy from my body. I watched and fought the inclination to let myself fall sobbing to the ground. Closer and closer the cloud drifted slowly towards the very edge of the sun. A half-mile away in the monastery, all had been set up on the assumption of bright sunshine. The sun would reach its zenith. The lenses would focus its beams on the piles of grey powder I'd placed in just the right positions. The powder would ignite, and would burn along the trails I'd laid to all the right places. Already, other lenses had started fires under the double kettle filled with the mixture. This would now be at boiling point – and would stay safely at boiling point unless . . . unless . . .

The cloud covered the sun. At once, the desert was plunged into shadow, and all the heat of the day was stopped. Still pointing up at the sky, I stood with shaking legs. Someone in the crowd was claiming that God had indeed sent His sign. No one paid attention. Meekal was already walking towards his own carrying chair. The Caliph was back on his feet, waiting for his people to move aside so he could step down from the platform. The cloud had covered the sun at its zenith, and seemed set to stay there until the zenith was past. I felt Edward lay a hand on my shoulder.

'Come, Master,' he said in English. 'We tried our best. Karim tells me that we can—'

There was a sudden flash over on my left. I turned and looked into the bright mushroom of orange that had erupted above the walls of the monastery. I watched as it swelled and swelled – a hundred feet, no, two or three hundred – above the walls. Even with my visor to blot out much of the brightness, it was like staring straight into the sun itself at noon. I watched as the great ball of fire that swelled still greater at the top of the bright column seemed to move within itself – here dazzling, here relatively dark. It was like looking at the ridged contours of a brain illuminated from within.

I could only have seen this for the briefest moment. But time seemed to have stopped as I stood there, watching as all my finished mixture and the thousands upon thousands of gallons of its raw materials were converted into a second and momentarily brighter sun. Then I heard the roar of the explosion. It filled the whole desert around me, and sounded as loud in my bad ear as in the good. Even as I noted for the first time how atoms of light travelled faster than atoms of sound, and thought to frame some hypothesis to explain the difference, I felt something that can only be described as a great, invisible hand. It slapped me hard in all parts of my body, and, cupped in its gigantic palm, I was thrown back ten – perhaps twenty – feet before landing with a hard bump on the sand.

Ignoring any damage I may have suffered, I pulled myself into a sitting position and gasped for breath as I looked again at the orange ball a half-mile away across the desert. It had swelled still larger, but now appeared to be losing its definite shape and solidity. I watched it gradually fade into an immense cloud of dust and smoke that I thought would linger for ever above the now vanished walls of the monastery.

'Master, Master – are you all right?' I heard Edward cry as if from a great distance. I jumped as I felt his arms about my chest and he pulled me to my feet. Had I gone deaf in the noise? I clutched hold of him and looked feebly about for my stick. It was now that stones and other debris began raining down upon us. I heard the thud of objects in the sand around me, and more distant crunching and screams. I felt myself thrown back on to the sand, and now Edward's body covering mine. Even as the hail continued of lighter stones that had been thrown higher in the blast, I struggled free and stood up. I looked around. I now saw the damage the explosion had caused, even this far away. The canopy had gone from the Caliph's platform. The platform itself had turned over. Every carrying chair had been blown apart. All the horses had bolted. Large stones and other debris littered the ground as far as the eye could see. No one else was standing. Everyone I could see was huddled on the ground. No one moved. I couldn't even tell if anyone else was still alive.

I saw my walking stick over by the shattered remains of the sound reflecting screen. I let go of Edward and walked towards it. I bent forward to pick it up. But Edward had got there first. He pressed it into my hands. I turned to him and smiled.

'I did that,' I said in English, pointing with my stick towards the still huge cloud of dust. Edward nodded. He made no other reply. I smiled more brightly and raised my voice. 'Yes, I did that,' I repeated. 'I'll bet no one else has ever managed the like. "Look on my works, ye mighty, and despair," ' I quoted in Greek from an ancient poet.

I turned again and found myself looking straight at the Caliph. Half his beard was gone, and there was a bloody gash on his face. I laughed as he tried to control the shaking of his body and get any words out at all. He sat down suddenly on the sand. He pointed weakly at the still growing cloud above what had been Meekal's project, and slumped forward.

' "Look on my works, ye mighty, and despair," ' I cried again. I held out a hand to help the poor man to his feet.

Well indeed might the mighty despair.

66

If you've seen one of them already, there isn't much to be said about any other prison. Every palace needs one, and the Caliph's palace was no exception. You got to it by going down the steps that lay the other side of a small door at the back of one of the main administrative buildings used by the Governor of Syria. Unlike in the Imperial Palace in Constantinople, these stairs hadn't yet had enough use to be worn. But it was the same melancholy descent from bright sunshine into perpetual darkness, and the same smell of unwashed humanity and of bottomless despair.

I rapped smartly with my stick on the desk of the little Syrian who was supposed to be keeping watch at the foot of the long staircase. He woke with a start and peered at me in the dimness of the lamp that shone from an iron bracket on the wall behind him. I fought to control my breathing and dropped a slip of papyrus on to the cluttered desk.

'This doesn't cancel the order that no one is to be admitted,' the man said in Greek.

I'd been expecting that. I unhooked a purse from my belt and took out five solidi. He looked at the golden discs and nodded. He reached behind him and pulled out the stopper from a water clock. He pointed at the first marker.

'You can have twelve minutes with him – no more,' he said. He opened his mouth to call for one of the guards.

I stopped him. 'The permit says I can see him alone,' I said, waving at the slip.

The Syrian shook his head. 'No private meetings,' he said firmly.

I opened my purse again and poured its entire contents on to the desk. Their sound made a dull echo within the room. When the man had finished his choking fit, he stood up and took a bunch of keys. He looked for a moment at an open ledger. He looked back at the gold and sighed. He gathered up the coins and put them back into the purse that I'd now dropped in front of him. Tucking the purse into a deep fold in his clothing, he led the way across the room to a door at the far end that was bound with iron.

Knowing exactly what to expect, I held my breath as the door swung open and we stepped into the deeper gloom of a long corridor. If you've ever had a cat, you'll know the beast's genius for finding your most expensive rug or silk hanging, and then shitting all over it. Imagine this, left to dry out and go stale, and then shoved under your nose. Imagine this, plus the cat's dead and putrefying body, and throw in a stinking fish – and you have some idea of how a prison smells. I clapped a scented cloth to my face and tried not to think about anything at all as I shuffled along that corridor. To the best of my ability, I blotted out the sound of sobs and whispered pleading from behind each of the wooden doors that we passed. Every time I've been in one of these places, I've told myself that this would be the last. It never had been yet. Perhaps even this wouldn't be the last.

'So, Grandfather, have you come to gloat?' Meekal asked as his eyes got used to the lamp. His own cell was larger than I'd expected. But the main floor was reached down a flight of steps, and was covered in a two-inch carpet of liquid filth. I looked at this briefly as I reached the bottom step. I nerved myself and continued splashingly forward to where Meekal was sitting. He tried to get up as I approached. But the chain attached to his iron collar was too short to let him move more than a few feet from the wooden bench where he'd been sitting.

I turned to the Syrian gaoler. He hadn't followed me down the steps. He stood in the doorway, still holding his lamp.

'Get out of here,' I said coldly. 'You can leave the lamp on the steps. I'll summon you back when I'm ready.' I heard the door swing gently shut. By then, though, I was already standing over Meekal. He looked up at me and tried to smile.

'I've spent the past few days trying to clarify when you started working for the Empire,' he said. 'Was it when you were still in your British monastery? Was even your confiscation and exile part of the plan?' He shuffled to the end of his little bench and made room for me. I sat down beside him, and tried to ignore the wet filth that soaked straight through two layers of silk.

'Your question is irrelevant,' I answered. 'In a sense, I never stopped working for the Empire. A better question is when I realised what I was supposed to do. Answering that would take longer than I fear we shall have.' I reached into the satchel I'd brought in on my back and pulled out a loaf of bread and some wine. I watched as Meekal ate his first meal since he'd been pulled, more dead than alive, from the wreckage of the Caliph's platform.

'You were a fool to disbelieve what I said,' Meekal began again. 'I really meant those words about joining the two empires. It would have been a fresh start for the world.'

I looked down at my feet and splashed them in the filth. 'The problem,' I said, 'is that I did believe you. And, in spite of all that happened to me there, it would pain me more than I can imagine to see the Empire fall. More than that, though – far more than that – would be the thought that the Saracens could then rampage without any real opposition through Europe. I would do all this again, and more, if it meant the call to prayer would never sound from the monastery in Jarrow. You are, of course, right that the Christian Faith means nothing to me. Your own new Faith has many advantages that we don't need to discuss. But, for all its original idiocy, and for all that has been added to it, the Church carries within itself the seeds of something that, sooner or later, will germinate into what may never quite have been, but what might yet be.'

'The Empire *must* fall,' Meekal insisted.

'I'm sure it will,' I conceded. 'But it won't fall until there is some other line of defence against your people. I bought time the other day. I did no more than that. But I bought time that I have no doubt will be used.'

'What do you suppose they will do to me?' he asked.

I looked at him and smiled. 'You may not have heard that Karim is now Governor of Syria,' I said. I waited for Meekal to finish his ironic laugh. 'Yes,' I went on, 'though it won't be his intention, the Empire will find him a most useful member of the Caliph's Council. The Caliph has declared you an Enemy of God – a traitor, a spendthrift, a sorcerer, and an unwise meddler with the old families of which he is, after all, a member. I spoke with Karim last night. He refused even to consider softening your punishment. Tomorrow morning, you will be taken from this cell to be racked and, after that, tortured all over with red-hot pincers. You will then be taken to the usual place of punishment. Your extremities will be cut off. You will be blinded in one eye, and have one ear cut off. Then you will be crucified. There are other incidentals. However, since you have passed that sentence many times on others, I don't need distress you with any further description.'

'It is the will of God,' he said, fighting to keep his voice steady.

I opened the satchel again and took out a battered scroll.

'I haven't just brought you physical comfort,' I said. 'I found this in Beirut, and was thinking to send it to a friend I made in Africa. It is the third book of Lucretius – his long meditation on death as the end of all things. You may remember that I tried to make you read it when you were a boy in Constantinople. It led to one of the few disagreements I ever had with my darling Maximin. I bring it to you now. It was copied by a Greek scribe, and he lapses into the Greek alphabet here and there. But I've corrected the few actual errors. I hope you find the time to read it this evening. I'll make sure you have enough light for the effort. I promise it will give you comfort – especially if you read it all the way to the end.'

I was done. I stood up and moved towards the steps that would carry me back to reasonably dry stone. At the top of the steps, I turned and rapped my stick on the door.

'But, Grandfather,' came the now laughing cry from behind me, 'you haven't asked what I was really doing when I fucked the dead boy.'

It was a question I had thought of asking. But since the boy's head had vanished in the blast, I saw no point in asking what exact use had been made of the body.

'Michael,' I said, looking back down at the hunched figure, 'I never imagined our parting would be of this nature. I did hope for so much that was better.' I stopped and controlled my voice. 'This is our parting. I shall not see you again.'

I might have said more. I might even have gone back down to put a hand on his shoulder. But the Syrian gaoler was now pushing the door open, ready to take me back to where my carriers awaited me above in the sunshine.

I sat a long time in my bath. I sobbed uncontrollably and rocked back and forth as the slaves sponged water over the tightly shrivelled skin of my back. For all he'd been a total bastard – for all he deserved everything that had happened, and more – he was still the son of the only child I'd ever truly loved. When Martin had brought the little baby from outside that church door in Constantinople, I'd adopted him on the spot. I'd taken him in my arms and called him my own. He'd been, throughout his life, the one consistent joy in my life. I'd wept for days in Carthage when I'd received that insolent notice from Michael of his death. Whatever lay in store for Michael – or Meekal: you say what you'd have me call him – it was richly deserved. It still didn't wipe out that he was the child of Maximin.

I took the refilled cup from a slave and drained it all in one go. I handed it back for more. There are some pains, however, that not wine – nor even opium – can wholly blot out.

67

'I don't see why I should answer – not, at least, within the Caliph's dominions – to an agent of the Emperor.' I looked stonily at Joseph until he shifted his gaze. I put my hands on the table and shuffled my feet on the floor.

'My Lord Alaric,' he tried again, still in his flawless Saracen, 'this is not in any sense a formal interrogation. I merely asked if this object was yours.' He nodded at the sharp little knife on the table. Still covered in blood where Meekal had opened his veins, it had done unexpected service ever since I'd borrowed it in Jarrow to sharpen my pens. I smiled and looked again into Joseph's eyes.

'I rather think it might be yours,' I said.

'I could have you killed for this,' Khadija snapped at me. Twitching away beneath her veil, she sat beside Joseph. I stretched my legs under the table until I kicked against one of the four legs opposite me, and laughed.

'Don't be silly,' I said. 'Karim would never allow such a thing, and you know it.' We fell silent. It was the morning appointed for the execution of the traitor Meekal. Sadly for all concerned but himself, Meekal had taken matters into his own hands. Now, the three of us sat together in my grandest audience room. Dressed as an officer in the Caliph's guard, Joseph had, so far as I could tell, made his way through the palace without challenge. I'd dismissed all the slaves to their own floor in the Tower of Heavenly Peace. I imagined Khadija had ensured that her own spies should have the day off from their work on the floor below that.

'My Lord Alaric,' Joseph said, his voice now conciliatory, 'this is altogether a most irregular situation, and I must ask both of you to show continuing restraint. The Lady Khadija acknowledges your part in removing Meekal from what might otherwise have been a commanding position within the councils of His Majestic Holiness. She does not hold against you the unfortunate death under torture of several of her closest associates, nor her own brief confinement in a dungeon. She accepts that the betrayal of her conspiracy was a necessary part of your ruse to keep Meekal from visiting the former Monastery of Saint Theodore on the morning of the demonstration, where he would surely have discovered your intention. You have single-handedly achieved a revolution within the Saracen Empire that has reversed the policy of His Late Majestic Holiness Muawiya, and returned power to those born and bred within the Desert Faith. You may be sure that the Emperor is also grateful – though for reasons that it would be indelicate to discuss too closely in the presence of the Lady Khadija.'

'Tell me, Joseph,' I broke into his emollient flow, 'how did you know that I'd do the Empire's work? You were sent out to Jarrow to keep me safe from Cuthbert and Hrothgar. When that failed, you were sent after me to make sure I never got here. The orders then changed to making sure that I did get here, and that the more intrepid attempts on me by the Angels of the Lord came to nothing. But you never bothered telling me what I was supposed to do.'

'As you said yesterday to Meekal,' Joseph said very smoothly, 'you never stopped working for the Empire.' He looked back into my scowl and allowed himself a cold, bureaucratic laugh. He ignored the feeble attempt that Khadija was making to be heard. Doubtless, she was less interested in how he'd got a spy into the prison than in his own presence in Jarrow.

'But, very well,' he continued, 'you deserve some kind of explanation. When Meekal first suggested your abduction from Jarrow, we heard both from the Lady Khadija and from our other spies. We quietly assisted the Lady Khadija's own conspiracy to have you murdered before Meekal could lay hands on you. However, we made sure that her plan was never likely to succeed. I did not choose Brother Cuthbert myself. But I am impressed at the ability of our French agents to find so heroically useless a man, and at such short notice. Even so, I went out myself to Jarrow to make sure that Cuthbert's plan failed and that Meekal's succeeded. I than put myself through the motions of a pursuit across the Mediterranean, and of various murder attempts in Beirut and in Damascus. We needed Meekal to believe you were not working for us. And we needed the Lady Khadija to confirm this belief should we ever decide to betray her to Meekal.' He allowed himself another chuckle as Khadija went into some kind of fit deep within her clothing. I poured myself a cup of wine. Joseph could stay with the water. He paid no visible attention to the slight, and continued with quiet enjoyment.

'As you know, the plan did not at first work out exactly as was hoped. As Cuthbert was trying to open the gate of the monastery – not realising that Meekal's people were now in charge outside – he was killed by the boy Wilfred—'

'Now, do tell me about that,' I broke in. 'It's something I guessed long ago. But I'd like to hear the details. What could have possessed poor little Wilfred to do anything so energetic?'

'I have no idea,' Joseph said with some faint recollection of the annoyance. 'But it was Wilfred. I have no idea what could have spurred him to that. I never thought him capable of lifting more than one of the lighter books in the monastery library. But Wilfred it was. This was an inconvenient act, as I now wanted the gate open. As the boy lay sobbing and calling on God to strike him dead for his sins, I did intend to open the gate myself. It was now that someone – almost certainly the boy Edward, whom I had never suspected of involvement – hit me hard from behind on the head. By the time I was able to get free of the monastery, you had all vanished.

'I caught up with you off the coast of Africa. What you were doing there was a surprise to me. But, since I expected you to continue from there to Beirut, we needed to give you cause to believe that we wanted you dead. Even so, you made your way to Caesarea. There, I might have spoken to you directly. But I had no reason to believe you would have cooperated. So I instead nudged you towards Beirut. What happened thereafter needs no explaining.'

I asked about the meeting Hrothgar had mentioned to Edward

in Kasos. I got no answer. I dropped this and moved to the more interesting question of how he'd guessed I would act as I did. Joseph permitted himself another laugh.

'There are some things that can be planned down to the smallest detail,' he explained. 'Other things must be left to the workings of Providence. God is on our side. We knew He would not allow you to do other than your duty. And you will not be aware of how much we had to trust to God.'

'I know about the earthquake in Constantinople,' I said with a look at Khadija. 'I guessed what was expected of me when you spoke behind me in Caesarea. When I heard about the earthquake, I understood the reason. Tell me – how serious is the breach?'

'The walls won't be ready to withstand another siege for at least another three years,' Joseph said. 'Every time we think the work is nearing completion, the engineers find more evidence of undermining. What we have was enough to stop some barbarians earlier this year. It wouldn't stop the Saracens if they turned up in force.' He turned to Khadija, who, now she'd removed her veil, was looking rather cowed. 'We had no idea, My Lady, how close Meekal was to success. We only knew that a renewed attack on the city – this time with our own weapons – would be successful. We were and are grateful for your own efforts to starve him of resources. But we could not afford to let him succeed in his project.'

'Do you mean we could attack next year and win?' Khadija asked. She sat bolt upright. I could see her whole body shaking with the horror of what she'd just heard.

'I mean, My Lady,' Joseph took up, 'that you *could* have attacked and won. You could have attacked next year, or the year after that, or the year after that. You could have removed Meekal, and, even under your own incompetent direction, your people could have conquered the Empire. Partly thanks to you, that is no longer possible. I have no doubt you will win a battle here and there against us. I share Alaric's view that we neither can nor should attempt the recovery of Syria and Egypt. You are welcome to Africa. But you really have now missed your chance to destroy the Empire. The next time you are in any position to go back on the offensive, we shall be waiting for you.' He laughed again, now with more genuine humour.

'Really, Khadija,' he said when her face stopped twitching as if she'd suffered a stroke, 'you have done yourself a considerable favour. One of these days, you will stand before Saint Peter. I am sure that, in view of how you have played your own unwitting part in our plan, he will overlook your noxious heathenism.' She now got up and paced about the room. Serves the old bitch right, I thought. But Joseph still wasn't finished. He looked back at me.

'And so, My Lord Alaric, the question remains of what is to be done with you.' He paused and smiled coldly into my face. 'You will appreciate that you cannot be left in Damascus or in any other place ruled by the Caliph. You are the most dangerous man alive. I spent yesterday looking round the site of the explosion you produced. Within what remains of those monastery walls, there is nothing but a crater twenty feet deep, and the sand there has turned to a sort of glass that cracks and splinters underfoot. We cannot afford to let you do anything like that again for the Caliph. For all the good they would then be to us, we might as well leave the walls of the city unrepaired.

'At the same time, His Majestic Holiness has already told Eusebius that you will not be allowed to return to Constantinople. The evidence of his own senses has told him not to allow you anywhere near your old laboratories in Constantinople.'

'So, which of you will arrange for my "accidental" death?' I asked. Joseph and Khadija looked at each other.

'Karim is Governor of Syria,' Joseph replied. 'We all have good reason not to alienate him. That means that you must be left alive until such time as God calls you to Himself. We cannot tell ourselves any longer with confidence when that might be. Even so, you are to be spared.' He paused again and smiled. 'Have you never missed all your dear friends in Jarrow?' he asked.

'Not particularly,' I sighed. I looked about at the heavy luxury of my audience room. I thought of the delights of Beirut. I thought of dawn prayers in that frigid chapel three thousand miles away.

'Nevertheless,' said Joseph, 'you leave tomorrow morning. This time, of course, you will not go without luggage. But you leave tomorrow morning.'

I pulled myself free from the renewed embrace and wiped the tears from Edward's eyes.

'Come, come, dear boy,' I said, 'this will never do.' I stared round at Karim and the crowd of young Saracens who stood modestly back from this horribly protracted farewell. 'You may be a regular Saracen now,' I continued in English. 'But do try to remember one last time what you were. You can at least try for a stiff upper lip.'

'I shall never see you again,' he cried disconsolately. 'What will I do? How shall I—'

'Oh, shut up, Edward,' I replied with an affectionate pat on his shoulder. 'I used you shamelessly from Caesarea onward. I've already explained myself at some length. Above all, I sent you and Karim racing into the desert with a pack of lies in your heads. No doubt, I saved you from what I had intended to be a suicide mission against Meekal and the Caliph and everyone else. But I sent you off as bait to draw Meekal away from my preparations. And still you cry like a little child to see me go?'

'Everything that I now am,' he replied with quiet ferocity, 'you made me. You are my lord and father. Let Karim put his foot down – he'll get all this cancelled. Won't you, Karim?' He turned away to Karim, who looked back and pursed his lips uncertainly.

'No,' I said, still firm. 'Jarrow it must be, and Jarrow it will be. Besides, after all this excitement, you won't grudge an old man some final peace?' I laughed and bent forward for one last embrace. I thought my bones would crack with its force. I pulled back again. 'Now, go,' I said. 'Go to your own people.' I'd already had my farewells with Karim. We nodded to each other. He took hold of Edward and led him, still weeping, among the other Saracens. The boy turned several times and looked back. I stood watching until he was completely lost in the crowd.

EPILOGUE

Jarrow, Wednesday, 4 March 688

I'll not trouble you with the details of my return. I was carried in a closed chair straight to Beirut, where an Imperial transport was already waiting. This, with its protecting fleet, carried me in reasonable haste and comfort across the Mediterranean to Caesarea, where we stopped for a few days, and I renewed an old acquaintance. From here, we made for the Narrow Straits, where a heavier ship was waiting. I was in Canterbury for Christmas, where I had to put up with an increasingly senile Bishop Theodore. I arrived back in Jarrow a day before I began the main part of this narrative. Word of my arrival had long preceded me, and the whole monastery turned out to receive me in state.

'God has surely blessed us all!' Benedict cried over and over as we embraced and he led me to my cell, which was crowded with various boxes that I surely had never sent on ahead. There was a whole day of quietly joyful welcoming, and then an evening of wiping away tears as I read the covering letter Edward had sent with the boxes. The following day, it was down to work.

And now the work is finished. The great stack of papyrus will soon go into its wooden box for whatever use the future may wish of it.

And, astonishingly, I'm still alive after all of it. I am undoubtedly smaller than I was the Christmas before last. But I can't say much more than that. Unless I look about me at all the things I now have to keep me happy in this otherwise ghastly wilderness, I might almost think it had been, from first to last, some extended dream. But it wasn't a dream. For eight glorious months, Alaric the Magnificent lived again – and once more saved the world he had for so long adorned.

This being said, I think I can risk two whole opium pills in heated cider. We'll see what glorious dreams of the East they can produce. If I'm still alive tomorrow morning, I suppose I should start again on what I did in Athens. I do assure you – even after seventy-five years, it's a story worth telling.